Building Houses of Cards

Alan Kemister

The Road to Environmental Armageddon

Book Two

Building Houses of Cards

Alan Kemister

In July 2027, the G20 countries announce a coordinated global commitment to stabilize temperatures. It catches everyone by surprise. Dan Delacour and two fellow graduate students at Nova Scotia's Dalhousie University struggle to understand the meaning of the promises made by national governments. The new programs and national aspirations are described in great detail. Procedures for accomplishing their goals and intergovernmental enforcement mechanisms are not.

Dan's romantic involvement with a mysterious woman masquerading as a fellow student complicates their efforts. Elena Llewellyn leads him into a world of intrigue where leaders of the world's largest enterprises manipulate the climate crisis for their benefit.

A decade later, the focus moves to the United States. Political divisions and a preoccupation with autocratic China's increasing commercial and military influence have superseded concerns for environmental degradation. Tomas Matthews, Luna Grange, and a new generation of climate change crusaders join the struggle to prevent a global catastrophe.

Building Houses of Cards

Cover image by Judi Risser and design by the author.

ISBN: 978-1-7753459-3-0
May, 2022

Prelude

Summer, 2051

Greetings, everyone. *My name is Tony Atherton. I'm a climate change scientist here to help you understand how humanity botched the simple task of controlling global warming. My colleagues and I began documenting our efforts several years ago. I played a major role in the first part of our journey. The Souring Seas: A Climate Change Saga, describes that effort. Now, as we move into the next segment, others will take the lead. I have a minor role, but mostly I'm here to provide continuity and help guide the reader.*

Sixty years ago, scientists knew we must reduce our carbon dioxide emissions. They voiced their concerns at the 1992 Rio Earth Summit. Twenty-three years later, the Paris Climate Accord signified political acceptance of their reality. It mandated large reductions for the major industrial nations. Those measures should have kept temperatures well below two degrees above preindustrial levels.

When this story begins in 2027, we'd made little progress. We faced a future with temperatures far more than two degrees above background. The increases were already generating sea-level rise, droughts, floods, wildfires, and increasingly erratic weather. We were headed toward the chaos we would experience in 2049, and humanity seemed unable to prevent it.

You shall see, if you choose to read on, that a solution for global warming was imposed in the summer of 2027. It provided a pause in the march toward Environmental Armageddon. By 2041, the supposed cure was spinning out of control.

Our civilized life came crashing to a halt in May 2049. North American survivors became subsistence farmers in a preindustrial world that relied on barter. In the summer of 2051, my daughter, Hannah, my granddaughter Alice, and I were living near Pemberton, British Columbia. It's in the Coast Mountains several hundred kilometres north of Vancouver. We arrived in 2049. Alice's father, Zeke Barlow, joined us in 2050.

Pemberton became an amalgam of a modern town and a pioneering village. We had modern benefits like electricity and landline telephones. Communication was improving as other communities established themselves in enclaves that supported human life. But oil and many other commodities were in short supply. We relied on animal power for most transport and labour. We stayed home most evenings, too exhausted for anything else after hard days with much manual labour.

Trade with outsiders was very limited. We depended on the resources of our small community. In that respect, we resembled a preindustrial town with cottage industries and complete reliance on the food we grew in our valley. Producing larger amounts of more varied foods was a constant battle.

The Pemberton valley's pioneering folk were optimistic about their future. They welcomed newcomers and developed solutions to their problems. Most of the influx were happy to be alive, and ready to pitch in.

I worked as hard as any, but I wasn't optimistic about our future. Three problems tormented me.

The first was the lack of communication. Satellites and networked computers were long gone. We had shortwave radio communication with scattered radio enthusiasts. Their ham radio messages documented massive explosions and fires in eastern North America. Survivors who struggled in from the Prairies confirmed these stories. But they had few details, and we knew nothing about Africa, Asia, or South America. If those areas survived the unexplained onslaught, shouldn't we have some evidence? We'd survived for two years after a mind-boggling catastrophe struck the globe in May 2049, but we knew almost nothing.

Early reports suggested hundreds of nuclear explosions triggered the catastrophe, but atmospheric radiation levels were much less than calculations predicted. Did that mean something else triggered the destruction? Or did the explosions release less than the expected levels of radioactivity? I should have been happy. If radiation levels were as high as we expected, we wouldn't have survived the initial exposure.

My colleague, Bill Robertson, monitored the ocean from his home on Haida Gwaii, an archipelago in the Pacific Ocean west of British Columbia. Radiation levels he measured were higher than we expected. That raised an interesting question. Why were atmospheric levels too low and oceanic levels too high? It also raised another problem. High radiation in the ocean made seafood unsafe to eat. People living near the coast would also be subject to contamination by aerosols generated by wind and waves. Could we rely on natural processes stripping the radioactivity from ocean waters? Or would humans be stuck with dangerous levels of oceanic radiation for centuries?

My other problem was the increasing concentrations of carbon dioxide. Bill's measurements showed much higher levels and a more acidic ocean. Temperatures were also warmer. Continent-wide wildfires would have generated massive amounts of carbon dioxide, but smaller, less industrialized populations in the following years should have slowed emissions to a trickle. What did his numbers tell us about world populations?

For years, I'd studied the effect of a more acidic ocean on phytoplankton productivity. Bill's latest numbers described conditions that would generate the massive plankton blooms I'd been predicting. Would they extract so much carbon dioxide from the ocean-atmosphere system that we'd soon experience serious global cooling? Could we survive a prolonged shift to colder temperatures?

Information my British colleague, Dan Delacour, sent to me from the Shetland Islands helped us address these questions. It arrived on a yacht that transited the Northwest Passage during the fall of 2049. Merlin's Childe, with her skipper, Claire Fitzwilliam, overwintered somewhere in Alaska. She left Dan's package with Bill Robertson on Haida Gwaii in the spring of 2050, but I didn't get it until the fall. By that time, Merlin's Childe had left for places unknown.

Dan collected climate monitoring data from the northeast Atlantic from 2045 until the cataclysm in May 2049. Bill and I collected similar data for the BC coast. I merged Dan's observations with ours. We then used tedious shortwave radio transmissions relayed by other enthusiasts to add newer results. Assessing the data with our now limited computing capacity would take time. Undeterred, we tackled the job with enthusiasm. We now had data that should help us understand what happened in May 2049 and generate useful predictions of future trends.

The package Claire delivered from Shetland contained a manuscript with Dan's description of events between 2027 and 2032. It complemented my record of events earlier in the 2020s. Between 2022 and 2027, I stood at the forefront of climate change research. Between 2027 and 2032, Dan carried the torch.

Claire and her crew, several of them participants in Dan's story, got so close without me meeting them to discuss their roles in the events leading up to 2049. I was unlikely to get another opportunity, but I could read Dan's depiction of a critical five-year period. This is Dan and his wife Elena Llewellyn's story, told in third person, as we'd agreed to several years earlier. It includes input from several others.

Part One

An Industrial Solution

Chapter One

Friday, July 16, 2027

Dan Delacour thumped his desk, rattling mugs and pencils and toppling a book onto the floor. "Yes!"

The Dalhousie University graduate student was on a roll. Three major improvements to his mathematical model for deep-water formation in the Labrador Sea worked flawlessly. One more change and he'd have the tool he needed to address the impact of climate change on a key process in ocean circulation.

He glanced at his watch. Four forty-five. Too early for dinner but too late to start that final tweak. He'd been working like a dog and deserved a little diversion.

He turned to the online news feeds. The headline, ALIEN INTERFERENCE IN SHELLFISH POISONING, grabbed his attention. A reporter invoking manipulation by extraterrestrials amplified his interest in an already hot topic. After digging into inconsistencies in several stories about Australia's latest harmful algal bloom, Dan checked the time. Now he was late, and he had a stupid commitment with his sister's carpenter.

He hurried to the Muse, the Dalhousie University Association of Graduate Student's pub on the campus in south-end Halifax. No way he'd let her carpenter destroy his Friday evening get-together with fellow oceanography students. Tonight, his visit would be shorter than usual, but he could be there for a while.

Elena Llewellyn, the non-scientist in their group, made room by shifting her chair. The free-spirited young woman was an animated Welsh pixie, a throwback to sixty years earlier, when flower power and free love prevailed. Her tie-dyed top and long flowing cotton skirt didn't mesh with the increasing regimentation and conservative Christian orthodoxy of North America in 2027.

She placed her hand on Dan's thigh and teased him with her pinkie. He placed his hand on hers and squeezed her fingers together. When she smiled and slid closer, the light dawned. She was sending him signals he'd totally missed. She was beautiful, feisty, and often had better insights than his science colleagues. He'd be a fool to ignore her advances. The realization distracted him from the pub-table speculation about the Australian algal bloom and accusations of sabotage in the sinking of a fishing boat.

His recent experiences proved he was a failure at balancing his interest in climate change and his thesis with his interest in girlfriends. Climate controversies were heating up. Could he avoid ruining another relationship by failing to find the right balance?

"They've gone overboard as usual," the hulking John Jeffries said. "A red tide with shellfish poisoning on the Great Barrier Reef is trivial. It will soon be forgotten."

Dan glanced at the others. He wanted to read their reaction to John's regressive perspective before responding, but no one said anything. He sighed. "Outbreaks may be commonplace, but no shellfish were involved. Direct transmission of algal toxins to humans is unusual."

"But not unprecedented," John replied, scowling while shaking his head. "Every time someone farts, your lot cries climate change crisis."

Dan rolled his eyes. "Jesus, John, don't turn everything into a confrontation. If phycotoxin poisoning without ingesting contaminated seafood is happening, someone must inform the health authorities. It may have nothing to do with climate change."

Madison Jeffries jumped in, defending her husband. "But Dan, the story went viral because reporters said aliens orchestrated the outbreak to highlight the climate change problem."

Dan snorted. "Gutter press. When challenged, they couldn't identify their sources."

"Or wouldn't," John added. "No reporter willingly reveals confidential sources. But it's the environmentalists' fault. They're always stirring the pot."

Two servers arrived with plates of fish and chips. Elena leaned toward Dan as the others tucked in. "I knew you'd make it and what you'd order, so I did the honours."

He smiled, another indication of her overtly solicitous and rather possessive behaviour. *I'm not complaining, but what caused it, and why now, when something strange is happening to our world?*

After an interlude when everyone focused on their fish, bespectacled Anna Pawlak brandished her fork like a conductor's baton. "Aliens threatening Earth's citizens if they don't curb carbon dioxide emissions is absurd."

"The story grabbed everyone's attention and caused panic because it sparked people's imaginations," Elena replied. Her carefully modulated English accent always grabbed everyone's attention. "Aliens arrive and notice global warming is out of control. They threaten the world with dire consequences unless we curb emissions. Governments downplay the significance of the reports and question the aliens' existence. That's a story with legs."

Dan chugged the last of his beer, slammed his glass on the table, and stood. "I agree with Anna. The story doesn't hold water. I hate to miss the discussion of its limitations, but I'm late. Gotta run."

Startled by his sudden movement, Elena spilled ketchup on her shirt. She struggled to clean the red smear as Dan grabbed his pack and charged toward the exit.

"Dan! Bloody hell, Dan!" Elena yelled minutes later as he strode toward his new digs.

He turned. She stood five metres away, bent over with her hands on her knees as she gasped for air. Several cloth bags lay beside her.

He rushed back. "You okay?"

"Crikey! Where's the disaster?"

"Sorry. You've been trying to catch my attention?"

The gasps became guffaws as she sank to the sidewalk, choking on her laughter. "Yeah! It's hot as Hades, and I've been yelling for ages. What's the bleeding hurry?"

"Late heading home to talk to a carpenter." He paused, eyeing the assortment of bags she always carried. "Give me some of your stuff. I'll deal with my problem, and then I'm all yours."

She pointed back toward the university. "But your flat's that way."

Dan hesitated. He'd only shared that apartment with his latest girlfriend for one month before they broke up. Moving on from brief relationships was an all-too-frequent occurrence he wasn't proud of. He hadn't mentioned it to anyone. *Does her knowledge mean she's been keeping track of my living arrangements?*

"My sister's new house. Being renovated and I'm looking after it," he said as he puzzled this latest conundrum.

"Lead on, Macduff," she said, while holding out several bags. "I need your help. Then you can impersonate the big bad wolf and have your way with me."

The sexually charged invitation, an amplification of the signals she'd been sending at the pub, surprised him. They'd been platonic friends for months and seldom alone. He'd been preoccupied with his work and unreceptive to her hints, but her interest was now perfectly clear. He shrugged his shoulders before grabbing her bags and hurrying home. *She's older and more interested in climate change than the undergraduates I've been dating. Will that make a difference?*

The carpenter was gathering his tools when they arrived. He kept glancing at Elena as he instructed Dan on the next morning's engineered flooring delivery.

Did her rapt attention and coy smiles suggest she was interested in his instructions, or was it flirtation? And what were they laughing about as she escorted the young stud to the door?

When she returned, Dan cocked his head and raised an eyebrow. "Well?"

"Would you explain a paper?"

"Explain a paper? Not what I expected."

"A serious science paper from the *Journal of Deep-Sea Research*. I'm not sure I understand it."

He sighed. The situation was getting crazier by the minute. "Where is it?"

She pulled a stack of documents from a bag. "A study of underground vents in ocean sediments. Here's the paper and several others it referenced."

"Sounds geochemical. You should ask John. He's into that sort of research."

Elena hesitated before handing Dan the papers. Her olive skin tone didn't hide her flushed appearance. "I, um, well, I'd rather you looked at it. John confuses me when he explains anything."

That couldn't be true. John provided clear explanations. Was the paper an excuse, a Trojan horse designed to breach his defences? *She's effing gorgeous, and I've no intention of rebuffing her advances, but what's her motivation?*

"Coffee?" he asked.

"If it's no trouble, but I would appreciate your ideas. You can read whilst I make coffee."

He showed her the construction zone that was the kitchen and assembled the laboratory funnel in a ring stand he used to make drip coffee.

Dan retreated to the minimally furnished living room, placed a Led Zeppelin LP on the platter of his outdated stereo, and positioned the tonearm. He attacked the first paper as the opening riff to 'Whole Lotta Love' filled the room. He smiled as he disappeared into the world of scientific research. *My kind of background music.*

Elena brought him coffee and bustled about the house and garden. As he neared the end of her stack of documents, she joined him on the sofa. She'd played both sides of *Led Zeppelin II* and replaced Led Zep with the Doors.

She poked him as Jim Morrison screamed the refrain from 'Light My Fire'. When he looked up, the Welsh beauty was snuggled next to him, stark naked, with a big grin on her face.

Dan took a deep breath and tried to relax his voice. "Lost your clothes, did you?"

"Had to deal with the ketchup you spilled on my top, and I wanted clean knickers for tomorrow." She snuggled closer and slid her hand under his T-shirt. "I washed them in your awesome bathroom and pegged everything to the drying rack on the deck."

"That means you're staying?"

"Well, yeah. You wouldn't kick out a naked girl, would you?"

He smiled, no longer in doubt about where their evening was heading. "Probably not. Gets nippy out there at night." He leaned over and kissed her.

She extended the kiss as she pulled him into an embrace that propelled them toward horizontal on his loveseat.

Seconds later, she pushed him away and sat with her hands folded in her lap. "Tell me about my paper."

"What, now?"

She pointed at two bulging, hand-rolled joints on an end table. "Patience, Romeo. I want your assessment before we get to my other entertainments."

Dan wilted in multiple ways as he struggled to understand her behaviour. *No way I'll manage a serious discussion with her sitting there naked.*

"I'll find you something to wear," he said before rushing upstairs.

When he returned, he handed her a T-shirt before retrieving the article. "What can I tell you?"

She pulled the shirt over her head. "What it says, so I can determine if I understand it correctly. Then I have some nutty ideas for you."

The paper described elevated concentrations of biologically important gases near the base of a mid-ocean ridge. The critical observation was oxygen escaping from tube-like structures.

"Is that normal?" Elena asked when he finished his description.

He shook his head. "Organic matter decomposition consumes oxygen and produces carbon dioxide and ammonia. You shouldn't see oxygen escaping from the sediments."

"What about photosynthesis? It generates oxygen when it produces organic matter."

"Photosynthesis needs sunlight. It can't occur on the ocean floor."

She grabbed the paper and pointed at a paragraph on the fourth page. "But Dan, they saw oxygen."

"They suggest an unknown biological process releases oxygen through those tubes. They admit they don't understand it."

"Good. That's what I hoped. Now, what about this one?" She stood and turned, bending forward stiff-legged as she fished another paper from her bags.

Dan stared wide-eyed as his Loverboy T-shirt rode up over her hips. It did nothing to hide her blatant sexual display.

The paper she handed him before sitting down was short, a one-page letter to *Nature*. It described a pod of deep-diving whales detected by sonar as investigators approached the same study site.

After a quick read, he returned it. "Biology. No idea what it means."

"But should whales be that deep?"

"Don't know how deep an individual whale might dive, but I doubt you'd see a whole pod at depth."

"What does it mean? The oxygen, the tubes, and the whales scarpering when the oceanographers approached?"

Dan scowled. She was teasing him mercilessly with unanswerable questions. "No idea."

"Here's my theory. Whales are the super-intelligent species on Earth. They congregate at places like the one your fellow oceanographers found and communicate by telepathy. The whales instruct less intelligent animals to build the tubes in the sediment and produce oxygen they breathe. They also plant thoughts in humans' brains that influence our activities."

"Good grief! What produced these crazy ideas?"

"Term assignment for my summer school course. The professor challenged us to imagine how different the world would be if we discredit a basic life premise." She looked up, her smile and twinkling eyes bewitching.

He nodded his encouragement. "I get it. You postulated whales are the most intelligent animals."

"Makes sense. They have the biggest brains."

Dan shook his head. Everyone knew brain size wasn't proportional to intelligence. "They don't manufacture tools, store knowledge, or have a sophisticated language."

"That's why I hypothesized non-verbal communication, and it needn't be a technological society. It could have an intellectual focus, like eastern philosophies. Anyway, it's not meant to be real. It's an exercise in logical thinking. But it would explain the Australian business we were discussing."

His brow furrowed as he tried to link this discussion with the earlier one at the pub. "How do super-intelligent whales come into that story?"

"Suppose whales are convinced humans allowed global warming to go too far and made the shellfish generate the toxins."

She was technically wrong. Phytoplankton, not shellfish, generated the toxins.

"Then," she added, "they instilled the idea aliens generated the toxicity and threatened humanity if we did nothing about global warming. That would explain our current worldwide drama. And I can explain other inexplicable events using intervention by whales."

His eyes widened as he considered her idea's screwy logic. "Okay, I'll give you one thing. If whales communicate in this way, it gives credibility to world leaders receiving strange messages no one can trace. If I played your game and imagined a basic premise is wrong, I'd imagine aliens with superior technology sent the messages."

"You could tackle that premise if you were taking the course, but I'm sticking to whales as the pre-eminent intelligence on Earth. I need your help searching for errors in my exposition."

Dan sighed, remembering her inaccurate reference to shellfish. "You want to start now?"

She grabbed a joint and skipped toward the stairs. "No, silly, not now. Time for a little diversion."

At the top, she leaned against a doorframe, twirling the T-shirt over her head. Dan picked her up, carried her into the bedroom, and lowered her onto his rickety bed.

Chapter Two

Saturday, July 17, 2027

Elena lay in Dan's bed feigning sleep while she enjoyed the warmth of the early morning sun streaming in the east-facing window. He rose, collected fresh clothes, disappeared into the *en-suite* bathroom, and turned on the shower.

Her newfound beau was open-minded and considerate, accepting without sarcastic comment her over-the-top behaviour. When she stood at the top of the stairs enticing him into bed, he took charge in the most masterful and delicious way. Complete opposite of public-school educated Brits she'd encountered. They were erudite, forceful, and demanding in public, then meek, mild losers in bed.

Brown eyes, short brown hair, slightly above average height, well-toned without bulging muscles. Her rather ordinary-looking Canadian lover might blend into a crowd, but he was attentive, sensational in bed, and whip-smart. *What more can I want?*

Someone pounding on Dan's front door interrupted her reverie. The sound of running water stopped, and seconds later, he rushed from the bathroom and down the stairs. Elena crawled out of bed, grabbed the Loverboy T-shirt he'd found for her the previous evening, and pulled it over her head. She checked its length before descending the stairs. *What if he sprinted down because he expects an irate girlfriend on the porch?*

Before she reached the bottom step, he'd pulled open the door. He stood soaking wet with dishevelled spiked-up hair, wearing only blue jeans. He looked so damned buff as he confronted two fit, clean-shaven men with close-cropped hair, dark suits, and aviator sunglasses. Their loutish demeanours reminded her of a dictator's bodyguards in a third-rate movie.

The older man pushed onto the threshold and presented his official government identification. "Mr. Delacour, we're from the Canadian Security Intelligence Service. The Prime Minister requires your immediate presence in Ottawa at a hearing on global warming."

Dan stared, a puzzled expression on his face. "He can't do that! What if I'm busy?"

The agent shook his head. "He can, and we have the means to ensure you obey. Yesterday's declaration gives the PM wide-ranging authority to address the alien demands. It includes co-opting the efforts of individual citizens."

"What?" Dan exclaimed.

Elena stopped, her mouth hanging open. Rumours suggesting aliens created the phycotoxin outbreak and threatened governments had gone viral in the blogosphere and the mainline media. Governments reacted, insisting alien control of the phycotoxin outbreak was a hoax. Was the Canadian government now responding to the hoax?

"Pack an overnight bag," agent number one said as he passed Dan a single sheet of paper.

Dan scanned it before passing the page emblazoned with the Prime Minister of Canada's seal to Elena. She glared at the agents after reading the prime ministerial letter *requesting* Dan's attendance.

"I can handle today's flooring delivery," she said as she returned Dan's letter. She was cheesed off with the way these plods ruined her meticulously planned weekend, but she wouldn't admit it.

The second officer nodded toward Elena. "Listen to the little lady. The sooner we leave, the sooner you return."

Dan shrugged and turned toward the stairs. He paused, staring at Elena, before heading upstairs.

"Make it snappy, and the young lady stays here," the older agent said while staring at her T-shirt. "Loverboy, eh? You weren't even born when they were popular."

She smiled, trying to ignore their sexist behaviour. First one called her 'little lady', then the second stared after making thinly veiled threats. She didn't want them sniffing around and finding her second chemically enhanced joint and the rest of her stash. Better to keep them here in the front hall, distracted by her appearance. "Dan's into these old rock bands. Isn't this one Canadian?"

"Yeah, Calgary. Wicked old band. Attended a Loverboy concert when I was a teenager."

Dan returned properly dressed and carrying his overnight bag. He diverted into the living room for his laptop. At the front door, he passed her his house key and followed the agents to their black SUV. At home, her uncle would contact the head of MI5 and sort a fiasco like this in seconds. Here, she was powerless. Dan apparently accepted his fate, but she was thoroughly pissed off.

Elena watched until they turned the corner, then she repaired to the living room to search for a Loverboy LP in Dan's extensive collection. She found *Keep It Up*, placed it on his turntable, and cranked the volume. She collected the joint still sitting on the end table and retrieved the clothes she'd hung outside. The flooring delivery could arrive at any moment. She didn't want to encourage another misogynistic performance like the one she'd just endured.

*****

In their vehicle, the first agent passed Dan a manila envelope. He stared at the bulky package, wondering what was really going on. Why had they appeared on his doorstep without notice, why him rather than someone more senior, and how the hell could he contribute to an ill-defined process without an opportunity to prepare?

Once he calmed down, he opened the envelope and perused the top sheet. It described emergency hearings in the national parliament on the scientific basis for climate change. The second page outlined the subject Dan would address during an afternoon presentation. After he looked up, he realized they were on the road to the Shearwater military airport.

When they were airborne, he wasted several minutes staring out the window of the executive jet. Several questions dominated his thoughts. Why was the government invoking interference by aliens? Why invite him to this high-level meeting?

The first was political. Aliens were not a credible driving force for the meeting. Were they introduced to divert a gullible public's attention from the government's real motive? Or was there something he totally missed?

He had a potential answer to his second question. Dr. Heinrich Keizer, his thesis supervisor, was a member of the national climate change task force mentioned in the PM's letter. The invitation must be his doing.

His other concern was personal. An opportunity to present his results to senior politicians should have been exciting. But his initial reaction had been annoyance at anyone interrupting his weekend with Elena.

After turning away from the window, Dan focused on his one chance to influence government action. It demanded a flawless description for a non-specialist audience, but he lacked time to generate a fresh presentation. He located his PowerPoint file for a recent talk he gave to high school students and tweaked it to suit the current situation.

In Ottawa, the hearing in a large meeting room in the Houses of Parliament dragged on. When the Minister of the Environment made her blatantly partisan opening remarks, reporters packed the room. Most of them followed the minister and her bevy of advisors when she left twenty minutes later. That left the twelve members of the special parliamentary committee, their eight science advisors, the expert witnesses, and a few reporters.

After half an hour of political posturing by the committee members and ten scientific presentations that described local or regional impacts, Dan got his opportunity to extend the scope to the global scale.

He described the impact of global warming on Atlantic-wide circulation patterns. Warming temperatures meant less cold water sank into the abyss and flowed towards the tropics. A direct consequence was weaker warm currents like the Gulf Stream that returned surface water to the north.

"Our analysis suggests the vertical transport will cease in 2045. That means a massive reduction in northward flowing warm water and an absence of the Gulf Stream as we know it. We'll see colder winters in Europe and more ice in the Barents Sea. Berlin is north of Saskatoon. Without the Gulf Stream, its winters will be as cold."

He concluded with a plea for oceanographic research into deep-water formation and ongoing monitoring of environmental conditions in the Labrador Sea. His graph with the drop-dead date for Labrador Sea Water prominently displayed remained visible on the screen behind him.

The chairman gazed at the government side of the committee table. "Questions?"

"Could we treat the formation region like a heat pump and withdraw valuable heat from these waters while keeping the circulation pattern intact?"

Dan stared at the member, wondering if he understood the scale. "The required heat removal would be massive and the distances vast. It wouldn't be practical."

The chairman shifted his gaze to the opposition's side. A New Democratic Party member raised his hand. "Your graph shows a range of dates for the doomsday you're projecting. Are you suggesting it could occur as early as 2035? That's only eight years away."

Dan smiled, happy to hear a question that showed a basic understanding of the problem. "My date represents the central tendency from the analysis, the most probable value. It has some uncertainty. The earliest date would be 2035."

After a few more questions, the chairman glanced at the clock and dismissed Dan before calling the next witness.

Dan muttered about the partisan nature of the questions as he hurried away. He almost collided with a clerk outside the hearing room. The modern-day Bob Cratchit handed Dan a sealed envelope.

"Plane ticket for your trip home and cash for your expenses. You're booked on an evening flight, but if you'd prefer to stay over, the airline will rebook you."

"Anything you need from me?"

The clerk consulted his tablet. "We have a copy of your slides, and your comments were recorded. You're good to go. Thank you for your contribution."

Dr. Krueger stepped past the clerk and accompanied Dan to the exit. "Don't be despondent. You gave us the input we need—a solid description of what you're doing and why it's important, without speculation or political diatribes."

Dan snorted. He'd contemplated a pitch for environmental action but deleted the extra slides as he listened to the talks. "But aren't we here to push for action?"

"We are, but we must accept the politicians' plodding, methodical ways. Your job was presenting a clear picture. The task force scientists will synthesize everything and make our case. You've made it easier, better than the less-focused presentations."

"I hope you're right. I only heard politicians trying to score points off each other."

"Trust me. It was worthwhile. And you're set to make an important contribution. Once you've finished your thesis, you'll have many opportunities."

"You think so?"

"The world's major carbon emitters will commit to reaching their Paris Accord targets by 2030. Your results will be critical for predicting how their improvements alter current projections."

Dan shook his head. "I don't believe it. The changes are too great. They'll have too big an impact on people and the economy. This panic will blow over, and government leaders will return to fancy talk and no action."

"Trust me," Dr. K repeated. "Governments are committed to major reductions in fossil fuel use. We'll see economic repercussions because the time frame's restricted. Environmental changes may be large and rapid, so you must gather the data and perfect your models. Get home and get to it."

A different Elena Llewellyn greeted Dan when he arrived home. A ponytail, plain yellow top, and walking shorts had replaced her long flowing hair, tie-dyed T-shirts, and wraparound cotton skirts. The simpler, more modern getup exuded sophistication.

She pointed into the dining room. "The flooring's stacked and ready for installation Monday. And I've been everywhere, clearing the debris and making it more liveable."

"You *have* been busy," he replied as he pulled her into a hug.

"I also fetched some clothes," she added, "and when I realized you were coming home tonight, I visited the greengrocer."

He pushed her away and cocked his head, eyebrows raised. She was playing the hausfrau role, but he couldn't determine her real agenda? "You're planning an extended stay?"

"It's quiet here. My place is pandemonium because one flatmate has two friends staying." She tilted her head, mimicking his posture. "I can leave if you want me to."

Dan shook his head before heading to the kitchen. "I'm not kicking you out, but what's the deal?"

This wasn't the Welsh nymph who lured him into wild marijuana-fuelled sexual adventures. More like the practical friend he'd known since she arrived in Halifax to begin graduate studies in political philosophy. *Either version is preferable to being alone, but why did she revert?*

She snuggled against him as he grabbed a beer. "Tell me what happened after those scary secret agents hauled you away."

He twisted the cap off his beer, tore open a bag of nacho chips, retreated to his living room sofa, and related the gory details of his trip to Ottawa. "Boring and anticlimactic," he concluded.

"Crikey. From the way they talked, I imagined the Prime Minister and half the cabinet soaking up your pearls of wisdom."

"Complete absence of VIPs except for the environment minister, and she only stayed for fifteen minutes," he said with a chuckle as he recalled the platitudes she'd spouted.

"So only committee and task force members like Dr. Krueger."

"And no discussion or debate," he replied, wondering how she knew Dr. K was there. "After we made our presentations, they whisked us away."

She snuggled closer. "Strange, isn't it? They go to the effort of getting you together—"

"At great cost."

"Yeah, really. Why couldn't you email your talk and participate by videoconference? Sending an executive jet for one participant is absurd." She shook her head. "Talk about reducing carbon emissions. And after all that, no discussion. Absolutely crazy."

"Dr. K said it's the way Ottawa committees work. We were part of a public data-gathering exercise that's mostly for show. They want the discussion later, behind closed doors. And they never give a damn about squandering the taxpayer's money."

"But governments have been subject to more disruptions and protests in recent months, and they're now ready to act. I hope their data gathering works. Wouldn't want them to make nonsense of it."

Dan bit his lower lip as he pushed her to arms-length. *She's too damned well informed.*

"That's what Dr. K said. They'll act, and it's our job to make sure they do it from the best knowledge base. But I don't believe it."

"Writing's on the wall. Things will change."

He scratched at the stubble on his jaw. "The United States has increased its carbon emissions since the implementation of the Paris Climate Accord. And economic expansion in countries like China and India has overwhelmed their efforts to control carbon emissions. How can these countries reverse course and reduce emissions in forty-one months?"

"Believe me, big changes are coming, and they'll happen in a matter of days and weeks, not months and years."

"But do governments have the will?"

Elena nodded. "They've gone to the precipice and realize they can't go farther without falling. We should be prepared."

"Prepared, how?"

"Oh Dan, don't be naïve. We need fuel for cooking and basic foodstuffs that won't perish."

"You're kidding. They needn't reduce greenhouse gases by that much."

"Think about it. We're facing restricted air transport, rationing or expensive fuel for vehicles, massive shifts from coal and heavy oil to lighter oil and natural gas. Think back to the beginning of this decade when first the coronavirus pandemic, and then the war in the Ukraine messed up the supply system. It's precarious, and disruptions will occur."

Dan shook his head. *Is she making mountains from molehills, or does she have inside information she's keeping from me?*

Chapter Three

Dan woke to the sound of someone tapping on a computer keyboard. He opened one eye.

Elena sat by the window wearing his Loverboy T-shirt. A mug rested on the windowsill.

Her delicate elfin features and flawless complexion looked paler in the early morning light. Sunlight streaming through her unkempt hair picked out the red highlights in the dominant brown.

He stretched. "You're up early."

She pointed at the clock on his bedside table. "It's gone seven. I was reading news from the old country. You want a report, or should I return to bed?"

She abandoned her computer without waiting for an answer, tugged the shirt over her head, and dropped it on the floor. He pulled aside the sheet. The news could wait.

Later, Dan had eggs sizzling on the stove. Elena appeared outside the deck door, naked and dripping from a morning swim.

"Forget your swimsuit?"

"Do I need one?"

"What happens if we invite friends over?"

She rubbed her wet hair with a towel. "Steve and Anna." She paused when Dan raised his eyebrows. "They're your most serious friends, and we'll need serious allies as we march forward."

"Allies? March forward? What are you talking about?"

"Countries will respond, but everything won't go smoothly. When opponents raise questions about the science, you'll need serious allies like Steve and Anna to help answer them."

The pint-sized Steve Matthews was thirty and older than most of his graduate student colleagues. He was a sometimes austere, physical oceanography student, studying fluid dynamics. The bookish Anna Pawlak was another pure scientist fascinated by the elegance of mathematical descriptions of sub-atomic particles. Dan couldn't imagine their role in a climate change battle. "Should we invite them?"

"Yeah, today. The weather's beautiful, and we can discuss your trip to Ottawa. No time to buy a bathing suit, but I'll organize dinner."

"I thought you wanted emergency supplies?"

"We'll be free in the afternoon. You agree?"

He shrugged. He should focus on his research project and the updated scenarios Dr. K mentioned in Ottawa, but he couldn't simply push Elena into the background. "I've nothing pressing."

She raced away and returned with her phone. She described the pool to Steve, but not to Anna.

After breakfast, they visited the home centre to buy disposable propane cylinders for Dan's camp stove. Others were buying propane and gasoline-powered electrical generators, but store shelves weren't stripped bare.

After a quick lunch at a trendy café, Elena visited the grocery store, and Dan returned home to devote a few hours to his project.

Anna and Steve arrived at four o'clock and wheeled their bicycles onto the porch.

Dan nodded toward the door. "You could take them inside."

"They'll be safe locked to the railing, and it's probably easier."

While Steve locked their bikes, Anna pulled her swimsuit from her backpack and turned to Elena with a gigantic smile on her face. "Steve told me about the pool. Must I assume you simply forgot to mention it?"

Elena headed inside. "I planned to go in without one. I thought you might join me."

"But you wouldn't give me a choice. And what about the guys? You expect them to join your skinny-dipping party?"

Steve followed with two bottles of wine from his bike bags. "I'm not interested in frolicking naked in anyone's backyard."

Dan took the bottles, putting the white in the fridge and the red on the counter. "The pool's secluded enough. You needn't worry about the neighbours."

Steve reddened. "That's not the problem."

Anna glanced at Steve before responding to Elena's suggestion. "I think not. Where can I change?"

Elena sighed before leading Anna to the bedroom. They returned a few minutes later with Anna in a one-piece Speedo suit and Elena in the tiniest bikini Dan had ever seen. She'd only been a few square centimetres less than honest when she implied she had no swimsuit.

After their swim, Anna stared at the house with furrowed brows. "So, Elena, what's the deal? You now living here."

Elena's response skipped important details. "I came over Friday to ask Dan about a paper and stayed because he needed someone to manage things whilst he was in Ottawa."

Anna scoffed. "More complicated than that."

"Stayed for the weekend. Now it's up to Dan."

Dan scowled, wondering why Elena suggested he was in charge. "No point. In a few weeks, I'll be apartment hunting."

Steve gazed from the house to the yard. "What's the story?"

"My sister's house. Her family's moving from Winnipeg next month. I've been holding the fort while they get renovations done."

"Then you'll move out?" Anna asked.

"Three kids and a bloody great dog. And no suggestion I stay."

Steve turned toward Dan with his head tilted to one side. "Winnipeg. Business transfers?"

"Yeah."

"I wonder if they'll move that quickly."

"Why not?" Anna asked.

"The web suggests governments plan to make reductions in carbon emissions from carbon pricing and regulations that reduce travel," Steve responded.

Dan's eyes narrowed. Steve always remained aloof from political talk. His sudden interest was as surprising as Elena's. "Why would that affect anything? If you're transferred, you go. If fuel goes up, you shrug your shoulders and pay."

"That's not what I'm seeing. Their employers may delay their transfers."

Dan turned to Elena. "You've been surfing the web. What are you seeing?"

He expected her to engage, but she remained silent, her eyes brimming with tears. *Something he said... or something else?*

Shortly after nine, Steve and Anna wobbled home on their bicycles. Dan and Elena turned to the kitchen.

"I'm amazed you pulled together such a fantastic dinner," he said as he surveyed the mess. "Hamburgers never tasted so good."

She organized everything into neat piles and loaded the dishwasher. "Three trips to the local greengrocer. You can discover my other secrets if we make this living arrangement permanent."

"But I'll soon be apartment hunting."

"I can't tolerate my place and Kim's scatty friends. I'm better here, and we can search for another flat together."

He stepped back, his heart racing. Where was she heading? They started with one steamy night together. Now, after two days, she was pushing a long-term commitment. "You sure you're ready for that?"

"You don't listen," she replied as she filled the sink with soapy water. "Big things are happening, and I plan to share them with you." She turned from the sink, beaming as she flicked suds in his direction. "And we know damn well it's what you want."

By Monday morning, the trickle of rumours had become a flood. Inflammatory tweets and blog postings by various rabble-rousers warned of drastic reactions from governments everywhere. Better-known commentators discussed the need for worldwide initiatives to reduce carbon emissions. They insisted concrete action was imminent.

Government spokesmen from the G20 countries denied every rumour. The similarity of the insipid replies smacked of conspiracy. They downplayed the need for urgency using almost identical words and ignored questions about local concerns.

Dan's immediate priorities hadn't changed. He trekked to the university and began reformulating his models. A new scenario where carbon dioxide increases for the G20 countries end abruptly demanded his attention.

He was busy writing computer code when Steve strolled into his office. "We wanted to thank you for yesterday. Jolted us from ruts we'd been living in."

"Thank Elena. It was her show."

"You can pass the message."

Dan nodded as Steve commandeered a chair. "I need to finish my thesis, and this crisis lets me add something practical."

"To a thesis focused on theoretical arguments based on physical principles? You want something from me?"

"Your latest models to illustrate the impact of my work in your real-world situation."

"Okay. The code's available. You can make your changes, rerun the models, and compare the results."

Steve held up his hand. "Your revised model that accommodates our new reality, the one we'll soon be experiencing."

"That's a new problem. It may take months to develop an understanding I can model."

"Come on, Dan, we know you've been thinking of little else since Saturday. You'll get it sorted."

Dan laughed, thinking of the distractions Elena provided. "Hope so, but I only started this morning, and life's getting complicated. I'll send you the code for the current model today, and you can help me develop new scenarios."

"You're on," Steve said as he strode to the door. "The paper we produce will make our marks in the field."

Dan shook his head. Steve was the third person in two days who'd said the new political machinations would make his career, but he was far from convinced.

He returned to his programming with greater enthusiasm. He looked up when Elena jangled a ring with a key and a small plastic figurine in his face. The six-centimetre-high figure looked like something from a sex toy store. "Oops, sorry, didn't realize you'd come in. Been here long?"

She laughed. "About ten minutes. You mutter to yourself when you're working."

"People have mentioned it. Only happens when I'm into something."

"You were definitely into something, and it wasn't pornography. I peeked."

Half an hour later, Dan transferred the results of his day's efforts to an off-site memory bank and gathered his stuff. He found a sticky note on his desk near where Elena had been sitting.

'See you at six. If you're late, you'll regret it.' No signature, just a tiny drawing of an elf or fairy.

He arrived home at ten minutes before six. Elena waited, wearing a knee-length black dress and diamond-studded gold earrings that didn't reflect the playfulness her note promised.

She accosted him before he kicked off his shoes. "Your sister phoned. Their arrival's been delayed by six weeks. There's also important new info on the web."

Dan's shoulders sagged. Had life's grubby details steamrolled another romantic opportunity? "Does Gabby want me to call back?"

"After nine. We should have dinner, and you must see what's happening elsewhere."

"Can't you tell me while I prepare something?"

"I'd rather go out. It might be our last chance."

"Things aren't getting that crazy..." Her pained expression suggested she thought it was a real possibility. "Okay, I shouldn't doubt your judgement when I haven't seen the evidence. Where should we go?"

"The Five Fishermen."

It was one of Halifax's most expensive restaurants, and they'd need a taxi to get there. "I can't afford that."

"It's on me. My flatmates returned next month's rent. Plenty for one big fling before austerity destroys our options."

Dan smiled, kissed her, and ascended the stairs to find more formal clothes. It didn't take an Einstein to realize she'd already made the reservation.

Chapter Four

Thursday, July 22, 2027

Tuesday, the rumours coalesced. Wednesday, hints of the G20 countries' climate change policies started trickling out. By Thursday, leaks of enough detail made the bad news obvious.

The formal announcement on what would later become known as Global Climate Action Day described three main thrusts. Emission reductions would make up for lost time and achieve the 2030 levels mandated by the Paris Accord. Coal and heavy oil usage would be severely restricted. Non-fossil fuel sources would replace coal-generated power. Their goal was the complete elimination of electrical power generated by burning fossil fuels.

Their next target was the heating of homes and other buildings. Natural gas, electricity, and various non-fossil fuel sources would replace coal and oil. No one mandated the elimination of fossil fuels for heating, but projections described significant reductions. The situation for transportation was similar. Regulations mandated severe reductions in petroleum as fuel for cars, trucks, and trains.

Dan sat in his office, mesmerized by the newsfeeds. He imagined buy-in from the European Union, Britain, Japan, New Zealand, and a few others. They'd long sounded progressive on climate change while making some, usually inadequate, efforts to tackle the problem. He couldn't swallow serious commitments from China, India, Brazil, Russia, Saudi Arabia, and especially the United States.

The US had been a serious backslider since Donald Trump became president in 2017. China and India had been worse, using increased reliance on coal to fuel their burgeoning economies. Would China, the United States, and India, the three largest carbon emitters and coal consumers, do their parts?

In Canada, government subsidization of heavy oil production had frustrated efforts to reduce emissions. The multibillion-dollar subsidies undermined efforts to appear progressive on climate change. Would this initiative result in rapid removal of these subsidies? If so, the reductions in heavy oil production would help Canada meet its greenhouse gas targets. A lack of action on the subsidies would suggest a lack of serious commitment.

Dan fetched a Coke from a vending machine before turning to the official sites promising details for targets, timelines, and mechanisms. Would they answer questions percolating through his mind after reading the formal announcements? He read while willing Elena to appear. At five, he shut down his computer and gathered together the fruits of his investigations.

He met her outside his sister's house. "Glad you're here. Masses of crazy stuff we should discuss. You keeping track?"

She theatrically wiped her brow. "Quick swim, then I'm ready to discuss the day's events."

Dan followed her, picking up clothes she shed on her way through the house. He stopped in the kitchen to pour himself a glass of wine. He carried the bottle and a second glass to the pool deck, where he settled back to watch his Welsh nymph.

Fog crept in as he sipped his wine. He slipped inside and fetched a towel.

Elena gazed at the sky after climbing from the pool. She shivered as Dan wrapped the towel around her shoulders. "What happened to my beautiful afternoon?"

"Fog."

"Late in the summer for fog?"

"Never too late for fog in Halifax. You'll get used to it. When the fog rolls in, everyone retreats inside."

Minutes later, Elena stood inside the patio door, rubbing her hair. Her clothes sat on a kitchen chair and her wineglass on the table. She didn't appear interested in either. "What do you make of today's announcements?"

Dan poured himself a second glass before responding. "National plans are detailed and comprehensive. Were teams working on them for months, not days, as suggested by various events last weekend?"

"Like your panic trip to Ottawa?"

From his perch at the end of the kitchen counter, he stared at the fog swirling around the pool. "That and the fuss about aliens. They make no sense if governments have been negotiating this agreement for months. And how did they keep everything quiet?"

"I find the secrecy fascinating."

He strode into the living room and sat on the sofa. An optimist might argue emission increases from the G20 countries had flattened since they signed the Paris

Accord. Now they were promising a 50% decrease in three years. "The real question is, can they keep it together and accomplish the ambitious goals they've set themselves? And will all twenty countries stay the course?"

Elena followed after picking up her wine. She smiled before settling onto the sofa and snuggling against him. "What does it mean for us?"

He wrapped his left arm around her, cupping a breast. "A terrible future where no one can afford clothes. We'll all be as naked as you."

She laughed as she leaned into him. "Sounds bad for population control. But seriously, the changes they're describing are huge. Can global economies cope?"

"Economics, political science, the psychology of groups, those are your fields. Most of the scientific and engineering changes they've described are workable."

"They'll have severe economic repercussions."

"I suspect that's part of their plan. Crash ahead with the big changes they've announced. Live with the inevitable recession they cause." He sipped his wine. "A recession will reduce carbon emissions. It'll kick start the long-term move to lower emissions from the proposed changes in electrical generation and transportation infrastructure."

"Crikey! Draconian. Will the citizens stand for it?"

Dan placed her now-empty wineglass on the end table and pushed her onto the sofa. He hovered over her. "God knows, but the scientists will have done their job when we put the brakes on our runaway carbon emissions. The politicians and you social scientists can determine how society deals with the new reality." He paused staring into her eyes. "I have another question about today's announcement."

She squirmed out from under him. "Time I got dressed, and we organized dinner."

He smiled. Had a little macho male muscle-flexing stopped her naked shenanigans when they had serious matters to discuss? "If you insist."

After getting dressed, Elena stir-fried accumulated leftover vegetables and laid out French bread and slices of deli meats and cheeses.

"What's your next big question?" she asked as they sat down for their meal.

"How did our global political leaders pull off this agreement? Did an external trigger like the implausible alien influence force them to act?"

"Or did they finally act on years of scientific advice?"

"Doubt it. Something sparked this remarkable agreement. What was it?"

Elena picked at her food. "Do you need a specific trigger? World leaders have communications pathways, and the Davos Conferences bring political, academic, and business leaders together."

After dinner, Elena stood by the pool, staring into the distance. When Dan joined her, she turned and strode inside without saying anything. *Is she hiding something related to my question about triggers?*

Friday afternoon, Dan squeezed into the space Elena saved for him at the grad house pub.

The aloof and introspective Steve Matthews was on his feet defending climate change action. "The models show we're facing a massive shift in global circulation patterns in the next decade. No one will escape the consequences."

John Jeffries leaned back, smirking. "You're fearmongering like Dan. We'll find technological solutions before your doomsday scenarios become a reality."

Steve challenged him, leaning forward with his palms flat on the table. "No way. You can't devise engineering solutions to global-scale change that prevents wintertime sinking of cold, dense water. Warm up the northern oceans, and deep-water formation ceases."

"Engineers will devise new ways to produce deep water or ways to take advantage of evolving environmental conditions," John said. "And hell, Canada's a northern country. We'll benefit more than most."

"You're dreaming in Technicolor," Steve replied. "You can't switch off the Gulf Stream and expect everything to go smoothly. We'll see chaos in Europe, and no one will escape without serious consequences. Halting emission increases is the only option."

John toppled his beer glass as he spun around to fetch something from his backpack.

His wife, Madison, almost fell as she lurched away from the tsunami of beer racing toward her. "Jesus, John, can't you be more careful?"

Others helped Madison stem the sudsy tide, but John carried on, oblivious to the mayhem he'd caused. He brandished the latest scientist turned journalist's fluffy coffee-table book about the wonders of new technologies. "Scientists, engineers, and entrepreneurs will turn these challenges into new products. Politicians too, they'll make sure everyone benefits."

"No way," Steve replied. "Big business and national government have done nothing, and the solutions we need won't occur without a concerted effort."

The conversation over the next hour included more consideration of the Australian phycotoxin incident and a short-lived green engineering development based on research conducted by Tony Atherton, an ex-Dalhousie student, into ocean acidification. Eventually, the discussion worked its way around to the previous day's political announcements.

Madison gazed from one face to another. "Why have governments finally tackled climate change?"

Dan smiled as he gazed at John's stylish blond wife. She usually restricted her comments to everyday topics and domestic duties, like organizing the meal orders. The sometimes-acerbic Steve Matthews once said Madison's only useful contribution was introducing her friend Elena. But she'd just raised the critical question.

Anna and Zach Abraham, a newcomer from the biology department, offered explanations. Elena even mentioned her theory about whales. Their explanations were mere speculations.

Later, Dan frowned as he and Elena walked hand in hand like teenage sweethearts toward his sister's house. "I'm surprised you mentioned your whale's tale."

Surprised was the wrong word. Puzzled would have been better. He didn't understand where her whales were taking her. That begged a larger question. He didn't understand where she stood on any important issues.

"Why not? It makes more sense than invasions by creepy extraterrestrials from Alpha Centauri."

"But a week ago, you outlined an intellectual conjecture generated by a philosophy class assignment."

"It makes more sense. You said you weren't qualified to comment on my article about sighting whales at depth. Zach looked into it. He said it was an interesting idea."

Dan hesitated, hoping to avoid appearing critical of her first foray into environmental science. "How's your paper coming? Didn't you want my comments?"

"Haven't worked on it," she said before turning away. "Week's been too crazy."

He pulled her closer, and they stumbled along the sidewalk like Siamese twins joined at the hip. "You can say that again. It's been one weird week, and you've had the added upheaval of moving in with me."

"You're okay with that, aren't you?"

He couldn't resist his new lover, the first one to understand his overriding concerns. If only he understood her intentions as well as she understood his. "At first, I thought you were crazy to abandon your old place for a few weeks at my sister's. Now we have all summer and perhaps longer."

"It's like they want us to stay."

"They need someone to look after the pool and energy-saving systems. But we'll be searching for new places after the undergraduates return and grab the best ones."

"We can search together for our love nest, our haven from the turmoil." She broke away from his embrace and skipped ahead. "We can, can't we?"

He smiled. "Yes, my Welsh nymph, we can."

Chapter Five

Monday, August 2, 2027

As July turned to August, anger and aggression replaced bewildered acceptance of the government's new plans. Everyone was unhappy. Consumers because the price of gasoline had almost doubled in one week. Merchants because wholesale prices for their merchandise increased as supply became unreliable. Industrialists because new government regulations were onerous and confusing. And self-styled saviours because everyone ignored their solutions.

Elena glanced up from her computer screen when Dan offered her a morning cup of coffee on Halifax's Natal Day holiday. "They're doing something right if everyone's equally unhappy."

"Elimination of a four-billion-dollar subsidy for heavy oil producers hits our oil industry harder than others."

"The restrictions on thermal coal are also Draconian." She shrugged. "They must target coal-burning and heavy oil production."

He leaned on the back of her chair, reading over her shoulder. "It only works if it happens everywhere."

"Trust me," she said. Simple words that carried massive responsibility. Could she honestly expect him to trust her when she was keeping so many secrets? "Coal for heating is toast. Oil and natural gas are also feeling a serious pinch. It's a worldwide phenomenon."

"Even China and India?"

She nodded. "Those industries are finished."

"Won't clamping down on coal and heavy oil boost lighter oil and natural gas production?"

"The experts disagree. New measures will cause a recession."

He laughed, wondering if she'd identify the sources for her inside information. "Governments will pump in stimulus money."

"Not if they're serious about reducing carbon emissions. They must decrease demand and force populations everywhere into less wasteful lifestyles."

"A major shakeup?" he asked.

"That's what my sources tell me."

He pulled up a chair and wrapped an arm around her shoulders. "Hell for people with expensive living costs and businesses to manage, but we'll be fine. What about your family?"

She snorted. "The epitome of expensive lifestyles, but they're minted."

He waited, hoping she might elaborate, but she sipped her coffee with a wistful look in her eyes. "And your family?"

"Dad has a secure academic position. That leaves my sister and her husband. They may be exposed to economic shocks, but they have valuable skill sets."

Tuesday morning, Dan arrived at the university determined to ignore the impending personal and economic disruptions. Describing the rapid transition to stable carbon dioxide emissions was causing more computing problems than he expected. He'd concentrate on the accumulating pile of minor technical problems with his revised model. Attention to larger issues, if any remained, would follow.

By five fifteen, he'd generated and tested cures for four issues. He'd been working for nine hours with only short coffee breaks. *Time to discover what Elena learned today and reconnect with society's newfangled problems.*

When he arrived home, the door was locked. "Elena." Silence. He dropped his pack and strode to the patio. She wasn't by the pool or anywhere in the yard.

He searched the house before checking his email and her Twitter and Facebook pages. *No sign of a physical or electronic Elena.*

Dan popped open a beer, grabbed a bag of nacho chips, thinking that his addiction to these bland tortilla snacks might be getting out of hand. He shrugged and returned to the poolside patio. He'd relax, and they'd scare up dinner when she arrived.

At six thirty, he abandoned his post, sent Elena an email, and headed for the pub. He wandered past a service station where motorists queued for gas. Stores also had many customers.

For years, Dan and his fellow climate change activists argued the public would accept the costs of progressive action. As Dan strolled into his local watering hole, the noise and bustling activity confirmed their contention. People were making adjustments, including paying more for the carbon costs of the products they used. They might grumble, but they'd go along.

Industry and government represented the other half of the equation. Would they accept the new reality and make meaningful changes? Or would they pay lip service to environmental concerns and sleaze out of real change? The reinstatement of his sister's move after a minor delay supported that idea.

The tanking oil stocks on worldwide markets argued for a more substantive shift in industrial activity. Those trends suggested a shift away from a fossil-fuel-based economy.

An hour later, Dan stepped from the boisterous pub into the cold damp of another foggy evening. Too damn cold for his typical summer attire of golf shirt and walking shorts, but somehow fitting for the negative feelings that plagued him through his lonely evening meal.

He returned to an empty house. At ten, Elena's cryptic email arrived.

<Sorry, Dan, I couldn't tell you in person. I've been called home.

I must go. At the airport, plane leaves momentarily.

I already miss you.>

His eyes widened. *Could this be real? Yesterday evening, she was ecstatic about apartment hunting. Today, she's gone with no earlier opportunity to contact me?*

He checked the email's timestamp and departure times at Halifax's airport. The daily flight to London departed before she sent the message. Was she taking a late flight to Montreal or Toronto, or possibly Boston, planning to catch her transatlantic flight tomorrow?

Wednesday morning, Dan rose early, hoping for a message from Elena. Nothing. After a quick shower, he hiked to the university. He needed to bury himself in his models to keep his mind off her.

Minutes after he arrived, Steve Matthews appeared with Tim Hortons coffees and a box of muffins. "New field measurements let me reassess approaches to microscale horizontal turbulence."

Dan tore his eyes from his computer screen. "This is important for me?"

"If you curtail carbon emissions and temperature flatlines, atmospheric turbulence should decrease. Ocean turbulence may become more important for your Labrador Sea deep-water formation."

"Doubt it. Your adjustments to vertical turbulence may be important, but advection is the major process moving heat into convective areas."

"That's not proven."

Dan shrugged. He could easily prove it. "Provide your modified diffusion coefficients, and I'll apply them after I get the new model running."

"That's all I ask." Steve picked up his coffee and headed for the door. He left one coffee and the muffins on Dan's desk.

At five, Dan leaned back from his computer and assessed his progress while the latest version of his new climate model digested the data. His long day, fueled by coffee and the four muffins Steve left him, appeared successful.

Madison Jeffries appeared as he powered down his computer. "Heading home? Time for coffee?"

"Will John be joining us?" He preferred a beer, but not without her husband.

"Not this time," she said while looking down, her fists clenched. "There's something I must tell you."

He took a deep breath. "Where?"

"The library atrium. I'm meeting John at six, so I'd rather stay on campus."

After a short walk from the oceanography building to the library, Dan purchased two mugs of coffee at a takeout counter. "What's the big news?"

"I saw Elena this morning. It was weird."

His chest tightened, and he shivered. "Okay..."

"I was downtown visiting a lawyer about some family business. As I left, I noticed Elena hurrying along the opposite sidewalk. I followed, hoping we'd have coffee together."

"This morning?"

Madison charged on, apparently oblivious to Dan's question and puzzled expression. "Before I caught up, she turned into the Prince George Hotel. As I arrived in the lobby, she entered an elevator. It went straight to the tenth floor."

"So?"

"The new tenth floor has long-term rentals."

"Perhaps she met someone?"

"How would I know? I lingered over two coffees in the hotel bar. She didn't return."

Dan hesitated, raking a hand through his hair. "She left yesterday. I got an email saying she was returning to England in response to an emergency. If she couldn't get a flight..."

"She'd return to your place or stay at an airport hotel, and she wouldn't be meeting anyone in a tenth-floor suite." Madison pulled out her phone and plugged in a number. "Hello. Elena Llewellyn's room, please." Another pause. "Oh, sorry. Must have the wrong hotel."

"This *is* getting weird."

"Yeah, weird. And there's more. I phoned the friend who rented a room to Elena when she first arrived in Halifax."

"She lived there until she moved in with me three weeks ago."

Madison shook her head. "She only stayed for two weeks. And one more thing. That course she's taking—it doesn't exist."

Dan's heart pounded. "No way!"

"I'm so sorry, Dan. I know you really liked her, and she was good for you." She put her hand on his. "Elena's involved in something sinister. I had to tell you."

Dan analyzed their conversation as he trudged home. Madison met Elena shortly after she arrived in Halifax, found her accommodation with three friends, and brought her to one of their Friday afternoon get-togethers.

Her British passport confirmed her name. Her heritage was Welsh, and she had a classy English accent. She told them she was an orphan raised by a bachelor uncle who ran a bank. Elena claimed a degree in political philosophy from the London School of Economics. She said she moved to Halifax to escape a suffocating home life while pursuing her interests in philosophy.

After he arrived home, Dan searched in vain for Facebook, Twitter, or LinkedIn accounts associated with the British Elena Llewellyn. Googling her name revealed an Elena Llewellyn associated with the Llewellyn Bank, a financial firm based in London, England. The next step was finding a picture linking that Elena with his mysterious friend.

His search yielded information about the bank and its chairman Gareth Llewellyn's role in London society, but no pictures of his niece. Dan did discover a link to Halifax. The Llewellyn Bank provided financing for the Prince George Hotel's recent expansion.

He kept digging and found her picture on a social website linked to the London School of Economics. It confirmed she'd graduated from LSE two years earlier and provided pictures of an heiress living in a social swirl far beyond anything Dan could imagine. He stared at the images, shocked by the message they carried.

Her deceit and the cavalier way she'd abandoned him should have made him angrier. But he didn't feel the anger. He'd arrived home, hoping she'd be waiting for him. Now, as he searched the web, he sought something to exonerate her, explain her behaviour, and presage their getting back together.

Rather than sit home drinking more beer after a dinner of beans and beer, Dan headed for the Prince George Hotel. A hotel brochure he found in the lobby described the recent expansion to add suites targeted at business customers on the ninth floor. New executive suites for longer-term rentals were on the tenth. He took the elevator to the ninth floor but discovered he needed a special pass to reach the tenth.

Thursday morning, Dan dressed more formally than usual and returned, hoping to see Elena. At noon, after a leisurely breakfast, an hour hanging about the lobby shops, and two more loitering outside, he abandoned his quest.

"How's it going?" Steve asked from Dan's office doorway late that afternoon.

"Lousy. Arrived at twelve thirty and accomplished bugger all."

"She's gone, hasn't she?"

"Who?"

"Come on, Dan, don't mess with me. Madison knows something bad about Elena but won't elaborate, and she's not taking calls."

Steve hadn't shifted from Dan's doorway. Did his diminutive colleague fear a violent reaction? Dan wasn't as intimidating as John Jeffries, but a ninety-eight-pound weakling would tower over Steve. "She's not the person we thought she was, and she's done a bunk."

"Should I leave? Or would talking help?"

Dan sighed. "I need someone to explain what she was doing here."

Steve finally entered and pulled Dan's extra chair to the spot Elena always chose. "Too big a question. Try something smaller, something tractable that leads us toward the big one."

"Okay, first question. Does the Llewellyn Bank have an executive suite on the tenth floor of the Prince George Hotel?"

"Leave it with me. You'll have your answer tomorrow morning. Now get working on your models. I need results, and so do you."

Steve strode away, leaving Dan wondering if he was as mysterious as Elena. He'd been a PhD student at Dalhousie years earlier, but left to manage a family firm. He'd returned to continue his studies. That made him older than his fellow graduate students, but not necessarily mysterious. But if he could extract privileged information from the hotel...

Steve reappeared at noon on Friday. "Can't stay, but I've answered your question. The bank has reserved a tenth-floor suite since the floor opened. Elena occupied it for the past six months. She checked out yesterday afternoon. Gotta go. Big weekend."

Dan slumped in his chair, struggling to breathe. She'd deceived them from the start. He could no longer assume she'd reappear with an explanation that blew away his doubts. And Steve's explanation of how he found out suggested his family engineering firm was larger and more important than he'd previously implied. The situation was getting crazier and crazier.

At home that evening, Dan had opened his third beer when Elena's message, a video attached to an email, arrived. His hand shook as he accessed it. Her face appeared on the screen, then she stepped back and held up a newspaper.

"Today's edition of the *Daily Mail*. Check it online if you don't believe I'm home in my London flat." She stepped aside to let the camera see into her apartment.

Her face returned to the screen. "I hoped to send this message sooner, but the travel restrictions caught me, and I couldn't leave Halifax on Wednesday. Finally got away yesterday afternoon. Won't bore you with the details, but I arrived in London two hours ago."

She looked away from the camera. "Checking my notes. I'm sending you this message to tell you I'm sorry. I didn't want to leave, but Uncle Gareth has a mission to save the world. Can't give you details, but when it comes out, you'll see it's an honourable quest, one you'll support."

Once again, she looked down. "He needed my help, and I couldn't refuse. I'm sorry I didn't handle it better. I can't explain. I just couldn't."

She stopped to dab tears before a sniff, followed by a wry smile. "You must be angry with me, but I couldn't avoid it." She wiped another tear. "I love you, Dan, more than anyone in the entire world. Someday, we'll get together. Until then, I'm thinking of you." She sniffed. "Please don't hate me. I know I'm doing right. Have to go before I completely dissolve into tears. Bye, but just for now."

The screen went blank. She was gone. The emotional, disjointed message appeared honest and heartfelt, but it explained nothing. Dan was as uncertain as he'd been three weeks earlier when she followed him home with her story about super-intelligent whales.

Chapter Six

Monday August 9, 2027

Elena gazed at the streetscape through a window in the apartment created by England's trendiest interior decorator. Custom-made ultramodern furniture and paintings by leaders in the avant-garde art scene made her London flat unique and the envy of her friends.

The twenty-five-year-old heiress should have been happy, but images of Halifax and Dan Delacour refused to devolve into sepia-toned memories. She had candid photos taken during the few weeks they lived together and money to burn. After staring at the photos on her cell phone, she reached a decision. She'd commission a magic realist portrait, a feminist take on Goya's Nude Maja, to keep his memory sharp until she convinced him to join her.

Elena turned her back on the early morning sunshine, strode to the kitchen, and activated her coffee maker. She'd missed her luxurious lifestyle during most of the six months she'd masqueraded as a student in Nova Scotia. Now, as she added a pre-packaged premium coffee pod, she imagined Dan pouring boiling water through spoonfuls of bargain-brand pre-ground coffee in a laboratory funnel. Somehow, those low-tech early morning pick-me-ups tasted better than the caffeine-rich masterpieces her space-age machine created.

After coffee and a breakfast bagel with cream cheese, a habit she'd acquired from Dan, Elena left her trendy flat for the Notting Hill Gate underground station. The Central Line train would take her to St. Paul's in the City of London and a short walk to the Llewellyn Bank of Wales. There she'd report to Chairman and CEO Gareth Llewellyn, her closest living relative, on her time as an undercover agent.

Uncle Gareth was more than the chairman of an investment bank. He was a key player in a consortium of industrialists with global ambitions. They were using their financial might to encourage government action on climate change.

Her clandestine mission had been part of that effort. It was a simple task for a sophisticated young woman. Befriend the graduate students and post-doctoral fellows in the oceanography department and report on their research activities. After four months gathering information, she focused on Daniel Delacour. The leader of the graduate students researching climate change succumbed to her womanly wiles.

It began as a lark, something to do after graduating from the London School of Economics and stodging around her uncle's bank for a year. She could channel Mata Hari and support his quest, one she'd accepted without question. Then something went seriously wrong. She had to abandon her mission and the lover she'd become devoted to.

Jeremy Groves, another of her uncle's agents, told her Uncle Gareth had recalled her to London. Had someone broken her cover? Or was Jeremy sent to extract her for unrelated reasons?

The questions festered as she made her first daily commute from her flat to the investment bank in a gilded building.

A note stuck to the front of a bulging file summoned Elena to her uncle's corner office.

Gareth Llewellyn, a dapper fifty-seven-year-old whose aura of sophistication projected an image much larger than his modest stature, gazed without rising. "What went wrong?"

"My cover story was inadequate. We need stories that withstand scrutiny."

Uncle Gareth drummed his fingers on his desk. "Time was tight, and we were dealing with university students, not professional security forces."

"Graduate students are curious by definition, and they discovered the flaws in my cover."

He shuffled papers and read for a minute. "But not your mission."

"They realized I was working undercover, masquerading as someone I was not. But they cannot know the reasons for my subterfuge. I would have mended the rifts if you hadn't called me home." She tried not to grimace, but she lacked the confidence implied by her words. *Would Dan have accepted my overtures?*

"Don't worry. You were an anomaly in our surveillance network because I needed a task to introduce you to our crusade. Others, like young Groves, are legitimate students. We pay them retainers to document research activities."

Elena tried to decipher her uncle's expression. Did he recall her after he discovered her romantic attachment to Dan? Or did the file on her desk suggest he needed her to address something else? "I saw the file but didn't have time to study it."

"We're moving ahead. You will assess the information we receive from our agents."

"I was an observer, a gatherer of data. You must have experts to analyze it."

"Dear me," Gareth said while shaking his head. "Whatever happened to my niece's unbridled confidence? You have field experience and a first in political philosophy. Make use of your capabilities and become an expert. Great changes are imminent, and you shall have a role."

She recalled the chaos gripping Halifax in the days before she departed. "The carbon taxes and restrictions on usage are part of your plan, are they not? Otherwise, it wouldn't be happening everywhere simultaneously."

"Governments responded to an external climate-related threat."

"We know that's a hoax. There were no aliens or other external threats. It was in my final report, and I suspect my fellow spies made similar comments."

A devilish grin spread across Gareth's face. "Fortunately, everyone isn't as perceptive. The ploy worked. The world accepts the critical need for immediate reductions in carbon emissions."

She stared. Her uncle's smug reaction was hard to accept. Did his organization have more than an advisory role? Were they involved in a monumental conspiracy that subverted the will of worldwide governments? "What comes next?"

"Remediation, engineering solutions to counteract carbon dioxide accumulation over the past decades. But that's not your problem." Gareth sidestepped his desk and headed toward his office door. "You're to analyze the scientific and social response to our efforts to control temperature. Focus on your task and let the politicians and engineers worry about theirs."

Elena returned to her desk and spread the file's contents across its pristine surface. What would she learn? Would it justify activities that appear clandestine, and frankly, immoral? Could her new task quell her fears, provide a challenging new focus, and a responsible role in their noble cause? Would it subsume her longings for Daniel Delacour? Or would it provide proof her uncle's means for achieving his 'noble' objectives were too underhanded?

*****

Six weeks later, on the western side of the Atlantic, Dan strode to his office, contemplating the changes he'd seen since Elena disappeared.

He was living alone in the attic of a renovated house. It was an interesting apartment extending from front to back with a little balcony. The floor area was huge, fifty square metres, but the sloped ceilings restricted standing room to a central strip.

He'd moved when his sister's family occupied their new house. The new travel restrictions had delayed their move east from Winnipeg by three weeks. Their experiences joined the list of inconvenient accommodations people were making as they learned to cope with their brave new world. They were real but not onerous.

The stock market presented a different story. The decline in worldwide markets was the worst since the 1929 crash. Shares of large companies associated with the fossil fuel industries had plummeted to one-quarter or one-third of their value several months earlier. Those of many smaller companies became worthless.

After spending the day reassessing atmospheric carbon dioxide and temperature data for the past sixty-five years, Dan arrived at Steve and Anna's for dinner. "Just a simple meal. A Polish goulash for the three of us," Anna insisted when she extended the invitation.

He had flowers in one hand and the results of his day's labour in the other.

Steve laughed as Dan passed the flowers to Anna. "No one else would bring a printout from his latest investigations to dinner."

Dan ignored him as he extracted a bottle of wine from his backpack.

Anna wrinkled her nose at Steve before turning toward Dan. "Flowers are nice, and we always appreciate another bottle. But, in this company, your new results are probably better than the others together." She smiled as she led the way into their apartment.

After dinner, Anna brought the discussion around to what she'd claimed was the best of his hostess gifts. "It's time for your new results."

Dan leaned over and fetched his sheets of computer printout from an end table. "The big question, are the changes governments mandated so quickly helping? In the past, scientists took their time getting their estimates of atmospheric CO_2 and temperature right. They provided an annual measure during the following spring."

"But that's no longer adequate," Steve interjected. "Two months and the public's clamoring for answers."

"So, Dan?" Her little smirk showed she was joking. "Are they working?"

Dan pointed with the spoon he'd used to stir sugar into his coffee. "You're as bad as everyone else."

"Get on with it."

"If we're to make estimates on sub-annual time scales, we must understand the variability. Carbon dioxide is straightforward because it shows consistent seasonal variability. We can produce seasonally adjusted monthly estimates of the year-to-year changes."

"And they tell us?" Anna asked.

Dan smiled, enjoying his dramatic presentation. "It's increased following the established trend until the merest hint of a slight reduction in the August data."

"Amazing. You suggesting you can see a break in trend from one month's data?"

He passed them graphs of his monthly atmospheric CO_2 concentrations for the past three years. "Only a hint, but it's a tantalizing suggestion. The temperature observations are more interesting, but the noise is a problem."

Anna rolled her eyes and thumped the table, rattling the crockery. "Get on with it."

"I've generated a smoothing function, and the results are fascinating. I'll need a critical assessment of my approach, but that's for later. First, you must see what I've discovered."

Dan distributed graphs of his smoothed monthly temperature trends and waited, sipping coffee and nibbling a piece of cake.

Steve shook his head. "Can't be. Your procedure must be wrong."

Anna looked up, frowning, "Are you suggesting we've had a progressive reduction in the rate of temperature increases since October 2026?"

Steve turned on his partner. "That's why I said it can't be. If CO_2 goes up, temperature must follow. They're intimately linked."

"Please educate a stupid quantum mechanicist," she said, turning to Dan for support.

"Steve's invoking the greenhouse gas effect of CO_2. It generates the well-established relationship between atmospheric carbon dioxide concentrations and global temperatures."

Anna pouted. "I know about the positive relationship between carbon dioxide and temperature. The entire world understands the greenhouse effect."

"It's the major driver of atmospheric temperature changes. But we have other drivers. That's why temperature trends are more erratic than carbon dioxide ones."

"You're suggesting something else is driving temperature, uncoupling it from the CO_2 trend?"

"Exactly."

"But what?"

"Don't know, but I have one final piece of evidence that may be important."

"And what's that?" Steve asked, scowling.

"NASA's admitted to problems with surface ocean reflectivity measurements in their global climate observation program. They're seeing increased reflectivity starting sometime last year. They claim it's a calibration problem, but they haven't resolved it."

Steve's scowl disappeared as he reengaged. "And you think this links with the weird temperature trend?"

"The timing's right, and we need something to explain a flattening temperature trend nine months before governments acted."

Chapter Seven

Friday, February 11, 2028

Four months later, on a cold, wet winter evening, Elena joined her Strategic Analysis Group colleagues at a trendy Farringdon Street wine bar in the City of London. They were celebrating results trumpeting a major reduction in global temperature increases.

Memories of Dan Delacour reacting to similar observations flashed through her mind. She shook her head after waving an arm. "We shouldn't jump to conclusions based on a few numbers."

Elena slumped into her chair when no one heeded her warning. Dan would have persisted, identifying traps they were falling into, but she lacked the expertise to argue her case.

She picked up her wineglass and tuned out the conversation. She was pondering ways to reconnect with her Dalhousie oceanography friends when Alfredo Rodriguez's loud but slurred voice jolted her from her reverie.

Alfredo was their team's brooding beast—a bulky man with a receding hairline, bushy eyebrows, and deep-set eyes. He glowered, saying little during social occasions, but he wasn't known for over-imbibing.

"They're screwing us around. The fiasco is a ploy to corner coal and oil supplies. The principals in our effing cartel will soon own every scrap of coal and oil on our blighted planet."

"Bollocks," someone replied. "The new regulations are killing markets for coal and heavy oil. Those resources will be worthless."

Alfredo rose and almost toppled onto the table. "They're buying them for nothing. Then, they'll publicize their global warming fix. The value of coal and oil will shoot up, and our bosses will own it all." He crashed into his chair, a solid piece of furniture that survived the impact.

Alfredo sat immobile with eyes closed while everyone gaped. He opened his eyes and continued his rant.

"Poor sod who works for Space Technologies tells me everything's in place. Once they receive the signal, they'll announce their cure, and global warming will become a footnote in the history books."

This generated another question. "Space Technologies? Are they one of ours?"

"German high-tech firm owned by one of the bloody conspirators taking over the effing world."

"You talking about the Company of Gentlemen Entrepreneurs?"

"Damn right. Two hundred industrial oligarchs who control over fifty percent of the world's wealth."

Brandon Newbury took Alfredo's arm and helped him to his feet. "Come, Alfie, it's time we saw you home."

Alfredo stumbled from the wine bar, leaning on his equally tall but leaner colleague. Brandon was an Eton and Oxford-educated scion of a family that probably belonged to the mysterious industrial association dedicated to solving climate change. He'd remained silent as Alfredo vented his anger.

The gathering broke up, and Elena returned to her apartment. She collapsed into her bedroom armchair and addressed the portrait she'd commissioned from the country's leading magic realist painter. It was hanging over the head of her bed.

"Please, Daniel," she said. "Talk to me. I've learned something startling. You'll understand the details. When I next contact you, please, please, respond."

Later, Elena fired up her laptop, but she didn't email Dan. She searched for information related to Alfredo's outpouring.

The background was relatively clear. Uncle Gareth and his colleagues in the Company of Gentlemen Entrepreneurs had a plan, one he didn't explain, to control global warming. Something convinced governments to commit to this plan. But what was it? When she questioned the legitimacy of alien threats, Uncle Gareth laughed at the gullibility of governments and the public. Did that suggest the company concocted the false threat?

Alfredo insisted coal and heavy oil were the primary targets. Market prices for these commodities plummeted. Share prices dropped and trading volumes spiked. Were company members amassing millions of shares?

Her research proved the concentration of ownership was as Alfredo described. Establishing the basis for his other claims was tougher.

The European Space Agency had launched small satellites into orbit high above Earth. Their website described a network joined by electromagnetic forces. They claimed it would mitigate greenhouse heating by deflecting solar radiation away from Earth. Astronomers discredited such a protective shield.

She'd linked Uncle Gareth and the Company of Gentlemen Entrepreneurs to the alien threats using unproven inferences. Was the company also responsible for this latest fairy tale? If Space Technologies was implementing a technological solution, it must involve their mysterious satellites. Astronomers said they couldn't provide a heat shield, but they must have a role in the company's global warming cure. What could it be?

Elena seldom regretted her lack of scientific knowledge, but right now, she was thoroughly confused. Alfredo insisted the company had a scheme to control global warming while manipulating the price of coal, oil, and gas. But carbon dioxide produced from the burning of fossil fuels generated global warming. Uncle Gareth and his colleagues could only gain from buying up the shares of these energy companies if they could control global warming without restricting carbon dioxide emissions. How could they do that?

She needed Dan's knowledge and insights. But she feared rejection if she called him or sent a message. She scoured the depths of her mind for a sure-fire approach he couldn't reject. She dared not contact him until she had that plan in place.

*****

The same afternoon, Dan joined Anna, Steve, Madison, and John in the Muse.

"What's new?" he asked as Madison poured the first round.

"Godbots," Anna replied.

"What the hell are they?" John asked.

Madison set down the pitcher. "Satellites launched by a privately held company in Germany. A cynic who questioned their real purpose gave them that nickname."

Dan glanced up from his beer. "Using the European Space Agency's launch capability?"

"First ones were," Madison replied. "More recently, American, Russian, and Chinese militaries have launched them."

Anna reclaimed her story. "The proponents say they'll create an electrostatic grid that covers the sky like a reflective parasol. It will track solar noon and deflect heat into space."

"Is that possible?" Dan asked.

"Sun-synchronous orbits are commonplace," Anna replied before shaking her head. "An electrostatic grid is not. They compare it to atomic structure where solid-looking material is mostly small atomic nuclei separated by empty space."

"Incredible. You're going from femtometres to megametres. That's a huge change in scale. Can such an analogy be valid?"

"Reminds me of the arguments about alien communications last summer," Anna said. "Insufficient info for a definitive assessment, but the scientific consensus says no."

Dan put down his glass and drummed his fingers on the tabletop. "When did the European Space Agency start launching them?"

"Eighteen months ago. Why?"

"That's when NASA's ocean reflectivity measurements went haywire."

"What about militaries taking over the program?" Steve asked. "Is that significant?"

Dan increased the intensity of the tattoo he was drumming on the table. Godbots launched from American, Russian, and Chinese bases suggested surveillance, but he couldn't ignore the coincidental timing. "Is this related to the disconnect between atmospheric CO_2 and temperature?"

"How?" Madison asked.

"CO_2 has continued to increase except for a brief pause last summer. When they announce the annual number for 2027, it will be higher than 2026."

John snorted, a harbinger of his first challenge in weeks. "Why hasn't the IPCC produced last year's number?"

Madison put her hand on John's arm. "IPCC?"

"Intergovernmental Panel on Climate Change," Dan replied. "They're responsible for assessing climate change science, but they're super cautious. Their 2027 numbers will be out soon. They'll show us CO_2 is up following the long-term trend, and the temperature is almost the same as 2026."

"What makes you so damn sure?" John said as he shrugged off Madison's hand.

"I needn't be as cautious as the IPCC when I assess the monthly results I've been compiling."

"You alarmists never are."

Dan glanced from Steve to Anna. *Would they object if he mentioned their investigations?* "CO_2 concentrations plateaued for two months last summer, then resumed their upward trend. Temperatures have been flattening since the middle of 2026."

Madison stared with a furrowed brow. "That makes no sense. How could last summer's political action designed to arrest the relentless increases in global temperatures influence temperatures a year earlier?"

"Indeed," Dan replied while watching John. *How will he respond?*

"For Christ's sake, Dan, what are you telling us? Someone started launching mysterious satellites in 2026. The reflectivity sensors went tits up, and the temperature stopped increasing. Why?"

"Thank you, John, for the concise summary. Steve, Anna, and I have struggled with this for months. We're sure our numbers are okay, but we can't answer your question."

Dan left the Muse an hour later. He slithered along icy Halifax sidewalks considering a factor he hadn't mentioned. In her goodbye video, Elena said her uncle had a secret philanthropic mission.

Dan spent days digging into that mission. He learned banker Gareth Llewellyn was well-integrated with the political-industrial elites. He attended high-level meetings like the World Economic Forums at Davos, Switzerland, where bankers, industrialists, and leaders of the world's major democracies discussed economic and social policy. In recent years, climate change had been a major concern. Did Llewellyn's mission provide the outside influence that galvanized governmental action?

An unseen natural decoupling of the temperature carbon dioxide relationship wasn't tenable. That left a massive scale technological disruption. Could Gareth Llewellyn and his industrial colleagues unleash such a fix? A completely unknown technical solution was unbelievable. Foisting their solution on humanity without anyone noticing was even more incredible. That idea was as far-fetched as Elena's suggestion whales ruled the world, or the equally impossible alien forces orchestrating the Global Climate Action Day announcements.

Elena Llewellyn was sitting in London at the heart of this phenomenal undertaking, if undertaking it was. In a fairy-tale romance, he and Elena would join forces to resolve the problems, vanquish their incredibly powerful enemies, and save the world. But this wasn't a fairy tale, and he couldn't forget how she left without making any effort to explain her actions. And the explanatory video she sent him two days later raised more questions than it answered.

Dan couldn't shake dreams of getting back together with Elena from his head, but she wasn't the answer. He, Steve, and Anna must solve the puzzle without her help.

Chapter Eight

Tuesday, April 18, 2028

Two months after Alfredo's outburst in the Farrington Street wine bar, Elena strode to the South End Halifax house containing Dan's new apartment. Her attire on the sunny spring afternoon was practical but elegant. None of the hippie garb she favoured during her sojourn in Halifax. She sported sandals, skirt, top, light jacket, and broad-brimmed hat from her favourite designer's casual springtime collection. She sat perched on the stoop when he arrived home.

"What are *you* doing here?" he demanded.

"I have critical information, and we must talk... about us."

He stood rigid, with his thumbs tucked under his belt, scowling. "You can't rationalize deceiving us and buggering off?"

"Please, give me ten minutes because you need the information, and I *can* explain."

"Why should I care?" Dan asked as he glanced toward the tops of wine bottles poking from a leather bag nestled between her knees.

"Because you don't understand my motives. I meant to help; my contribution to the war against global warming."

His scowl hardened. "I'll give you ten minutes. This better be good."

He helped her up, and they climbed the stairs to his apartment. The steeper stairs from the second to third floors reminded Elena of the narrow staircase to dingy servants' quarters in her grandparents' English country house. The bright, spacious room they entered surprised her.

She held out her bottles of French Beaujolais. "If you'll allow me a few extra minutes, we could sample one."

Dan perused the labels. "Nice wines. But you're not buying me off with forty-dollar bottles of wine. Tell your story and leave."

"Dan, please, be a gentleman. Open a bottle and offer me a glass. One glass whilst I explain the situation. Then, I promise, I'll leave."

He shrugged his shoulders. "Waste of time, but if that's what you want..."

She gazed across the narrow street at the tightly packed Edwardian houses while he located corkscrew and glasses.

He returned with an opened bottle, wine glasses, and a plate of crackers and cheese. He pulled a second chair close to the low table where he deposited his tray and pointed to the unoccupied chair. "The floor is yours."

Elena took a deep breath, trying to decipher Dan's response. He'd talked tough but bent to her will surprisingly easily. *Does that mean I'm winning?*

"My uncle shares your conviction global warming must stop. He sent me here, and colleagues to other universities, to discover the latest scientific research."

"Bullshit! No one sends spies to learn about our research. We publish it in journals anyone can read."

"We can't wait years for the publication of your results. And we weren't tapping phones or reading emails. I just listened to your discourse."

"You deceived us. Your story about taking a summer school course before starting grad studies was a farce." He gazed at her elegant clothes and grunted. "And that crap about being a poor student escaping an unpleasant family situation—total crap. You're a fucking rich bitch, probably worth ten million dollars."

Rich bitch annoyed her, and she almost forgot her resolve to hold her temper. Her net worth was closer to three hundred million pounds, but admitting it would be a disaster. "So, I'm wealthy. It's not a big deal, and I never said I was poor. I said I was escaping an awkward family situation, and that was true. I dressed down because I wouldn't fit in at the grad house pub wearing designer clothes."

Dan grabbed the wine bottle. "Unbelievable. Pretending to make an effort with the wine. It's trivial, a bagatelle."

"My behaviour was wrong," she admitted as tears pooled in her eyes. *How can I put this disastrous red herring behind us without dissolving into tears?*

"I realize my mission was suspicious. I don't care if you forgive me..." She took several deep breaths. "No, that's wrong. I do care, but right now, it's unimportant. I've learned things scientists must know."

He leaned forward and put his hand on hers. "Okay, I'll suspend my disbelief. This better not be a repeat of your whale tale."

A few tears escaped as she smiled, imagining his portrait on her bedroom wall. "That tale led to the happiest weeks of my life. Couldn't it happen again?"

Dan shook his head. "Get on with it."

"After I returned to London, Uncle Gareth gave me a new job." She hesitated, staring at her glass. She was already skirting around uncomfortable realities. "I've learned some disquieting things."

"Sometimes," he replied as he leaned back, sipped wine, and nibbled cheese. "It's best to cut the crap and just say it."

Elena described how her uncle's efforts to fight climate change might be less honourable than she first thought. She ended with the Company of Gentlemen Entrepreneur's scheme to reduce global temperatures while expanding the burning of coal and oil.

"Whoa, stop there," he said. "Do you know how this works?"

"They've subverted the political process and cornered the coal and oil markets. But I don't understand how they can control global temperatures while expanding burning."

Dan leaned forward and topped up their wine glasses. "Go through what you know."

She choked back the urge to emit a victory whoop. "First, my uncle's colleagues are responsible for the satellites designed to shield Earth from solar radiation."

"That's bunk. They cannot shield the planet."

"But Space Technologies is preventing warming. If it isn't those satellites, what is it?"

"Space Technologies, you're sure?"

"They've built a specialized plant, and the entire production disappears without a trace. I thought it was satellite production. Is it something else?" She stared into his eyes, hoping he'd understand her sincerity.

Dan drained his wine glass and sighed. He leaned forward, his eyes engaging hers. He summarized his understanding of the disconnect between temperature and carbon dioxide that he, Steve, and Anna developed over the preceding months.

Elena stared. He'd confirmed things she'd guessed at. They led her straight to an unpalatable conclusion. "If they've broken the link between carbon dioxide and temperature, we can return to a carbon economy. They'll make a killing."

"By they, I presume you mean this cartel of sinister industrialists."

Elena wrinkled her nose, reminded of her uncertainty about her uncle's motives. "I'm not sure they're all equally guilty."

"Stick to the science."

"We resume burning coal and oil, but don't increase temperatures. Then what?"

Dan clapped his hands on his knees. "Don't know, but I have two questions to ponder. How are they doing it, and what's the impact? You've finished your wine, so you should go."

She stared, shocked by his rapid shift in behaviour. "I could stay, make dinner, and..."

Dan shook his head. "You're pushing too hard. We can meet for dinner tomorrow, and I'll tell you what I've discovered."

She leaned over and gave him a quick kiss. She'd figured it out. The careful scientist had an idea he wanted to work through before saying anything. "'Till tomorrow. I'll find somewhere quiet and let you know."

She flew down the stairs, through the main door, and onto the street. "Mission accomplished," she said when she was safely on her way to the Prince George Hotel.

*****

Dan opened his computer search window before Elena reached the street. He started with stock market activity of companies involved in fossil fuel industries. His investigation confirmed her statements about the concentration of shares in the hands of mega-investors already dominating the industry.

His next observation was more surprising. The increased trading volumes began in the summer of 2026, one year before the worldwide interventions that depressed prices. Questions about why investors were in the market a year before the crisis hit didn't interest him. The critical discovery was more evidence the game began a year before Global Climate Action Day. And game was the correct word, a gigantic chess game with humanity as pawns.

He couldn't identify the players moving the pawns on the global chessboard. Were the major industrial countries running the show? Was Elena's Company of Gentlemen Entrepreneurs a force behind the thrones? Or was another human, animal, or alien mastermind pulling the strings?

He paused, checking the darkening sky. Nine o'clock. He'd been engrossed in his task for three hours. Time to enjoy a beer, heat a pizza, and tackle the problem of Space Technologies. He'd save the second bottle of wine for another occasion.

After pizza, Dan carried his second beer to his computer desk. He plunked it by the monitor and typed Space Technologies into his search bar. The company website highlighted technology for the development and production of nanoparticles for various commercial applications. Reflective nanoparticles that increased the brightness of freshly laundered fabrics were their most successful product.

Next, he located the mysterious Space Technologies factory Elena mentioned. The company website called it their new product development centre, but didn't specify what products they were developing.

Dan located the factory near Brunsbuttel, on the Kiel Canal. It had docking facilities for three undersea cable laying vessels they'd converted for oceanographic research. Google Maps showed one ship, approximately seventy metres long, alongside their dock.

The final gem he plucked from the Space Technologies website was a brief reference to electrostatically linked satellites the company built between 2023 and 2025. The company awaited an assessment of the success of the twelve satellites launched by the European Space Agency. *Were these the Godbots Anna mentioned at the Muse?*

He closed the website and searched for additional information on the company. The pickings for the privately held company were slim. When he abandoned his search at three, he'd uncovered several significant facts. The company was involved in satellite development, and they had serious interests in nanoparticles and oceanographic research.

After insufficient hours of fitful sleep, Dan returned to the fray. His target was the work of several oceanography students who studied at Dalhousie six to ten years earlier. The main players were Jacinta Lopez Martinez and Tony Atherton. Jacinta investigated the response of phytoplankton to acidic ocean waters between 2019 and 2023. Her simulations of a future acidic ocean generated huge increases in biological production. Between 2022 and 2025, Tony conducted studies that quantified the removal of organic carbon from Jacinta's more acidic ocean.

Dan had ignored their work because the environmental impacts of the changes they observed in aquaria wouldn't manifest themselves for decades. Upheavals Dan expected from the cessation of deep-water formation meant they may never encounter such low pH conditions.

But the mysterious mechanism controlling global temperatures could delay or even circumvent the changes in ocean circulation he'd been studying. If carbon emissions kept increasing, ocean acidification would follow as night follows day. Jacinta and Tony's elevated primary productivity could become the next watershed event in the climate change saga.

He imagined a crazy scientist sitting in a control centre juggling temperature, pH, and primary productivity to generate a stable climate. It would be a disaster waiting to happen.

Tony and Jacinta were former students of Dr. Heinrich Krueger, Dan's supervisor. Their PhD theses would be available in the department office, and he could consult Dr. K when he returned from his latest trip. But Dan only had ten hours before dinner with Elena.

As he poured boiling water into his coffee funnel, he remembered Steve Matthews was a graduate student at Dalhousie between 2021 and 2023 before suspending his studies for several years so he could return home to rescue his family business. He must have known Jacinta and Tony.

When Dan arrived in his office doorway, Steve glanced up from his computer screen. "Checking out the chatter on social media. No one's addressing the disconnect between the CO_2 and temperature trends."

"That's so annoying," Dan replied. "NASA must see the trends we're seeing. Why aren't they saying anything?"

After discussing NASA's odd reaction for several minutes, Steve shifted the focus of their conversation. "That question didn't bring you to my doorway…"

Dan placed the two PhD dissertations he'd collected from the department office on Steve's desk. "I'm looking into Jacinta Lopez and Tony Atherton's thesis projects."

"Jacinta Lopez. Feisty little woman." Steve smirked. "Your type, but she's married with a child."

"Be serious. What can you tell me about her work?"

"Biological study of phytoplankton's response to the lower pH ocean we'll see in sixty years. She focused on changes to their physiology." He tapped his index finger on Tony's thesis. "You'll be more interested in this one."

"What did he discover?"

"Increased phytoplankton productivity Jacinta observed translates into increased transport of organic carbon to ocean sediments. His modelling efforts suggest the transports will impact carbon dioxide concentrations."

Dan picked up Jacinta's dissertation and flipped through the pages. "I should return this one and concentrate on Tony's?"

Steve nodded. "If you're interested in transport. I hadn't given their work much thought. Tony's calculations showed the elevated primary productivity in a more acidic ocean won't have an ecological impact until 2100."

"But if temperature's controlled while carbon emissions continue to grow, we release more CO_2 into the atmosphere and drive down ocean pH—"

"And the doomsday scenario Tony describes in his thesis comes into play."

Dan picked up the heavy volume. "It could become… important."

Chapter Nine

Wednesday, April 19, 2028

Elena sauntered into the upscale boutique hotel wearing an elegant navy-blue cocktail dress. She surveyed the lobby and pseudo-Victorian dining room with tables tucked into alcoves. They were perfect for the dinner conversation she imagined.

Dan arrived wearing dress pants, a shirt and tie, and a sports jacket. The leather satchel slung over his shoulder matched his tan-coloured trousers and gave him a professorial appearance. He wasn't as elegantly dressed as she was, but he'd tried, and she appreciated it.

She stepped forward and hugged him before nodding to the *maître d'*. He led them to the table she'd chosen. Waiters with appetizers and drinks followed.

"Quite the performance," Dan said as the *maître d'* held Elena's chair for her. "But don't you let your guest choose?"

She smiled, imagining Dan escorting her to parties in the homes of her influential society friends. "When we attend London dinner parties, they'll serve the most popular cocktail and canapés they prefer. Tonight, it's my party, so my choices."

Dan sat back, sipping the martini-like drink the waiter poured from a metal dispenser. "Visiting London seems like a distant possibility. Shouldn't we focus on more immediate concerns?"

If that was his choice, she could provide a serious concern. "A group of ultra-wealthy businessmen usurped political power from governments. The political consequences are enormous."

"You're changing the spin. Weren't they responding to an unsolved global problem?"

Elena shook her head. She'd have preferred more small talk, but he wanted to get serious. "So they claim, but are they manipulating the climate issue to control the energy markets?"

"I'm confused. You with them or against them?"

"Skeptical," she replied. "I must be able to oppose them if necessary."

"And I'm supposed to explain how scientific evidence impacts your political story? Helps you determine the truth?"

"From your droopy eyes, I'd guess you've been up late studying it."

Dan took another sip of his cocktail. "I have been busy."

"Good. Let's hear it."

"First, Space Technologies are nanoparticle manufacturers."

"So?"

"Nanoparticles add sparkle to products. I jumped to surface ocean reflectivity and wondered if they're related."

She leaned forward, eyes wide. "Is that what Alfredo was referring to?"

"Alfredo? Who's he?"

"A colleague whose drunken outburst inspired my search. He claimed Space Technologies controlled temperature."

"They have ships. Could they seed broad swaths of ocean with their nanoparticles? It could explain the increased reflectivity."

"What?" she exclaimed. He spent the next few minutes explaining what he knew about NASA's problems with their ocean reflectivity measurements.

"Is it the answer?" she asked.

"It's a hypothesis," he replied. "I'll work on it."

"And I'll investigate the company."

Dan smiled when Elena offered him the final appetizer. "That was last night. Today, I investigated something that may have more serious consequences."

"More serious than industrial conspirators usurping power from major governments? At best, they're subverting legitimate political oversight. At worst, they're manipulating the environment for personal gain."

Dan waited as the waiter whisked away the empty appetizer tray and martini glasses. He replaced them with salad bowls, a bread tray, and white wine. "Explain how they're doing that."

Elena sighed before stepping through her arguments. She outlined the conspiracy to use government action to facilitate their move to control temperature. After expressing her concerns about how culpable her uncle might be, she launched into her immediate problem. "I fear they're using temperature stabilization to increase coal and heavy oil usage. And your nanoparticle reflectors make it possible."

"We haven't proven the nanoparticle linkage."

"But the disconnect between temperature and carbon dioxide proves they have a temperature lowering technology."

Dan shook his head. "You're jumping to conclusions."

"That's my story, and from my perspective as a political philosophy student, it's a frightening development."

"Your uncle's Company of Gentlemen Entrepreneurs is calling the shots, and governments are doing their bidding. Is that what you're saying?"

"Governments may be directing them. But what if they *are* calling the shots?"

"We could have a political crisis." Dan glanced around as waiters arrived with the main course. "I'll try to establish the link between surface ocean reflectivity and these presumed nanoparticles. That would remove one uncertainty from your story." He stared at the array of platters. "But this looks wonderful. Shouldn't we focus on dinner?"

She clinked her wine glass against his and sighed. Earth might be in crisis, but her little corner was unfolding as it should.

Later, Elena stopped in the Prince George Hotel lobby. "Come up to my suite. I'll brew tea, and we can discuss the remaining issue lurking behind your troubled brow."

In the suite that seemed twice the size of his apartment, Dan prowled while she prepared the tea. She entered the living room several minutes later, carrying a silver tea set.

"Herbal tea with no caffeine. I'm dying for a cuppa, so you must join me."

"Always follow the conventions," he replied, his eyes laughing.

She poured. "Now, tell me what's bothering you."

"I unearthed research with serious implications for the Draconian future you're imagining."

He waited while Elena made herself comfortable, then described Tony Atherton's study of the global carbon balance in a more acidic ocean.

She leaned against his shoulder. "Ramifications?"

"Enhanced production and burial will begin in fifty years when acidity reaches a threshold."

"And we'd never reach this level if we reduce carbon emissions. But, if Uncle Gareth and his friends have their way, temperatures stabilize and carbon emissions surge, and we reach it sooner. Then what?"

"CO_2 concentrations drop, and temperatures decrease."

Elena sat up and reached for her teacup. "How quickly?"

"Unknown, but the trend would be downward."

"What does it mean for the nanoparticle reflectors?"

"Another tough question. A drop in CO_2 concentrations enhances the reflector's cooling effect."

"Earth cools rapidly, sending us into a new ice age?"

Dan's pained expression telegraphed his answer.

"Oh God, Daniel, I came here hoping Uncle Gareth and his friends had things under control. I wanted to rekindle our romance and solicit your help understanding the science."

Dan pulled her close. "I think you succeeded."

"Maybe, but the big picture looks worse than I imagined."

Dan carried her to the bedroom, laid her on the bed, and snuggled beside her. "Increasing CO_2 emissions are the main problem. You must convince your uncle to abandon their nanoreflectors before the temperature drops. But the real solution is getting everyone to stop emitting ever-increasing quantities of CO_2."

"How can we trust conspirators who lust after wealth and power?"

"God knows. Technologies for reducing CO_2 concentrations exist, so they may prefer that option. But trying to balance emissions and removal in an uncertain political climate will be tricky as hell."

Elena wasn't a scientist, but she appreciated the complexity of global environmental manipulation. *How can anyone, or any group, hope to navigate a path through those scientific and political minefields?*

******

The next morning, after breakfast in Elena's suite, Dan wandered to his university office. She was incredibly wealthy, with endless opportunities to pursue whoever and whatever she chose. Why would she bother chasing an unremarkable graduate student struggling to produce the research results that would lead to his killer thesis and a career as an obscure university professor? Not an ambition that should resonate with someone in her exalted position.

Her betrayal the previous summer incited his colleagues. They wanted her hanged, drawn, and quartered. At first, he disagreed, but the evidence piled up, and he begrudgingly accepted their perspective. More recently, he'd softened his view as he looked for explanations that vindicated her. Now she'd returned with another tale that was too fantastical for words. But she dispelled his skepticism and dragged him into her latest schemes. *How does she do it?*

The answer was obvious—he remained madly in love. But the potential pitfalls were also obvious. Her world of high finance and international intrigue was foreign to Dan, and he couldn't envisage a role for himself. This visit could easily become a rerun of her ruinous sojourn in Halifax a year earlier. And it left him with so many unanswered questions.

Who was the Company of Gentlemen Entrepreneurs? And what did she mean when she said they'd usurped the power of democratically elected governments? Presidents and prime ministers led their governments, opposition parties opposed, and courts and other checks and balances functioned. Business leaders had always exerted pressure on governments, ensuring their partisan interests got preferential treatment.

Dan couldn't answer the political and economic questions or alter Elena's unwavering hold on his heart, but he could address the science issues she raised. To do that, he needed Steve and Anna's help.

He found them hunched over a computer in Steve's oceanography department office. Dan addressed them from the doorway. "Elena's resurfaced."

"Jesus," Steve replied. "She has a nerve returning after screwing us around."

Anna poked him before stepping away from Steve's computer. "What did she say?"

"Why do you care?" Steve asked. "I wouldn't even respond if she tried to address me."

Dan snorted. He'd expect Steve to engage an enemy, not turn the other cheek. "She stopped on her way to the US, hoping to mend fences."

"No way! What did she want?"

Anna jumped to Elena's defence. "Steven. Stop. Think. Dan still likes her, and she helped us." She dragged a chair from a corner and motioned Dan toward it. "She had something for us, didn't she?"

"Garbage," Steve said. "Like the alien scare, her stupid whales, or those Godbots."

Anna folded her arms beneath her breasts and glared. She was no Brunhilda, but she appeared capable of manhandling the diminutive Steve. "Dan, tell us what she said."

Dan related the relevant parts of Elena's message. He mentioned Godbots and nanoparticles, and the company, Space Technologies, that produced them before turning to their primary concern—the increasing pace of CO_2 emissions.

Anna responded to the Godbots as Steve fumed. "But Dan, we've proven Godbots aren't involved in heat transfer, so what's the link?"

Dan shook his head. She'd raised another of his puzzling questions. "There must be one."

"Accelerating rates of CO_2 emissions are more interesting," Steve said. "Does the data you're collecting support that idea?"

"Not clear, but we can reassess the NOAA data."

"Difficult, isn't it," Anna interjected, "to prove a change in trend for noisy results that are increasing so rapidly?"

Dan nodded his agreement. "But we must try."

"And if the concentration increases are accelerating..." Steve gazed toward the ceiling while drumming his fingers on his desk. "We'll get to where lower pH alters phytoplankton dynamics faster than my old buddy, Tony Atherton, predicted."

Anna shifted to the corner of Steve's desk. "This matters?"

"It does." Steve glanced at Dan. "You read his thesis, didn't you?"

"He predicted a new carbon sink that would reverse the upward trend."

Steve shook his head. "But not rapidly. Natural biological changes take time."

"You can't defend that. Some occur quickly."

"I'll contact Tony. He must have an idea."

"He's a professor somewhere?"

"Went from here to the University of Victoria's global climate modelling group. Then he landed a professorship at the University of British Columbia."

"You contact Atherton," Dan said. "And I'll see if the NOAA data support Elena's suggestion of accelerated CO_2 discharges."

He leaned forward with his right hand on the desk as he rose. Anna put her hand on his arm. "Wait. Much of Elena's message was economic or political. Should we focus on scientific issues?"

"We understand the science."

Steve rose from his chair and glared at Dan. "We trusted Elena, and it led to shit. We can't now accept everything she says without checking."

Steve was right. Elena's claims needed confirmation.

As he approached his office, Dan returned to a question bothering him since Tuesday. If Elena's Company of Gentlemen Entrepreneurs had access to engineering expertise and endless capital, why hadn't they tackled sequestering carbon rather than dampening temperature increases? Temperature increases were a symptom of the real problem, the carbon dioxide buildup. A proper solution would address the problem, not the symptom.

Many proposals for carbon sequestration existed. One that appealed to Dan involved sinking dry ice to the ocean floor. The cold temperature and high pressure would keep the CO_2 in liquid or solid form without additional intervention. Those solutions shared an important downside—they were expensive to implement. But money wasn't a problem for these guys.

Were they really so intent on making money, they avoided these obvious solutions and put the planet at risk?

Chapter Ten

Wednesday, April 26, 2028

A week later, Elena and Penelope Fitzwilliam sipped cocktails in a trendy restaurant near the Boston Common. They'd been best friends at their English public school and co-conspirators during Elena's various dalliances in the intervening years.

When Elena described her latest amorous adventure, Penny demurred. "You're beyond this, girl. Tell your uncle you're going your way, or accept his foreign princeling or English lord with a fancy title and precious little else."

Elena snorted. She had her plans for her future in hand, but she needed to keep them from Uncle Gareth by keeping the myth of a search for a suitable aristocrat alive. "And have him run off as your Milton did with whatever. Do you even know?"

"Weird, vaguely feminine person he found while trolling the depths of the latest European alternate lifestyle mania. They chose gender elimination, nothing to identify them as male or female."

Image of members of the Russian Skoptsy sect that advocated the removal of the external genitals of both men and women flooded Elena's mind. "You mean they both appear androgynous? And for him, it wouldn't only be appearance. They must have emasculated him."

"The ultimate step in the movement toward a genderless society," Penelope said as she passed Elena a photo. "Neither of them even has nipples."

Elena stared at the photo before turning it over as a server approached. "These cults attract the dissolute sons and daughters of our aristocratic families. You expect me to risk something similar? No way, darling, I'm not doing it."

"They can't all be like Milton." Penelope paused while the waiter served their appetizers, then changed the subject. "I have money and Claire, and I'm building a life in America's lone bastion of progressive thinking. We're developing a Bostonian response to creeping repression in what my American compatriots call Earth's greatest democracy."

Elena's oldest friend had never expressed an interest in progressive politics. Did her newfound commitment suggest money and her daughter were inadequate compensation for the trauma Milton imposed on her life?

"Don't forget your friends on the old sod," Elena said as she wondered about potential synergies between fights for social justice and action on climate change. "We're also concerned about the world's future."

Penny laughed. "But right now, you need something else. What's my role in your latest adventure?"

"Cover from tomorrow afternoon until Saturday, when I collect my luggage before an evening flight home."

*****

Dan stood outside the glass doors that separated the Halifax airport's boarding concourse from the baggage claims area. He waved when Elena strode through.

"What now?" he asked after an embrace that confirmed he'd overcome the apprehension he displayed on meeting her nine days earlier.

"We'll rent a car because we have an hour's drive before dinner."

"Where we headed?"

"Old Orchard Inn."

"But why?"

"I wanted to be with you, but I didn't want anyone to know."

Dan rented a car, and they headed onto the highway to Halifax. He made the turn onto a second four-lane highway without consulting a map.

Elena gawked at the bleak early spring scenery as they accelerated after sweeping from one highway to another. "You said you'd never made this trip."

"Our highway system's simple. Checked the route while you were in the washroom."

"We'll be there by six," Elena said after consulting her phone. "Time for dinner and a discussion of everything I've learned. Tomorrow and Saturday morning we'll be tourists—Cape Split and Wolfville. It apparently has a cute little university."

"Acadia. It's early for hiking, and the Cape Split trail will be muddy and cold."

"I've hiked the UK in all seasons and all weathers. Switzerland, too. Muddy and cold are not problems. If we need extra gear, we buy it."

"Too expensive," he said as he pondered her choice of tourist entertainments. They explained her odd suggestion he bring his hiking gear, but was she actually interested in small towns and hiking through the backcountry? Or was this another of her complicated ruses?

Elena laughed. "Everything's on me, and money's not a problem."

Dan shook his head. The pieces of this latest puzzle weren't fitting together. "A trail of credit card payments will blow your cover."

"You rented the car because they demand a credit card. From now on, I'm paying with cash."

After dinner in the Old Orchard Inn dining room, they retired to the adjoining lounge. Elena ordered liqueurs and settled back. *Is she ready to unburden?*

"I hoped to learn how tightly Uncle Gareth's colleagues were tied into the US government and if, as I speculated last week, they're manipulating government action."

"I guessed that was your goal."

"It's worse than I imagined. The industrialists are calling the shots in their effort to counter China's growing economic might."

Dan relaxed, taking the first sip of his Irish coffee. She was describing a massive geopolitical upheaval that had its roots in climate change and global economic developments, but her reasons for this latest visit were unclear. "I can see how it happened. Scientists tried to convince governments to act on climate change, but they never made progress. Now your group's taken the initiative and forced a solution on them, a solution that suits your purposes, not the government's or the people's."

She shook her head. "We can assume they had Earth's welfare in mind. But they're subverting the political process, abandoning democracy's basic premise."

"We have elections, the courts, and the other checks and balances."

Elena picked up her liqueur glass, glanced at it, and stood. She took two steps toward the bar and returned to lean on her chair-back. "They face minimal constraints. And we have another problem, a power struggle within the Company of Gentlemen Entrepreneurs."

She strode to the bar and returned with a server close on her heels. He carried one coffee and two pieces of cheesecake.

"One group sides with the American, Chinese, and Indian governments. They want to expand coal mining and coal-fired generation of electricity. The second group, my uncle's, wants to focus on less polluting types of fossil fuels for uses that cannot be replaced by cleaner energy sources."

"Hang on a minute. You're being inconsistent. First, you said American members of your company joined with their government leaders to oppose the growing dominance of China. Now you're saying one group is working with American, Chinese, and Indian governments."

Elena spent many minutes explaining the conflicts that developed within the company when the economic battles between the US and China overwhelmed their original environmental concerns. She also described the conflict developing between herself and Gareth Llewellyn. He was her closest living relative and her guardian during her teenage years. They'd been really close, and he'd been preparing her for major roles in the bank and his quest to save the world from global warming. Now, as she developed a deeper understanding of the intrigues within the company, she feared an irreparable rift.

Dan scanned the room before staring at Elena. "What's my part?"

Two days later, as the bus trundled toward Halifax, Dan struggled to understand developments since Elena's return. If she wanted scientific knowledge, she had better options than a clandestine visit. If her reasons were personal, another step in her attempts to rekindle their relationship, why didn't she mention their future?

He strode from the bus stop to Steve and Anna's apartment.

Steve opened the door seconds after Dan knocked. "Elena returned, didn't she?"

"Appeared and gone again. Makes no sense."

Steve stepped aside and gestured for Dan to enter. "Why not?"

Dan described her efforts to avoid her phone and credit cards before mentioning a conundrum. "But her flight from Boston must be documented."

"False passport?"

Dan snorted as Steve led the way to their living room. A false passport would up the intensity of the intrigue. "What's she hiding? And from whom?"

"Forget your bloody spy fantasy. Did you learn anything we can use?"

He hesitated. Their conversations had focused on her political concerns rather than his scientific ones. "She offered nothing on their temperature controlling mechanism."

"No problem. We'll sort that one. Anything else?"

"She acknowledged their scheme—create a crisis that drives down the value of energy companies and buy up the shares. When everyone realizes they have temperature under control, they'll expand production and make a bundle."

"It fleshes out what she already told you."

Dan nodded. Some things were clearer, but others were murkier. "My final observation is more interesting."

Steve looked up from the tablet where he'd been recording notes. "Well, what is it?"

"One group is fixated on expanded fossil fuel use. The second recognizes the importance of controlling carbon emissions but doesn't see any need for urgency."

"How did you come to that conclusion?"

"She became agitated when I mentioned serious negative impacts of rising CO_2."

Steve stood and headed to the kitchen. "That is interesting. Are they unaware of the consequences?" he asked, but he didn't wait for Dan's response.

He returned with two steaming coffee mugs. "It shows we must convince people the climate change problem isn't solved."

"Hopeless! Scientists fought for forty years to convince everyone global warming was serious. Now, we're back to square one."

Steve grabbed his tablet and called up Tony and Beth Atherton's ClimateChange&U website. It documented a highly successful campaign to encourage individual North Americans to lower their carbon emissions. "The public was mostly receptive. Governments were the problem. These latest developments have ruined all their progress." He turned his tablet toward Dan. "We need to reconnect people with sites like this one."

Dan shook his head as several of Elena's revelations came tumbling into focus. "Won't work. A bunch of industrialists have outflanked us, initiated an imperfect solution, and sold it to governments everywhere. Eureka! Problem solved. Everyone rejoices and returns to their wasteful ways."

"Don't be so negative. Countries haven't removed their carbon taxes. They'll slow fossil fuel consumption, and the next crisis, Tony Atherton's pH-induced plankton explosion, won't kick in for decades. We have thirty or forty years."

"You're dreaming. Consider our situation. What happened to the plan to end government subsidies for heavy oil production?"

"Shelved because it would kill jobs."

Dan nodded. "Business as usual. Elena's expansion of coal and heavy oil consumption will overwhelm any benefits from the consumption taxes. And their temperature solution must be metastable."

Steve stood as Dan finished his coffee. "Another?"

"No, thanks. I should go home and decompress."

"Other aspects of her visit were... more interesting?"

"Confusing," Dan replied before changing the topic. "Have you heard from Atherton?"

Steve shook his head. "Hasn't returned my call."

Anna strode up as Dan stepped from the apartment. She grabbed his arm and dragged him back inside. "Welcome home, Romeo. We've much to discuss."

Dan sighed, another delay before he could return to his languishing investigations. "Okay, but make it quick."

Anna entered her kitchen, dumped homemade chocolate chip cookies on a plate, and turned toward Dan.

"Chill out, have a cookie, and I'll describe my successes."

She described a conversation she and Madison had with an American economics student, starting with the student's adventures escaping increasing suppression of her trans lifestyle.

"Confirms our impression the US is cracking down on alternative lifestyles," Dan replied.

Anna held out her plate of cookies, and Dan accepted a second. "When I learned what she was studying, I asked her about the concentration of ownership in the fossil fuel industries. She confirmed what Elena told you."

"You didn't mention her?"

"Course not. I just asked a simple question. She took off giving us detailed information on the companies that are consolidating ownership."

Steve grabbed a cookie and waved it at Anna. "Tell him about the Godbots."

"Space Technologies designed the satellites and manufactured the first dozen in one of their plants."

Mention of manufacturing facilities reminded Dan of Space Technologies' plant and extensive ship berthing facilities on the Kiel Canal. "Near Hamburg?" Dan asked.

Anna shook her head. "Bavaria. They call them Sunlight Reflecting Drones, SRDs, and initially claimed they would lower global temperatures by tracking the sun and reflecting away incident energy. They now argue they'll coordinate reflection of sunlight by an integrated array of reflectors."

Dan twisted around and almost tipping his kitchen stool. The pieces were fitting together. "Could they be monitoring the effectiveness of nanoparticle reflectors in the ocean and guiding the ships deploying them?"

Steve fussed with his coffee maker. "Unproven."

"But it fits."

Steve refilled their coffee mugs and brought tea for Anna. "Monitoring effectiveness and guiding slow-moving surface ships would only need a few satellites. Their original explanation was sci-fi fantasy, but it gave a rationale for an array of satellites."

"You suggesting surveillance satellites?" Anna asked.

Dan stared at his mug. He didn't need the coffee Steve kept pushing his way, but the conversation was becoming more interesting. "If Russia, China, and the US are working together in a clandestine spying operation, who's the target?"

Chapter Eleven

Tuesday, May 2, 2028

Elena recalled Dan's disquieting comments about rampaging plankton blooms as she joined the throng of commuters heading toward her underground station. His concerns could destroy Uncle Gareth's temperature control scheme. Raising them may cause a confrontation, but she had to do it.

"Profitable trip?" he asked as Elena entered his palatial office.

"Private conversations with colleagues sharing your concern about your grand adventure and listening to the views of your opponents. I also consulted with our scientific surveillance operatives in Washington and Boston."

"Recent developments from your scientists?"

"The altered temperature trend has invigorated efforts to estimate when deep water formation will cease."

"Not important. Our nanoparticle reflectors postpone that day of reckoning indefinitely. Gives us time to develop an economy that's less dependent on fossil fuels."

Elena hesitated before settling into the comfortable chair in front of his desk. Uncle Gareth's explanations of the Company of Gentlemen Entrepreneurs' motives had never been fulsome or convincing. Was he now offering her a different take on his grand adventure? "Is that your dream—a transition away from fossil fuels? If so, it flies in the face of those pushing for expanded coal and heavy oil production."

"I'm acquainted with that problem. We have time to address it."

She stood and leaned forward with her hands on his desk. "Perhaps less than you hoped."

He scowled, eyes piercing into Elena's. "Why?"

"Another crisis looms—a carbon dioxide crisis. Research suggests we'll reach a CO_2 tipping point in fifty years. If we expand carbon emissions, we'll reach it sooner."

"How much sooner?"

"Not clear. Twenty-five to forty years from now."

"A new deadline will keep my colleagues focused. Keep me informed."

She stifled her desire to hammer away at Dan's latest concern. She'd raised the issue, and he'd asked her to keep him informed. That was probably all she could expect. "Will do," she said as she sat down.

Uncle Gareth's newly expressed perspective raised as many questions as it answered. Most obviously, how did they plan to profit from their investments in coal and oil if their long-term goal was replacement of these energy sources? And how would Dan's concerns about a transition to lower temperatures fit into their plans? More than anything else, could she trust him? *Too confusing, and I need a better understanding before I confront him.*

"Your visit with Penelope was more agreeable," Gareth asked moments later.

"Stayed for three nights. Caught up on old times, simpler times when we weren't mired in international intrigues of unprecedented proportions."

Gareth sighed. "School days should be times for simpler adventures, but our current situation is not unprecedented. Business and political leaders have solved major challenges through coordinated action. We'll do so again. But tell me, how is Penelope?"

Elena frowned. *Is focusing on Penelope a diversion to deflect my concerns about the controversies within his grand conspiracy?*

"Managing. Her daughter helps, as do investments from her divorce settlement. But she'll never get over the implied criticism from her family and his, or the sacrifice they foisted on her. Taking custody of the son she and Milton had and refusing to let her visit is intolerable."

"Difficult. And I agree, one shouldn't blame Penelope."

"Difficult! It's a bloody crime," she exclaimed before slapping the revealing photo of Milton and his paramour on Gareth's desk. She wanted to play along with her uncle's attempts to find her a suitable husband, but Pen's photo had destroyed her resolve. "His parents and hers let him wallow in his perverted fetish after they produced an heir. And you wonder why I reject the scions of aristocratic families."

He looked away, his expression wistful, with a hint of moisture in his eyes. Not the reaction Elena expected. "Since your parents' unfortunate deaths, I've tried to do what's best for you. Milton's the exception. Another eligible young gentleman will bring you the best of all worlds."

Young gentlemen, Elena muttered outside her uncle's office. Most were rogues, and many, not so young. They reminded her of the crooks in Uncle Gareth's Company of Gentlemen Entrepreneurs who'd taken advantage of the climate crisis to amass wealth. Gentleman was a misnomer for too many members of both groups.

Elena's concerns began with Alfredo Rodriguez's drunken outburst at a Farringdon Street wine bar. He was the first to mention Space Technologies and the plans to corner coal and heavy oil production. How did he discover these things long before they became known to anyone outside a tightly constrained inner circle?

Brandon Newbury stepped forward when Alfredo needed a friend. The bank's director of industrial loans would know how to contact his senior financial analyst. She turned toward his office.

"Morning, Brandon. Can you spare a minute?" Elena asked from his open doorway.

He grinned. "For my favourite spymaster, as long as you want."

"Spymaster?"

"I imagine your operatives skulking about university laboratories in their lab coats, taking photos of complicated equipment, and stealing critical results."

Elena scowled. She didn't appreciate Brandon's attitude, belittling her endeavours on behalf of the bank. Was it a sleazy come on, or an attempt at one-upmanship, showing her he had his finger on the corporation's pulse? "Nothing like that. I didn't even own a lab coat. My standard disguise was long skirts and tie-dyed T-shirts."

He motioned toward the chair on the far side of his desk. "Can dig your image—headband, granny glasses, loose-fitting tie-dyed shirt, and a long translucent skirt floating in the breeze."

"Yeah, right? I don't wear spectacles. Seriously, I'm looking for Alfredo."

"Alfie. Weren't you present when he ranted about various things?"

"I was, and I've learned his rantings were accurate."

"Alfie's dedicated, an incredibly honest person."

Elena shook her head. Dedicated and honest didn't necessarily lead to unearthing secrets. "How did he learn about Space Technologies' temperature modifications before anyone else?"

"Simple. We loaned them the money for a ship. Alfie investigated their creditworthiness."

"Doesn't Space Technologies belong to one of Uncle Gareth's co-conspirators?"

"Conspirators, is it? I'd say collaborators, partners in a noble cause."

She wrinkled her nose, convinced Brandon sympathized with the company's goals. *Could his family be in the cartel?*

"They're not above employing underhanded tactics, so I prefer conspirators," she replied.

He shrugged his shoulders. "Regardless, the bank has a fiduciary responsibility to its shareholders."

"And now he's disappeared."

Brandon held up his hand. "He's working on a special task for your uncle. When it's complete, he'll be back at his old job." He wiped the hand across his brow. "In time to investigate three major deals we're anticipating."

"If I want to contact Alfredo, I should talk to Uncle Gareth?"

"Afraid so, or wait until he returns."

Thursday morning, Uncle Gareth appeared in Elena's office doorway at ten thirty. He settled into an armchair and pointed to another on the far side of a small circular table.

"Tea's coming. I must bring you up to speed on our challenge." He placed the photo she'd left in his office two days earlier on her table. "But first, here's your picture. It got me thinking—"

Elena stumbled, almost falling into the second chair. "Oh, God. You weren't involved, were you?"

"Not a party to that travesty."

He stood after someone knocked on Elena's door. She picked up the photo and placed it in a drawer while Uncle Gareth admitted his tea-tray-carrying secretary.

He waited until she left. "It got me thinking about romance. Mine and yours."

"How does that photo generate such thoughts?"

"Made me reassess my motives when I pressured you to find a suitable husband."

Elena hesitated, troubled by the direction the conversation was heading when she wanted to discuss Alfredo Rodriguez and his startling revelations. "You were taking your duty as guardian seriously."

"I overreacted to my ill-fated foray into matrimony and interfered when I should have stood aside."

Elena choked on her tea, stunned by his mention of a secret marriage and the suggestion he would stop pushing her toward a society match.

"I didn't know you were married," she said after regaining her composure.

"Many years ago, I went against your grandparents' wishes and married the girl I loved. She was a shop-girl, a nobody. Our family refused to accept her. We had a fairy tale romance for several years, but a problem arose, as it does in fairy tales. We wanted children, but it didn't happen."

"That's so sad, but couldn't you adopt?"

He held up his hand, a gesture that reminded Elena of her conversation with Brandon. "She died. They called it an accident, but I thought otherwise. She blamed herself for our lack of offspring." He grabbed a tissue from the box on her desk and blew his nose. "A mess that spiralled toward disaster until you were born. Things settled down, and I immersed myself in running the bank."

Elena reached for one of the upmarket butter cookies that accompanied all tea services at the Llewellyn Bank. "Then, my parents died in a crazy accident while living the life of wealthy adventurers, and you found yourself responsible for a precocious preteen girl."

"It went well until I become too involved in finding your perfect husband. I apologize for that terrible mistake. It won't happen again.

"That took a painfully long time," he said, after glancing at his watch. "I must leave soon, but before I do, I should outline my problem with the Company of Gentlemen Entrepreneurs. You already understand the basics?"

"I suspect so," she said before pulling back, surprised and puzzled by his sudden decision to explain the big conspiracy. Did he hope to fend off criticism by presenting his side of the story? Or was it an honest attempt to bring a member of their team up to speed?

"The primary group, the partners your grandfather brought together, consider our endeavour as mercantile altruism. Banking and most traditional enterprises function best in a stable environment. Our efforts over the past ten years have produced environmental and financial stability. That's good for business, but it's also good for humanity because we've controlled global warming."

"But you haven't solved the carbon emission problem."

He stood, walked to her window, and gazed into the City of London financial district. "We've postponed the day of reckoning. You must convince me there's a pressing problem."

"I welcome the challenge. But what about the other faction?"

"The second group, I call them cowboy capitalists, wants to milk the fossil fuel business for all it's worth."

"You must convince them their approach is self-destructive."

"Brandon and Alfredo Rodriguez are working on understanding the situation. You should approach them." He extracted a card from his wallet. "Here's Alfredo's contact information. Visit him, discuss what he's learned. Same for Brandon."

Elena closed her door after Gareth left, returned to her desk, and sat with her chin cupped by her hands. She had no clear understanding of Gareth's latest moves? *Is offering me free access to Brandon and Alfredo helpful? Or is his apparent helpfulness an attempt to mislead me?*

Chapter Twelve

Elena woke early. After breakfast, she rode the underground to the Richmond auto repair shop that maintained her car. She'd inherited the automotive classic, a Lotus Elise roadster, from her father. That wasn't quite true. Uncle Gareth preserved the canary-yellow convertible until she was old enough to own a car. The garage owner, a connoisseur of vintage British sports cars, kept her seventeen-year-old roadster in perfect working order for whenever she needed a car.

Some might consider it an expensive affectation, but it was her father's prized possession. Memories of riding with him, often at excessive speeds, dominated her few fond memories of her parents.

Elena plugged her route into her GPS and meandered south along suburban roads to Leatherhead, where she picked up the M25 and then the M23. On the highway, she opened the throttle and experienced the thrill of driving her lightweight road warrior.

Minutes later, she slowed as she pulled onto a secondary road. It would lead her to the Turner's Hill pub Alfredo chose for their meeting.

At five to twelve, she parked beside an elegant Jaguar sedan that was probably Alfredo's.

Alfredo pointed at her Lotus as he opened the pub's door. "Nice motor," he said before leading them to a table in the front window.

Alfredo got down to business after Elena ordered a pot of tea and a Danish pastry. "Your uncle's drawn me into his grand enterprise. I've compiled financial histories and recent business dealings of everyone involved. They control enormous wealth focused on financial services and basic industries; no dotcom billionaires."

She focused on his words, her eyebrows furrowed. "Is that significant?"

"It shows a long-term commitment, a grand plan to concentrate wealth and power in the hands of traditional industrialists. They're involved in agribusiness, resources, chemical industries, transportation, and finance."

"Industries that supply the infrastructure modern businesses need."

Alfredo raised his wine glass after the server arrived with Elena's tea. "Exactly. Dotcom companies need power, infrastructure, and basic resources to produce their gadgets."

"And this grand plan includes using their industrial might to influence government response to global warming?"

"Some would say perverts government action, twisting it to their advantage."

Elena pondered Alfredo's statement. When he said some, did he include himself? Or was he now aligning himself with Uncle Gareth and the company? "Something went wrong?"

"Your grandfather and several European collaborators formed the company in 2002. Gareth continues his father's *noblesse oblige* scheme to reap profits while solving the world's global warming problem."

Elena sipped her tea and had a dainty bite of pastry. Alfredo was more talkative than she expected. She might learn more than she expected if she didn't challenge his story. *Stick to light-hearted comments that keep him going. I can worry about its credibility later.*

"Our family isn't part of the nobility," she said.

Alfredo smiled, an indulgent grin on his face. "They share that quintessential British characteristic that combines the aristocrat's right to wealth and privilege with an obligation to protect the masses. Stopping global warming is good for everyone, but their real goal is financial stability."

"Profit rather than altruism?"

"Profits, wealth, return on equity. Those are the motivators." Alfredo replied, laughing. "They needed active participation by worldwide governments to make the scheme work."

"How does this translate into a split within the company? That's what we're talking about, isn't it?"

"A significant split, but their goals are not that different. One faction wants rapid wealth accumulation. They're less concerned about environmental consequences and think they can deal with them later. The second has a longer, more integrated view. They want to control global warming to provide a stable environment and slower wealth creation."

"So, it's all about wealth creation?"

He drained the last of his wine. "Business decisions always are. I appreciate the sincerity of your uncle's altruistic intentions, but the bank and its success will always be of paramount importance."

She returned to her Richmond garage at a slower pace, too distracted by her thoughts for high-speed motoring. If Alfredo's most recent explanation was correct, she could relax and join her uncle's quest, knowing she'd be part of a grand adventure. But only three months earlier, Alfredo said the Company of Gentlemen Entrepreneurs was part of a monumental conspiracy. Had he learned that his earlier opinion was misguided, or had they convinced him to join the conspiracy? She could see only one way forward. She must accept Uncle Gareth's expressed views until she proved they were erroneous. But that didn't address the science questions. For those, she needed Dan's input.

Four hours later, Dan's face on the video link improved her spirits. "Beautiful here. I roared about the countryside investigating country homes."

Dan laughed. "Assuming the role of landed gentry?"

"Tell you later," she said before outlining her growing uncertainty about Uncle Gareth's motives. She concluded with, "What have you discovered?"

After describing his recent efforts, he looked away. Was he scanning his notes to make sure he'd missed nothing or planning a broadside? "We're busy, and tomorrow, Steve, Anna, and I will meet with Tony Atherton and Beth Manville. They're Steve's friends from six or seven years ago—"

"From his first time at Dalhousie?"

"Yeah. They're both active in climate change issues. We hope they'll become active collaborators."

Elena sipped her tea. Dan's investigations of the underlying science were important, but she needed to focus on the links to political issues. "The biggest problem is the continuing expansion of coal-burning. Pinpoints China, India, and the United States as the main offenders."

"I'd include Venezuela and Canada, two major bitumen producers, but this is nothing new. The US, China, and India have always produced the most emissions."

"And the Americans are increasing their use of coal."

"As are China and India," Dan added, his brow furrowed because he probably failed to understand why she was belabouring this well-understood point.

Elena tapped a finger on her computer. *Time to bite the bullet and tackle the big problem.*

"The US is a modern industrialized democracy," she said. "We need them onside before we move to include India and other emerging economies."

"And China?"

"We can't control China, but if the US joins us, and we accommodate India, we can isolate China. That's why you must stay in North America, hopefully in the United States, and join others pushing our agenda."

Dan scowled as he looked away from his computer. He may understand her logic, but he obviously didn't like it.

Elena saw through his attempt to hide his disappointment. "You must understand the dire nature of the American situation."

"In Canada, we're aware of their fortress America attitude."

"But not its extent. The US is hunkering down for a protracted battle with China for global domination."

Dan snorted. "Old news, been happening for a decade."

"We have proof the US is establishing an unprecedented integration of government and industry."

"I presume your uncle's partners are central players in these American alliances. And what about China? Are they also involved?" He paused his barrage of questions, but only for a few seconds. "Is it anything new? Government and key industries have always worked hand in glove."

This was not going as well as she hoped. She knew secrets she dared not divulge. *How can I convince my skeptical scientist without presenting my data?*

"Unprecedented integration, unprecedented manipulation of the political process," she said. "Alfredo Rodriguez claims they're making a mockery of American democracy by manipulating government actions whilst conspiring with Chinese industrialists."

"Don't believe it. US checks and balances always cause clashes between the president, congress, and the courts."

"Window dressing," Elena said before outlining her limited understanding of the internal schism. "The company worked behind the scenes to solve the global temperature crisis. But in the US, industrialists Uncle Gareth can't control are exploiting the situation. They're not working toward climate stabilization."

"Jesus, that's so depressing. What's the good news you've been hinting at?"

Elena took a deep breath and embarked on a rambling explanation of her uncle's efforts to find her a perfect husband. She concluded with his recent promise to abandon his misguided efforts. She paused for another deep breath and added, "now, we can get together openly, and with the amount of money I'm making, frequently."

"But you want us to continue our separate quests."

"More important than ever. We need you inside the ramparts of fortress America. And I must convince Uncle Gareth and his European allies to fight harder for reduced CO_2 emissions."

He stared at his screen before taking a deep breath. "All right, I accept your arguments. I'll be your science mole in America, but carbon emissions are the critical issue. Your uncle and all his shady co-conspirators must clamour for reduced carbon emissions. Otherwise, we're pushing dangerously close to a tipping point caused by ocean acidity, something that could make all your efforts moot. That's why tomorrow's meeting with Tony Atherton is so important."

She slumped in her chair when he ended the call. *Poor start, but in the end, it went far better than I expected. Time for the killer thrust that solidifies our commitment to each other.*

*****

Saturday morning, Dan followed Anna along the walkway to her Halifax apartment.

"Emergency trip for milk," she said, as he rushed to catch up. Inside, they found Steve, Tony Atherton, and Beth Manville huddled in the living room, admiring photos of Tony and Beth's two kids.

Steve looked up as they entered. "Ah, Dan, you've arrived."

Tony strode forward with his hand extended. "Howdy. Missed your talk at the AGU, but I've done some digging since Steve contacted me."

"Me too. Read your thesis and various papers. Fascinated by your modelling."

He turned to his wife. "Beth Manville, my partner in our efforts to publicize the need for climate change action."

Dan 'met' Tony through studying his work, including one paper with Achara Zhu, a biologist from Thailand who was his first student, but didn't know Beth. Anna said she was an actress turned journalist who'd developed an abiding interest in environmental politics.

"Do you follow ClimateChange&U?" Beth asked.

"I've seen your website, and it's mentioned by the other students. Slim pickings for a bike-riding environmentalist living in a rented garret."

Anna edged into the room, carrying a large tray. "Sandwiches plus coffee and cakes to keep us going. We should start because Tony and Beth have a plane to catch."

Dan extracted his laptop and accessed the illustrations describing the results of his recent collaboration with Steve and Anna.

Tony reacted to Dan's brief presentation. "Others have noted your core observation. We must be cautious speculating on trends based on one year's data."

"But we have two years' data," Dan said. "Smaller increase from 2025 to 2026, and 2027 is hardly warmer than 2026. Carbon dioxide increases in both years follow established trends."

"A single year with no temperature increase while CO_2 marches upward is not proof."

Dan looked up, puzzled. Was he playing devil's advocate, or did Tony actually dispute his results? "But when I combine it with our other observations—"

"It produces an enticing scenario. But you must proceed cautiously. You'll need more data to convince the skeptics."

Beth jumped into the standoff between two generations of climate change modellers. "But Tony, everyone in Nigeria agreed the temperature trend has broken."

"They glossed over the fact we lack proof."

Steve intervened to keep things moving. "Perhaps that's where we should go next. What did you learn in Lagos?"

Tony motioned to Beth. She took a deep breath before describing the UN-sponsored meeting that brought together climate scientists, politicians, government bureaucrats, and community groups from Africa and Southeast Asia. "The objective was a look toward a future with constant temperatures."

Tony nodded. "Annoying for the scientists because they ignored us whenever we mentioned the uncertainty."

Anna asked a critical question. "They're assuming the policies implemented by governments will be sustained?"

"Correct," Tony said. "Scientists will document this monumental change in global warming, not question it."

Beth frowned. "I found it disconcerting. Everyone was jubilant, celebrating the end of global warming and unwilling to accept voices of caution."

"Even delegates from Pacific Island nations were saluting the victory over warming," Tony added. "But they ignored the fact that continued CO_2 increases will doom their coral reefs."

Dan snorted. The annoying tenor of the meeting was obvious from Beth and Tony's synopsis. "But rising sea level won't inundate them."

Beth nodded. "That's the crux of the problem. The immediate issue, increasing temperature, is solved if you trust the politicians to stay the course. They're focused on that victory and willing to ignore the dark clouds lurking on the horizon."

"How do we reengage everyone?" Dan asked.

Tony drummed his fingers on the table. "That's the billion-dollar question. Short term, we can do nothing. Once the euphoria dies down, we're back to the tedious job of convincing first the progressive elements of the public, and then their governments we haven't conquered climate change."

First Interlude

Winter 2051/2052

Hello again. *Tony Atherton here with a quick update.*

December 2051 brought cold, snowy weather to Pemberton. By March, old-timers were shaking their heads, saying this was the worst winter they could remember. I didn't share most people's frustration with the blustery weather because it would add to the snowpack on the surrounding mountains. They'd been suffering snow loss for years. We needed more snow.

I discussed potential causes for the cold weather with Bill Robertson, my oceanographic colleague on Haida Gwaii. Was it a regional anomaly, a random fluctuation that confounded global temperature trends? Or could it be a sign of my long-anticipated shift to a cooling trend?

The reduced industrial output during the last three years should have slowed carbon emissions. But the burst of emissions from the explosions and wildfires in 2049 could have overwhelmed the reductions. If so, continuing ocean acidification would soon lead to increased carbon removal. More removal would mean less CO_2 in the atmosphere and lower temperatures. Did the last three years move the date when we reached a tipping point between global warming and global cooling closer?

The long winter months gave us time to ponder our latest observations. The cold weather was most likely a regional anomaly, but we had insufficient data for a solid conclusion. Our only choice was a watching brief until we acquired more evidence. The tipping point that seemed so close in 2048 was probably years away, but we couldn't be sure.

Here, after Beth and I first appeared in Dan's story, is a good place to explain how our various interests in climate change converged. It's my chance to explain how Beth and I, Dan and Elena, and Steve and Anna evolved into a ragtag team fighting to save the world.

Dan and I started our oceanographic careers in Dr. Heinrich Krueger's climate research group, me in 2020 and Dan in 2025. Steve bridged the five-year divide. He was an oceanography student when I arrived, left to solve a family crisis in 2024, and returned two years later. After graduating in the summer of 2025, I moved on to a professorship at the University of British Columbia. Several years later, Dan went from Dalhousie to the University of Southampton. Steve and Anna went from Dalhousie to Boston, Massachusetts. He took charge of his family's engineering firm, and Anna became a professor.

I began working on the impact of a more acidic ocean on plankton in 2021. The next spring, Jacinta Lopez discovered phytoplankton grew far more rapidly in a more acidic ocean. I studied the removal of that excess growth and estimated its impact on global carbon budgets. For five years, we stood at the forefront of research into the effect of primary productivity on global warming. We learned plankton removal would produce a transition from global warming to global cooling. My work put the date seventy to eighty years into the future. I soon realized other climate change crises would intercede before we got there.

In 2027, Dan was a next-generation graduate student working on one of those problems. He was studying the effect of global warming on the transport system that moves seawater through the world's oceans. That process is driven by the sinking of cold, salty surface waters in several critical northern and southern locations. The sinking water flows toward the tropics where it resurfaces and produces currents pushing surface water toward the poles. That closes a giant circulation system that moves water throughout the oceans.

Dan predicted an end to deep-water formation in the Labrador Sea fifty years before our estimate for the transition to global cooling. The shutdown would play havoc with ecological and socio-economic systems.

The global warming 'cure' foisted on the world in the summer of 2027 threw our calculations into disarray. If temperatures stabilized at less than two degrees above preindustrial levels, Dan's predicted end to deep-water formation would not occur. Other negative impacts, like sea-level rise, would be reduced or eliminated. Weather patterns would stabilize. Extreme events would be less frequent.

Observers saw these improvements and shouted, 'Great! The problem's solved'. They were very short-sighted. The mysterious intervention did nothing to reduce carbon dioxide emissions. More atmospheric CO_2 meant higher concentrations in the ocean.

In water, CO_2 dissolves to form carbonic acid, thus increasing ocean acidification. The increased acidity would destroy coral reefs. Other problems, like the low pH super blooms I'd been studying since 2020, would arise. Their slowly developing impacts would be far-reaching but not immediate. The public was too busy celebrating temperature stabilization to worry about concerns that were decades in the future.

The public may have been oblivious, but the study of a lower pH ocean surged back into the scientific limelight. This change invigorated my career and those of my Dalhousie University colleague, Marc Lavoie, and my first UBC student, Achara Zhu. We resumed work with renewed enthusiasm and established greater collaborations with colleagues in the United States and Great Britain. Beth and I had new ammo for our fight to convince the world important climate change problems remained unsolved. Earth's long-range prospects were murky, but our immediate objectives were clear. We had to stop the never-ending increases in global carbon emissions.

Beth's climate change fight became more political. She ventured into retail politics as a Green Party candidate. She joined Elena Llewellyn and Steve Matthews on the political side of our multi-pronged fight to save the world from human-induced climate change. Dan's efforts also became more political. Our quest remained the same. We had to convince world leaders to take the problem seriously.

Chapter Thirteen

Saturday, June 17, 2028

Six weeks after her meeting with Alfredo, Elena returned to Crawley. This time, her destination was Gatwick Airport, not a pub in Turner's Hill. She arrived at North Terminal with time for a coffee before Dan's overnight flight arrived from Canada.

In early May, when they parted at the Halifax airport, she had such positive views of the monumental quest they were undertaking. Now doubts clouded her vision. She'd learned too many disquieting things about the rifts in the Company of Gentlemen Entrepreneurs and kept too many secrets from Dan. It had to stop, but she couldn't risk losing him and his commitment to their cause.

"What a zoo," Dan said after he bounded through the doors isolating everyone from the international arrivals area. His shoulder bag slid down as he gathered her into his arms.

She smiled. Typical Dan, no romantic overtures, just a big hug and a comment on the immediate situation that erased her fears. "But worth the effort?"

He leaned forward and kissed her. "Worth the effort."

Elena stepped aside as passengers jostled by. "Pit stop, or you ready to roll?"

"Train to London?"

She smiled. His upbeat attitude suggested it was time to commit to her overly complicated plan. "Carpark and drive to Winchester."

"Winchester? South of here, with a big cathedral? Already bought your country house?"

"I thought we could be tourists and scope out country houses." She paused, her uncertainty resurfacing as she contemplated the array of sensitive topics they must cover before Dan met Uncle Gareth. "Let's hit the road. I'll explain after we find somewhere for lunch."

Dan followed her through the terminal and short-term parking garage to her canary yellow sports car. "Wow, is this yours? Will there be space for my stuff?"

She popped open the trunk, revealing the mid-vehicle power plant ahead of a small storage space.

He shrugged off his backpack, squeezed it inside, and added his shoulder bag. "Where's your luggage?"

"Inside, behind the seats."

Elena chose secondary roads through the farms and forests of the extensively cultivated South Downs National Park. She chatted about her friends, the London parties she frequented, and activities at the bank. She said nothing about their immediate plans until she drove the Lotus into a Winchester parking garage.

"Restaurant's around the corner. After lunch, we can visit Winchester Cathedral."

"And the news that's struggling to burst forth?"

She pointed at a Tudor-style timber-framed building with dark brown beams and white stucco wall covering. "After we've ordered."

Finally, the server took their orders and produced a pint of the local ale for Dan and tea for Elena. She put her hand on his. "Uncle Gareth has started his estate planning. As a first step, we're setting up a foundation sponsoring research into global environmental issues."

"And you won't be short of lolly to pay for the luncheon we've ordered."

She smiled. "I see you're working on your British slang. No problem affording lunch and anything you desire. You'll be minted and living the life of Riley."

"Isn't that American?"

She nodded. Happy with the way her plan was unfolding. Before she left Halifax in May, and during their transatlantic conversations since, they focused on their commitment to the climate change battle. During the next few days, they must resolve more personal aspects of their life together. The first one was now on the table, hidden underneath banter about British and American slang. "American soldiers brought it across the pond during World War One. Seriously, you and I will never be short of funds, but we must use our money wisely. Not like the way my father squandered his inheritance."

After lunch, they strolled across the river into Winchester, along Main Street past the King Alfred the Great statue to the Winchester Buttercross. They turned left along Great Minstrel Street to the cathedral.

*****

81

Three hours later, they retraced their steps, slid into Elena's car, and joined the commuters crawling from Winchester to the northwestern satellite community of Sparsholt.

Dan shook his head as they pulled into the circular driveway of an exclusive hotel. "Unbelievable. I'll never get used to it."

Elena smiled as she emerged from her low-slung car. "You ain't seen nothin' yet."

Dan struggled to escape from the confined space and turned toward the trunk before realizing his error. He rushed after Elena.

A doorman held open the door. "Welcome, Ms. Llewellyn. I'll have a footman collect your bags before parking your car. Lotus Elise Series 2, isn't it?"

She handed him the keys. "Well observed. A 2011 Series 2. One suitcase and a garment bag behind the driver's seat and two bags in the boot."

Dan stared. "You're a regular here?"

"Never. I told them when we'd arrive and the make and colour of my car. It's pretty distinctive."

"No kidding, but still..."

"You'll get the hang of it. Easier than understanding why the climate's going pear-shaped."

Dan leaned over and whispered. "Sure you don't mean tits-up?"

"Daniel! That's vulgar, not an expression for polite company."

Upstairs, Elena smiled as Dan checked out the elaborate furnishings in their suite. "For a French Canadian, you seem unusually familiar with British slang."

"Hah, no French accent, and almost as British as you. My parents emigrated to Canada in the 1990s, but the family has deep roots in Dunbartonshire."

"Interesting and perhaps useful."

"Why?"

She ignored his question. "Strange how names can be misleading. When Cristina Rodriguez heard my name was Elena, she assumed my mother was Spanish. Not so, just as British as my father, but it led to some confusion."

"Christian names mean nothing because parents choose them for crazy reasons, but surnames are different. The original Scottish Delacours were Huguenot refugees from Louis the Fourteenth's France, so I do have French heritage. But many generations ago."

Elena smacked the sofa. "Sit here. I've something important to tell you before we go down for dinner." After he joined her, she clasped both his hands. "Please, stay calm, no angry outbursts."

"Your furrowed brow and the twinkle in your eyes say you're happy but apprehensive."

"Very perceptive." She took a deep breath. "Daniel, I'm pregnant."

Dan's jaw dropped. A baby, their baby. She wouldn't have invited him if it wasn't their baby, and it explained her interest in a country home.

The shocking but wonderful news changed everything. Moving to England became priority one, and restarting his career in the UK would become job two.

Then the doubts reared their ugly heads. They'd been together for one night on her way to the US and two more nights during her return trip. Did she appear, hoping to get pregnant, or was it an accident? Could it be someone else's baby? His questions spewed forth in a disjointed stream that didn't convey his true feelings.

Elena gripped his hands tighter and stared into his eyes. "Eight weeks, and I've been with no one for months. It must have happened during our night in the Prince George Hotel."

"You stopped taking the pill?"

"After I returned to London, I felt moody and in no relationship, so I give them a rest. I was far into my cycle and worried about my period starting when I was in Nova Scotia. It must have been that first night."

"You're sure you're pregnant."

"Oh Daniel, what a typically male question. I felt awful on the plane coming home, and I've had morning sickness for weeks."

Dan pushed her away. During the last six hours, he'd been inundated with fantastic news. Now he was throwing it away. "Please, can we push restart?" He waited until she nodded. "Wonderful news, the best thing for us. But I'm overwhelmed and making a complete mess of everything."

"Are you sure? I've had such terrible doubts. Two demons battling it out, one on each shoulder."

"More like Welsh pixies. I can see them there, whispering conflicting advice in your ears."

"Then I was euphoric at our reunion. I so much want us to be together." She paused. "I can't imagine us not having a family."

He gathered her into his arms. "Hasn't gone as you planned, has it?" She shook her head, and he continued. "It's the impetus we need to reassess our plans and begin life together."

Elena jumped up, but wobbled and sagged onto the sofa. "God! Pregnancy is driving me crazy. First, I had morning sickness, and now it's dizzy spells." She sat upright. "We can't abandon our quests. The more I learn, the more I'm convinced they're our destiny."

After an elaborate dinner in their hotel's ostentatious dining room, she reiterated the importance of their two-pronged battle.

"I've focused on the incestuous relationship between rogue members of the company and certain critically important governments."

Dan hesitated while the server cleared away plates from the main course. "But my role is science advisor. Why shouldn't I finish my degree and find a position in England? Several topnotch universities around London, and the University of Southampton has a big oceanography department. The government's National Oceanographic Centre is also in Southampton. I won't be sacrificing my career."

"Because the United States is the key. We can't control the situation in China, and Uncle Gareth and his trusted partners have the inside track in Europe."

"How does me being in North America help?"

"We need you inside the US science system because they're abandoning collaboration with their allies."

Dan paused, sipped his coffee, and tasted a forkful of the chocolate cheesecake the waiter delivered. "It's getting harder to access US data, but it's not impossible. The University of Southampton won't be worse than Dalhousie."

Elena shook her head. "The restrictions you've seen are the first step. They'll increase, and you won't have access to critical US data."

"How do you know?"

"It's already happened in commercial and political spheres. Trust me, it's coming in science, and arts, and everywhere else."

Dan offered Elena a sample of cheesecake. "It's good."

She reached across with her coffee spoon. "Hmm, it is good, but I'm serious. You mustn't change the subject."

"Now we're having a baby, a long-distance relationship won't work."

"We'll buy a house somewhere south of London. I'll hire a housekeeper and a nanny for our child. I'll continue to work in England. You'll finish your degree and find a post-doctoral fellowship or a short-term position on the US east coast, and you'll come home as often as possible."

"It's a lousy solution."

She snagged another spoonful of cheesecake. "Two years, maximum three. Then I'll have my foundation set up. We'll know what we're up against, and you can move permanently. We'll use foundation resources to continue the fight."

"Three years! I'll miss the first three years of our child's life."

"All you'll miss for the next seven months is me bitching about being pregnant. In our worst-case scenario, she'll be twenty-nine months, and you can fly here every few weeks. We can buy a bloody jet if that's what's necessary."

Dan checked the empty plates and cups. Her solution was unpalatable, but a life together with his Welsh pixie, millions of pounds, and a critical quest was irresistible. "More coffee?" She shook her head. "Back to our room? Time to bury this. We can't let it ruin our fortnight together."

"A stroll on their grounds," she replied. "Acres of property, and it won't be dark for ages. We can find somewhere nice to talk about our next few days."

He stood and helped her from her chair. "And not worry about climate change or economic crises."

Except for one afternoon at Stonehenge, they devoted their days to visiting country homes for sale in Hampshire. Elena called them modest, but to Dan's eye, they appeared enormous. And the associated grounds, downright intimidating.

On Wednesday evening, they entered a different world. London was the home of the Llewellyn Bank and Elena's swirl of sophisticated friends. Dan expected social experiences he was unprepared for and a return to the climate change battle they'd ignored for several days.

Chapter Fourteen

Thursday June 22, 2028

At 5:30 a.m., Elena stood by the bed in her London flat. The early morning light illuminated her naked lover. She gazed at the painting above the headboard, comparing it to the real thing. Dan opened one eye, stretched, and assumed a pose that mimicked his portrait.

"Last night, you didn't comment on my painting?"

He gazed at Elena, not at the painting. "A tad distracted."

"Well, what's your verdict?"

"Erotic, very personal, and so realistic. Tonight, when I meet your friends, they'll recognize me immediately. I'll feel like I'm standing there naked."

Elena smiled. The male egotists she'd known would be proud of such glowing exposure. *Is Dan really that different?* "Only my closest girlfriends have seen it."

"Like how many?"

Elena fidgeted, shifting from one foot to the other. "Quite a few. I'm so proud I show it to everyone."

"Men too?"

"No man has entered this room since the workman installed it. They're modern women of the world. They can't wait to meet you."

"You're not helping. Confirms I'll be on display."

She climbed onto the bed and pulled the sheet over them. "You'll sweep them off their feet and have them prostrated before you. Like me one short year ago."

He gathered her in his arms, and they drifted back to sleep. It was too early for anything else.

Two hours later, Elena sat in her kitchen, savouring her day's first cuppa. His reaction to his portrait confirmed her commitment to her beloved. Dan displayed none of the overwhelming confidence that characterized the Oxford-educated sons of the rich and famous. And he lacked their ability to utter without forethought the socially sanctioned platitudes for all occasions. Dan may be parsimonious with his words of endearment, but when he talked about their relationship, his studies, or anything else, they were heartfelt comments, not empty words. When it came to the crunch during the party, he'd wow them.

At 7 p.m., an ancient London hackney carriage delivered them inside the gates of a stately house. A liveried butler ushered them into a crowded reception room.

Dan gaped as Elena approached a woman whose bizarre dress had more gaps than gown. Elena smiled. "No subtlety tonight, my dear. Diedre, this is Daniel Delacour. Dan, Diedre O'Donnell, our hostess."

"Delacour. A Huguenot clan of that name settled in Scotland. Involved in the weaving trade. Relatives of yours?"

Dan nodded. "My parents emigrated to Canada from Dunbartonshire. Could have weavers in our history."

She turned to Elena. "Your North American savage is not quite what we thought. Does he have a highland dirk tucked into his kilt?"

"For you, he might need a halberd."

"Hardly. Two quick flicks with his dirk, and I'd be standing here naked."

Laughing, she focused on the next arrivals, and Elena led Dan into the room.

"Lowland rather than highland Scots," Dan muttered as two more of Elena's friends approached. "And no dirk to attack anyone's dress."

They laughed at Dan's comment and pulled him toward the bar. Elena found a chair where she could rest her surprisingly weary bones after four hectic days searching out the perfect home for their child. It was brilliant, as she knew it would be. He'd slay her friends, but she had nothing to worry about. She had the lolly and his baby growing inside her.

*****

Friday morning, Dan followed Elena into her Uncle Gareth's office.

Gareth rose as they entered. "I finally meet my favourite niece's valiant defender of climate change research."

"Your only niece, Uncle Gareth. Makes favourite meaningless."

He smiled but didn't respond to her gently critical comment. "Welcome, Daniel, to the Llewellyn Bank." He motioned to four armchairs arranged around a low table overlooking London's financial district. "Alfredo Rodriguez will join us to discuss the relevance of your work to our mission, but his train's delayed."

Several minutes later, Alfredo knocked and entered the room. He placed a sheaf of papers on the table and launched into his observations without waiting for introductions. "Our current situation mimics George Orwell's Nineteen Eighty-Four. Progressive Europe, lined up against fortress America and autocratic China."

Gareth held up his hand. "I wouldn't classify Russia as progressive."

"But important as Europe's dominant supplier of oil and gas." Alfredo nodded toward Dan. "America's domain encompasses the Americas, including Canada. Chinese influence spreads to much of Asia and Africa."

"Japan, India, Australia, and New Zealand?" Elena asked.

"Japan, Australia, New Zealand, and several others are aligned with Europe. India's a separate case, unaligned, but a major user of coal. We cannot ignore her."

Gareth sighed. "What does this mean for controlling global warming?"

Alfredo extracted another sheet from his stack. "Before Dan describes the science, I have several observations."

"Proceed."

"China has serious issues related to their control of minorities and opponents to their regime. Evidence suggests the Americans are headed in a similar direction. Your company colleagues are implicated."

"Document your concerns about US policies and the role of the Company of Gentlemen Entrepreneurs. Your next observation?"

"Space technologies are experiencing unexpected losses and the necessity of reseeding the ocean."

Dan's eyes widened. A loss term for their nanoparticles could become an important factor. "Do they explain why?"

"No explanation. Their latest financial statement has a new line for replenishing lost particles."

Gareth turned to Dan. "Is this important?"

"Could be critical. Increased acidity will lead to increased biological removal of carbon. When that happens, they'll need a mechanism for shutting off the nanoparticles."

Gareth held up a restraining hand. "Acidity keeps popping up, but my engineering colleagues claim the ocean is buffered. Added carbon dioxide should not affect acidity."

Dan sighed. As part of his joint quest with Elena, he must address science questions, but they agreed he shouldn't push too hard during his first meeting. "The ocean has limited buffering capacity. Industrial CO_2 inputs have overwhelmed it. As a result, we've seen increases in ocean acidity over the last century."

"Summarize the scientific arguments and forward them."

Elena jumped in. "We've already compiled the consensus view on the scientific arguments. I'll prepare a report."

Gareth smiled at Dan. "Looks like you're off the hook. Give us the bottom line. When does this happen?"

"Our initial assessments put the time when enhanced carbon removal produces a reduction in global temperature at 2080 to 2100. Newer evidence suggests carbon emissions are increasing more rapidly than we expected. That pushes the deadline closer."

Gareth scowled. "But no firm estimate. I can't tell my colleagues, 'this will happen if we don't stop increasing atmospheric concentrations of carbon dioxide by...'"

"Not yet. But the past year's events have given impetus to scientists working on this issue. They'll produce better numbers."

In the underground, heading toward Notting Hill, Dan raised a festering issue. "Time you stopped pussyfooting around the Company of Gentlemen Entrepreneurs and your uncle's role."

She jumped up as they approached the Marble Arch underground stop. "Come, we'll find somewhere in Hyde Park."

They strolled to a café by the Serpentine. Dan ordered a beer and Elena tea and biscuits.

She described the European origin of the company and the dynamic nature of the interaction between industrialists and governments before addressing the controversy that dominated company thinking.

"Before our scheme launched, leaders of the major European powers insisted on a global effort, with all the major players marching to the same drummer. The original partners and the European governments had consistent agendas. When they tried to bring in others, the cohesion fell apart on both sides of the partnership. They could accommodate some countries, but the United States, China, and Russia weren't willing partners."

He placed his glass on the table and leaned back. "The US has never trusted Europe's capitalist model with extensive regulation and control. China would be even less likely to buy into a European model. Russia and others are still living the cowboy capitalism of the nineteenth century. How could anyone imagine such a plan working?"

"It was a hard sell, but we were standing on a precipice and needed drastic actions. They made it work."

Dan stared at people rowing boats on the Serpentine. "So that's what you imagine we're up against—China, a country that's beyond your control, Russian oligarchs who are also uncontrollable, and the United States. The US has the world's largest economy, a large, wealthy, independent-minded, and well-educated population focused on personal freedom."

"We can't fight every battle. We must fight the ones we can win. And we can influence battleground USA."

He turned away from the water and drained his beer. "If we're talking about winnable battles, what about my country?"

"Canada's important because it's the eighth largest carbon emitter, far more than you'd expect from its modest population. It's an enigma, progressive by some measures, but so closely tied to the US, it has limited ability to chart a different course."

Dan snorted. He had little confidence in the integrity of Canada's political and business leaders. "If it even wants to."

"Valid point, so until we have compelling counterarguments, we lump Canada with the US."

"Strange bedfellows, given their trade disputes."

"Until the Canadian government stops subsidizing heavy oil production by predominantly US corporations—"

"Led by renegade members of your Company of Gentlemen Entrepreneurs..."

She sighed. "All extremely confusing, but we must choose our battles."

"But you aren't explaining our battles, the ones that will keep us apart for the next three years."

Elena pushed back her chair, stood, and took a few steps toward the Serpentine. "We can't address those without Uncle Gareth's input."

"Yes, Uncle Gareth," Dan said as he steered her to a bench overlooking the water. Uncle Gareth was an ill-defined enigma. "You've clarified my picture of the company, but not his role."

She stared at the water for several minutes, and Dan wondered if she would say anything. "Uncle Gareth's father, my grandfather, was the company's leading light when the company was European, and Britain was part of the European Union. Later, when Britain left the EU and Gareth became responsible for the family's involvement in the company, the important players were in the EU, America, and China. Britain became a secondary player, but Uncle Gareth refused to accept it."

"You're describing family honour, not the Llewellyn Bank's role?"

"It's become his battle using his fortune. The bank's interests are secondary."

"And it's your duty as his heir and future Llewellyn family matriarch to play your part."

She turned to face him with tears brimming in her eyes. "I may worry about the tactics the company employs, but it's my grandfather's mission, my uncle's mission, and mine. I cannot abandon it. That's what you're getting yourself into when you join us. It becomes your mission, and in time, we'll pass it along to our children."

Gareth postponed their Monday morning meeting until Wednesday. He presented Elena with a thick dossier. He insisted she store in her office safe and invited them to lunch at his club. He didn't mention Elena's concerns with company ethics until she'd retired to the ladies' room after a long, involved luncheon.

"Elena worries about the depth of our integration in the political process. The dossier I've given her proves our involvement is necessary and effective. Most of us remain committed to our goal of stabilizing the global environment by reducing our dependence on fossil fuels."

Gareth paused for a breath, holding up his hand when Dan opened his mouth. "We have a serious problem. Several members, Americans mostly, have abandoned our cause. They're focused on making quick profits from expanded exploitation of fossil fuels."

"That's already evident in the monitoring data, and it will lead to an environmental crisis."

Gareth nodded. "One we must avoid, or our mission becomes a woeful failure. We need you and Elena to join the battle to ensure that doesn't happen."

When Elena returned, Gareth stood and extracted a yellowed document from the inside pocket of his jacket. "It's time for me to welcome Daniel into the Llewellyn family and our grand adventure." He passed Dan the document. "We'll call it a wedding gift, although such a designation is premature and perhaps not consistent with Elena's wishes."

Dan unfolded the stiff document, realized it was a property deed, and passed it to Elena. Her reaction was a stifled squeal. The present was a country house near the border between Hampshire and Sussex that had been Elena's grandparents' home. She recounted fond memories of extended childhood visits.

Dan learned Gareth had Hafen Ddiogel, the stately house near the village of Winchfield, modernized, and a swimming pool added. The location was perfect for Dan and Elena. Near enough for a one-hour train commute on the South Western Railway to London in one direction and Southampton in the other. It was near Fleet and Farnborough, two larger towns, and close to the M3 highway between London and Southampton.

While Elena stared at the deed, Uncle Gareth presented Dan with a ring of keys. "The renovations will soon be complete, and you and Elena can move in."

Thursday morning, Elena pulled her bright yellow Lotus to a stop before her grandparents' Victorian-era country house. She'd hadn't been there for ten years, but navigated the byways after exiting the M3 without consulting the maps on her phone.

She leapt out, intent on exploring the house and grounds. Her visit brought back memories from her childhood. For Dan, it provided a shocking picture of the life Elena was offering him.

Chapter Fifteen

Tuesday, July 4, 2028

On his first day back, Dan arrived at his Dalhousie University office before eight. It was already hotter than England, and his windowless office, closed up for two weeks, was stifling.

Steve joined him before he was halfway through the electronic messages he'd neglected during his fortnight in England.

"Elena has an unbelievable fortune and a vast array of rich and influential friends," Dan said when Steve asked about his trip. "Her uncle and his cartel of financiers and industrialists do control global temperatures with nanoparticles."

He described his understanding of the Company of Gentlemen Entrepreneurs, their incestuous relationships with various governments, and the problems developing in the United States.

Steve snorted. "What else is new? My fellow Americans always take the blame."

"We can discuss the details once I clear my backlog, but that's where the political problems lie."

Steve stood and walked to Dan's open doorway, where a hint of a breeze disturbed the stale air. "If you read Beth Manville's editorials on ClimateChange&U, you'll see she also focuses on the American government and how your government aids the US cause."

Dan wondered if they could influence the website's direction. He logged on and scanned the recent activity. "She may not realize the importance of string-pulling industrialists, mostly owners of energy companies," he said.

"Nothing new. An unholy alliance between robber barons and the government is old news. America's constitution keeps it under control."

Dan looked up from his computer and stroked his chin. They were not, as Steve suggested, in a business-as-usual situation. "There's an enormous difference. These industrialists control global temperatures. Governments are beholden to them."

"The president controls the military, and Congress can shut down unruly industrialists. They've done it before. They can do it again." Steve glanced at his watch. "Catch up on your mail and join Anna and me for coffee. We'll continue this conversation."

"How's Elena?" Anna asked when Dan plunked his mug on the coffee room table.

He hesitated, wondering if she was aware of Elena's pregnancy. "Working hard on our new focus—convincing the Company of Gentlemen Entrepreneurs they must tackle CO_2 emissions."

"Provide a cure like the one they produced for temperature?"

"If countries won't reduce emissions, another industrial fix becomes the only solution."

"Is it doable?"

Dan placed his hands on a chairback. The scientific answer to her question was simple. The underlying politics, complicated. "Carbon dioxide removal from the atmosphere has been feasible for ages."

Anna looked up, puzzlement furrowing her brows. "Why didn't they go after CO_2 at the beginning?"

"Cost may be the issue. Or the magnitude of the removal." Dan hesitated. Those explanations were valid, but they didn't account for the serious economic perturbation Elena'd uncovered. It suggested making money from whipsawing oil prices was the real reason for tackling temperature rather than CO_2.

Steve strolled in as Dan took his seat. "Just ended a call with Tony Atherton. He has a student working on carbon removal in his low pH environment but says funding more work may be difficult."

"Where does that leave us?" Anna asked.

Dan grimaced, remembering tensions the topic generated at the Llewellyn Bank. "With a fight on our hands because the timing for increasing CO_2 removal is critical."

Anna turned to her partner. "Steve?"

"Familiar ground. I remember having this discussion seven or eight years ago. If scientists stick to developing the basic understanding, they'll be okay."

Dan glared at Steve. "We're in a different world. Governments and a cartel of businessmen are controlling temperature while letting CO_2 increase. They've mollified people who argued we must tackle global warming. But CO_2 increases will cause another ecological catastrophe. We can't sit back and focus on the scientific principles."

"Then how should we proceed?" Steve asked, refocusing Anna's question.

Dan grabbed a sheet of paper someone left on the table and started scribbling notes. They must develop a solid plan of attack to prevent Steve from falling back on his standard academic excuse for avoiding action. "We're developing a better idea of our opponents and the forces lined up against us."

Steve stood and leaned forward with his hands on the table, then shook his head while resuming his seat. "Sorry, I let my American ego get the better of me. By forces lined up against us, you mean the American members of this industrial cartel?"

Dan hesitated, trying to avoid a confrontation by choosing his words carefully. "Rogue industrialists in the US, more in China, Russia, India, and probably elsewhere. But America's the world's biggest capitalist economy."

Anna placed her hand on Dan's. "Where does Elena fit into this?"

"In a tough spot. She's working inside a fractured industrial cartel with suspicion of everybody and everything ingrained in its core. Hard to know who she should trust."

"God, that sounds ominous. We'll do what we can, and believe me, you can trust us. Please, Steve, tell me you agree."

"No question, we must contribute, but we have our priorities. We'll be graduating and looking towards our futures."

Dan smiled, remembering Elena's exhortations when she convinced him they must focus on the US. "If you settle in the US, it should help her cause."

"Why?"

"Having allies, American scientists with industrial and commercial credentials, working inside their system may be invaluable."

Anna collected the empty coffee cups. "And you? What are your plans?"

"To follow in your footsteps. I'll also search for a postdoctoral position in the US."

"Not in England?" she asked over her shoulder as she rinsed the cups.

"The near-term battlefield will be in North America. We must convince the Americans and their Canadian compatriots to focus on reducing carbon dioxide emissions."

Steve laughed. "We get the message. The problem is real, it hasn't been solved, and we all have roles to play. And I can offer you one extra morsel."

"What's that?"

"While you were in England, Marc Lavoie, another Dal grad, told me about research he's doing on silica cycling. It's linked to Tony's work. He's currently working at the University of Connecticut, so another US science ally for you."

Five weeks later, Dr. Krueger stormed into the lab before Dan's morning coffee cooled. "Drop everything and prepare for sampling the mystery bloom."

Dan looked up from his computer screen. He was struggling with revisions to his thesis. A new sampling effort was the last thing he needed. "What?"

"Ocean colour satellite shows a major bloom centred over Emerald Basin. I've chartered a ship. John Jeffries, Melissa, you, and I must sample it. CTD for T, S, and oxygen, water samples for pH, alkalinity, nutrients, and chlorophyll, net tows for zooplankton. The works."

Dan shook his head. Had too many days in Ottawa, working on government task forces, adversely affected his research supervisor? "Bloom? Everyone knows about spring and fall blooms, but midsummer?"

"Unusual, and possibly related to acidity, field observation of processes we've only studied in aquaria."

"Explains why you want John involved. But can Melissa handle the biological effort?" She was an undergraduate in her first summer working in a research lab and unfamiliar with the activities Dr. K was describing.

"I'll ensure she survives. Others are unavailable, and we must get on it."

Dan sighed. "I'll manage the physical measurements and organize the sampling gear. What ship, which CTD?"

"MV Phoenix, a basic supply ship for offshore rigs with capability for hydrocasts and net tows, nothing more."

"So, our portable CTD. Depth capability is two hundred metres; the basin depth is three hundred."

"No choice, but plankton will be in the top fifty. Should give an adequate picture of the physical environment."

"When, and how long?"

"Tuesday for two sampling days, and two more during the next week."

Dan shook his head. That meant two weeks snatched away from his thesis. "I'll coordinate with John and Melissa. We'll get it done."

When Dan boarded the Phoenix on Tuesday morning, the wind howled, and the rain pelted. He'd worried about summer student Melissa's reaction to the accommodations, a single cabin with four bunks, but she appeared unconcerned. Now, she waited inside the ship's laboratory space, decked out in brand new work boots and wet gear, equally unconcerned about the lousy weather.

"Ready to roll?" he asked.

"All set. I snagged the most isolated bunk, and a crewmember added a privacy curtain. She told me about meals and stuff."

"Seasickness meds?"

"Under control."

"Good. I'm checking the equipment we tied down because it'll be bumpy."

"We still leaving at eight?"

"Should be. Once we get going, you should lie on your isolated bunk until you get used to the motion."

She nodded. "I'll be okay. But what about the others? They're not on board."

"They'll make it. Try to relax. We'll be busy once we get to our sampling station."

"When's that?"

"Noon, then another station later in the afternoon, and all the sample processing. We'll be going until evening."

The weather cleared before they reached their sampling station, and the ship's motion had been milder than Dan expected. Everyone was ready for action as Dan clamped their CTD to the hydrowire. He monitored its progress as the winch operator lowered it into the abyss. He'd conducted dozens of CTD casts during his three years as an oceanography student but always shivered as the expensive piece of gear disappeared into the murky depths.

The basic electronic probe recorded conductivity, temperature, and depth. CTDs generally had an oxygen sensor and theirs, an experimental, often unreliable, pH sensor. The package, when it was working properly, gave a continuous record of the changes in salinity, temperature, oxygen, and acidity with depth.

After its ponderously slow round trip from the surface to two hundred metres, Dan unclamped the device, carried it into the laboratory, and downloaded the data.

When he returned to the main deck, Dr. K was unclamping the last of their six water samplers from the hydrowire. "CTD data okay?" he asked as he passed the ten-litre sampler to John.

"Looks good, even the pH numbers."

"I'll get you the real numbers from these water samples," John said as he disappeared into the lab.

Dan laughed. John, the great defender of modern technology, preferred old-fashioned chemistry bench methods for oxygen and pH.

Dr. K turned to Melissa. "Okay, Melissa, your turn. Three tows, one from the surface to fifty metres, a second from fifty to one hundred, and a third from one hundred to two hundred."

Dan was pouring over data they'd collected during their first day's sampling when Dr. K strode into the lab shortly after nine. "What have you learned?"

"The TS profile is unlike the one they observed on the Bedford Institute's spring monitoring cruise. And the ocean colour satellite showed a patch of almost clear water a month ago."

"Something brought deeper water to the surface, and we've had a bloom growing since then."

"Deeper water means a nutrient input, and if it was unusually acidic..." Dan paused, unsure of where his observations were taking him.

"That could be the answer. Melissa's chlorophyll measurements are at the upper end for a spring bloom, and pH is below the normal range." Dr. K stood for several minutes, drumming his fingers on the benchtop. "We may have exceptional productivity sparked by low pH conditions. Just what Jacinta's experiments of six years ago predicted."

"Jacinta Lopez? I forgot about her. I always attribute the discovery of high productivity to Tony Atherton."

"Jacinta's discovery. Tony modelled it and made predictions of ecological impacts in a future low pH environment."

"And you think we may have encountered those conditions? Temperature and salinity suggest a Gulf Stream ring."

"Too soon to make claims. We understand high nutrient, especially silicate, concentrations in the deeper waters, but why would those waters have low pH?"

Their second day's sampling added nothing to the picture they'd developed on day one. When they returned to the area during the next week, the phytoplankton bloom had dissipated. Copepods, small zooplankton that forage on phytoplankton, had taken over, but pH remained lower than normal.

Chapter Sixteen

Saturday, December 9, 2028

Dan arrived in England at 8:30 a.m., his third trip across the pond in five months. The first, on a midsummer charter jammed with hundreds of tourists, landed at Gatwick Airport and cost most of his meagre graduate student savings. Elena purchased the business class tickets for the more recent flights landing at Heathrow.

He spied Elena leaning against a pillar when he emerged from the international arrivals area. He rushed forward, dropped his bags, and held her at arm's length. "Looks like that baby could be born at any minute."

She sighed. "Four weeks, but I wouldn't complain if she arrived a little sooner."

"Did you drive here?" She nodded. "Not the Lotus. A hire car, or your new estate car?"

She waddled toward the exit. Dan collected his bags and followed. "Estate car," she said. "Arrived a fortnight ago. It's amazing. Forty miles this morning, and it still shows an available range of five hundred kilometres."

"They found you an electric model. They said they wouldn't have one until February."

"Uncle Gareth gave them hell, and presto, it arrives—one with all the features we wanted."

"Nice," Dan said as they approached the silver Range Rover SUV. "No problem finding space for my luggage in this one."

"We managed with the Elise on your other trips."

"Staying longer, so I have more stuff. Last time, we could barely pry you into your Lotus. It had to be your new car, a hire car, or the train."

She stopped and wagged her index finger. "Dan, think! Not my car, our car. Our car, our house, our life together."

He looked from Elena to their shiny new car. "You're right, our car. We chose it together, we'll use it to drive *our* baby around, and I can contemplate owning a car. But the house, I'll never get used to that. And the Lotus was your father's car, so it will always be yours."

She laughed. "It's a start, and you can begin by driving our car home to my house because I'm tired."

"You okay?" he asked after she stopped at a washroom.

"Fine, the ongoing joys of pregnancy. I'll be so happy when it's over, and I can return to my real life."

Forty minutes later, they arrived without incidents where Dan forgot to drive on the wrong side of the road. Elena retired, and Dan wandered the grounds of what would one day be his home. He was preparing coffee with her fancy espresso machine when she reappeared.

"What's new in the North American war zone?" she asked.

"Not much. Funding for climate change research is drying up, and the US is digging in deeper in their bilateral trade war with China."

Elena smiled, a told-you-so sort of smirk. "Alfredo's prediction of a 1984-like scenario is happening, but it's a trade war, not a military confrontation."

Dan shook his head. The proliferation of the damn Godbots hinted at military machinations, but for now, they should thank their stars. It was only a trade war. "Both sides are sabre-rattling, and every year their military budgets grow larger. But so far, it's only talk and aggressive posturing."

"Where does Canada fit into your picture?"

"We haven't been a military factor for decades, and no sign that's changing. For Canada, it's about new trading patterns. We were always America's major trading partner, but they've cut us out of most beneficial arrangements. They dump stuff in Canada when it suits them and buy our raw materials on their terms. They're treating us like a vassal state."

She reached for the teapot, dumped in a teabag, and filled the kettle. "Canada should reject unfair trade with the US and join with Europe and Japan in trading partnerships that isolate China and the US. You already have a trade deal with the EU, and you're part of the Trans-Pacific Partnership. It should be an obvious solution."

Dan shook his head. A European-led policy of isolating the US and China had no chance, and most evidence suggested European states are comfortable trading with

China. "We can't ignore the globe's two largest economies, and I suspect governments and big business in Canada and the US are in this together."

"That," Elena said as she poured boiling water into the pot, "is the crux of the matter. The Canadian government is playing both sides of this issue, pretending to be progressive on fighting climate change whilst expanding heavy oil production they export to the US."

"And the oil company owners must be part of your Company of Gentlemen Entrepreneurs."

Elena slumped into a chair. "It's driving Uncle Gareth to distraction. I'll give you the latest, but before I do, any update on your high growth event from last summer?"

"The coastal ocean colour satellite shows no other episodes. But we're convinced the one we observed was a real-life occurrence of the high growth events low pH will cause."

She glanced at Dan as she swirled her teapot. "But you can't say when they become the norm."

Dan retrieved his coffee from the espresso machine and turned toward her. "It's a harbinger of our uncertain ecological future, but we can't say when. Tony Atherton's thesis and papers contain our best estimates."

Elena poured her tea. "Gareth needs scientific certainty to convince reluctant colleagues to change tack. They agree in principle, but won't move until they see a deadline."

Dan slapped the table with his palm. Everyone's inertia was impossible. Nothing new, but mindboggling nonetheless. He blamed politicians and business leaders' short-term perspective and a willingness to cut their losses and move on when something went wrong. Problems festered, hidden beneath natural variability, and when they erupted, they couldn't fix them with a new law or a business write-down. "If we can't convince humanity to cap emissions, we need major efforts to sequester the CO_2 we're producing. Otherwise, we *will* push global ecosystems into a long-term downtrend, and it could take decades, perhaps centuries, to reverse it."

"You're talking environmental chaos, and Uncle Gareth's imagining economic and political chaos if we can't patch up the schism in the US."

"What about China and India? They're growing rapidly and still dependent on coal and oil."

She glared. "India's not a problem. They'll cooperate with reasonable accommodations for their emerging economy status. China's an outlier, but against a united free world, they'll play along. They were already reducing their dependence on coal when this began."

"Because of their notoriously poor air quality."

"The reasons don't matter. We need the Americans onside to isolate China and force them to cooperate."

Dan hesitated. He'd arrived for the birth of their baby. It should have pre-empted discussion of the global controversy they were mired in. He wanted to put it aside, but knew he wouldn't succeed. Before he returned to Canada, they must corner Gareth and convince him to refocus his company on reducing carbon emissions. "But industrialists who were partners in your company are major contributors to the current American intransigence."

"Renegades. No longer members of the club. They, along with politicians of both political stripes, are taking the US down this impossible road."

"So, how do you escape the impasse?"

"Uncle Gareth is reorganizing his forces, including new collaborators, dot.com billionaires, and others who've benefited from the new web-based commercial economy. We need people like you and American scientists who support us fighting alongside our financial and industrial allies and supportive politicians."

The next month evolved slowly, a strange hiatus from the crazy eighteen months since July 16, 2027, when Elena pushed her way into his world and overcame his reluctance to focus on anything but his thesis project. Then on Friday, January 5 at 2:15 p.m., Elena went into labour.

Dan called the doctor. The midwife and her assistant arrived at Hafen Ddiogel within minutes, with Dr. Jamieson not far behind. Mrs. Baxter, the housekeeper, and Marcie, the nurse Elena hired for her unborn daughter, had roles to play. Even Cook was involved, but Dan and Gareth were exiled from the second floor and sent to wait in whatever main floor room they preferred. They chose the library and settled back with the first of several glasses of scotch.

For several hours, Dan and Gareth conducted a wide-ranging conversation that included many of Dan's questions about the Company of Gentlemen Entrepreneurs. Nothing was resolved, and no harsh words were spoken, but when Mrs. Baxter interrupted them to say a light dinner awaited them, Dan felt he'd reached an important milestone. Issues worrying him for months were on the table. He was sure Gareth would consider them in due course.

After dinner, they returned to the library with the coffee carafe, and Gareth described his global political issues. Dan smiled. They'd turned a corner, tackling the first of many things they'd discuss over the coming days.

As the hours dragged on, and Gareth refused to call it a night, Dan realized he was participating in a time-honoured tradition of the British ruling classes. Birthing was the business of the mother and her womenfolk. Men waited outside the birthing chamber, providing a security blanket for the important activities unfolding inside.

Carys announced her entry to the world at 2:05 a.m. on January 5, 2029, almost exactly twelve hours after Elena's labour began. Fifteen minutes later, Dan was permitted a brief visit with mother and daughter. Then the household retired.

A week later, as he prepared for his return to Canada, Dan put his arm around Elena's shoulders and pulled her closer. "My thesis is almost ready for submission, and I've a job commitment in Georgia. I'll be on the frontline of your battle with America within six months."

His visit for his daughter's birth harboured a single disappointment. He'd hoped Carys' birth would alter Elena's perspective, but she remained committed to the company's monumental battle to win the hearts and minds of Americans. Dan now knew she wouldn't be swayed. He must accept her battle would keep them apart for two more years.

Chapter Seventeen

Thursday, March 7, 2030

Fourteen months after Carys' birth, Dan drew fractals on the computer in his Skidaway Institute of Oceanography office in the coastal wetlands southeast of Savannah, Georgia. He'd been on his job as the scientific leader of their sector of the American government's coastal monitoring program for seven months. His team was currently at sea, and they had interesting results.

He waited for his opportunity to raise a critical issue during the National program's monthly conference call. Finally, the chairman intoned in his deadpan way, "Any additional issues?"

Dan jumped in. "Our spring survey is generating unusual results."

"If you're planning to harangue us on satellites underreporting biomass, I'll save you the bother," the NASA coastal ocean colour group leader replied. "We accept your contention, but need more field data."

Dan ignored the interjection. "We're finding reduced biomass, observations more like those in central gyres."

The background noise on the NASA node increased. "On your shelf?"

"The latest satellite images show reduced colour."

"I can confirm that," someone at NASA added. It might have been Olivia Grange, one of their data analysts. "We're seeing reductions all along the coast."

The chairman's voice showed more animation than usual as he brought order to the conversation. "Dan, is this an information item, or are you expecting input?"

"Heads up for NASA to give the coastal scanner data a more rigorous assessment. And if anyone has field data, they should produce it."

"That it?"

Dan shook his head, a pointless, involuntary gesture during an audio call. "Our field party found huge numbers of salps. Could be responsible for the low phytoplankton biomass."

"Salps!" Olivia Grange yelled over the sound of a chair crashing to the floor. "Tell Dan I'll phone him."

The chairman, a computer specialist, not a biologist, came on chuckling. "She rushed from the room. Dan, can you describe a salp?"

"Gelatinous planktonic tunicates and voracious predators of phytoplankton. They're pelagic and move by pumping water through their barrel-shaped bodies, filtering plankton as they go. They grow faster than most planktonic predators and often accompany major phytoplankton blooms."

"Animals, not plants?"

"Animals, like jellyfish, but more advanced. They have spinal cords."

"How big?"

"Maximum ten centimetres, but they congregate into strings many metres long."

After several seconds of silence, the chairman asked an important question. "Is this related to climate change and your observations of elevated phytoplankton biomass?"

"Possible, but too soon to jump to conclusions."

The chairman laughed. "Right, don't jump to conclusions. I've heard myself say that." He took an audible breath. "Anyone else? Anything to add?"

Another silence. "Let's be on the lookout for salps in our soup. And Dan, don't miss Olivia's call, or you might get yours dumped over your head." He chuckled at his joke. "Thank you, everyone. We'll meet again on the first Thursday of next month."

After the conference call, Dan updated his boss on the meeting and the latest news from their survey ship.

"The story's broken," Ben Oldham, the monitoring program manager, said after Dan's briefing. "Citizens are reporting slimy deposits on the shoreline."

"We talking tourist beaches?"

"Not yet, but that's the worry, especially if it persists. We need someone to show the flag and tell them we're working on the problem."

"By someone, you mean me."

He shrugged as Dan's phone beeped.

The screen announced an incoming text from Olivia. He tapped 'display' and read the message.

<Dan, Olivia. On my way to the airport. Plane arrives at 1945 hours. Pick me up.>

"Olivia," Ben exclaimed when Dan relayed her text. "Is that Olivia Grange?"

Dan nodded. "A coastal zone colour analyst at NASA. She rushed from today's meeting when I mentioned salps."

Ben gazed heavenward, extending his arms like he was offering thanks. "Perfect. Dr. Grange is a verifiable expert. Get to the beach and give the reporters our normal crap about working on the problem. Tell them we have a world expert arriving this evening."

"You know her? We can defend this?"

"Trust me. She was a graduate student studying salps when I worked at Florida State. She's brilliant and a walking encyclopedia."

"Okay, I'll face the press and meet her at the airport. Strategy meeting here first thing tomorrow morning?"

Ben snorted. "Fat chance. She'll have you in the field this evening and before dawn tomorrow. You have lots to learn about Olivia."

When Dan turned to leave, Ben called him back. "She's mercurial, always charging from one seemingly disjointed idea to another. You'll have your hands full, but I promise you one thing. You'll learn everything you could need about salps."

Dan smiled as he stepped through the door. He'd only seen Olivia Grange during two conference calls when someone opted for a video link. He understood the suggestion she was flighty. Her departure when he mentioned salps and other behaviour fit that characterization, but he couldn't credit the rest. He saw a gawky undergraduate who lacked social skills. But if she'd been a graduate student a decade earlier when Ben worked in Florida, she could be in her thirties. Her appearance and behaviour suggested she was several years younger than his twenty-eight. Ph.D. and NASA work experience and Ben's comments negated that idea. She'd be his contemporary, or even a few years older, and more than a satellite data technician.

That afternoon, Dan made preliminary observations of the slimy mess clogging one shoreline. He finessed impromptu interviews with several reporters before heading to the airport.

Seconds after he arrived, Olivia bounded into the arrivals area. Dan understood why Ben claimed she was a force to be reckoned with. With her unmistakable joie de vivre, she stood out from the other passengers.

The woman he'd never met greeted him with enthusiasm befitting lovers reuniting after an extended absence. She stepped back and rewarded him with a bewitching smile. "Your lab for sample jars and then the beach with the salp carcasses."

"What, now? Shouldn't we delay until tomorrow and check you into a hotel?"

"We're in the vanguard battling the world's fiercest predator, and there's no time to lose."

Dan laughed. "Like Cervantes' Don Quixote and Sancho Panza?"

"*Daniel*, this is no joke, and we must join the battle. We aren't tilting at windmills."

"Surely you exaggerate."

"No joke. You've berated us about the increases in biomass and how they're harbingers of larger increases as the ocean becomes more acidic."

Dan nodded. "Results from the university where I did my PhD suggest that's an inevitable consequence of climate change. But those results predict no acid-related increases for decades."

"I've studied those papers. Exposing plankton to intermediate acidity will also generate increased primary production."

"What are you suggesting?" he asked as he led the way to his car.

"The increased biomass you've observed results from extended exposure to intermediate acidity. Our satellites show it's widespread along the entire eastern seaboard and persistent."

"We can't know the cause."

She stopped and glared with her hands on her hips. "You asked me what I was suggesting. That's what I'm telling you. Some parts need confirmation."

"Okay, sorry, please continue."

"Increased primary production attracts increased predation. Your results suggest salps are responsible for the low biomass you're currently observing."

"Your voracious predators are on the job, like locusts attacking a cornfield." Dan laughed, thinking of an earlier occasion when a colleague made an apocryphal allusion to lemmings. This time, he decided his biological comparison was more accurate.

"They are. Are we seeing a major shift in the ecological structure? One with serious implications for climate change?"

"The original research suggested increased phytoplankton growth will lead to increased carbon removal that will mitigate the impacts of fossil fuel inputs."

"Exactly. Humanity has failed to make progress reducing carbon emissions. We're seeing salps riding to the rescue and saving us by gobbling up phytoplankton and transporting them to the sediments. It's happening right here, right now."

That comment reminded Dan of the Gaia Hypothesis. "You're getting ahead of yourself because we only have a few disconnected observations. If we establish your larger picture, you could defend a significant role for your little blobs in our ongoing climate change saga."

"That's why we must get to work."

"All right. I can find torches, mason jars, and scoops to collect the muck. What else?"

"A large sieve, and trays we can use to separate the salp carcasses from the other beach junk. And a shovel."

An hour later, they stood at the back of the beach where large accumulations of salps were first spotted.

She stared into the darkness. "Not a tourist beach?"

"The outer beaches with surf and sand only have a few salps in the normal tideline debris. The town had their crews out cleaning them this afternoon."

"A bayou without surf." She pointed to the east. "Barrier islands with ocean beaches out there?"

Dan shook his head. "A more complicated shoreline with protected areas like this and exposed ones that develop into tourist beaches, but no bayous."

She scanned the beach with her torch before kicking off her sandals and unfastening her skirt. A lace shawl she'd draped over her shoulders joined the pile of clothes on the sand by their sampling gear.

She'd transformed from a modestly attired retro-looking woman into a beach bunny in shorts and a T-shirt. The sight reminded Dan of Ben's mercurial comment. If Ben was referring to this devil may care attitude, he'd handle it.

"Shovel, six jars, scoop, and tray," she said as she strode toward the water's edge, flashing her light before her. She turned at the tide line. "Come on, Sancho, step to it."

When Dan arrived a few seconds later with the gear she requested and a felt marker clutched between his jaws, she laughed. "You're pretty good at following orders for a project leader and someone far above me in the hierarchy."

He dumped his burden on the sand. "What? I thought all federal employees consider themselves several steps above their state colleagues."

She laughed again while flashing the torch in his eyes. "I'm totally enjoying working with you. You hold the lantern and keep the records. I'll do the sampling."

Dan stood aside, supplying scoop and bottles as required and keeping notes as she shoveled muck into a tray. She separated residues of salp carcasses from the sand using the sieve and deposited them in bottles. Once she filled the sixth jar, they returned to the bin with their sampling gear.

When he rose from checking his records and storing their jars, she stood before him with her arms above her head.

"Help me with my shirt," she said.

"What?"

"Next step is sampling the bottom beyond the surf line, but my hands are contaminated with salp goo. I don't want to touch my clothes."

"It's too damn cold. Why not do it tomorrow when we're better prepared?"

"Now," she replied without explanation.

Dan rubbed his hands on his pants and gingerly gripped her T-shirt between thumbs and forefingers. "Last chance," he said before pulling the bottom hem over her bra, head, and fingers she'd scrunched together to avoid contamination.

"Now, my shorts."

Seconds later, she stood before him in her plain white bra and panties. "See, no problem, totally modest." She grabbed the sieve and scampered into the bay, wading until she was waist-deep. "Bring the remaining jars to the shore," she yelled before ducking from sight.

Dan followed instructions and stood knee-deep with a jar at the ready as she emerged and waded toward the shallows. Her soaking wet bra and panties no longer qualified as modest. Dan's concept of a serious scientist with a devil-may-care attitude flew away as movie trope images of naked or scantily clad women emerging from the waves invaded his brain.

Olivia, fortunately, kept her mind on the job as she scooped salps from the sieve to a mason jar. "Masses of salp goo. It seems thick, and pretty much everywhere I walked."

She collected five more samples before they abandoned the beach, returned to the lab, and refrigerated the samples.

At 11:05, they headed toward Dan's apartment without discussing where they were going. It was too late to find a hotel, and her free-spirited behaviour signaled she'd be open to bunking down in his flat.

She kicked off her sandals and dropped her backpack in the apartment doorway. "Shower first, then something to eat, because I'm ravenous."

Dan pushed her pack farther inside before closing the door and pointing toward the bathroom. "Second on the right," he shouted as he corralled her stuff. She disappeared, leaving her shorts and T-shirt in the hallway. Her behaviour reminded him of the first night Elena Llewellyn stayed in his sister's Halifax house. But the circumstances were very different. He was now married with a fourteen-month-old daughter. How would Elena react when he told her about this aspect of his two-year sojourn in America.? *Will she reconsider the commitment she's so keen on?*

Chapter Eighteen

Friday, March 8, 2030

When Dan's alarm jangled at 6:30, Olivia had already risen.

Before they crashed, they'd discussed their observations and made preliminary plans for today's sampling. Olivia's various speculations reminded Dan of a transient occurrence of elevated phytoplankton concentrations he'd observed on the Scotian Shelf two years earlier. Unusually low pH triggered that event, and a massive zooplankton bloom ended it. They'd shown elevated silicate concentrations contributed to the bloom, and the marauding zooplankton were copepods, not salps. No suggestion elevated silicate triggered this bloom, but the other factors were similar.

"Your survey ship's due this afternoon to load gear for near bottom sampling and measuring colour," she announced when Dan appeared in the kitchen.

"Did someone say how they plan to sample?"

Olivia passed him her phone. "Read the texts. A pumping system."

"That figures, but it takes a crew to install it and electronic techs to set it up. They won't get it done this afternoon."

"Benny says they'll be out this evening. And he's setting up a similar system for us to use in inshore waters."

"Benny?"

"Your boss, Ben Oldham. Around FSU, he always hummed an old Elton John song, *Benny and the Jets*, so students called him Benny behind his back."

"If that's the situation, we'd best grab a bite, head for the lab, and give Benny a heads-up on today's sampling plans."

That afternoon, at a station in the maze of channels behind the outer beaches, they encountered soupy black sediment reeking of hydrogen sulphide.

"Eureka," Olivia exclaimed when she pulled a discoloured salp from the muck. "The final piece in the puzzle. All day, we've seen evidence of phytoplankton predation and transport to the bottom. Now, we have salps contributing to the formation of highly organic inshore sediments."

Samuel Sparkes, the gnarled old boat operator assigned to their trip, spoke up for the first time. "If you want rotten egg gas, you should visit Bartlett's Hole."

Olivia kept picking salps from the black goo. "Can we go there?"

Bartlett's Hole was an almost legendary anoxic depression, but Dan didn't know its exact location. He looked at Sam for guidance. "Can we?"

Sam smiled a gap-toothed grin. "Near here, only twenty minutes if I open 'er up."

"Make it so," Dan said.

Thirty minutes later, Sam cut the motor, and they drifted toward a strange sight. The almost circular basin devoid of the eelgrass choking most of the backwaters had gases bubbling from its surface. Dan's nose detected hydrogen sulphide in the air downwind of the bubbling cauldron.

"Out," he yelled, pointing back.

Sam shifted into reverse, and they backed away from a potentially dangerous situation. Hydrogen sulphide is extremely toxic, and the human nose is an imperfect detector. It's sensitive to non-lethal concentrations, but not the higher ones that could prove fatal. That meant the only safe reaction to smelling the rotten egg smell of hydrogen sulphide was immediate departure.

"Can we approach from upwind?" Olivia asked.

Sam turned the boat and shifted into forward. "Usually smells like a swamp, but I never seen it like this. You want the far side?"

"If possible," Dan replied. Olivia wouldn't abandon this sampling opportunity, but they must keep it safe.

Sam navigated narrower channels until he encountered a larger one that returned them to the cauldron. All three sniffed the air like frightened deer as they approached.

Dan held up his hand as they slid up to the edge of the bowl-shaped basin. No hydrogen sulphide smell, but bubbles of gas escaping from the surface were visible ten metres ahead. "Quick sample here, then we're heading home."

He deployed the sampling device that vacuumed anything sitting on or floating above the sea bottom and watched the video display as it descended. A few seconds later, the picture went black. "Bottom depth?" he asked.

"Forty feet," Sam replied, using the old imperial measures that were still commonplace among non-scientists in the United States.

"We're only down three metres, and we're already in the black muck."

"Start the pump," Olivia demanded. "We're in a ten-metre-deep layer of unconsolidated sediment."

Dan engaged the pump. "Very soupy if the depth sounder doesn't detect it."

Olivia held the sampling sieve ready as clear water spewing from the hose turned murky. The soupy sediment flowed through the screen, and within seconds, blackened salps appeared. "See, salps everywhere we go. We're onto something important."

She scooped sievefuls of salps into a sampling jar as Dan lowered the hose into the muck. He stopped it at five metres, where Olivia collected another sample containing salps. When he lowered it to ten metres, they found no salps. He raised the hose to the surface and motioned for Sam to withdraw.

Dan breathed a sigh of relief as they sped away, but Olivia gazed back longingly. He shook his head. She'd risk life and limb to collect more samples farther into the basin—a risk he couldn't authorize.

Sam opened the throttle and drove the workboat at top speed. Once they were ashore, Olivia took charge of the samples, and Dan headed for his office.

He fired up his computer and logged into the website supporting secure personal video conferencing. He entered Elena's web address and waited for her reply.

"Sorry for the unscheduled call," he said when she logged on. "You free to talk?"

"Timings good. Busy day. Home relaxing with Carys sleeping here beside me." Elena turned her camera so Dan could see his daughter's cherubic face. "You could have phoned."

"And missed an opportunity for remote contact with Carys." He shook his head. "I need these video calls. Without them, I'd go crazy down here amongst the alligators."

She laughed. "Another close encounter with an alligator, is it? Not the reason you called."

"No. Big development unfolded yesterday. Important for both professional and personal reasons. Check out this video."

He switched from the selfie camera to a segment of video recorded by their sampler.

"Can't see much, amorphous blobs in murky water."

"They're salps, predators ravaging a huge bloom that extends from Florida to Massachusetts. It shows the future predicted a decade ago by Tony Atherton is real, and it's happening here, now."

"You suggesting the environmental Armageddon Atherton predicted is imminent?"

"Must be an isolated occurrence, but as CO_2 concentrations increase, they're bound to become more frequent. I'd call it a harbinger of disasters to come."

"Harbinger, is it? That's becoming your favourite word."

"No way. My favourite words are Elena and Carys, and I miss you both."

"Which gets us to the personal aspects of this call."

He paused, wondering how he'd telegraphed his concern. "I've been overwhelmed by a scientist who arrived to study them."

"Young, female, pushing herself into your personal space?"

He sighed. "Female, chronologically not so young, but young at heart. She arrived yesterday evening. We worked until late, and then she bunked down in my apartment. She's settled in for the weekend. Thought you should know."

Elena smiled as Carys stirred. "Does she resemble another young woman who wormed her way into your life three years ago?" She held their slowly wakening baby in front of the camera. "I trust you, Dan. You can handle it. Gotta go. Carys is awake, and dinner awaits."

Dan returned to his lab and listened as Olivia waxed poetic about their results. They tidied the lab and drove to the commercial harbour to discuss plans for their two extra days of ship time.

At eight thirty, they stood with Ben Oldham, watching their survey ship pull away from the Savannah waterfront. Ben bid them good night, and Dan turned to Olivia. "A pub or my apartment?"

"Your place. Your fridge has beers, and we have much to discuss."

After a short walk, he unlocked the passenger door. "What's on your mind?"

She waited until he pulled into the traffic. "I need somewhere to stay for the next week. I'm hoping it's your place."

"Not Washington and work on Monday?"

"Took a week's vacation. We're onto a big story, and I want to stick with it."

"I have a second bedroom and a cot in my storage locker. We can set it up."

"It's your computer room, and we'll need a command centre."

"Wouldn't my institute office with access to library and support staff be better?"

He drove in silence until they escaped the downtown traffic. "Something else bothering you?"

"You're still skeptical, but this really is important."

"It may be a chance occurrence, something we don't see again."

She banged the dash, and he tensed, anticipating a swat. "It's a harbinger of our future as carbon emissions continue to rise."

That word again, but this time someone else is using it.

"We've proven nothing, but it's an interesting idea."

She twisted toward him, straining against the seatbelt. "That's why I must stay involved."

"How?"

"I'll work here for the next week. I'll help your team process the samples we've collected, do more sampling, and search for a way to stay involved."

"You could stay longer or visit regularly if NASA covers your salary, and our budget, or the state's coastal resources program, provides travel and operating funds."

"Can we make it work?"

"Possible. But no singing *Benny and the Jets* around the lab."

With laughter in her voice, she sang the song. She knew the tune and all the words.

"I'm guessing you plan to stay with me when you're here," he said as they approached his apartment. "We need to get something straight—"

"I'll be on a tight budget."

"And your comment about my second bedroom being a valuable command centre suggests you anticipate continuing to share my bed. You must know from my pictures I'm married with a small child."

"It's okay," she said as he unlocked the door of his ground-floor apartment. "I also have a child. Her name's Luna, goddess of the Moon. She's eleven, so older than yours, and very independent. I must stay involved with the experiment, and I must minimize my expenses. I'll accept whatever living arrangement you choose."

Olivia was so into investigating her salps Dan couldn't turn her away. And he understood her little beast's potential significance in the rapidly approaching climate change crisis. He couldn't allow her to become his lover, but she could become a valuable ally in their fight to understand the ecological significance of CO_2 emissions. An expanding quest could make his exile easier to endure.

Chapter Nineteen

Wednesday, August 21, 2030

One year after Dan moved to Georgia, Anna Matthews watched from the front porch as her husband Steve drove up the dusty drive to her great uncle's farm. For the past month, the eastern Pennsylvania farmhouse had been the final waystation in her decade-long exodus from difficult times in her native Poland.

Her troubles began in 2020 when she became a teenage mother impregnated by her second cousin. A year later, she emigrated with her parents to England but left baby Tomas behind with his father's parents. She finished school in England, studied mathematics at a redbrick university, and moved on to Dalhousie University for her PhD.

In Halifax, she met Steve Matthews. He was another Dal graduate student with a complicated past. They became an item, and in 2028, they married. She changed her name from Pawlak to Matthews and hoped to leave her unhappy past behind. Except for one thing. She hadn't forgotten her son, Tomas.

Leaving him with his paternal grandparents had been a terrible decision. He was neglected and eventually rescued by one of her Polish aunts. He was now living in the United States with other members of her extended family. She vowed to become reunited with her son, but issues related to his citizenship status meant it couldn't happen until she established a domicile in the US.

That began in mid-June when Anna completed the requirements for her PhD. Her oral exam went well, and the final changes to her thesis were trivial.

On June 27, she, Steve, and their eight-month-old baby, Nicola, entered the United States. They rushed from the Holton, Maine border crossing to Steve's family home in Somerville, Massachusetts, and spent the next two weeks finding a home for themselves.

They arrived at the Pennsylvania farmhouse on the morning of July 16 for Tomas's tenth birthday celebration. Anna and Nicola remained. Steve returned to Halifax to complete the last requirements for his PhD.

Tomorrow, their family of four would drive to their new home in Plymouth, Massachusetts. Anna could begin her life in America reunited with her husband, daughter, and son. Her exodus from Poland would be complete.

The six-hour road trip on Thursday, August 22, went smoothly. During the five weeks Anna and Nicole lived on the farm, Tomas got into the idea of having a baby sister. In the car, he entertained her whenever she woke up. When she slept, he chattered about things he saw along the road and asked questions about the house they were heading to.

"Will I have my own room," he asked, "and my own computer?"

"With a window?" he added when Steve assured him his bedroom waited for him.

Steve shook his head. "What sort of life is he remembering?" he whispered to Anna.

As Steve pulled out to pass a slow-moving truck, Anna recalled the remote corner of Poland and the farming village where she grew up. That, and the nearly identical neighbouring village where Tomas lived for his first seven years. The hovels they lived in were tiny, overcrowded, and crude—no electricity, no running water, and no sanitation. Moving to the crowded farmhouse with two dormitory-like bedrooms, one for boys and one for girls, must have been a shock. Their new house would be another.

"Your room with a window that looks over our yard," Steve said. "Smaller than the farm, and no animals, but a nice lawn and some garden. We'll grow strawberries, and I don't know what else. You can help us decide."

"Flowers," Anna added. "I want lots of flowers."

They arrived at their Plymouth house nine hours after leaving Pennsylvania. The six-hour drive plus stops for lunch, dinner, and other breaks were too much for Tomas. He took one sleepy-eyed trip around the garden, found his bedroom, and crashed.

Nicola was livelier because she'd spent most of the day sleeping in her car seat. She gawked and gurgled and made other baby noises as Anna carried her on their first trip around their new house. They'd purchased it two months earlier, but the closing was very recent. Steve's mother and siblings had managed the logistics.

They'd done a splendid job. They'd emptied the shipping pod Steve packed in Halifax and added surplus furniture from their various Boston houses. As Steve unloaded the car, Anna imagined a rosy future living in Plymouth with their mishmash of furniture from Halifax and Boston.

*****

In September, a letter from the University of Georgia terminated Dan Delacour's contract. The letter praised his efforts to understand plankton ecology on the southeastern US continental shelf. It blamed changing government regulations, not problems with his performance, for the decision, but offered no hope of continued employment.

He was neither surprised nor concerned. Program managers in Washington were using an old and often neglected preference for Americans to purge aliens working in the US. One more example of America's isolationist trend. When Ben Oldham told him Olivia Grange, a well-qualified American who'd become his friend and collaborator, would assume his duties on November 1, Dan could leave with few misgivings. The dismissal was a blessing in disguise. It would speed up the reunion with his wife and daughter.

On Thursday, October 3, Dan loaded his possessions and headed north on Interstate Highway 95. He had an emigration interview in the British Consulate on Tuesday morning. That left time for a side trip to Boston.

On Friday afternoon, he found a family immersed in its new life. Steve Matthews was busy with his post-doctoral fellowship at the Woods Hole Oceanographic Institution and the family engineering firm in Somerville. Tomas was enrolled in grade five in the neighbourhood elementary school and enjoying life in a modern American suburb. Anna had her dream appointment, a post-doctoral fellowship in the mathematics department of prestigious Harvard University.

She waited at the front door of their large house nestled in a well-treed suburban lot with her ear tuned for any noise from inside. Dan bounded from his car and engulfed her in a hug. "Not what I expected for two young scientists struggling to make their way in academia."

She sighed. "Our story's getting complicated, but we should leave it until Steve gets home. I'll collect our younger one, and we can stroll around the garden. When Steve arrives, we'll break out the beer."

She scurried inside and returned seconds later with sleepy-looking Nicola cradled in her arms. They wandered around the garden while she explained how Tomas, her much older first child, became part of their family. She looked up when Steve and Tomas appeared. "They're home. We can start the barbeque and catch up on the sixteen months since we last saw you?"

That evening, when Anna was getting Nicola to bed, a strangely philosophical Steve Matthews brought Dan up to date on his side of their family story.

"Life never unfolds as one expects," he said as he spread his arms wide and gazed into the evening light filtering through their trees. "We've done okay."

"Looks pretty nice."

Steve nodded. "Strange how we got here. You know I started studying engineering at MIT."

"I didn't. I assumed your undergraduate major was physics."

"Must have told Tony Atherton I started in engineering. I switched into physics, so you're right, my BSc's in physics. At first, I expected to join the family firm, but I became disenchanted with that future and switched into science with academia in mind."

"And that led to oceanography at Dal in what, 2022?" Dan added to keep Steve talking.

"Twenty twenty-one, but it also led to a strained relationship with my family. My father didn't accept that I would abandon the firm with, in his view, the vain hope of becoming a professor. Fast-forward three years. My father's gone, and the company's in trouble. I abandon my academic dreams and return to help rebuild the company."

"Before my time."

Steve nodded again. "Jump forward to 2026. You're at Dal Oceanography for the first time, and I'm back for a second try. I graduated and found myself a postdoc at Wood's Hole. Anna also had her PhD and a postdoc at Harvard, so we thought we were on our way. When I started applying for teaching jobs, I learned I was too old. Faculty appointments in oceanography were going to young lions, not thirty-three-year-olds with a few detours along the way. In a few months, I'll be back running the family firm. This time, I understand it's where I belong. And Anna's on the shortlist for a tenure-track position as a mathematics professor at Boston University."

"So, it's working out okay."

"Yeah, an interesting job, two kids, and hopefully one professor in the family. And I haven't lost sight of our fight to control global carbon emissions. I'm now approaching it from a slightly different direction."

Dan looked up from his empty glass. Their battle to understand climate change had become more complicated since it began in 2027. "Elena's Company of Gentleman Entrepreneurs' technological fix has stabilized global temperature, but major industrialized nations have done little to reduce carbon emissions. The environmental stress gets worse, and their temperature cure must be metastable."

Anna joined them in their main floor den as Steve refilled their glasses from his bottle of single malt scotch. "Modern technological man always accepts remedies without adequate consideration of their durability. He has unfettered confidence in our ability to come up with another cure for developing situations."

"Bloody lousy approach," Dan said before savouring his drink. "Waylays any hope for a proactive effort to address the problem."

Anna settled back with the tea she brought with her. "I'm a newly Christened American and trying to imagine how the United States fits into your battle. My early observation is we're in a difficult position."

"No question," Steve said. "America's mired in an existential battle with China for commercial and industrial domination. It pits our democratic, free enterprise system against China's autocratic state control."

"But," Dan asked, "how does our battle to reduce carbon emissions play into your picture?"

"Cheap energy is critical." Steve paused, gazing at Dan. "That and a go-it-alone attitude that explains the University of Georgia's decision to cancel your contract. Everything suggests the America First mantra that surfaced fifteen years ago is thriving."

Sunday morning, Steve bade Dan a hasty farewell before speeding off to solve a crisis that developed overnight at Matthews Engineering. Dan wasn't in such a hurry. He and Anna enjoyed second cups of coffee before he hit the road north toward Halifax.

Anna sighed as she accompanied Dan to his car. "You and I may stay focused on academic issues. Steve's loyalties are now split between an academic career and his interest in the family firm. His dedication to your battle against ever-increasing carbon emissions may waver a little, but we'll still be here, fighting on your side." She paused and raised Nicola's arm. "Wave bye-bye to Uncle Dan."

Thursday afternoon, after days spent solving logistical problems from selling his car to final emigration formalities, he boarded his flight to London.

"Daddy," twenty-one-month-old Carys yelled as Dan wrapped his arms around Elena outside Heathrow's international arrivals area on Friday morning.

"Is she happy to see me?" Dan asked as he scooped the toddler into the hug.

"I think so," Elena replied as she took charge of his baggage cart. "She's talked about little else for days."

An hour later, Elena turned onto Hafen Ddiogel's manicured drive. As usual on his visits to their Winchfield estate, Dan felt like an outsider—getting comfortable with his new home would take time.

Chapter Twenty

Friday, October 11, 2030

At 5 p.m., Dan and Elena left Carys in the care of Mrs. Baxter, the housekeeper, and Marcie, the nurse. They repaired to the local pub for Dan's first pint as a resident of the United Kingdom.

Elena glanced up as Dan placed her glass of white wine on their table. Her furrowed brow telegraphed concerns she'd been hiding all afternoon. "Your stint in the United States wasn't as successful as we hoped."

He hesitated as he savoured his first taste of the pub's premium bitter. "Rather shorter than we planned. Didn't give me time to get the States back onside in your fight to curb CO_2 emissions."

Elena sipped her wine. "Too much to hope, but your sojourn wasn't a total waste."

"Some insights into how the US science system works, and a useful study I conducted with Olivia Grange on salp ecology. The papers will enhance my CV," he said as he recalled his first hectic week working with Olivia. They'd developed a good working relationship despite her obsessive nature and lack of empathy.

"But nothing's altered the Americans' conviction climate change is a non-issue. One that's solved by the successful control of global temperatures."

Dan nodded. "That's the core science problem. Academic scientists are well supported, but applied research gets bugger all." He paused for another swig of beer. "Lowering carbon emissions needs scientific effort, international cooperation, and coordination by federal government institutions. Not happening in the US. No federal funding, and they're inhibiting efforts by restricting access to their large environmental datasets. They've also become very slow and cautious when they draw conclusions based on their observational programs."

"Why?"

Dan shrugged his shoulders, wondering why she was focusing on the structural problems he'd encountered. "Their government's actively denying change is an issue and exerting undue influence on a process that should be science-based."

"A topic for Sunday when Gareth and Alfredo visit. Anything else? We need something positive."

"Afraid not. I had upfront personal experiences with two disquieting trends. The first was the starving of applied research. The second is the massive purge of foreign scientists working in government facilities. Same goes for government-funded positions in universities. They cannot be good trends."

Elena smiled. "It got you home nine months sooner than we agreed." Her smile turned into a frown. "They're broad-based trends we see in many areas, and definitely negative." She gazed around the pub while she sipped her wine. "Any positive news?"

"Positives for us or your big fight?

"Either."

"Let's start with the big fight. I generated joint projects with several scientists doing important work on climate change." Dan described his collaborations with Olivia Grange, Tony Atherton, Marc Lavoie, and several others. "They'll help us define the problem and identify the best routes forward. That's a positive."

"And Beth Manville, Tony's wife, continues to push the cause on their website."

Dan nodded. Beth had her finger on the political pulse in Canada. She could become another important ally. "So, you have science-related allies within the North American enemy camp."

"And for Dan Delacour?"

"A fellowship with teaching responsibilities at Southampton University. It may lead to a permanent research position or be a stepping stone to a tenured teaching position."

"And you'll provide input to our efforts to save the world."

He smiled. That became an unstated commitment when he linked his future to the Llewellyn clan. "You'll say it's my duty."

Dan watched Elena stride to the bar. They had the evening to reconnect after ten months with only two visits. It was time to forget climate change and consider more pleasant subjects. But he couldn't suppress his misgivings about the global euphoria after the National Ocean and Atmospheric Administration published numbers, confirming the world had broken the upward trend in global temperatures. Countries using stabler temperature to justify abandoning their carbon dioxide emission targets would generate serious repercussions.

After luncheon on Sunday, Elena dispatched Dan to meet Gareth Llewellyn at the Winchfield train station. He pondered the changes since Global Climate Action Day as he waited.

Dan's thoughts turned to the future when the youthful-looking Sir Gareth of Penarth bounded from his first-class carriage. They returned to a poolside party in full swing. Southern England was revelling in an unusual weather condition that was more common in North America. Their Indian summer day was bright, clear, and reasonably warm, but late in the year for swimming by anyone but hardy youngsters.

Alfredo Rodriguez was there with Cristina, his wife, and Carlos and Isobel, their two children. Dan and Gareth joined Alfredo at a table sufficiently far from the pool to be outside its splash zone. Elena arrived with a tray.

Alfredo glanced up as Elena distributed glasses of lemonade. "Christina will supervise our children, and I see your girl is entertaining Carys in a baby pool."

Elena glanced at the pools. "They'll be fine whilst we discuss the issues facing us. Later, I've promised Carlos and Isobel a tennis match."

Gareth shook his head. "It's Dan's third day home. Should we postpone this discussion?"

"Best get on with it, Uncle Gareth. He has meetings all week in Southampton."

Dan nodded. He yearned to start family life in England with Elena and Carys, but Gareth and Alfredo were there to discuss geopolitical issues. Their meeting provided his opportunity to spend a few hours convincing them they must focus on carbon dioxide emissions, not global temperatures. He couldn't pass it up.

Gareth smiled. "We have issues that could keep us occupied for days. Who will start?"

Elena looked at her husband. "Let's begin with Dan. He might provide new insights into problems you, Alfredo, and I have pushed around for months."

Gareth Llewellyn nodded his agreement. He turned to Dan. "The floor is yours."

Dan reviewed the evidence linking high productivity to real-world occurrences of low pH and enhanced carbon removal. He finished with the ecological importance of low pH super blooms. "They'll occur more frequently as the ocean becomes more acidic."

Gareth held up his hand. "For clarification, more acidic because we continue to pump carbon dioxide into the atmosphere."

"Yes."

"We're already at the crisis you anticipated?"

Dan shook his head. "We've seen isolated examples of a future where this behaviour dominates. We've yet to reach the point where removal exceeds inputs."

"When does this occur?" Gareth asked after a theatrical sigh. "I need a solid estimate to convince my colleagues we must act."

Dan paused. Gareth was raising a problem they'd banged their heads against several times. People, governments, and Gareth's Company of Gentlemen Entrepreneurs would only act when they had a deadline they couldn't avoid. "I'm sorry. We're in uncharted territory. We don't know."

"Then what should we do?"

Despite the lack of a concrete deadline, Dan felt compelled to risk annoying Gareth by stressing the need to act. "A sensible observer would realize we must address the situation—"

"You suggesting we aren't sensible?" Gareth shouted, attracting the attention of Catrina and Marcie.

Dan started, surprised by the vehemence of Gareth's reaction, but refused to back down. "I'm suggesting society behaves like someone who can't appreciate the severity of the situation. It can't bring itself to take the correct course."

Alfredo jumped in. "We've ventured from the scientific to the political."

Gareth thumped the table. "We have. Let's talk business and politics and return to the science if appropriate."

"We should start at the beginning," Alfredo said. Gareth groaned, but Dan smiled. They'd never adequately explained the Company of Gentlemen Entrepreneurs. Perhaps he'd learn something important. "Your father formed the company thirty-three years ago. They knew climate change would become the formative issue of the twenty-first century."

"Yes, fine. My father, Elena's grandfather, the previous owner of this house, was a visionary. We can say, looking back, that he was mostly correct. But he didn't anticipate our current situation."

Alfredo passed around copies of a flowchart he extracted from his satchel. "I'll get to it after I put everything into its historical context for Dan's benefit. The original group was European. The major players, progressive countries. Together, the government leaders, and the core members of the company, developed a plan to control global temperatures."

Gareth waved his copy of the flowchart. "We needn't review this."

Alfredo ignored the interruption. "We must consider their motivations. They were prepared to proceed with a European initiative in 2015. Their goal was economic stability, an important factor for the traditional industries they led. Government leaders had a broader vision, one that involved the entire world. They insisted on buy-in from the United States, China, India, Russia before enacting the plan."

Dan turned, distracted by squealing from the pool. "And that's where it went wrong?"

"Not initially. Barack Obama was elected President of the United States in 2008 and awarded the Nobel Peace Prize in 2009. European governments and the company supported his nomination, and he began a progressive shift in America. Several American industrial leaders joined the company, and the plans to seed the ocean with reflective nanoparticles became a reality. Everyone knew China was a dubious partner. With the United States, Europe, and almost everyone else united, they thought they could manage China."

Dan silently thanked Alfredo. The Spaniard was giving him a valuable summary of how the plan developed, one that softened Dan's jaundiced view of the venture. "Then Donald Trump became president, and everything changed."

"Oversimplification. Trump represented a trend that blossomed during Obama's second term. Trump rode that conservative Christian, inward-looking trend to victory. He was at the vanguard of the move to fortress America and the mercenary bilateral trade deals that have characterized the last decade of American foreign policy. American members of the company aided and abetted him."

Elena entered the fray, defending her uncle's vision. "Not all. We have American partners who share our perspective."

Alfredo shook his head. "Here, the company works with governments. In the US, the rebels work with the government."

"Where does that leave us?" Dan asked, hoping they'd return to Alfredo's history lesson.

"With major problems. The global political situation is unstable. We have three major factions—Europe and a bunch of allies vs. the United States and its allies vs. China and theirs."

"The *Nineteen Eighty-Four* analogy you often mention," said Elena.

Alfredo described his favourite political philosophy for several minutes. Then Isobel approached the table and pulled on Elena's sleeve. They suspended the discussion while Elena engaged ten-year-old Carlos and eight-year-old Isobel in a tennis match.

Gareth provided his perspective as they watched the tennis. "I'm transferring management of bank operations to Brandon Newbury. It will allow me to spend my remaining years struggling to remedy the harmful effects of the instability we've inflicted on the planet. We've generated the uncertainty that's anathema to good business planning."

He stood staring into space as Isobel ran to collect errant tennis balls. "And you, Dan, you've added scientific uncertainty about the impact increasing carbon dioxide emissions could have on the global ecology."

Dan stooped to pick up a ball and toss it to Isobel. He then described carbon capture techniques and other interventions that could buy time to resolve Alfredo's political issues. It was a change from his normal perspective, but one Gareth probably needed.

"Oh, the optimism of youth. For Carys' sake, I hope you're right, but I cannot share your enthusiasm. We're headed for a cataclysmic showdown between the United States and China. The next decade and forward-thinking Americans' ability to turn around a tense situation will be the key."

"So, you agree with Elena," Dan replied. "The critical battleground is in America."

"The political structures protecting their democratic capitalism are being challenged like never before. But you lived there for a year. What did you observe?"

Dan mentioned his relative isolation from political machinations while working in Georgia. He focused on their tendency to favour fundamental scientific research over more applied work. He moved on to a general topic. "I noticed some disquieting social changes impacting young people."

"University students?"

"University students, young working people. First, fundamentalist Christian dogma is playing an ever-increasing role in social life. Second, the urge to explore, to be young and adventuresome, is being beaten out of undergraduates."

"Interesting. Social behaviour we should add to our new appreciation of climate change science and Alfredo's disquieting political-economic trends. Unless we escape from that morass—"

A lightning flash from thunderheads that amassed unnoticed cut off Gareth in mid-sentence and truncated the tennis match. Everyone raced for the house as the first drops of a late afternoon thunderstorm hit the ground.

"Chaos, utter bloody chaos," Gareth said as he followed the more fleet-footed younger people to the house. "Are we approaching Armageddon?"

Dan grabbed an umbrella and ran down the broad flight of concrete stairs that led from the house to the poolside patio. He handed it to Sir Gareth and followed him into the house.

Gareth's Company of Gentlemen Entrepreneurs unleashed the chaos when they stabilized temperature rather than carbon emissions. They were treating the symptom rather than the cause of human-induced climate change. The company members' desire for short-term commercial gain before they tackled the carbon emission problem generated that misguided approach.

Their quest for commercial gain was having unexpected consequences. It was fuelling America's renewed confidence in its ability to challenge China for commercial domination of the world. Would it lead to a serious confrontation that would make Sir Gareth's current chaos pale by comparison?

Chapter Twenty-One

Monday, February 10, 2031

Four months later, Dan trudged up the drive of their Hampshire estate. When he arrived in October, England was experiencing the benefits of warmer, more stable summers that extended well into fall. Then it started raining. He'd yet to see snow, but he'd seen plenty of rain. Today, the sun was shining.

In November, the German scientist managing the European seeding program resigned. He was in his sixties and struggling with the aftereffects of a heart attack. Gareth Llewellyn exerted pressure, and Dan found himself responsible for nanoparticle additions to the eastern North Atlantic and the entire South Atlantic. He didn't even know how the program worked.

Hours studying Space Technologies' internal documents solved that problem. German, American, Chinese, and Japanese ships were spreading billions of buoyant nanoparticles. The microscopic mirrors reflected incident light from the ocean's surface. Surveillance satellites monitored the success of the reflectors. They also guided ships adding new particles to the ocean.

In his first months as program manager, Dan focused on fine-tuning the seeding patterns. Over time, he hoped to expand his role, but he was moving cautiously. Their efforts to focus on the major ocean currents were key. They dumped massive amounts in currents like the Gulf Stream. Nature helped them by spreading the particles with little effort on their part. If they perfected that part of the process...

That was his long-term agenda. Tomorrow, he'd travel to Paris to help solve a major problem with the temperature control program. It would be his first venture into crisis management.

He found Elena lounging on a patio chair. She was wearing a light jacket and soaking up the surprisingly warm February sunshine. "You're home early," she said when he stepped onto the patio.

Dan dropped his briefcase on a table. His nanoparticle management job was consuming too much of his time, but he didn't want to dump his concerns on Elena. "Emergency trip to the European Space Agency headquarters in Paris. Should be home Friday afternoon."

"Good. Uncle Gareth, Alfredo, and Brandon will be here on Saturday at noon."

"I'd not forgotten. This trip adds another issue."

"A problem with the monitoring satellites?"

He shrugged. The problem was a sticky one, but unrelated to the operation of their handful of European satellites. "Ours are fine, but the Americans have disabled theirs."

"They've withdrawn from the tripartite agreement?"

"I'd say yes, but they'll argue they've improved things, made it cheaper."

Elena set aside the document she'd been reading. "Quit beating around the bush. What's the problem?"

"We rely on satellite monitoring data for ocean colour, temperature, and reflectivity. We use them to establish our seeding patterns and check the success of our efforts to seed the large ocean currents."

"Didn't realize that, but it makes sense."

"For several years, we've kept temperature in a tight band, within two percent of our target. Suddenly, it's six percent below target, and we've lost a major management tool."

"The average temperature has dropped?"

Dan hesitated, surprised by his unconscious use of the word we when describing his predecessor's results. "We've had a few low years, but until this year, we've kept them within our target band. The downward pressure on temperature worries me, but the immediate problem is the uncertainty introduced by a major decline."

"This happened because the Americans shut down the satellites in their sector?"

He grabbed a chair and sat with elbows on their patio table and his chin cupped in his hands. "They replaced the established protocol with a simpler one using carbon emission rates for the past year."

"Shouldn't it work if carbon dioxide produces the temperature increases?"

"It's cruder. They've abandoned our fine-tuning efforts."

"When Alfredo hears this, he'll claim it's another example of the United States abandoning international cooperation."

"One that causes our temperature management program serious grief."

Elena glanced at her watch. "Cook had a personal problem, so I gave her the afternoon off. Mrs. Baxter and Nurse Marcie will look after Carys. We're on our own. The local okay with you?"

Dan laughed, his mood brightening as thoughts of domestic bliss chased away his occupational worries. And the way Elena jumped at opportunities to give Cook an evening off. She was getting into the pleasures of simple evenings at the pub. "I'll never master the lord of the manor lifestyle. But I can handle the local for bangers and mash with a pint or two of their best bitter."

An hour later, they strolled along soggy country lanes to the Barley Mow pub on the Basingstoke Canal. Dan checked the taps and selected a dark ale, one of many specialty brews they brought in on a rotational basis. Elena, as usual, chose white wine.

Elena returned to their patio conversation after a server took their food orders. "Is your Paris trip related to getting the American satellites reactivated?"

Dan shook his head. "Not happening. Ask Alfredo about getting the US to reinstate abandoned commitments. We must replace the American ones for the western Atlantic and rethink the international collaboration. Right now, the Chinese appear more reliable than the Americans."

"You're talking about half of the North Atlantic. Aren't they managing a much greater area in the Pacific?"

"The critical areas are broad continental shelves. We're focused on the Gulf of Mexico and the east coast of North America, where American cooperation matters."

"And the Caribbean?" she asked.

"The shelves are more broken, but still important. We must replace the Atlantic coverage westward from the southern tip of Greenland if we're to manage the situation."

"What about the Pacific?"

"Different dynamic. And they aren't involved in the Indian Ocean program."

The always friendly waitress stopped to chat when she delivered their food. Elena resumed their conversation after she wandered away. "How will you manage the satellite reset?"

"We'll determine the availability of satellites and launch windows. I'll discuss getting the EU to fund them with Gareth on Saturday. Hopefully, Canada will become a partner. The new satellites will re-establish coverage of their waters. If that doesn't work, we may look to our Asian partners for the redeployment of several Indian Ocean satellites."

"And the Americans will accept this move?"

"They'll balk at redeployed Chinese satellites. Should be okay if the EU or Canada sponsors new ones."

"As you say, a topic for Saturday. I have another question, but before I get to it, one minor point."

"Okay."

"Your comments suggest China could be a better partner than America."

Dan hesitated, wondering if he'd subconsciously shifted his position. "I doubt it. Just frustration with American secrecy."

"Good. Because both are self-serving. Chinese cooperation suits their purposes. The actions of neither China nor the US show a true common front with the other nations."

"Okay, I accept. What's your other question?"

"Has their military redeployed the satellites?"

Dan glanced up from the steak and kidney pie he'd been devouring. "Interesting. Makes the science managers appear less villainous, but it begs a more important question. Why would the military withdraw the few satellites our program needs? Military cost-cutting?"

Elena choked on her fish. "Don't make me laugh. The Americans must have more important uses for the satellites."

Dan drummed a fingertip tattoo on the tabletop as he tried to sort out the implications. "Makes no sense. Space Technologies has licenced hundreds of these satellites for use by Russia, the US, and China. And all three countries have their own satellite development and launch capabilities. They don't need the few satellites our program uses."

"Then what are they doing?"

"I see much coercion, including infringement of American liberties in their battle with the Chinese. Are they sucking temperature management into that battle?"

"Could they be worried about you using the data from those satellites to see something they're trying to hide?"

Dan shook his head. "They control the satellites. No opportunity for us to change what data they collect."

"They're hiding something," Elena replied. "Seems like too much of a coincidence."

She described the resurgence of religious denominations stressing family values, hard work, and purity of spirit. She also mentioned the increasing regimentation in postsecondary education and how all the changes perverted their efforts to manage climate change.

Dan compared Elena's image of US society with the one he'd developed during his year in Georgia as he headed for the bar. He'd seen hints of the embryonic dystopia she was describing, but didn't see how they could be related to his latest development. Several minutes later, he returned with more wine and beer. "How have your renegade company members and their political partners orchestrated these changes?"

"In the 1950s, irrational fear of the Soviet Union allowed the Un-American Activities Committee to play fast and loose with American liberties. Citizens ignored the problem, lulled into complacency by their post-war prosperity. Nothing's changed. The new threat is commercial domination by China, and our solution to global warming has generated a new era of prosperity running on cheap fuel. Once again, the public's sleeping at the switch."

"But why mess with their freedoms?" Dan asked.

"They've always considered themselves underdogs who must motivate a unified populace to challenge implacable foes."

Elena's view of the motives of the American government and their industrial backers reminded Dan of his downward spike in global temperatures. Were Elena's socioeconomic considerations and his scientific ones linked?

In 2024, Tony Atherton predicted a downturn in global temperatures if ocean acidity continued to increase. His date for this change from increasing to decreasing temperatures, was fifty years in the future. Newer results produced by Achara Zhu and Marc Lavoie were pushing the date several decades closer.

Dan made real-world observations of elevated productivity during unusual episodes of low pH waters in 2028 and 2030. Were these isolated events harbingers of a frightening future that was creeping ever closer? Or did they suggest America was orchestrating another spike in their carbon emissions?

Could these changes be part of a conscious effort to push the world toward environmental Armageddon? Was it part of the American's battle with China for commercial domination?

Had they deactivated their satellites to hide their new approach? Or was it part of a scheme to control the public when problems arose? Would their satellites provide the guidance system for weaponized drones that would control American citizens?

If these possibilities were even partly true, they turned Alfredo's imagined intrusions into normal commercial transactions into child's play.

Chapter Twenty-Two

Wednesday, April 23, 2031

On a bright spring morning, Achara Zhu boarded the jet that would take her from Vancouver, British Columbia, to Bangkok, Thailand. After four years studying with Tony Atherton, she'd completed the requirements for her PhD and cleaned out her UBC office.

Achara had big plans for her job as a professor of oceanography at Chulalongkorn University. She would revitalize the oceanography department and conduct ground-breaking research on the effects of increasing acidity on planktonic organisms in the South China Sea. Her ongoing collaborations with Tony at UBC and Olivia Grange at Skidaway would anchor her work. The students she trained would take it ahead. She imagined a future where they conducted definitive work in her field in Thailand.

Her euphoria lasted for one week. The department head dropped by her office to remind her that the university would close for two days in honour of May first, their Labour Day holiday. He handed her a copy of the formal agreement that governed start-up grants for professors.

The document ruined her day. When she accepted her job, she'd been promised funds to establish her lab. The university would provide her basic infrastructure, and she would secure operating funds for her research. She didn't realize the infrastructure money didn't come from the university or the government of Thailand. It came from the People's Republic of China.

What was she to do? For more than a decade, Africans and South Asians had lived with China's approach to international diplomacy and development. China's generosity always had a steep price. Accept their approach and join their team, or face the consequences.

She wasn't naïve. She'd already approached the Lewellyn Foundation for a research grant. It would provide financial support for several students and operating funds for her lab. The grant application was submitted, and Tony Atherton, her PhD supervisor, assured her it would succeed. But her funding request assumed she would have a laboratory with basic equipment and the benches, electricity, and water she needed for biological research. Must she accept this Chinese incursion into her work?

She was proud of her independent spirit and hated appealing to Tony for help so soon after she arrived in Thailand. But she couldn't face the parties her parents organized for the four-day Labour Day weekend without getting his input.

*****

Before Tony answered Achara's call at nine thirty in the morning, he calculated the time in Bangkok—11:30 pm. "Evening, Achara. Rather late for a social call. You still struggling with the time change?"

"No privacy at my parents' house, so I waited until everyone was asleep."

Tony hesitated. For four years in Vancouver, she'd displayed overwhelming confidence. Now, after one week in Thailand, she sounded uncertain. "Problems?"

"Hope not, but I'm overwhelmed by how much everything's tied to China. Chinese research funding with requirements to share data was expected, but lab benches?"

Fifteen minutes later, Achara ended the call. She'd vowed to proceed carefully, always mindful of the Chinese eyes and ears lurking everywhere, but not to alter her plans.

He returned to the computations he'd set aside during the call. His efforts to predict when acidification would reverse the trend to ever-increasing carbon dioxide concentrations demanded international cooperation. Chinese and American efforts to stifle the flow of information and knowledge hampered progress, but he couldn't abandon efforts to work together with Achara and many others.

Something to discuss with Beth when he got home. The problem was more political than scientific, and she may have ideas about how they could best address it.

At home, Beth focused on the bigger political implications. "Achara's concern is serious, but small potatoes. The Americans offer American-style democracy as an incentive for cooperation. The autocratic Chinese system is different. They buy the allegiance of their vassal states. Different approach, same goal—global domination. Small fry like Achara get caught in the crossfire."

"The decades-old battle for commercial domination."

Beth shook her head. "More than that. China's convinced its governance model is superior to democracy and free-market capitalism. They aim to dominate the globe, establish a new world order that follows their model with them in control."

"Until Global Climate Action Day, they were succeeding. No one stood up to their relentless onslaught."

"It shouldn't have worked that way. The major free-market economies dwarfed China, but they couldn't work together. Their views of democracy and their social objectives were too divergent."

"How did GCAD change that?"

"The American's saw through the objectives of your colleague Dan Delacour's grand plan to control global temperatures. They saw an opportunity to strengthen their economy and unilaterally challenge the Chinese."

Dan nodded. Beth's explanation was simple, logical, and undoubtedly accurate. "It allows the Americans to ignore the interests of Canada and everyone else. Where do your new political insights take us?"

She shrugged her shoulders. "It's making life difficult for everyone. And, as I said at the beginning, Achara's caught in the crossfire. Right now, crossfire is the operative word. The Americans and Chinese are heading for a military showdown in the South China Sea."

*****

One week later, and thousands of kilometres to the east, church clocks struck midnight in the southern English countryside. Elena Llewellyn arrived at Hafen Ddiogel after a long and stressful day at the Foreign Office in London.

"The crisis in the South China Sea?" Dan asked as he handed her a nightcap. "Not returning first thing, are you?"

She shook her head before sitting by the fire's dying embers. "Outside advisors are on call tomorrow, but not expected back at 0800. That pleasure's saved for their wage slaves."

"Hope none have long commutes."

She laughed. "Most are prepared. They have changes of clothes and places to kip. Enough small talk. I must fill you in before we retire."

He already understood the basis for her concerns. "American, Australian, Japanese, and Indian military exercises in the Bay of Bengal have caused Chinese conniptions for weeks. Another development?"

"The Chinese can't ignore four democratic countries presenting a united front against Chinese aggression along their borders." Elena stood and walked to windows overlooking the darkness that hid their lawn, pool, and tennis court. "The exercises ended today. The Australians will sail through international waters to Perth. Two Japanese ships will also call at Perth on their way home. The Americans have announced they will sail through the South China Sea to Japan."

"An obvious provocation. The Chinese claim the South China Sea is their sea, and much of it's within their territorial waters."

"They can't allow five American warships through without making a show of force. What will it be? Will either side back down? If not, we'll face a confrontation akin to the Cuban Missile Crisis."

"Surely not!" Dan said. "The Americans aren't carrying nuclear missiles they'll install on Brunei or the Philippines."

"Perhaps not, but the Chinese always overreact to these perceived slights."

"What can anyone do?"

"That problem kept us at loggerheads for hours. Our two superpowers appear willing to flail away, and no one can intervene."

"Russia?"

Elena laughed. "They have more nuclear weapons than anyone, but no credibility as an honest broker. Neither will listen to Russia."

"EU, Britain?"

"Europe. In my grandfather's time, the Company of Gentlemen Entrepreneurs saw Europe as the saviours of civilization. It wasn't to be. Cohesion they once had no longer exists. Unless they can regain the sense of common purpose they temporarily achieved when the Russians invaded Ukraine in 2022, they'll remain impotent. And they'd have to bring Russia into their fold to provide the military muscle Europe lacks. How likely is that?" She shook her head. "I see no hope."

"So what happens?"

"Today, tomorrow? We hope they find a way to back down without either side losing face. For the next year, the next decade, I don't see our escape route."

Midnight in England brought the following day's early morning light to the eastern approaches to the Malacca Strait. Five US warships steamed in a southeasterly direction toward the Singapore Strait at standard speed. They were 450 nautical miles and less than twenty-four hours away from a confrontation with a larger contingent of Chinese warships in the South China Sea.

Chapter Twenty-Three

Friday, April 25, 2031

A few days earlier, the sun was sinking low across the river as program director Ben Oldham prepared to leave his Skidaway Institute of Oceanography office. Olivia Grange, their new scientific leader for the southeastern sector of the American government's coastal monitoring program, poked her head in without knocking.

"I'm off next week for six months in Papua New Guinea," she said, before turning away.

"Wait," he called, and she returned, closing the door behind her. "I've seen no paperwork to cover this trip and no plans for how your survey team will manage in your absence."

"Trip's critical for my research, a golden opportunity to join an elite team led by a Harvard University expert. I sent you the program description last week."

"A description, yes, but nothing about a request for you to join the mission. It's too short notice. What about the program we hired you to run?"

"Widmark can handle it. Plane ticket's purchased, gear's shipped. I'm all set."

"What about Luna?" Ben asked, thinking of Olivia's strange daughter. She must have been eleven or twelve, but she appeared to lead a vagabond existence, wandering wherever she wanted, whenever she pleased.

"She's coming with me."

"What about her schooling?"

Olivia laughed. "She'll learn more on Panaeati Island than she does in the stupid elementary school she seldom attends."

"Leave her with someone here, or her father, until the school term ends. It's only what, five or six weeks. She can spend the summer with you and return to school in September."

"Not happening. See you in October." She turned and strode away while Ben scrambled through his files, looking for shipping and travel authorizations.

He found the travel authorization buried in a communications package from the Coastal Zone Monitoring directors at the National Oceanic and Atmospheric Administration headquarters in Washington. The University of Georgia's financial office in Athens approved the plane ticket and shipping bills. Olivia secured funding for this adventure from NOAA without consulting him, and the University of Georgia gave it their approval.

Problems associated with working in a small institute with too many bosses were getting worse. Eight months earlier, the University forced the cancellation of Dan Delacour's contract. He'd been the most reliable program scientist they'd had in years, but they dispatched him for political reasons. NOAA had insisted on Olivia Grange as his replacement, and now, six months after she arrived, she was gone for another six.

That left Charlotte Widmark, a young marine biologist Dan hired to complement his expertise in physics and chemistry. After Olivia replaced Dan, the monitoring program had two biologists but no oceanographer. And Olivia's interests didn't align with their monitoring program. That left Charlotte managing it on her own. She'd done a good job. Dan insisted she was a rare find before he left, and he'd been right. For the next six months, she'd have extra responsibility.

*****

Olivia found her twelve-year-old daughter on a dock helping an old fisherman clean his catch. "Pack your bag with clothes for a tropical climate."

"The weekend?" Luna asked as she rinsed her hands in the bay.

Olivia shook her head. "Longer trip, months."

"What about school and friends?"

"Bugger school and friends. You skip half your classes, and who was your last school friend?" Olivia turned and strode to the shore.

Luna scurried after her. "Where we going and for how long?"

"Papua New Guinea."

"Where's that?"

Saturday morning, they boarded a plane to Atlanta with a connection to Los Angeles. There, they caught a flight to Sydney, Australia, with another connection to Port

Moresby, Papua New Guinea. After two days in airplanes, they had a room in a Port Moresby hotel. Olivia sat with a textbook in the lobby, waiting for the rest of Professor Tilbury's research team. Luna, the fearless explorer, disappeared into her strange new world.

On their second day, Luna skipped into the hotel at dinner time. "Saw weird houses in the bay standing on sticks. Can we live in one?"

Maggie Brown, a fellow team member sitting in the lobby drinking gin cocktails with Olivia, laughed. "Not where we're going, darling. We'll sleep in thatch-roofed huts, standing on stilts on a white sand beach. Earlier, your mum and I talked about us sharing one. What do you say?"

"On a beach? Where?" Luna replied without answering Maggie's question.

Maggie responded, unperturbed. "Panaeati Island, a tiny island off the southeastern tip of Papua. It's isolated and beautiful, with a large lagoon surrounded by a coral reef that's perfect for our research."

"How do we get there?"

"Three hundred and fifty nautical miles, so a long boat trip. I suspect we'll fly to Misima Island and take a boat from there."

The next day, when Professor Tilbury arrived, he demanded that Olivia send Luna home.

"Can't do it," Olivia responded. "No one to send her to. If I had someone, I wouldn't have forked over seven thousand dollars of my money to bring her here."

Her new friend Maggie jumped to Olivia's defence. "You have Olivia and me on the Panaeati Island team. We can share one hut, so Luna's accommodation costs you nothing. Food's never an issue. Masses go to the native population anyway, so one more mouth's insignificant. Olivia and I, along with the two guys on our team, can keep Luna's schooling on track, and she can come with me when I help at the native school." She stood and positioned herself in Dr. Tilbury's way as he paced. "Not an issue and a lot less disruptive than losing a team member at this late stage."

"But I mustn't be responsible for a ten-year-old child at one of my field stations."

Olivia jumped back into the fight. "She's twelve, not ten, and you're not responsible. I'm her mother and I'm responsible. I brought her with me because I had no choice. We'll make it work. Think of the educational opportunity we're giving her."

Dr. Tilbury folded. On Thursday, May 1, as American and Chinese warships approached a standoff 3000 nautical miles away in the South China Sea, his team flew to their field headquarters on Misima Island. Various subunits dispersed by boat to their experimental sites.

Before the units were in place, the confrontation in the South China Sea was over. The Chinese yielded, saving face by escorting the five American ships into the Philippine Sea.

Olivia, a thirty-three-year-old scientist from the US, and Maggie Brown, a twenty-seven-year-old post-doctoral fellow from Great Britain, led the team studying plankton biology in Papua New Guinea's Louisiade Archipelago. For the first four months, two American undergraduates on summer work terms joined them. They spent most of their time working in Panaeati Island's lagoon but often disappeared, sometimes for several days, to Misima Island or one of the other lagoons.

Luna never left Panaeati Island. Except for the few hours she spent bored by the daily US middle school lessons her four *de facto* guardians taught her, she went totally native. She played with the native kids, swam in the lagoon, and explored every inch of the island. But she also worked. The native children from a very young age helped with the tedious and often back-breaking labour of their subsistence economy. Luna pitched in with her new friends, working alongside them. She also helped out at the Mission school, teaching the littlest ones to speak English. They taught her the native language.

The six months flew by, and on Wednesday, October 29, Olivia and Luna arrived in Savannah. Friday morning, they found themselves in a battle in the principal's office of Luna's middle school. A school system administrator, the school principal, Luna's teacher from the previous year, and a social worker sat at a table. Olivia faced them, with Luna lingering off to the side.

"Test her," Olivia said. "You'll find she belongs in grade eight, not seven. Four academic scholars guided her through the middle school curriculum. She's already familiar with the grade eight requirements. She could pass the final exams for those courses today."

The social worker whispered to the principal, who whispered to Luna's grade six teacher. She stood and walked over to Luna. "Come, Luna, we'll go somewhere away from these arguments and talk about everything you learned in Indonesia."

"Papua New Guinea, not Indonesia," Luna said as they walked away. "The Papuans aren't friends with the Indonesians."

The social worker stood as the door closed behind her. "We aren't here to discuss how much Luna learned while she was away. These are the relevant facts. One, Luna has a terrible attendance record at her previous school." She stared at Olivia. "Two, you've made no effort to encourage her to attend school. Three, you buggered off last spring without informing the school. Four, you didn't enroll her in any school for two months at the end of the last term and two months at the beginning of this one." She sat down again. "You will either provide us with the name of a suitable relative who will undertake to raise Luna responsibly, or we will take her into care."

*****

Once again, Luna found herself flying off to live with her father. The court-appointed lawyer was pleasant, but adamant. This wasn't a short-term fix they could unwind. Until she turned eighteen on December 12, 2036, her father would be responsible for her welfare.

Her dad was a better parent than her mother, but it was so unfair. Her mother had taken her to live in paradise. Six months when her mother and three other adults really cared about her welfare. Six months with dozens of strangers who treated her with kindness and respect, and expected and received the same in exchange. Six months when the teachers at a funny little school taught her stuff and appreciated that she taught others in return.

The happiest months of Luna's life were entirely her mother's doing. And what was her reward? A judge told her she couldn't provide for her daughter for the next five years.

Her computer-scientist father was okay. He'd provide a more stable home, and if he caught her hooking off school, he'd convince her with his irrefutable logic that she must try harder. If she claimed, as she usually did, that school was boring, he'd challenge her with the most difficult but intriguing problems, ones she couldn't resist. Yeah, life with her father would be interesting, and she'd do better in school, but he'd never take her to Panaeati Island. In fact, she doubted he'd take her anywhere outside Washington, District of Columbia.

Luna spied her father, Richard Muldoon, waiting in the arrivals area of Washington National Airport. She was surprised to see him anywhere outside his apartment, but quickly regained her composure. Her keeper, a social worker from Savannah, had paperwork they must complete before she returned.

Richard led them to a nearby Starbucks, where they ignored Luna as they worked through their stack of documents. Half an hour later, they left the Starbucks, Luna's now ex-keeper to her return flight to Savannah, and Luna and Richard to his apartment in Riverdale Park. She'd begun her life in Washington

Chapter Twenty-Four

Saturday, May 1, 2032

Steve Matthews watched Nicola scamper into their Plymouth, Massachusetts, kitchen. She was yelling instructions to Anna about the mixture of breakfast cereals she wanted. It was May Day, the first anniversary of the largest, most potentially inflammatory naval confrontation in several generations.

"Don't have to remind me," Anna replied when he mentioned the day's significance. She compared it with the Soviet Union, its geopolitical ambitions, and the 1962 Cuban Missile Crisis. "Reminded me life in the United States isn't quite the idyllic existence we imagined when growing up in Poland. It appears closer to the picture the Soviets painted of their cold war enemy."

Steve waited by the kitchen counter for his coffee cup to fill. He didn't accept the Cuban Missile crisis as an apt comparison. In 1962, Soviet ballistic missiles on Cuban soil were a serious threat to the US. In 2031, China created a phony crisis when American warships transited through international waters on an internationally recognized shipping route. "They had no grounds for preventing our passage, and they had to back down. We called their bluff, and they folded."

"Chalk up one for America," Anna said, a smile brightening her gloomy countenance. "But the similarities exist."

Steve sighed. He had to tread carefully because anti-Soviet feelings were engraved on her Polish soul. He described the subtle differences, as he saw them, between the cold war and the current situation. After World War Two, Germany and France were destroyed. Britain was broke and exhausted. America alone could challenge the Soviets. Now, America stood alone in opposition to another totalitarian regime set on global hegemony. "This time," he concluded, "our erstwhile democratic allies could support us, but they lack the will to join our fight."

"Need more milk," Nicola demanded as Anna stared into their garden without saying anything.

"I got it, Mom," eleven-year-old Tomas piped up. He turned to his little sister. "Say when."

When Nicola returned to slurping her cereal, Tomas gazed at his stepfather. "Our teacher says America must stand up to her enemies, but we should also protect the environment."

"Does your teacher say we should pay more attention to environmental issues?" Steve asked Tomas. He suspected Tomas' teacher would stress the patriotic side of the question rather than the environmental one. Tomas may only be eleven, but he was already an environmentalist.

Tomas shook his head, his brow furrowed by a puzzled frown. "She says we must stand up to our enemies. I say we should worry about the environment."

"Well, I say good for you," Anna said before shifting her attention back to Steve. "Are you breaking with Dan and other climate change scientists on carbon reduction?"

"Reducing carbon emissions is a priority, but it isn't an urgent one. We must rein in Chinese belligerence first, then address climate change."

"Can't we do both?"

Steve shook his head. "Too great an adversary, and they're gaining too much influence. We must focus."

"The Soviets were throwing their weight around and had a huge sphere of influence before they fell. That's what happens to dictatorships that get too big. Same should happen to China."

"We can hope so. The Soviets were buying influence with money they didn't have and running a bankrupt economy. The Chinese have a strong economy and the support of their masses. They won't crumble so easily."

"So, America must defeat them industrially and commercially."

"That's how I see it. But I'm not severing ties with Dan. In fact, I sent him a message yesterday."

Nicola looked up from her now empty cereal bowl. Anna turned to cleaning up the mess their daughter created, and Steve took his coffee to their kitchen computer. He opened his favourite news site and began scanning the stories. After Anna released Nicola from her chair, she returned to their conversation by asking Steve why he needed to contact Dan.

"Your future as a professor at Boston U is secure," Steve replied. "My future as a part-time scientist at Woods Hole with a bigger commitment to Matthews Engineering is less certain. I must talk to Dan about research."

"You're okay with focusing on the family firm?"

Steve hesitated. He didn't want to burden Anna with his uncertainties about his future. "We're making progress against China, and Matthews Engineering is prospering. Been discussing this with the family. They agree we have a unique opportunity, but it will take more commitment."

Anna's brow furrowed. "A big expansion?"

"New vision rather than physical expansion. We must focus on our strength, innovative, high-value products. That's where we have an opportunity—engineering design and fine machine tooling for the products of the future. They will lead America to victory over China."

"We'll continue to buy the bulk of our manufactured goods, the run-of-the-mill-stuff like refrigerators, from China? Doesn't sound like the road to success."

Steve turned away from the computer screen he'd been using to avoid making eye contact. They disagreed on very few things, but one was his faith in American democracy as the gold standard for government. It was being challenged by China's autocratic governance model. He was confident America would prevail if they all pulled together. Anna's scowl showed she wasn't convinced.

"We must shift to other low-cost sources—Mexico, Indonesia, India—it doesn't matter where provided we freeze out the Chinese," he said.

"So that's the plan. Buy our consumer goods from low-wage countries but not China and focus our industry on high-end manufacturing we export to the world. Sounds like the model European countries like Germany and Sweden have been following for years."

"We have two huge advantages. We needn't support their burdensome welfare states nor the excessive regulation of the European Union. Reinvigorated American firms, including Matthews Engineering, will make it happen."

Three weeks later, Steve contacted Dan Delacour via video link. After a few questions about various family members, Steve turned to business. He began by describing his proposal for a study of surface turbulence and the efficiency of Dan's reflective nanoparticles. It was almost ready, but he had a few questions.

"Need Llewellyn Foundation funding?" Dan asked.

Steve shook his head. Dan and others in the international science community had no idea how inward-looking the US funding process had become. He needed funding from the NSF or another American agency. "Damned annoying," he concluded after describing the American situation. "But it's our reality."

"I can understand your government's resistance to Chinese incursions into your scientific research. Their history of stealing industrial secrets and undue control of projects scares everyone, but that shouldn't apply to other international funding agencies."

Steve shrugged. "Nothing I can do. Isolationism is running rampant."

"Not surprised. Globalization has problems, and no sense the world's working together on the big issues."

"Problems with your efforts to control temperature."

"That's holding. On Elena's political and economic fronts, cohesion is crumbling. We keep asking why can't Europe, America, Japan, and the other free-market-loving democracies unite in opposition to the Chinese juggernaut?"

"A problem I must consider as I focus more on Matthews Engineering."

"We've gotten off track. How can I help with your project proposal?"

Steve launched into his understanding of Dan's downward-pointing buoyant nanoparticles with a pyramidal shape and reflective square bases. "It's a good qualitative picture, but I need details that let me calculate righting moments and other physical characteristics. Also, access to samples."

Dan paused while he scribbled a note to himself. "The scientist running the US seeding program may be able to supply the quantities you need. I'll also get you a name and contact information for someone in Space Technologies in Germany."

"That's good. Should help me tie up loose ends before I submit."

"Have you considered the particles' effect on surface tension, like the way an oil slick affects the surface characteristics?"

Steve smiled. "It's in the proposal as a question I can address."

Hours later, as Steve strode from his Woods Hole lab to a nearby parking lot, a fellow student from their undergraduate days accosted him.

"Time for a quick beer with an old engineering school buddy?" he asked.

"Chris?" Steve replied, not quite sure he recognized the classmate from his days seventeen years earlier when he was an engineering student.

Christopher Perkins smiled. "A little water under the bridge, but have I changed that much? Where's the nearest pub?"

Steve headed for a popular tavern at the corner of Luscombe and Railroad, where Chris launched into a prepared spiel. "I'm working with Representative Carstairs, a member of the progressive Republican caucus in congress. They need a comprehensive background paper on the climate issue. Your name came up."

"Because I'm both a climate scientist and a businessman?"

"Someone who'd understand the Republican Party's perspective. Interested?"

Steve hesitated, reminded of his conversation hours earlier with Dan Delacour. Circumstances were pushing him toward greater involvement in the political process. Now may be the time to make a move.

"Yeah, interested. Give me the details," he said as their server arrived with two beers.

Chapter Twenty-Five

Wednesday, November 24, 2032

As Thanksgiving and a time for celebrating the year's successes approached, Steve struggled to focus on the positive.

Weeks after he submitted his assessment of the climate change crisis to the progressive Republican caucus, Representative Carstairs invited him to a meeting of New England caucus members. He'd jumped at the opportunity. *My chance to influence the political process.*

It wasn't to be. The politicians didn't look past their short-term objectives.

After the meeting, he focused on getting the longer-term environmental problems onto the politician's agenda. His efforts included consultations with Dan Delacour and Tony Atherton. Dan brought Marc Lavoie, an old colleague of Tony's now working at the University of Connecticut, and Olivia Grange from the Skidaway Institute of Oceanography, into the conversation. Together, they formed a formidable team with expertise in physical, chemical, and biological oceanography. His next step would be engaging colleagues in other areas of environmental science.

Steve saw his role as the link between the working scientists and Carstairs politicians. With Anna's help, he'd provide a valuable perspective that could make a difference. He soon realized turning his team's scientific insights into practical advice for the politicians wouldn't be easy.

He mentioned his ruminations to Anna when she arrived home on the eve of the Thanksgiving weekend. The following morning, they took Nicola for a late-season seaside outing. Anna asked him to explain his concerns as they walked along the nearly deserted beach.

"Major uptick in heavy oil consumption," Steve said as Nicola splashed in a pool isolated by the retreating tide.

"Cheap fuel to spur the economy and meet the Chinese challenge. Isn't that your mantra?"

Steve shook his head. Things were never that simple. He favoured the short-term exploitation of fossil fuels, but, as usual, the devil was in the details. "Cheap fuel's important, so that explains expanded coal consumption. Heavy oil isn't cheap, but its production has skyrocketed."

"And it has a heavy environmental cost."

"So that's my first concern."

"But not your last."

"Our political leaders are weaving this need for cheap fuel into their picture of the US as a lone warrior, the only staunch defender of democracy and free enterprise. I'm also worried about their distortion of our basic freedoms."

Anna's brow furrowed as she watched Nicola. "Sounds like a continuation of the post-WWII effort to get the world to accept the American dream?"

"Don't think so. That was a different era. A magnanimous America wanted to draw others into our fold by offering them American-style prosperity."

"Now you see a lone crusader fighting against implacable foes."

Steve nodded. "We've withdrawn from our role as leaders of the free world. It's now a solitary fight, us against the forces of evil. We cannot engage our autocratic enemy without access to unlimited cheap energy."

"But not a withdrawal from the world stage like after World War One."

Steve was a patriotic American. He relished his image of America standing tall and defending everyone's freedoms. "It's our battle, but we're fighting it on our own."

"No longer interested in cooperation with our European allies or Japan?"

"We need two things for our battle with autocratic countries like China and Russia. First, a dedicated Christian populous committed to democracy, free enterprise, and the American dream. Second, cheap energy to fuel a robust economy."

"But why wouldn't we engage our natural allies in this battle?"

"We've rejected the European-led push toward the capitalist welfare state and their willingness to coexist with our implacable enemies. Our only option is a solitary battle with the Chinese dragon."

Anna looked up, a puzzled frown on her face. "You think it's an acceptable development?"

"It's what we must do."

She shook her head. "I see America slipping into a regimented autocratic state that appeals only to undesirable dictatorships, like Brazil. We need allies if we're to defend democracy, free-enterprise capitalism, and our way of life. We won't get there by rejecting collaboration with Europe, Japan, Canada..." She let her list of natural allies tail off as she gazed at waves lapping on the shore.

Steve pointed at a lone raptor, likely an osprey, circling high above the beach. "We should work with our allies, but our basic democracy is safe. The separation of powers enshrined in our constitution won't fail us."

"But you said the Dems and Republicans have merged into one party. You have obvious concerns about their approach to climate change and many of their social policies. Countries slide into dictatorship when they venture down those roads. It's happened in sophisticated European countries, and it could happen here."

Steve leaned back, his hand resting on the sand behind him. He also worried about the concerns she was raising. "We don't know what awaits us, but our political and industrial leadership is unconcerned."

He watched the bird swing closer and decided it was definitely an osprey. "The public will rise up against unreasonable social regimentation. There's still time for progressives like Representative Carstairs to accept the advice he's getting on climate change. He can push for changes that bring America's economic policies into line with sound environmental ones."

"The problems are huge. What sort of changes can Carstairs hope to implement?"

Steve shook his head as they retrieved Nicola from the pool she'd been playing in and resumed their walk along the beach. "They aren't insurmountable, and there's no need for a single massive solution that won't get through congress. Solutions will include conservation measures, new technologies, and more carbon capture. They can be implemented incrementally. Over time, they'll do the job."

"And your group of scientists will keep the progressives focused?"

Steve nodded. "That's the role I see for myself. I'm worried, but still optimistic. We can make this work."

*****

North of the border in Vancouver, British Columbia, Beth Manville had a different perspective. "We're in deep trouble," she said to Tony Atherton as they tidied their kitchen after breakfast. "Any pretense the US and Canada are friendly allies defending the interests of capitalist democracies is toast. We've become a vassal state. We supply agricultural products and raw materials at prices they set."

Tony waved a serving spoon in Beth's direction before stuffing it in the dishwasher. "You're exaggerating, but the problem is real. Politicians say we must reduce our dependence on exports of oil and other raw materials to America, but we never make progress. What can we do?"

It was a good question, one that always came up when the political parties failed to fulfil their duty of representing the public good. "Bugger all. If you filter out the political crap, we're left with two parties whose policy statements and political actions are virtually identical. They're like Tweedledum and Tweedledee, pretending to oppose one another."

"Better than America, where they only have two parties."

"Garbage," she said as she flicked soap suds in his direction. "The Bloc's only active in Quebec, and the NDP's destined to remain a fringe party forever. That leaves the Greens, and they're too damn small."

Tony stopped loading the dishwasher, turned toward Beth, and cocked his head. "The small one now will later be large..." he sang to an old Bob Dylan tune.

"That's not how it goes," Beth replied, but she accepted Tony's contention.

He smiled. "It's what you're thinking, isn't it?"

"Possibly. If global environmental problems get worse and our economic prospects don't improve, the Green Party may be our only hope."

Tony closed the dishwasher door, turned it on, and pointed at their back door. Beth nodded, grabbed a jacket, and followed Tony into their garden.

He returned to his preoccupation with climate change science as they wandered onto the street for a short stroll around the neighbourhood before they got on with their busy days.

"Global Climate Action Day shifted the agenda. Its temperature cure killed public interest, but carbon emissions have continued at an accelerating pace. Achara's now established in Bangkok and convinced she's seeing the transition to decreasing temperatures."

"Your ocean acidification story will be back in the scientific limelight?"

"And your Green Party may be our only hope if we're to bring it into political prominence."

*****

Halfway around the world, Elena Llewellyn arrived home after another afternoon meeting at the Foreign Office ran into the evening. Politics and long meetings were playing an ever-larger role in her life. She shouldn't have been surprised. The Company of Gentlemen Entrepreneurs' plan to control global temperatures was inherently political. Her grandfather was a key architect of that scheme. Now, she carried the family's torch.

"The rifts are getting worse," she said to her husband, Dan Delacour, when she arrived home.

"Are you surprised?"

"I shouldn't be," Elena replied before describing the evolving situation. Europe, Japan, and a few other countries were taking the situation seriously. They accepted the stable temperatures as an interim measure that gave them time to reduce their carbon emissions and prepare for the post-carbon economy. Several major emitters didn't accept the temporary nature of the cure, and most of the third world took it as a God-given opportunity to expand their economies without concern for emissions.

Dan summed up the problem from his perspective. "The net result is accelerating emissions globally, and a harder job keeping temperatures within reasonable bounds."

"But you're managing."

Dan nodded as he approached the drinks tray. "So far, but it will get more difficult with time, and Tony Atherton keeps revising the date when a more acidic ocean contributes to carbon removal."

"That should help, shouldn't it? Extend the life of your temperature control program?"

"In theory, but we'll be into a new ecological paradigm, one we don't understand so can't control or accurately predict. But that didn't keep you late at the Foreign Office."

She smiled as she accepted the glass he offered her. "The focus was political, but we couldn't ignore the environmental considerations. We spent much of our time on the US-China situation. Cheap power's a core concern for both countries. The last hour focused on unrest in the equatorial countries of Africa and Asia. They're demanding we hold global temperatures constant while they close the GDP gap."

"And they'll also be exploiting cheap power that emits greenhouse gases."

"That's what we're up against. Increases in the United States, China, India, and the developing world swamp the emission reductions in Europe and Japan."

Second Interlude

Summer, 2052

By the summer of 2052, Hannah, Alice, and I had been living in the Pemberton Valley for three years. We had adequate food for our expanding population, more and better choices of crops, and improving infrastructure.

We were proud of our transition from a farming village, depending on Vancouver, to a self-reliant town. We had our power station, our lumber mill, and our blacksmith shop. We'd developed the capacity to repair and refurbish vehicles and appliances. Various other cottage industries were supplying goods and services we once brought in from outside. We lacked many skills, but we were making progress.

Stragglers wandered into Pemberton from various directions. They brought tales of wildfires and widespread desolation. They also mentioned clusters of survivors in enclaves that escaped destruction. The pictures they painted were bleak.

I tried in vain to reach those settlements via shortwave radio. I often talked to Bill Robertson on Haida Gwaii and maintained sporadic contact with radio operators in Alaska and northern Canada. But I heard nothing from anyone to the east or south. Did none of them have electricity? Or had I missed some important aspect of our new life?

The escape route we carved through mountain passes to the head of the Toba Inlet was our first physical contact with another area that escaped destruction by the wildfires. The village at the river mouth grew to several hundred when workers trapped at a logging camp joined the original homesteaders. They were establishing what could become a viable community based on trading, fishing, hunting, and logging. As they cleared more land, they would expand their capacity for farming. Our road was becoming a well-travelled trading route.

I worried about the fish they were catching. Bill Robertson detected toxic levels of radioactivity in fish caught in the Pacific Ocean off Haida Gwaii. Were Toba Inlet fish also contaminated? A grueling trip through the mountains ended my fears. Measurements I made on freshly caught fish were clean.

Encouraging news because Toba Inlet and other villages were growing phoenix-like from the ashes around the Salish Sea. Many would rely on fishing.

Our observations were puzzling. Why were fish caught in Toba Inlet and, we assumed, the rest of the Salish Sea safe, while those caught in the open Pacific were not? Radioactivity was presumably entering the ocean as atmospheric fallout. That would introduce it to surface waters where it would be subject to the vagaries of ocean currents. Could the currents in fjords and inland seas be transporting the contamination offshore before it got into the food chain? It seemed unlikely, but how else could the inshore fish avoid contamination?

Those questions weighed on my mind as we ventured to the southwest. The closest communities were Whistler and Squamish. Whistler was a skiing community high in the mountains. A few hardy souls were eking out an existence in the once-thriving resort. Squamish was an industrial town of 20,000 at the head of Howe Sound. It was abandoned when wildfires swept through the area in May 2049. Survivors were rebuilding in the ruins of the key port halfway from Pemberton to Vancouver.

We cleared the road between Pemberton and Squamish of burnt-out cars and repaired the most damaged sections. It was now passable for SUVs and other high clearance vehicles. The trip along an important thoroughfare in our expanding world took only two hours. Trivial compared to days on the trail between Pemberton and the Toba Inlet.

The mountains between Squamish and Vancouver were steep. Repairs to the seriously damaged road south were beyond our limited capacity. Without a road, contact with survivors around the Salish Sea would rely on slow-moving sailboats.

The combined road and water link was a godsend. It allowed trade with a growing number of coastal communities. We added them to our trading network with nearly ten thousand residents of Haida Gwaii.

We were now linked with several hundred thousand people from the Salish Sea to the Gulf of Alaska. Limited success, considering the population of BC before the cataclysm was over five million, but good compared to our success with the rest of BC or anywhere in eastern North America.

That summer, Zeke joined explorers venturing into the BC interior, a region that had suffered for years from extreme drought. They emerged from the Coast Mountains at Lillooet and turned north towards Prince George. At 100 Mile House, they diverted east and then south past Kamloops, Vernon, Kelowna, and Penticton before returning to Lillooet. They saw nothing but devastation during their month-long trek.

Other forays broadened the search area. Team One found few settlers before they reached the farming areas around Prince George in the north. They brought back reports of growing trade routes and contact with survivors in the Yukon and Alaska. Team Two found survivors in the large river valleys to the east of Prince George.

Near the Alberta border, they made a surprising discovery. The grasslands on the eastern foothills had regenerated. Populations weren't as large as pre-2049, but many communities had rebuilt. They claimed a population of two million on the Canadian prairies.

In southern Alberta, our explorers encountered armed militias pledging allegiance to the New American Republic. Apparently, the new political entity controlled the cultivated areas of Alberta, Saskatchewan, Manitoba, and the Great Plains states to as far south as Nebraska. They didn't claim ownership of the boreal forests that swept across the continent north of the prairie grasslands. They weren't interested in communication or trade with BC or, it would appear, the northwestern US states.

That fall, I reflected on the period before the cataclysm. I remembered our exuberance in 2022 when Jacinta Lopez Martinez, Rosie Parker, and I made a big discovery, and our frustration after 2027 as everyone sleepwalked into the future. Dan Delacour and the other nanoparticle program managers manipulated the world's weather. They created an extended period of stable temperatures and placid weather. It was an unstable solution because carbon dioxide emissions continued to increase.

The focus in the second half of the 2030s should have shifted into the second part of their grand plan to control climate change. The anticipated move from fossil fuels to other forms of energy didn't happen, but we encountered no catastrophic impacts. We were in the calm before the storm as the US and China increased the intensity of their Battle of Titans. The bottom line; we missed our golden opportunity and made almost no progress in our fight to reduce carbon emissions. I found this failure depressing, but Beth wouldn't let me abandon hope.

We now move to the next segment of our narrative. Our focus shifts to the United States. Steve and Anna Matthews provide the glue that holds this part of our story together. As time marched into the 2040, their son Tomas, and his girlfriend, Luna Grange, assume greater roles.

We rejoin the story after the four-year-long doldrums between 2032 and 2036. Tomas is preparing to attend the University of Massachusetts in Lowell. He will study marine biology and be drawn into the critical role biology plays in the climate change saga. Luna will study economics and political science and join crusaders looking at socioeconomic aspects of the climate change fight.

Tomas and Luna prepared this text during their long 2049 transit on Merlyn's Childe from the Shetland Islands through the Northwest Passage to British Columbia. They were aided and abetted by their boatmates. It also has sections I added more recently in consultation with Dan Delacour as our narrative became a team effort.

Part Two

Houses of Cards

Chapter Twenty-Six

Saturday, July 19, 2036

On a sunny summer afternoon, The Matthews family visited the Cape Cod National Seashore. They made the trek from their suburban home on the southern fringe of Plymouth, Massachusetts, to celebrate Tomas's sixteenth birthday, but he wasn't in a celebratory mood.

While his mother, Anna, fussed with their picnic lunch and his much younger sister, Nicola, constructed villages in the sand, Tomas launched into his concerns about the lack of progress on climate change. He was a studious young man with a passion for biology. Like many teenagers who became obsessed with issues, he focused on one side of the argument. He couldn't understand why they were making so little progress.

"We aren't getting anywhere," he said as he accepted the sandwich his mother offered him. "By 2000, everyone agreed we must stop the endless increases in carbon emissions. Agreements were signed, promises made, but emissions increased. And the rate of increase gets faster and faster."

He paused, taking a swig from his coke. He expected a response from his father, a scientist who'd been active in climate change research in the 2020s. When Steve Matthews said nothing, Tomas continued his rant.

He described events starting in 2010 when a bunch of fat cat industrialists and bankers, mostly Europeans, but some Japanese and others, got together. "They established a cabal, or is it a cartel, I don't know the right word, to control coal, oil, and gas production. This group, they called themselves the Company of Gentlemen Entrepreneurs, had a Victorian sense of duty. They'd exploit the resources that fueled our carbon-based economy, but use some profits to save the world. They'd orchestrate a transition to less polluting fuels they'd also control."

Tomas paused for breath and stared at the sandwich his mother handed to him. He devoured most of it in three gigantic bites. "It started well. Their global-scale engineering solution halted global warming. They convinced enough powerful countries to implement their cure—"

"How did you learn this?" Steve demanded.

Tomas gasped, surprised by the sharp tone of his stepfather's voice. "Climate change club at school. We search everywhere for info and discuss what it means at meetings."

"Climate change club," Anna added. "I don't remember that being a school club."

"It's not official. The principal refused to recognize us, even though a teacher supported us. But we continued doing our research and meeting at... one member's house." Tomas looked down, happy he'd caught himself before mentioning the guy's name. They'd caused such a fuss when they tried to form an official group that the six who continued promised they'd never reveal each other's names.

Steve sighed. "Better continue."

"They blanketed the ocean with reflective nanoparticles, but countries haven't reduced carbon emissions. We've been one of the worst offenders. Our emissions are way up since we agreed to reduce them as part of the Paris Climate Accord." Tomas held up his hand, hoping his father would let him finish before butting in. "At first, we made progress, then we pulled out of the agreement. Later we returned but never made enough effort."

Tomas stopped talking rather abruptly. He leaned over and grabbed another sandwich from the plate his mother prepared.

"My turn," Steve said, looking at Anna, not Tomas. "Your description of the Company of Gentlemen Entrepreneurs is accurate. Some American members remained committed to their cause, but our government, and most of its industrial backers, recognized a bigger issue—"

"China?" Tomas interjected.

Steve described the situation in the 2020s when China challenged the US commercially and pushed their military might wherever they could. "They ignored international agreements, broke all the rules, cheated at every turn, and behaved like the autocratic rogue state everyone now agrees they are. We never disputed the wisdom of Sir Gareth Llewellyn, the driving force behind the company. He may be a throwback to Victorian England and Kipling's 'white man's burden', but he'd analyzed the situation correctly. The problem was China. Europe and America could not solve this on their own. China had to accept their role in the fight before we brought the developing countries in Asia, Africa, and Latin America onboard."

"But we're facing a crisis—forest fires, floods, crazy weather, all those things. We can't delay reducing emissions."

Steve shook his head. "The scientists managing the nanoparticle program stabilized temperature. We have twenty years before other climate-related problems surface. Twenty years to convince China and India, the two largest emitters, to play their roles. Then we develop accommodations for the developing nations."

"Why not start here, start reducing emissions like they have in Europe?" Tomas asked. His father was defending the official American position, but he must understand the environmental stresses.

"Because America's not Europe. We've never trusted the European model of capitalism dominated by socialist or pseudo-liberal governments. The German government can say 'trust us, lower your carbon emissions, and we'll find common ground with China'. Their public buys it."

"Why can't we do the same?"

"That sort of manipulation of capitalist principles for the common good won't sell here. We must strengthen our economy by giving our corporations cheap power and the freedom to grow until we beat China into submission. Then we can deal with carbon emissions, a problem with well-established solutions."

Anna spoke up for the first time when Tomas turned toward her, his expression pleading. "Efforts the government's making to encourage the public to buy into this process remind me of stories my parents told me about the Soviet Union. Their efforts to control the population came to an abrupt end when the people finally threw off their shackles. The same thing could happen here."

*****

A month later, on the other side of the Atlantic, Elena Llewellyn welcomed her guests to Hafen Ddiogel. The list for the extended weekend visit included Tony and Beth Atherton with their children, Michael, thirteen, and Hannah, eleven. Penelope Fitzwilliam arrived with her nineteen-year-old daughter, Claire. Alfredo and Christina Rodriguez brought their children, Carlos, eighteen, and Isobel, fourteen. Achara Zhu rounded out the guest list. Elena's aging uncle, Gareth Llewellyn, husband, Dan Delacour, their children, Carys, seven, and Paul, four, were also present. The party from three continents strained the resources of the Llewellyn family home, but her stately house handled it.

Dan, Tony, and Achara were scientists. Beth was an environmental activist turned politician, and Elena, Alfredo, and Gareth were trained in political science and economics. Christina was a stay-at-home mother, and Penelope, an heiress with a bent for political agitation that often involved her daughter. She was also Elena's lifelong friend.

All participants shared an overriding passion. They knew climate change deserved serious attention. Their views on the best solutions varied.

Hafen Ddiogel's library, billiards room, nursery, and several acres of grounds with a swimming pool, tennis court, and maze entertained children and adults. Elena planned focused discussions of the issue that brought them together in the early evenings when the adults gathered for drinks before dinner. They would extend into the after-dinner period.

Friday evening, Claire, Carlos, and the older generation gathered in the larger drawing room for the first climate change discussion. Claire and Carlos drifted into a private conversation before Elena asked Achara for her southeast Asian views on the epic battle between America and China.

"Difficult for me," Achara replied. "I sound American, and my Chinese name makes Thais suspicious. My mother is Thai, and my father arrived in Bangkok when he was a small child, but we're labelled as Chinese. Makes me a poor choice to answer your question, but I'd say people throughout southeast Asia are quaking in fear. They don't trust the Americans to come to their aid if the situation deteriorates, and no one thinks the Chinese will be fair."

"Anything Britain or Europe can do?"

Achara shook her head. "We see a battle between Chinese tigers and jaded American lions for control of peace-loving herbivores living in the region. Europe's accommodation of Chinese aggression seems ineffectual."

Elena turned to Beth. "What's the Canadian perspective?"

"We no longer consider China a trustworthy state. China and the US have the world's largest economies. We can hardly ignore them, but we must scrutinize every agreement. In recent years, US actions have become more erratic. We don't fear serious repercussions from our dealings with either, but we must tread carefully."

"And what do you think?" Elena asked, turning toward Tony. "Messages I'm hearing from my contacts in the US suggest they will delay attention to climate change until they resolve the Chinese situation. How does that affect environmental management?"

Tony sighed. "Should ask Dan, not me. Oscillations suggest a poorly damped system. If Dan's nanoparticles can keep temperatures stable, they may have twenty years to deal with China. If we lose control of temperature, all bets are off."

Mrs. Baxter appeared and announced dinner. Elena turned to her guests. "We've asked some important questions and set the stage for discussions tonight and tomorrow. Right now, it's time to eat."

She took Tony's arm, and they led the way into dinner.

Chapter Twenty-Seven

Tuesday, May 12, 2037

She emerged from the shadows and matched Steve Matthews' pace as he strode along Summer Street in the Boston suburb of Somerville. The CEO of Matthews Engineering was *en route* to his wife Anna's Boston University office on the south side of the Charles River. He wasn't expecting another surprise visit from the enigmatic stranger who first appeared several years earlier.

Penny was an odd woman, perhaps five years younger than Steve's forty summers. She approached him after he submitted a letter bemoaning the lack of serious attention to climate change to the Boston Globe. That approach, like this one, and several others, was clandestine. She'd asked for his opinion on science issues, but never pushed him for anything else. It made all the cloak and dagger stuff hard to understand.

Unbeknownst to Steve, the British expatriate was a backroom influencer on the US political stage. She sympathized with Steve's concerns about climate change and America's assault on personal freedoms. Penny, however, favoured a right-leaning libertarian approach to solving these problems.

The previous summer, she'd taken part in her friend Elena Llewellyn's weekend retreat at Hafen Ddiogel. She sat on the sidelines, listening to the eclectic group of advocates for progressive action on climate change. Their discourse helped clarify her perspective. She spent the next six months in the old country assessing her future.

She'd now returned to Boston, intent on implementing her plan. Personal freedom and unfettered free enterprise were the only way forward. Until she and her libertarian colleagues were ready to move, she'd keep her plans to herself. Penny had a role for Steve Matthews, so she had to keep him engaged.

She grabbed his arm and pointed at a coffee shop, but said nothing until they were seated in a dimly lit corner. She leaned forward and whispered in her posh English accent. "The government hassles everyone who objects to their social policies and infringement of basic rights. A few strident advocates have disappeared."

"Disappeared," Steve repeated. Her statement reminded him of Anna's stories about the overpowering presence of the police in Soviet-era Poland. "That can't happen in modern-day America."

"Don't bet on it. They're using drastic measures to suppress opposition to their new American democracy."

"What about advocacy for climate change action? That's where I've been vocal and contributed to your Phoenix Group."

She shook her head. "Focus is on social policy and political activity. No sign they're cracking down on scientists."

"Not surprised. Neither the government nor the public see our importance. Why this meeting?"

"A warning. They're tightening the screws. We must expect a more heavy-handed approach to the social engineering experiment they're forcing on the American public. Opponents must tread carefully because they cannot rely on their vaunted freedoms." She gulped the rest of her coffee. "I'm off. Give me five before you leave. Don't deviate from your route to BU and then home. You won't hear from me until we understand our enemy."

Steve watched as Penny strode from the coffee shop. He knew nothing about her, not even her surname. Her accent and mannerisms reminded him of Elena Llewellyn, a young woman he met nine years earlier when he was a student at Dalhousie University. He detected similarities between the cloak and dagger game Elena played in Halifax, and the one Penny played in Boston. *Was Elena, not letters he'd submitted to the Boston Globe, responsible for Penny contacting him?*

Five minutes later, Steve left the coffee shop. He marched down Webster and Columbia streets and skirted the MIT Campus. He crossed the Boston University Bridge to Anna's math building office. On the train to Plymouth, Steve described his encounter with Penny.

*****

Anna listened to Steve's description, feeling more foreign than she had for several years. Her experiences growing up in Eastern Europe after the Soviet Union collapsed highlighted the fragility of political and economic structures. And her personal story showed that family and social structures, including the mighty

Catholic Church, were equally vulnerable. Everyone looked toward America, the land of opportunity. It was also the land of freedom and constitutional protection of their rights.

After seven years living in the United States, she had serious doubts. She no longer trusted the American constitution to protect her rights and freedoms.

Steve shook his head after she expressed her concerns. "Our separation of powers and independent courts has served us well for two hundred and sixty years."

"And the British point to their very different system. It's functioned without serious problems for longer than the US system. They're both vulnerable."

"Describe the vulnerability of our system."

Anna held up her hand, index finger extended from her fist as her precise mathematical mind catalogued her talking points. "Environmental uncertainty and instability that arises from increasing carbon dioxide emissions."

"We've been fighting that for decades. It won't topple governments."

Her second finger joined the first, making an old-fashioned peace sign. "Corruption and the obscene wealth accrued by industrialists colluding with the government."

"I agree. Three consecutive administrations have encouraged the concentration of wealth. Large firms have exploited the opportunities provided by stabilized global temperatures. What else?"

Her third finger joined the first two as she squeezed them together in a Girl Guides salute, with her thumb constraining her pinkie. "Excessive religious zeal that's perpetuating their false prosperity."

"Hard sell because we've always had a religious bent that matches the current drive to prosperity and commercial dominance. Next?"

She released her pinkie, letting her fingers spread out. "Subjugation of young people."

"Another one I accept. They're being forced into an unwelcome box that's stifling them. It's something I dread because Tomas will soon be caught up in it, but what can we do?" He paused while a Boston-bound train rushed by on the adjacent track. "Everyone's convinced we can't win without a cohesive, coordinated, and committed population."

She considered the reaction of the vast majority of Americans to her factors. "Those are the main vulnerabilities. Next, we must consider how America's already gone astray."

Steve offered her a rueful smile. "Let's hear what you've decided."

"I've decided nothing, just a few observations."

"Okay, give me your observations."

She began a decade earlier with events surrounding Global Climate Action Day and their interaction with Dan Delacour. While students at Dalhousie University in

Halifax, they made two critical observations. First, an industrial cartel with widespread government support implemented a technological fix for global temperature increases. Second, carbon dioxide emissions continued unabated.

"They're important," she concluded before pausing for a breath. "But we must focus on the past nine years."

Steve expressed his impatience. "Just tell me where you're headed."

"We've had Republican and Democratic presidents and several changes in leadership in the house and senate. Government focus hasn't altered one iota. And a select group of industrialists has accumulated obscene wealth."

"Okay. These reflect your first two vulnerabilities."

She paused as another train rushed by. "My other observations reflect the social manipulation that's accompanied the prosperity we've seen for the last seven years. And the new Christianity we seem so keen to embrace. It's generating a false euphoria that can't last."

Steve scowled. "And your last vulnerability, the forced regimentation of youth?"

"Don't understand it. Government elites are building this house of cards based on unsustainable economic prosperity, a new Christian ethic, and brainwashing young people. It can't last."

"Retrenchment is inevitable, but our system will handle it."

"Hope you're right," Anna replied. She understood his faith in American democracy, but remained unconvinced. "The parallels to the fall of the Soviet Union are frightening. And there's an international aspect we haven't considered."

"What's that?"

"America's abandonment of various international institutions while hollowing out several others."

"Yeah. World Bank, World Health Organization, the General Agreement on Tariffs and Trade."

Anna smiled a rueful smile. She could add several others to his list. "I'm worried about the International Atomic Energy Agency. It's much less effective than it once was, and most observers suggest the nuclear threat is growing."

"And the United Nations' ability to maintain world peace is shaky at best."

Anna was immediately drawn back to eastern Europe when Steven mentioned the UN's peace-keeping role. It was only fifteen years since Russia's invasion of Ukraine caused worldwide disruptions. "Especially when one combatant is a veto wielding member of the Security Council."

"We must remain vigilant and avoid losing what's good about America when we cast off your shackles and tackle these global problems."

"And that, my love, is what your vigilante friend Penny wants. We must be ready to contribute."

Chapter Twenty-Eight

Thursday, September 3, 2037

Four months later, Steve and Anna wandered into their suburban Plymouth backyard after a pleasant afternoon at the seashore. The tranquil, almost bucolic scene clashed with their negative feelings as their son, Tomas, prepared for his first year at university.

Anna slumped into a patio chair and stared into the thicket of trees beyond their yard. "Living at home while studying in Boston would yield better academic results. Why force university residence life on him?"

Steve placed the piece of driftwood he'd lugged home against a wall and joined her by their patio table. He worried as much as she did about how her often introspective son would fare living in a university dormitory, but he failed to see what they'd accomplish by revisiting the subject. "Tomas won't be the life of a party, but socialization and networking are important for the newly minted ideal American. He must work on them."

She straightened her back and leaned forward with her hands on her knees. "Are you defending the regimented existences our leaders are pushing down our throats?"

Steve shook his head. He was a patriot who gave the country's leaders the benefit of the doubt, but he had serious misgivings about several of the recent trends. "In my morbid moments, I imagine a diabolical plot to generate a homogeneous population of drones."

Anna stood, placing her hands on her hips as she listed the restrictions imposed on university students. Attendance at a university outside their immediate metropolitan area. Accommodation in a university residence for all four years with endless rules. Identification with one of twenty-three accepted churches and mandatory attendance at weekly services.

"Do you wish this for our son?" she asked.

"No options for an academically oriented youngster. He'll figure it out and make the most of his opportunity. You'll accomplish nothing by hammering away at our government's misguided integration of university education into its fight for commercial domination."

Anna checked her watch and gazed into the kitchen. "The kids will be home soon. I'll make tea. Or would you prefer beer?"

Steve snorted. "Iced tea, the drink of the complacent masses, but go easy on the sugar."

Twenty minutes later, when Nicola bounced from the house with Anna and the tea tray close behind, Steve was pulling weeds from the flower beds surrounding the patio. Nicola threw her backpack on a chair and plopped down beside him.

"Get what you wanted?" Steve asked.

"New sketch pad, three 6B drawing pencils, and a tube of Hooker's green."

"Hooker's green?"

Nicola favoured him with a don't you know anything stare. "It's the perfect colour. The stupid art teacher thinks any old green is okay for leaves, but my tree craves Hooker's green leaves."

Steve smiled. His eight-year-old daughter was so sure of herself and adamant about anything art-related. She must drive her teachers crazy. "Tomas brought you home?"

"He bought masses of school supplies. He'll be down soon. It's so hot we got super thirsty." She made a face as she gulped the tea Anna offered her. "More sugar."

Tomas arrived and dumped several spoonfuls in his tea without tasting it. "Waste of time. Almost everything was standard school supplies. Could have bought them next week in Lowell instead of wasting a day taking the train to Boston."

Nicola looked up from a scrap of paper she was drawing on. "But I wanted to visit my wicked art supply store."

"Come on. You can buy sketch pads and pencils in Plymouth."

"Not Hooker's green. I looked."

"Buy it online."

Nicola scrunched her nose. "I'd rather go to my Boston store."

Hours later, Tomas was hanging with his friends, and Nicola was in her room drawing or reading. Anna caught Steve having a wee nip from the single malt scotch bottle Dan Delacour brought him on his most recent US trip.

She stood in his study doorway, leaning against the frame, a scowl creasing her brow. "It's much broader than the problems plaguing university students, isn't it? It's afflicting everyone."

He raised his glass, bringing attention to one of those impacts. "Look at me, sneaking a drink in the privacy of my home. It's not illegal. We haven't returned to last century's prohibition, but it's become frowned upon to drink anything but dealcoholized wine and beer."

"The government encourages that trend, but it's led by the evangelical and fundamentalist churches."

"All churches," he replied. God didn't play a big role in his life, and their church no longer provided the social structure he once appreciated. "Since evangelical fervor infected ours, I no longer feel like I belong. It provides a stable environment for Tomas and Nicola, but my interest is minimal."

Anna entered his enclave, lifted a pile of paper from his easy chair, and settled in with her feet resting on the ottoman. "When my young life imploded in Poland, I abandoned my church because it threw me aside but welcomed the people who ruined my life. Since we arrived in Plymouth and joined your church, I'm stronger, more anchored in my world. Now, that anchor's slipping away."

"Episcopal Church traditions are being pummelled, but we must stick with it. This mess won't last forever."

"You tried again to make your case with Tomas, didn't you?"

Steve smiled. "He listened as always. I'm sure he understands, and he's strong enough to resist the irrational appeal of the crap the system's forcing upon us."

"And Nicola?"

He paused, staring into the evening twilight. They had nine years to ensure she had the strength to find the life she wanted. But the problem was far broader than the fate of one young woman. It affected the whole country. "If we don't reverse course, we'll face an unprecedented environmental catastrophe. We must regain the freedoms we once valued so highly and join humanity's fight to control carbon emissions." He held up his scotch bottle and pushed in the cork. "If not, little pleasures like Dan's bottle of single malt will have no value. We'll be fighting for our existence."

*****

On the eastern side of the Atlantic, Elena Llewellyn watched her daughter Carys and Carys' friend Toby cavort in the pool. She glanced away as Dan Delacour strode from their majestic country house. The eight-year-olds were sensible kids and strong swimmers. They didn't need constant surveillance.

Dan set his lowball glass on the table by her lounger and pulled up a lawn chair. "Toby's mum not here today?"

Elena checked her phone. "Doctor's appointment. She'll pick him up, Mrs. B will take charge of Carys, and we can relax."

"Tough day?"

She shook her head, but her sagging shoulders told a different story. "Brandon has the bank ticking along, and the struggle to bring stability to our chaotic world hasn't changed."

"What's today's problem?"

"We're making so little progress. Five years ago, you discovered the Americans had abandoned the agreed-upon protocol for controlling global temperatures."

Dan shrugged, wondering why she'd focused on the scientific side of their ongoing disputes with the United States. "A problem, but we solved it, and temperature's back in control."

She turned toward him, poking at his chest with her forefinger. "Don't diminish its impact. Recovery took two years and cost us millions. We had to bring Canada on as a partner. It was not trivial, but the American's reason for refusing to honour their commitments was." She inclined her head toward the kids in the pool. "They're more mature than the US government."

"I fault them for failing to consult their partners before taking action that affected everyone. Everything else is uncertain."

Elena scowled. "They're constantly going their way without considering their allies' interests," she said before walking to the water's edge to check on the kids.

Dan sipped his whiskey. He launched into the contentious topic when she returned. "You're too focused on the big split in the company. You must consider the constraints your US contingent faced."

Elena reached under her chair and slid out an ice bucket with a bottle of white wine. She filled her glass and stared at it for several minutes. "America's been an unpredictable partner with suspect motives for decades."

Toby's mother arrived before Dan responded. While Elena and Glennis struggled to corral two kids with no interest in changing from their swimsuits to their regular clothes, Dan refreshed his drink. He settled back to enjoy the late-afternoon sunshine. Fifteen minutes later, Elena returned to the poolside table. "Where were we?"

"The split and what caused it?" Dan replied.

"Seems like going over old ground."

"Not to me. You, Gareth, and Alfredo Rodriguez skirt around the details, and the details are always important."

"Something's bothering you?"

He nodded. The motive of the original company members, mostly Europeans, was controlling global temperatures. They wanted environmental stability, fewer floods, fewer droughts, fewer wildfires, less erratic environmental conditions of any kind. That would lead to more economic stability and better profitability for their companies. "Your company members' profit margins are up, so they've achieved their objectives. Capital gains from the coal and oil companies they snapped up are funding their temperature control program."

"We know this. Where are you taking us?"

"Your American partners had different objectives from the beginning. They identified an opportunity to make fortunes expanding the use of coal and heavy oil with no commitment to reducing carbon emissions."

Elena sat for several seconds with her head cocked to one side. "If that's true, they hid their real motive from Uncle Gareth and his colleagues. But it would appear, in retrospect, that your contention's correct."

"That raises another question. The American attitude has thrown the original European program badly off track, and we've struggled to stabilize it. We need to go back and work through things from the beginning, but none of the current team knows the background."

She sighed. "Remember that day, years ago, when Uncle Gareth gave you the deed to this house?"

"Summer of 2028, almost exactly nine years ago."

"He also gave me a history of company activities. It's in my desk. Gareth said it was a family matter you needn't read. Major misjudgement. My desk, top right drawer."

Dan tossed back his drink, jumped from his chair, rushed to the house, and returned with the dossier. He scanned the pages describing agreements the original company members had with European governments. The plan was laid out in great detail. Step one was stabilized temperature. Step two was reduced carbon emissions. Inclusion of the United States and other countries introduced conflicting agendas that jeopardized the original plan. It had been quietly spiralling out of control ever since.

Dan took Elena's hands in his. "I wish you'd shown me years ago."

"Why?"

He summarized the company's twenty-year-old programs to control temperature with nanoparticles. Key components were teams focused on nanoparticle research and development of innovative ways to lower emissions. "Why aren't the nanoparticle researchers part of our temperature management teams, and what happened to the work on emission reduction strategies?"

"Do you need them?"

Dan stood and began pacing. "This dossier makes some of the science clearer. It will help with ongoing management. Not easy without the Americans onside, but we can do it. Emission reduction is a different issue."

"Why?"

"Why? For God's sake, can't you see? If those scientists make a breakthrough, we have a completely new take on the climate change problem. It would be a total game-changer."

"But that would be good news."

Dan shook his head. Secrecy had always been the Achilles' heel for the Company of Gentlemen Entrepreneurs. Had it hammered them again? "Not bloody likely. It would mean someone is playing off the group managing the temperature control program against another secret team planning a carbon emissions breakthrough." He paused. Something similar might apply to a breakthrough in nanoparticle technology. "Does your Uncle Gareth know about this? Is he playing me for a bloody dupe, someone who's keeping their house of cards from falling apart until they're ready to spring their ultimate cure on the world?"

"And if those teams were abandoned for some reason?"

"We'd have another monumental failure." He paused again, thinking about technologies for trapping carbon. They worked, but they were inefficient and expensive. Abandoning research into better technologies made no sense. "I'd want to know who made that decision, and why."

Chapter Twenty-Nine

Thursday, September 23, 2038

The summons from UMass Lowell's Campus Cooperation Council at the beginning of Tomas Matthews second year meant trouble. Its name sounded innocuous, and its mantra, Empowerment through Collaborative Investigation, emblazoned across the building's facade, uplifting. Its real purpose was more sinister.

He approached the receptionist's desk in the psychological assessment office. He presented his summons to the stern-looking, middle-aged woman sitting behind the desk.

She scowled at his form. "You're ten minutes early."

"Expected preliminary paperwork."

She pointed to utilitarian metal chairs by the entrance door. "Sit over there. I'll call you when we're ready."

At three forty-five, she looked up. "Dr. Sarah Cruickshank, third door on the left."

Tomas strode down the hall and knocked on the doctor's door. *The damned secretary was just being a pain in the ass, insisting on sticking to the timetable for no useful purpose.*

"Enter."

He stepped into the room, expecting another frosty reception. A younger, friendlier-looking brunette nodded toward two armchairs separated by a small table.

"Give me a moment to complete my notes."

Tomas pointed toward the door.

She shook her head. "Sit down, make yourself comfortable. I won't be long."

Dr. Cruickshank ended with a flourish of keystrokes, snapped her laptop shut, and brought it over to the empty armchair.

"I suspect you understand why we called you in."

Tomas struggled to maintain a neutral expression. He had lots of experience convincing high school guidance counsellors that everything was okay. Fooling Dr. Cruickshank may not be so easy. "Not making the progress you want on the friendships front."

The educational system mantra stressed collaboration and cooperation, but the positive-sounding buzzwords hid another message. A certified network of nurturing friends was a prerequisite for admission to anything but the most menial levels of the workforce.

She tapped her computer screen. "I have your high school transcript. Stellar record, but no lasting friendships."

Tomas had seen the document. An extensive narrative accompanied the standard listing of courses and grades. "I focused on the school's priorities of sports, artistic activities, and solid academic achievements. I wasn't good at athletics or art, but I persisted with reasonable success. My academic record is better, including evidence of collaboration with others."

"And during your freshman year at Mass State Lowell?"

"Similar story, but no athletics. I've continued my interest in computer-generated art as a complement to my academic studies."

"We noted your collaborations, but see no effort to develop the friendships critical for success."

Tomas sighed. "I've focused on goal number one, graduating at the top of my class. I'll develop the mandatory support network."

"You must work on it, show progress."

"Last week, I began a team project. One of my partners is nice. Something may develop."

Dr. Cruikshank shook her head. "Developing friendships doesn't differ from achieving good grades. They don't just happen."

Tomas looked down without commenting. He figured the best approach was to appear cooperative and then ignore her message while getting on with his life.

She droned on. "You *must* try, or we'll assign you to psychological assessment and reorientation. Trust me. You don't want that."

Tomas kicked an empty soda can along the pathway to his university residence. After unsuccessful attempts to fit in with the crowd and establish romantic relationships during his first high school years, he abandoned thoughts of friendship and focused on his other activities. He wasn't antisocial or painfully shy. Adolescent social networking just wasn't his priority.

Two successful high school and one university year followed. His approach worked, but circumstances now dictated a strategic reassessment. He remained certain friendships would evolve when the time was right, but he needed a visible effort to show he was trying.

Fellow second-year student Luna Grange appeared as he entered the lobby. She was four or five inches shorter than him, and he was no towering brute. Despite her timid demeanour, she was cute, a dusky little pixie who needed to smile more often. "Is it my fault? Did I say something?"

Tomas started, shaken from his musings. "Sorry. Don't follow."

"I saw you entering the psychological assessment office. At their reorientation camp last month, they badgered me about my relationships with others, but I couldn't have said anything bad about you. I hardly knew you existed until this term's project together, and it started after the stupid boot camp."

Tomas stared. She must have noticed him during their first year, but he bit his tongue. Was it serendipity or the devil testing him? Less than half an hour after he'd described project partner Luna as a potential friend, here she was begging for attention. He gazed around the almost empty lobby, spied a suitable sofa in a quiet corner, and took her hand.

She followed and sat with a space between them, but didn't release his hand. "During the psychological assessments everyone endured as frosh, they identified me as a misfit who must attend a social orientation program. Infuriating intrusion; fluffy stuff and feel-good exercises."

"What sort of stuff?"

"You know, that pop psychology crap about the wonders of friendship. The web's flooded with it."

"Seen it. Meaningless garbage, no substance to it."

She slid closer. "Last spring, they deemed me unreformed and insisted I arrive two weeks early for reorientation before this term began. That boot camp was horrible. During the first days, they beat us into submission."

"Beat you?" he asked. This conversation was definitely taking a surprising turn.

"Figuratively, not literally. They exposed all our hang-ups and fears until we were naked snivelling wrecks crawling on the floor."

"Not literally?"

"Yeah, literally."

"Naked?"

"Some. Ones with phobias about being caught naked in school or other public spaces were naked. They reduced the rest of us to similarly exposed states, ones that reflected our phobias."

Tomas stared, imagining her naked. He shook his head, trying to dislodge the inappropriate thought. She looked up with tears trickling down her cheeks, so he offered her a tissue while willing her to continue.

"Being caught naked's not my phobia. My problem is an inability to get close to people. I must keep everyone at arm's length, or I get really hyper."

"You talking about guys? Do we frighten you?"

"Anyone, but especially guys. During those first sessions, they had the guys get close, all touchy-feely, and I freaked out."

"You're close to me right now."

She snuggled closer. "And it's okay. You don't trigger my fear. We've been hunched over a computer screen when we work on our project. I only have the slightest shiver, more from surprise than fear."

Tomas smiled. Shivers could have been a realization she was attracted. "Should we get together and chalk up two of those friendships we're supposed to develop?"

"Could we? It doesn't have to be intimate, a platonic relationship where we explore this friendship business."

Tomas couldn't read her expression. He was hopeless at deciphering expressions, and her tear-stained face defeated his meagre efforts. Was she expecting more than a platonic relationship? Did he want more? He'd avoided romantic liaisons for the past three years. Was it time to change?

"Clean up the tears. We can meet for dinner in, what, half an hour, and talk. Okay?"

Her face brightened. "Yeah, perfect."

*****

Luna danced up two flights and grabbed her shower kit. She'd go all out—shower, change into her favourite outfit, nothing too fancy for an informal occasion but nicer than her usual attire.

Forty minutes later, she encountered Tomas pacing the hallway outside the cafeteria.

He smiled when she appeared. "Thought you changed your mind."

"Sorry, my transformation from frog to princess took longer than I expected." She twirled. "Will I do?"

He laughed. "For this dive? No dress code."

"No, silly. Do I meet with Tomas Matthews' approval?"

He held the door, and they joined the cafeteria queue.

At a table overlooking a courtyard, Luna gazed into his eyes. "Tell me about yourself."

"Me? I'm in second-year science majoring in chemistry and biology."

"I already know what you're studying. Who are you? What interests you?"

He described his mother, stepfather, and sister in a few cryptic sentences, then paused while he swallowed a few mouthfuls of his dinner. "My stepfather's family are Bostonians. Their engineering company develops specialized machine tools and manufacturing systems. Mom's from Poland."

Luna glanced up from her almost empty plate. He spelled his name with no aitch, and had a funny accent, definitely not pure Bostonian. And he'd avoided saying anything about his early childhood. But she was most interested in his recent past and his interaction with the Campus Cooperation Council. "What makes a nice guy with a standard suburban upbringing a target for the psychobabble Nazis?"

His expression changed, suddenly more relaxed, without the tension around his eyes and in his shoulders. She wondered why he should find a subject that tormented every day of her life relaxing.

"Mom was seventeen when I was born in 2020," he said. "I don't know who my father is. Her family emigrated to England, but I stayed with relatives in Poland until my mom and my stepfather settled in Plymouth. I was ten, and I've struggled to fit in with life in America."

"You're seventeen or eighteen. That could explain why you appear less macho than most."

Tomas shook his head. "Eighteen in July, but age isn't the issue. I'll never be your typical he-man."

"I think you're perfect." She sighed when he didn't react to her overexuberant comment. "And here at Mass State?"

"High school was tough, but the academic environment suits me."

"But you didn't escape the psychopigs' clutches."

"Bad strategy. I learned to stay below the radar in school. Should be easier here. Will have to try harder."

"Like you're doing right now."

He smiled. "Maybe I'm interested." He gazed at the noisy students filling the room. "Should we find somewhere quieter? Then it's your turn to reveal all."

She hesitated. He'd been open about his worries. Was it time for her to reveal secrets she'd kept hidden for years? *Go for it,* her subconscious voice said. "We better find somewhere really private if you want me to reveal everything."

He blushed. "I didn't mean that. Just like, tell me about yourself."

She nodded toward the courtyard. "We can find a quiet spot..."

Luna watched Tomas share a joke with two guys as he carried their trays to the wash-up area. He was friendlier than she and capable of avoiding further confrontations with the Cooperation Council. If she was to become more than a token friend, she must make an effort.

Tomas located a secluded bench in the residence's private garden. "Okay, your turn."

She sat on the six-foot-long bench in a little alcove surrounded on three sides by flowering shrubs. When she realized she'd positioned herself as far from him as possible, she sighed and slid closer. She was responding to her fear of getting too close to anyone, a habit she'd have to break if they were to become friends.

"My bohemian upbringing attracted psychologists like vultures to a cadaver," she said.

Tomas put his arm around her shoulders, and she leaned against him, surprised by how pleasant it felt. "My parents weren't married. They didn't even live together, but they were friends. I lived with my mom until I was eleven. After that, I lived with my dad."

"What happened?"

"My mom was so involved in her work, she ignored me. We had ready-to-eat food or microwaveable stuff. I wandered in and out, found myself something to eat if I was hungry, fell asleep if I was tired."

"That's storybook stuff. No one lives like that."

Luna sat up, shaking her head. "That's how I lived."

"Then something went wrong?"

"Really wrong," Luna said as she remembered the gigantic trip seven years earlier that took them from Savannah to Panaeati Island. "I'd been to school and then wandered off somewhere. Mom found me on a dock helping a fisherman clean his catch. 'Pack your stuff. We're going away,' she said as she dragged me home. Three days later, we arrived in Papua New Guinea."

"Wow."

"Yeah, really." She described the ancient old plane that looked like they held it together with baling wire and the boat that completed the journey to a tiny island within a tropical lagoon. "It was beautiful—white sand beach, huts on rough-hewn platforms with thatched roofs, and no walls."

"Wow," Tomas repeated.

"Mom left me with the native kids and got on with her studies of salps, stupid jellyfish-like creatures that are her life's work. After living like a native in a stone-age culture for six months, we returned to Georgia. At school, all hell broke loose because she'd told no one we were leaving. They tried to take me into care."

"What happened?"

"Dad rescued me. I lived with him in Washington until I started university."

"A more stable environment?"

She snorted as she recalled her shift from one bohemian existence to another. "He's a freelance computer specialist who works from his apartment. He has food delivered and buys everything online. The only structure was meals. We had breakfast together most days, and one of us would prepare dinner."

"Wow."

Luna pushed away, wondering how many times he would say wow. "That's my life."

"I can see how fitting into our structured society is difficult. But why do you fear closeness to people?"

"The psychiatrists say it represents mistreatment I've blocked from my consciousness, but I don't believe them."

Tomas leaned back and studied his phone. "I've got an assignment to finish. If you're okay, we should get back to our routines."

She sat bolt upright, shocked by his sudden change of focus. "Tomorrow or the weekend? Can we find something interesting?"

"Sorry, part-time job with a biology prof. In the field from tomorrow afternoon until Sunday evening."

"Next week, then?"

He smiled. "Next week, we'll find something interesting."

Chapter Thirty

Friday, September 24, 2038

After his Friday afternoon lab, Tomas rushed to the Biology Department's loading area. Blond, blue-eyed Jessie Gordon, one of two graduate students in their regular field team, stood by the department's van. She had a trailer with their runabout hitched to the back. "Dr. Wilson insists on speaking to you before we go."

Tomas threw his backpack into the van. "I hurried so you could get going."

"Appreciate it, but we must wait for Dr. Wilson."

"And the others? They left already?"

Jessie shook her head. "Only you and me on this trip."

Dr. Wilson arrived a few minutes later and dragged Tomas aside. After a brief discussion about Tomas's comfort level with the arrangements, he and Jessie departed. She put the peddle to the metal as they sped north-eastward to a nature reserve on the Maine coast.

Three hours later, Jessie nosed their runabout onto the pebble beach on the landward side of a small island. Their experimental site was a well-protected bay on its more exposed eastern side. They could work in anything but the most severe weather.

Tomas leaped ashore and tied the painter to a tree. She joined him on the beach. "Take our gear to the usual campsite. I'll retrieve my traps before it's too dark to work."

Tomas unloaded the boat, pulled it higher onto the beach, snugged the painter, and lugged their gear to the campsite. When he arrived with his final load, Jessie had her six sediment traps aligned on the foreshore. She lit their campfire and crouched beside it, shivering in a wet swimsuit after her late evening swim. Tomas erected two tents side by side on the only bit of flat ground.

Jessie disappeared into the first tent before Tomas had it secured and reappeared several minutes later in a jogging suit and down jacket. She watched as he boiled water on their camp stove.

"Sorry," she said after he dropped a tea bag into a steaming mug and passed it to her. "I barked at you and left you with the hard work. Now you reward me with a cup of tea. I wanted to recover my traps and pissed with Dr. Wilson, but I shouldn't have taken it out on you."

They settled on flat rocks by the fire Tomas had crackling.

"Something I should know about?" he asked.

She shrugged as she watched Tomas heat stew on their camp stove. "The others pulled out, and Dr. Wilson couldn't make it, so she wanted us to cancel. I argued against the disruption of my sampling and suggested I go by myself. She refused to allow that, and I had a hard time convincing her the two of us could handle it."

"Why?"

"Some crap about her having a pseudo-parental responsibility for undergraduates who accompany us. I mean, we're both adults, aren't we?"

"Barely eighteen, but I guess that's good enough."

She smirked. "Ooh, younger than I thought, and such a sweet guy. I better be on my best behaviour."

"Cut it out. I'm trying to be serious."

"And really hard working. Look at this campsite. We've been here an hour, and everything's assembled. Even my gear for sub-sampling my traps."

"You need to do that tonight?"

She nodded before reaching for the bowl Tomas held out. "Dinner, then transfer the trap samples to their storage jars and clean out the traps so I can redeploy them Sunday morning. You know the cleaning routine, don't you?"

"Did it last trip."

"Good. Then it'll be time for bed because tomorrow we'll have a full day."

Later, after they finished processing Jessie's samples and setting up their gear for the morning, she returned to their earlier discussion. "Our screwed-up world got to me today."

"Have I missed something?"

"Dr. Wilson's fussing and too much forcing everyone into a common mould. It's stifling creativity."

"But that's about social interactions and the classroom environment. Can't you ignore it when you're pursuing your research project?"

"I wish," she said. "Similar restrictions apply to scientific research."

"But it depends on freedom to pursue understanding wherever it leads you, and America leads the world in scientific research."

"We lead the world in pure scientific research, but we're not free to pursue topics related to the country's social fabric."

An owl's hooting distracted Tomas as he watched waves lapping on the shore. "You mean environmental concerns, pollution, ecosystem loss, that sort of thing?"

"And climate change. The work we're doing here relates to how carbon dioxide emissions are changing the ecosystem. No freedom to follow that idea."

"They insist climate change was sorted twelve years ago."

"That's the problem. Global temperatures have been stable, but we should investigate other impacts."

"Like the differential heating of land and sea," Tomas replied. "It generates unstable weather that society has learned to handle."

"We're coping, but that's only one potential issue. Your dad's an oceanographer, isn't he?"

"Yeah, part-time at Woods Hole."

"Ask him the next time you're home. He can fill you in. But now it's time to crash."

She disappeared into her tent, but Tomas stayed outside watching for the owl. He wondered why she broke off the conversation without describing her concerns. Society's intervention in people's personal lives, and the way they interacted with one another in learning and work situations, was annoying. Did that meddling extend to how scientists worked and the subjects they could investigate? Was she afraid to talk about it?

Homecoming weekend was one week away. A crazy time on campus when the big football game and other festivities made productive work impossible. He'd return home and accost his father.

When Tomas arrived in their residence common room at 4:30 on Sunday afternoon, Luna waved him over. "Good trip?"

"Only two of us, so harder than usual, and I hate tents." He nodded toward the cafeteria. "You eating here?"

She gave him a quizzical look. "Paid for, and I'm struggling with an assignment."

"Give me thirty minutes, and I'll join you."

"Good. I learned something important."

He hoisted his backpack and strode toward the stairs. "Me too."

At 5:30, they lucked out as they entered the dining area with their meals. Another couple was just leaving one of the coveted small tables. They grabbed it and Luna stood guard while Tomas collected cutlery and glasses of water.

"What's your news?" he asked after they had everything organized.

"Wild demonstration on Saturday. It scared me."

"I heard nothing about a demonstration."

She grimaced before poking at her lasagna. "Unauthorized, and it sure generated a reaction from the administration. Cops arrived in force and arrested the organizers."

"But not the bystanders?"

"They were rough, forced us to clear out."

Tomas gestured with his fork. "What was it about?"

"Claire said they were protesting the death of democracy."

"Claire? Should I know her?" he asked as he placed his fork on his plate.

"Claire Fitzwilliam, a friend from last year who's sympathetic to the demonstrators. I suspect she planned some mischief." Luna paused before glancing around like she was checking for eavesdroppers. She described Claire's aggressive behaviour at an off-campus protest rally during the previous year.

"So you would provide cover," he suggested after she said Claire wasn't registered as a student this year.

"Yeah, I'm pissed about that, but they're onto something."

Tomas shook his head before defending American democracy. "Free elections, division of powers, a strong court system, an active press, and an informed electorate. It can't be in danger."

She pushed her empty plate away and grabbed her dessert. "If we're as free as everyone says, we wouldn't need a regimented society where everyone must fit into a narrow pattern of acceptable behaviour. And why must everyone attend church?"

"You can opt out."

"That's the problem, isn't it?" Luna leaned forward, tapping the table with her index finger. "We're being sucked into a tightly controlled existence if we wish to enjoy the prosperity we've seen for years. They don't need guns and military might. They rely on our greed."

Tomas picked at his dessert for several minutes. He saw disconcerting parallels to Jessie's complaints about restrictions on scientific research. He gave Luna a precis, concluding with, "I'm going home this weekend to ask my dad about Jessie's complaints. If something's wrong with scientific research, he'll know."

Luna scowled. "This weekend?"

"Yeah, why? Something wrong?"

"I hoped we could go to the homecoming pep rally and football game."

"Friday night and Saturday afternoon. You really want to?" Tomas asked. Homecoming was fodder for the sheep that bought into the administration's repressive agenda. He didn't expect outsiders like Luna to support it. He'd skipped most of the previous years' homecoming events and had no real interest in this year's version.

"Yeah. I missed them last year. It should be fun."

Tomas drummed three fingers on his temple as he contemplated the logistics— leave after the game and return early Monday morning. "Yeah, doable. Okay, let's join the Homecoming festivities."

"Dumb, isn't it, given what we've been talking about, but I want to go."

After the football game, Tomas caught the Boston train with seconds to spare and opened his tablet to study recent US history. After he reached North Station, a short subway ride took him to South Station and the train to Plymouth.

"Brief visit?" Steve Matthews said after their usual perfunctory greeting at Plymouth station. His stepfather wasn't an effusive person, so the abrupt question didn't faze Tomas.

"Yeah, sorry. Told Mom I'd be home for tomorrow's birthday bash, but a new friend wanted to attend the Homecoming game."

"No problem, just surprised by the last-minute change. What's up?"

Tomas considered his options as he opened the passenger door to their car, a relic from the early years of functional electric vehicles. "Something weird I learned from a biology grad student."

"About climate change?"

"Yeah, how did you know?"

Steve twisted around, checking for traffic before he exited his parking spot. "Just a guess."

Tomas summarized progress with his part-time job and Jessie Gordon's concerns about government support for climate change research. He described her study of the transport of organic matter to the sediments in an almost landlocked bay and ended with a direct question about her difficulty getting funding.

"Universities focus on education and fundamental research," Steve replied. "They see climate change research as applied work, not within the purview of academic institutions."

"But Dr. Wilson and others apparently think it's important."

Steve pulled their Tesla sedan from the train station parking lot. "Twenty minutes before we get home. Sit back, and I'll explain."

"Okay."

Steve, with the academic thoroughness that characterized all his explanations, summarized the battle against global warming from the 1990s to the Company of Gentlemen Entrepreneurs' technological solution.

He stopped, trapped behind a car, trying to turn left. "It worked too well. They kept average global temperatures in a narrow range since 2026. Scientists realize

177

carbon emissions are still a problem, but the public thinks the global warming problem's solved. Several countries have taken advantage of the situation and expanded carbon emissions. We're now heading toward another environmental crisis."

"Why don't we address those emissions?"

Steve described America's emergence as the dominant progressive democracy after the Second World War and its success leading worldwide international cooperation for seventy years. He outlined America's shrinking competitive edge and China's challenge for economic and political dominance. He mentioned Make America Great Again, the inward-looking approach that depended on cheap energy and stable temperatures. The global warming fix, he concluded, materialized when they desperately needed it.

Tomas became increasingly agitated as they crawled through the heavy traffic. His stepfather was revisiting old arguments but putting a confusing new spin on several aspects of the restrictive existence he was struggling with. "But we've enjoyed years of technological advance and unusual prosperity."

"Our government and their industrial supporters have ridden a wave of cheap energy to economic expansion. We've experienced none of the usual periodic downturns of economic cycles. But nothing comes without a cost."

"Where's the problem?"

"China's an autocratic country with tight control of all aspects of their society. We've spread wealth to our increasingly uniform public and convinced them to accept a prosperous but more regimented society. Research into climate change and global carbon emissions have been casualties."

Steve was explaining things Jessie refused to discuss, but something didn't compute. America was the biggest player, but it wasn't the only one. "What about Germany, Britain, Japan, and others more concerned about climate change? Wouldn't funding agencies in those countries support the work Jessie's doing?"

Steve mentioned the obvious impediments. "First, they have their scientists to support, and second, our government won't allow it."

"Why not?"

"National security."

Tomas strained against his seatbelt as he turned to face his stepfather. "National security? How does conducting scientific research affect national security?"

"It hurts their ability to control national agendas."

Hah! Control brought them back to Luna's concerns. "Controlling the public. That came up at last weekend's campus demonstration. It means we rely on others to conduct research we should be doing."

"It does, but American scientists have maintained collaborations with foreign colleagues. Mine include Daniel Delacour and Tony Atherton, old colleagues from my days at Dalhousie University. They're researching the impacts of lower pH on plankton, so aligned with the work Jessie Gordon's doing. You can look up their papers."

"But we're the world's richest country. Shouldn't we be involved?"

Steve shook his head. "It's the way it is."

Chapter Thirty-One

Wednesday, June 1, 2039

Eight months later, on a sunny early summer afternoon, Carys Delacour greeted her father outside Hafen Ddiogel, their English country house in Winchfield, Hampshire. "Dump your stuff and relax by the pool. When Mummy gets home, we're going for dinner."

"What's the occasion?"

"Half term break, and I want to go to your laboratory."

"You don't want to hang around the pool or do something with Toby?"

"He's at school until next week, and I want to do something helpful."

Dan's ten-year-old daughter, with professionally styled hair and an elegant frock, followed him into their extensive garden. She carried a tray bearing scotch on the rocks for Dan and lemonade for herself and her little brother, Paul. All were in their socially approved glasses.

After the dinner Carys hosted at the Winchfield Inn, Elena marvelled as she and Dan relaxed at home with cups of tea and biscuits purchased at the nearest Tesco. Despite the family's nine-figure net worth, they lived by Dan's almost bohemian middle-class standards. Dinner for their family of four at the local inn was his idea of a celebratory meal. The family outing cost barely one hundred pounds, but they enjoyed it immensely.

Dan had little interest in fancy toys or elaborate vacations. If one ignored their country house and small staff, their lives were pretty simple. They lacked nothing, and money from her extensive investments kept rolling in. The excess flowed into her foundation, supporting research into scientific, political, and economic approaches to climate change mitigation. It was an ideal arrangement, much better than the tempestuous lives of her society friends.

Dan brought the conversation back to their daughter as she poured the tea. "Carys is maturing so quickly, so sophisticated and aware. This afternoon, she asked me how she could help in our battle to save the planet."

"What did you suggest?"

"She's coming into the lab to learn about our efforts to control temperature."

Elena glanced at Dan leaning on the fireplace mantle. She smiled, thinking he was finally learning how to play the part of the English country squire. "Sounds more interesting than anything we're doing in the bank. How did she react?"

"Enthusiastic, full of ideas, ready to take over our mission. No challenge is too daunting for our daughter."

"And you have something for a precocious preteen?"

"She can help collate the data from our expeditions."

"Will it be interesting?"

He stepped away from the fireplace, collected his tea and a biscuit, and sat opposite her. He described the challenges they'd faced since the Americans abandoned the established temperature control protocols. "I'll show her how we use our field data to fine-tune the seeding process. I can turn it into a game."

"That's a relief. Better than questions about what Alfredo and I are doing."

"Why?"

"A crisis is brewing."

"Should you explain?"

Elena took several deep breaths. Their family dinner at the inn, Carys' first attempt to play hostess at a public venue, had been a huge success. She didn't want to spoil the memories by wallowing in her fears. Uncle Gareth had accepted her as a full-fledged partner in his fight to solve the global warming problem a decade earlier. She cringed whenever she learned about the latest Company of Gentlemen Entrepreneurs' meddling in the affairs of sovereign countries, but interfering in the affairs of nations was standard procedure for the company.

"Warring factions haven't changed," she said. "The US, with much of North and South America tagging along, versus China and their vassal states in Africa and Asia. Europe and its allies have lost influence in this battle of commercial behemoths."

"Anything new?"

"Chaos in the Americas. Venezuela's a failed state and ready to blow. Another revolution disrupting oil deliveries to the US is imminent."

"And where does Canada fit? They've always been America's largest trading partner."

"No longer. Far behind China and even Mexico, but important because they supply oil, minerals, and agricultural products."

"You suggesting Canada should cut off resource exports to the US and exasperate the expected shortages? The company and their European government partners would support this move?"

When Elena nodded, Dan abandoned his tea, strode to the drinks table, and poured himself a generous scotch. "Not surprised you want to keep Carys from such unethical intrusion into the affairs of sovereign countries. Our lab is better."

Elena ignored his attempt to bring the conversation back to Carys and her visit to the university. "We must bring Canada and the US back into the progressive democratic fold. Step one is severing the hold renegade industrialists who won't deal with carbon emissions have on both governments."

"Industrialists who were once members in good standing of the company."

Elena rolled her eyes. The activities of the renegade American industrialists illustrated the behaviour she abhorred. "We know that's the case, and it's tormenting Uncle Gareth's waning years. We'd be doing everyone a service by removing a malevolent influence."

Dan shook his head. "You can't have it both ways. Displacing those renegades with your uncle's more honourable colleagues won't save democracy."

"And what will save democracy?"

"Politicians who listen to an informed electorate and act on their wishes."

*****

Friday evening, Carys bounded into Hafen Ddiogel after a second day when she was enchanted by activities in Dan's laboratory. She'd shown amazing stamina and surprising insights for a preteen.

"It was so much fun," she exclaimed as Elena followed Mrs. Baxter into the foyer. "Dr. Atherton's report on the project he's conducting using the money we gave him arrived today. I read the whole thing and sent him an email with my question, and I entered Daddy's data into his computer. Tomorrow, he'll show me how we analyze it."

"Monday, sweetie," Dan said. "It's like school. We stay home on the weekend."

She posed hands on hips, offering him her most condescending look. "That's silly. You said it was important."

Mrs. B took her hand. "Come, young lady. It's long past teatime."

"But Mummy," Carys wailed before Elena helped herd her into the kitchen.

Elena returned a few minutes later and Dan followed her into their sitting room. She sighed as she settled into her favourite chair.

"Why the hangdog expression?" he asked.

"Uncle Gareth's seventieth birthday. We need something to make it memorable."

"A major development on the science front or a political breakthrough with the US?"

"Can you provide something?"

Dan's thoughts were drawn to the Tony Atherton email Carys mentioned a few minutes earlier. "Something he's been demanding for years, but it won't provide the good news you're seeking."

Elena frowned. "What is it?"

"A target date for the transition from increasing atmospheric carbon dioxide concentrations to decreasing ones."

"Isn't that the major development to relieve Uncle Gareth's perpetual melancholy?"

"Tony Atherton's project report predicts a turning point in fifteen to twenty years."

"The one including your old flame, Olivia Grange?"

Dan ignored her dig about Olivia. They'd worked together a decade earlier, but Olivia had been nothing but a colleague. "His take-away message; sedimentation of enhanced low pH plankton productivity will soon balance carbon emission increases."

"You don't sound as pleased as I expected?"

Dan slumped in his chair. Tony's report provided no insights into the dynamics of the transition or the potential impacts of future reductions in CO_2 increases. "They're talking about natural biological systems we can't control."

"We controlled temperature."

Dan sighed. An engineering fix based on simple physical principles like the relationship between ocean reflectivity and heat absorption was simpler to understand and control than natural biological processes. Could anyone control the complex interaction between environmental conditions, primary biological production, predation, and sedimentation? It seemed impossibly difficult.

"Observations suggest significant increases in plankton growth as pH decreases. That leads to more carbon sedimentation and lower CO_2 concentrations. Global temperatures should head down."

"How quickly?"

It was the question he dreaded; the one Gareth would inevitably ask. "Exactly. We're pushing the world toward an uncertain future when temperatures drop. Will the transition take years, decades, or centuries? We just don't know."

After the youngster's tea, Elena read Paul several chapters from Harry Potter, then skipped off to their bedroom. She returned moments later wearing sandals, a long cotton skirt, and a tie-died T-shirt with her hair in a ponytail. It was her latest summer go-to-the-pub attire, and it reminded Dan of the months she spent masquerading as a student in Halifax. Those were interesting times, but less fascinating than the eight years he'd spent masquerading as a country squire on their Hampshire estate.

They arrived at the pub after a pleasant stroll along rural paths and byways—a jaunt they could manage with their eyes closed. Elena socialized with several Barley Mow patrons, then repaired to a table in the garden. The late evening sun lingered above the horizon, and the temperature remained balmy. She sat back, soaking up the waning rays while waiting for Dan to arrive with their drinks.

Dan set wine and beer on the table. "Happy?"

"We stabilized global temperatures fifteen years ago, but I'd swear England's getting warmer."

"Stabilized weather patterns allow good weather to settle in."

"Which brings us to the political instability the US is causing."

Dan smiled. She used such unusual ways of introducing a topic. "American attitudes make our goals hard to achieve, but what can we do?"

"More than you imagine. Their two-party political system is vulnerable to political and industrial elites taking over. And don't tell me their separation of powers and an independent court system will prevent any excesses. They haven't worked in the past, and they aren't working now."

"Where are you taking this?" Dan asked.

"Donald Trump. He's the quintessential outsider, and many consider him the godfather of the current US regime. Consider how he took over US politics."

Dan hesitated, thinking back to 2016 when the Americans elected Trump. Dan was only fourteen at the time and uninterested in politics. By Trump's second election campaign, he'd developed an interest fueled, in part, by the 2020 coronavirus pandemic. "He identified several issues that struck a chord with voters and convinced millions he could address them. But he lost that election."

"Issues the elites were ignoring. They're ripe for another outsider who identifies problems the current elites are ignoring and drums up public outrage like Trump did twenty-four years ago."

"But it must arise from within the US. You can't impose it from outside."

Elena nodded before raising her wineglass. "When their new political leader appears, we can ensure he has the information to expose the problems."

"And I suppose you'll stir the pot of civil unrest."

"Like the 1960s, when students opposed the Vietnam War. Been done before, and we can do it again."

"But how?" Dan asked. Gareth frequently advocated intrusions into various countries' internal affairs. In the past, Elena had opposed such measures, now she appeared to be endorsing them. "Alfredo's been describing an American public that's committed to their new prosperity."

"Their prosperity is an unstable house of cards that must fall. We can aid in its inevitable collapse."

"What are your points of vulnerability?"

Elena held up her hand, index finger extended from her fist as she began stepping through her list. Environmental uncertainty and instability arising from increasing emissions of carbon dioxide followed corruption and the obscene riches accrued by industrialists colluding with the government. Dan objected when she listed excessive religious zeal because he felt America's religious devotion was too well-entrenched. He nodded his agreement when she added the subjugation of young people.

"I'll buy that," he said. "Many are ready to rise up and escape the box they're trapped in. Social media and instant communication will ensure they become a greater force than the one that ended the Vietnam War."

Elena lowered her hand before picking up and draining the last of her wine. She pushed her empty glass away. "We must wait for the right moment and offer our help. It's coming because they must constantly increase the pressure to maintain control."

"Don't wait too long. In another decade, we may have passed a point of no return onto a long path to lower CO_2 emissions and colder temperatures."

Chapter Thirty-Two

Sunday, September 4, 2039

At 11 a.m., after three months of consistently beautiful summer weather, Elena met Uncle Gareth at the Winchfield train station.

The aging banker had retired from active management of his bank but continued the climate change fight his father started forty years earlier. Strategy sessions with Elena, Dan, and Alfredo Rodriguez were an important part of a personal battle Gareth refused to abandon.

He passed Elena his overnight bag before descending from the train. "You didn't send Dan."

"At sea on your new nanoparticle spreader. Work finished yesterday, so they're steaming home."

Twenty minutes later, Gareth and Elena poured over pages of computer printout Alfredo spread on a poolside table outside Hafen Ddiogel.

Alfredo extracted the second page of his printout. "The Venezuelan situation is unravelling. Cronies of President Montez have sold to a European consortium."

Gareth's head jerked up. "Why would we get into heavy oil production?"

"Better technology," Alfredo responded. "They'll produce the lighter oil we need with carbon emissions that are almost as low as Russia's." He described the benefits of reducing Europe's overreliance on Russian oil and gas before shifting to the deteriorating American oil dynamic. He described depleting US reserves and increasing dependence on Venezuela and Canada. "They're supplying American needs at rock-bottom prices," he concluded. "We can disrupt that fiasco."

Elena frowned. Alfredo's explanation failed to answer Gareth's question and raised several others. "Why would they sell their oil so cheaply?"

"Montez relies on American military muscle to keep him in power. He accepted the price the Americans offered for his oil. Now his cronies and the Venezuelan public have risen up."

"With our help, because we've given them an alternative market for their dirty oil," Elena added.

Alfredo nodded. "And we're immune to US pressure."

Elena shifted to the more critical international relationship. "What keeps Canada in their fold?"

Gareth snorted as he appeared to recover from a private reverie. "They've been problematical for years. They've maintained a progressive line and signed various international agreements. But they provide massive subsidies to heavy oil production from the Alberta Tar Sands and don't build pipelines to take their oil to offshore markets."

"It's difficult for a small economic power living so near the world's largest one," Alfredo suggested. "But I agree with Gareth. They've failed to establish economic independence."

"So, they're stuck selling oil to the Americans at prices the Americans set," Elena concluded before she leaned forward and took the empty teacup Gareth had been fiddling with from his hand. She filled it from the pot steeping on a solar-powered warming plate. "Canadian political elites have always sided with the Americans. How do we change that?"

"That's the core question," Gareth replied.

Elena nodded as she filled the other cups. Time to get the discussion back to CO_2 emissions. "Last month, Dan told us health effects related to air pollution are forcing China and India to stabilize their emissions."

Alfredo consulted one of his charts. "Their reductions are minor."

"But the trend is right. The United States is now the only major player with increasing emissions. They're a democracy, so they should be an ally. How do we make them reverse course?"

Alfredo banged his stack of documents. "If Venezuelans overthrow their government and switch oil exports to Europe, other Central and South American countries will reassess their trading relationships with the US. If we convince the Canadians to follow suit, we'll isolate them."

"How would it help to reduce their trade with the Americans?" Gareth asked.

"We'd target exports of resources at sub-market prices."

Elena sighed. Alfredo could be so annoying. He gave them far too much detail about some issues and too little about others. And he continued to ignore the ecological hazards of increasing CO_2 emissions. His economic and political projections relied on Dan keeping global temperatures under control. They refused to consider new ecological risks. "How?"

"Canada's our key. Their democratic principles are being usurped by power-abusing politicians. We must convince the Canadian public to reassert control."

Elena's sigh became a frown. "Difficult. Replacing one bunch of industrialists controlling oil resources with another is one thing, but influencing the democratic process..."

Alfredo pulled another document from his briefcase. "Business as usual for the Company of Gentlemen Entrepreneurs."

Gareth staggered to his feet and leaned on the table. "Thirty years ago, the company undertook temperature stabilization because it was good for business. We convinced political leaders to join our effort, but we never usurped political power or subverted democracy. We mustn't lose sight of the moral obligation to use our economic power for the good of mankind."

"What about the potential for Chinese incursions into political and economic developments in the Americas?" Elena asked. "That can't be a positive development."

Alfredo nodded. "A potential, perhaps, for Europe to re-establish the influence it once had in South America. But not Brazil. It's a hopeless case."

An incoming text on Elena's phone attracted her attention. Her eyes brightened when she realized it was perfect for defusing the building tensions.

"A message from Dan. His experiments went well. They've compensated for American over-seeding and stabilized the fluctuations we've seen over the last few years. Does that help?"

"It gives us time," Alfredo said as Gareth slumped into his chair. "We can mobilize our allies in Canada and then the United States. We'll overcome twenty-five years of misguided rule, reassert democratic control, and re-establish international cooperation in the free world."

Elena cursed silently. They needed to focus on reducing carbon emissions rather than perpetuating economic expansion that relied on unstable mechanisms to control global temperatures. She kept her thoughts to herself because she needed Dan's technical expertise to win arguments with Gareth and Alfredo.

*****

In America two days later, Tomas and Luna huddled together on the first day of the fall term. They were mere specks in the crowd of twenty-five thousand undergraduate students at the mandatory football stadium rally. At midfield, UMass

Lowell's Vice President of Student Affairs struggled to generate enthusiasm for the restricted life of university students.

Tomas scuffed the concrete as the VP, the one responsible for the Campus Cooperation Council, droned on. "Why must we live in stupid university dormitories and follow their stupid rules?"

Luna provided the standard response. "Wastes minimal time worrying about trivialities like food, laundry, and whatever."

"During the summer, one of the grad students described his much freer life at a Canadian University."

"Is he Canadian? I didn't think we had foreign students at US universities."

Tomas responded with a litany of additional complaints about their increasingly regimented society. "We're all American, and we live in segregated residences until we graduate. We live sober, celibate lives that follow the strictures of our new religion. And we bow to idiots like this fool who heads the CCC."

Luna gazed both ways along their bench, then turned to check behind them. "Careful what you say. Someone may be listening."

"That too. Big Brother's always watching."

She sighed. "What's your point? Your family bought into the prosperity that accompanied these restrictions."

"I liked the camaraderie of living in a house with a group of students. If you'd been there, it would have been perfect. Why can't we do that during school terms?"

"And ruin my chance of participating in our country's prosperity."

Tomas slid his arm around her shoulder. This was important. He couldn't let it slide away. "Why can't we lead less structured, less restricted lives and still contribute?"

She pushed him away before reciting the government's standard mantra about the existential crisis America faced thirty years earlier. China's autocratic regime was using millions of slave labourers in a massive commercial enterprise to swamp the world with goods. America couldn't fight this foe without organizing its population and focusing its industrial effort.

"And we did it without destroying our democratic principles or our civilized society," she concluded.

"But are we free?"

"We have the world's greatest democracy. If you don't like the program, you can follow my parents. No one stops them from doing what they want."

He shook his head. The pablum they were forcing down everyone's throats ignored an important consideration. "They don't share the prosperity."

"They earn plenty to live on, and they follow their muses. And we're winning the trade war with China."

He paused, head cocked to one side. What happened to her fighting spirit? "We need the freedom to follow different paths to the national goal."

After the rally wound down, Tomas strode toward a beer tent in the campus's central square. Last term, Luna became enchanted by her friend Claire's exhortations to rise up, and he'd been reluctant to join them. Over the summer, he'd become more sympathetic to their views, but Luna had backed off. What changed during her summer home in Washington?

Luna hurried after him. "What's happening? Drinking's not allowed on campus."

Tomas didn't break stride. "Non-alcoholic beer and wine, and they're actually drinkable. They'll have stuff to eat."

He paused outside the tent. The administration had gone all out, providing an extensive display of culinary inducements to encourage everyone to accept their increasingly dystopian society. Why would they spend money on this publicity stunt rather than making small but longer-lasting changes that make students' lives better?

Tomas fumed as he loaded plates with canapes. Luna queued for beer and wine. When they met at a table under an oak tree, he noticed she was close to tears.

"Did I do something wrong?"

She contemplated her glass of white wine. "Our stadium discussion reminded me of things I learned this summer. I may need another."

He jumped up. "Don't go anywhere. I'll get us another round."

Tomas returned with another glass of wine and a second beer. During the rally, he couldn't understand why she'd spouted the administration's crap like she meant it. Then he hurried away when she appeared ready to reconsider. *Was giving her an opportunity for further thought a stupid mistake?*

After tipping back the dregs in her first glass, Luna sighed. "My dad echoed what you said earlier. Complaints about the lack of foreign students and not giving students breathing room. He claimed he learned more from the mistakes he made than from his lessons."

"We need the freedom to explore. We're not getting it."

She gazed around the square, and the tent crowded with students. "If Dad's so unhappy about universities, why did he encourage me to attend his alma mater?"

He relaxed, realizing nothing had changed. She'd been confused by conflicting messages during the summer, but they hadn't changed her perspective. "Because it's your gateway to the future. He wants you to have the opportunity. That's what my parents keep telling me."

"I suppose, but my mother said the most disquieting things."

"About marine biology?"

She gulped her second glass. "What else. She never says ten sentences about anything other than her stupid salps."

"What's wrong with her salps?"

"Nothing. They're apparently in bigger numbers than ever doing their usual thing."

"What's the problem?" he asked while wondering why the conversation was flying off in an unexpected direction.

"Salps are disturbing the normal ecological balance. Mom says it's a critical problem, and no one listens to her."

Tomas' brow furrowed. How could these scientific considerations explain her unhappiness? "The students I worked with this summer never mentioned salps."

"They may not live up here, but they're a big deal off Georgia. Her stupid salps didn't unnerve me. She's paranoid about government agents spying on her, controlling what she does, and how she communicates her results."

"Paranoid?"

"When I returned to Washington, I asked my dad. I told you he was an expert in electronic surveillance, didn't I?"

"Yeah, you did."

"If anything's wrong, he'd know."

Tomas reached out and placed his hand on hers. Infringement of personal freedoms, not science, was her real concern. That made much more sense. "And?"

"He was evasive—didn't deny it, but didn't confirm it. Evasiveness isn't normal for Dad, so I conclude there's something to it. And remember my friend Claire? She thinks we're being screwed, with spies everywhere."

"But—"

"Why would the CIA care about scientists studying salps?"

Chapter Thirty-Three

Friday, September 9, 2039

Less than a week later, Elena and Alfredo met Gareth for a late-afternoon strategy meeting in Gareth's neighbourhood pub. It was a public house in name only. The ornate pseudo-Victorian watering hole catered to an exclusive clientele of the rich and famous.

The frequency of their meetings had increased as the aging Gareth focused on the Company of Gentlemen Entrepreneurs' fight to save the world from climate change. Old age was making him impatient and insistent. It hadn't reduced his dedication to his lifelong task.

Alfredo turned toward the bar after he and Elena entered the taproom. "White wine?"

She nodded and scanned the room for Gareth.

"Update me on the science front," Gareth demanded as Elena approached his table in a quiet area that may have once been a snug.

Elena described Dan's success compensating for the Americans' altered approach to nanoparticle seeding. She ended with his fears of an ecological tipping point. As always, his concern was ever decreasing pH.

Gareth tore a chunk off his cinnamon roll and stared at his teacup. His current battle with old age and poor health meant he must avoid booze. It also generated a surprising desire for sugary treats. "Dan's damn tipping points. He knows we can't sell them to my business colleagues."

"But you must convince people we'll reach a point where the outcome becomes uncertain."

Alfredo placed two glasses and a bowl of bar nuts on the table. "That day may never arrive."

"Why not?" Gareth asked.

"New technology for the conversion of carbon dioxide to alcohol. Not bioconversion of corn and other crops we need as agricultural feed. Direct conversion of carbon dioxide gas."

"Commercially viable?" Gareth asked.

"They're working on it. It's something you *can* sell to your colleagues. If China and India adopt it, you'll have a single outlier in your battle to control carbon emissions."

Gareth pushed away his cinnamon roll. "We can't put our faith in unproven technologies. We're back to the recurring question. How do we bring America into the fold?"

Alfredo distributed sheets headed 'Venezuela' from his latest stack of computer printouts. "No reason to change our plan. The Venezuelan government fell three days after our last meeting, and the new government signed a partnership with the European Union. We'll modernize their oil upgrading capacity and import their oil to Rotterdam. First shipments are dirty, but future ones will be cleaner."

Gareth set his copy aside without reading it. "And the American reaction?"

"They declined to intervene in the revolt, and their opportunity, if they had one, is past."

"What's next?"

"Canada. An election call is imminent, and their most progressive party, the Greens, should make major gains. We must help them win seats."

Elena joined the exchange between Alfredo and Gareth. "When did intervening in a long-standing democracy's election become acceptable?"

"Difficult," Alfredo replied. "We may not find another opportunity."

Gareth looked up with an old person's wistful expression. "In the 2020s, we faced a worldwide crisis. The company intervened in the European political process. You'd say it was unethical, but we had no choice. The current situation is worse. A monumental political crisis atop an environmental one."

Elena shook her head. Why did Gareth and Alfredo always focus on political interventions that might, at best, produce partial or interim solutions? Why couldn't they tackle the core problem? "A political crisis of your own making."

Gareth sighed. "We must accept some responsibility because several company members lost sight of our goal."

Alfredo tipped back the last of his beer. "I disagree. Your colleagues understood European governments and their goal of a united Europe with regulated capitalist economies. The Americans never accepted such government intervention. They believe in unfettered capitalism."

Elena hesitated on her way to the bar until she heard Gareth's response.

"We must accept social responsibilities in mature capitalist societies."

A few minutes later, Elena returned with beer, wine, and a fresh pot of tea. "Alfredo will have argued America's response to the Chinese threat was unavoidable. But why did they revert to a high carbon economy and repressive social policies?"

Alfredo defended his perspective. "Americans never abandoned coal, and they've always had a strong fundamental Christian movement. Their business and political leaders channeled pre-existing tendencies."

Gareth poured his tea. "Enough of this. What's your plan for the Canadian election?"

Alfredo itemized his three-pronged approach to support the Green Party. It included endorsements by Canadian company members, a high-profile presentation in Canada by the world's preeminent naturalist, and a study of Canadian oil production by a leading progressive economist.

"The Greens will love them," he concluded.

On the train home, Elena considered Dan's potential reaction to their intervention in the Canadian election. Her Canadian husband had colleagues in the Canadian scientific community, and they knew a Green Party candidate in British Columbia. Would he favour informing her of the company's schemes?

"No way," Dan replied after Elena completed her report. "We can't give their opponents ammunition."

"What are their chances?"

"They're solidly in third place. If present trends continue, they'll have three or four times their previous best showing."

*****

The volunteers in Beth Manville's Vancouver Quadra riding were primed for action when Canada's Prime Minister dropped the election writ on September 13. Her chances appeared far greater on her second try running for the Green party. Within hours, her teams were in the neighbourhoods canvassing voters and installing campaign signs on supporters' lawns. Tuesday evening, seventeen-year-old Michael and fourteen-year-old Hannah, with their father riding shotgun, hit the West Point Grey area immediately east of the University of British Columbia.

Tony Atherton followed his kids to the first few houses, thinking they might need support, but he quickly realized they had their pitch under control. After house number three, he broke off and began his task, placing Beth's campaign signs on the front lawns of people who'd agreed to take them.

Three hours later, they'd covered their assigned territory. Tony dropped Michael at a meeting of Beth's youth workers before he and Hannah returned home for a late supper. Beth arrived minutes later. She slumped onto a kitchen chair as he prepared couscous and heated left-over curry in the microwave.

"Something wrong?" Tony asked, puzzled by her defeated look so early in the campaign.

She shook her head without the animation she normally displayed. "We're off to a solid start, and nationally the Greens are doing well."

"You could hold the balance of power in a minority government. So why the long face?"

"I should be happy because it shows they consider me a serious threat, but I don't like it."

Tony sighed. She was becoming exasperating. "What don't you like?"

"The personal attacks. At meetings, occasionally at people's doors, in the media. Mostly it's on reactionary social media sites."

"Why follow them?"

"Someone logs every time my name's mentioned. It's standard practice for serious candidates."

"Okay. What's upsetting you?"

Beth described the attacks. They included questions about their house, and what opponents assumed was a lavish lifestyle, ClimateChange&U, the Goddard fiasco, and her new television program. "Worst of all, they're onto my acting past and how I was young and, well, foolish sometimes. Except they don't see it that way."

Tony shook his head. Their lifestyle was so boringly middle-class anyone trying to make something of it would surely fail. "Take them in turn. You'll see they're nothing."

"Okay. The lavish lifestyle."

"Bunk. Our house is modest, smaller than the neighbours, and we've lived for years on my professor's salary."

He explained how she could turn the down payment nest egg they'd gained from his high-tech start-up company to her political advantage. He described other adventures from their Halifax life decades earlier, showing how she could spin some, like her involvement in ClimateChange&U, to her advantage and minimize the impact of others. Tony ended with their confrontation with The Reverend Terrence Goddard, a firebrand Evangelical Christian.

Beth shook her head. "You're being the logical scientist when there's nothing logical about this."

Tony sighed. She was making too much of manageable problems, but his arguments weren't bearing fruit. Better to switch tactics. "We'll appear *en famille* at your community barbecue on Sunday, and everything will be fine. You must focus on the big issues. They're trending in the Green Party's favour."

"Decades of prosperity have kept the revolving door of Conservative and Liberal governments in power."

"Nothing like the prosperity in the US," Tony said as he turned to check his cooking.

"Thirty recession-free years and less debt than we see in the US," Beth replied before outlining her concerns about the similarity of the old-line party policies. They both focused on expansion of fossil fuel industries and tight collaboration with the US despite them screwing Canada on almost every issue. She ended with the Green Party's complaint about the state of democracy in the country. "The notion we're exercising voter choice is a farce. They campaign from their traditional perspectives but govern like they're one party."

Tony called out, "dinner's ready," as he laid bowls of couscous and two different curries on the table. He added tar sands exploitation to her list of issues. "On Climate Action Day in 2027, the government announced an end to subsidies for heavy oil production, but nothing happened."

Hannah skipped into the kitchen. "What will end the revolving door of Conservative and Liberal governments?"

Tony smiled, realizing she'd been nearby, listening. "Chaos in America."

Beth shook her head. "There's no chaos in the US. Canadians are sleepwalking, accepting an alliance that subverts our democracy. It's worse down south. Americans are committed to their new world order. It's become central to their existence."

"Bubbles grow larger and larger, and then they burst."

"Gimme the pin!" Hannah said, her eyes glinting.

Tony gazed at Hannah, thinking a coming crisis with oil supplies may provide her pin. "Their ever-expanding economy is depleting their oil and gas reserves. They're becoming dependent on foreign supplies, and if we refuse to sell our petroleum resources at below-market prices—"

Beth pointed with her fork. "Canada won't change its policy? We sell cheap oil to the US because we can't ship it elsewhere. That hasn't changed. It got worse when environmental regulations outlawed oil transport through the Strait of Juan de Fuca. They ship the oil in the pipelines to Vancouver and the US. It can't go to overseas markets."

"That bloody law," Tony said. "Another example of collusion with the US, and the way environmentalists bought it. Disgusting. But the real issue, the one that will break the camel's back, is their refusal to pay royalties on oil we send to the United States. How can our government justify sending them oil without provincial governments collecting royalties?"

Hannah stood and carried her plate to the sink. She'd inhaled her dinner at typical teenager speed. "Easy. Jobs, jobs, jobs. That's what they say whenever they want to give away the taxpayers' hard-earned money. And it always works."

"Not this time," Beth replied. "We have a winning issue. One we'll ride to a future where the Conservatives and Liberals lose their stranglehold on our democracy. We'll resurrect real democracy and escape from the yoke of US suppression."

Tony smiled as he scraped the dregs from three serving bowls onto his plate. Beth had shaken off her lethargy. He'd never be as hopeful as Beth and Hannah, but on this issue, they had his wholehearted support. "If the Americans don't join the battle to control our climate, the world's in serious trouble. We must join the progressive countries and limit CO_2 emissions, and we must do everything we can to drag the Americans into the fold."

Beth nodded as she gathered the empty serving bowls. "Ending subsidies for heavy oil production is the obvious first step. It may become another futile fight, but we must pursue it."

Chapter Thirty-Four

Sunday, October 16, 2039

Beth flopped onto their living room sofa at 11 p.m. after a grueling month on the hustings. The outgoing prime minister had chosen the shortest legally possible campaign, hoping to catch the Green Party unprepared. The Greens started quickly, and their momentum increased steadily through the short campaign. Tomorrow, they'd learn if they'd gathered enough support.

"One day getting our voters to the polling stations, and we're done," she said.

"Been worth it, hasn't it?" Tony asked as he closed his laptop. "You'll win, and nationally, the Green Party will have its best showing ever."

Beth laughed, thinking of the standard political axiom to never celebrate before they count the votes. "It appears I'll be searching for an Ottawa apartment and piling up the air miles."

"Nightcap?" he asked.

"A small one. Help me relax."

She smiled as he headed toward the liquor cabinet. They'd left Nova Scotia fourteen years earlier, but she remained a Nova Scotia working girl. A drink meant Captain Morgan's dark rum and coke. He was no better, favouring the Ontarian's traditional rye and ginger, but his brand loyalty wasn't as great.

"You've seen the latest poll?" Beth asked when he returned.

"Studying them when you arrived. Close third in the popular vote but that poll's several days old. Your momentum's positive, the Liberals and Conservatives are sliding, and the NDP's far behind. You can pull this out."

"Unbelievable, but it could happen."

He passed her a glass and sat beside her. "Like it was preordained. Started before the election call with the American's latest stupidity, announcing American companies would be exempt from Canadian resource royalties. And barricading our half of the Juan de Fuca Strait to protect the environment. I mean, who are they kidding?"

"The final straw in longstanding American disregard for our sovereignty, but the meek acquiescence of the Liberals and Conservatives really mattered."

"Strange level of political blindness."

"And trying to out green us using bogus environmental claims."

"But it continued throughout the campaign, and not just American gaffs."

Her smile broadened as she sipped her drink. It did feel like something preordained. "Nine major Canadian corporations, including several in resource industries, have endorsed our approach to economic and environmental stewardship."

Tony described the progression of events as more oil producers joined their team, and Reginald Archibald, the darling of the international environmental activist set, endorsed their approach to resource development. He described prominent European economist Wolfgang Koerner's data showing the latest extraction techniques made Canadian heavy oil almost as environmentally friendly as lighter fossil fuels and much better than coal. Beth's head swam when Tony trudged through Koerner's statistical arguments, but the bottom line was clear. The pieces were in place for a monumental upset.

She grabbed her husband and hugged him close, stifling his scholarly arguments. "I won't relax until we see the actual results."

Monday, when the BC polls closed at 8 p.m., they'd been closed for four hours on the east coast and shorter periods elsewhere. Phone calls from the east gave Beth hints of unprecedented support for the Green Party, but the media blackout meant the information was spotty.

Beth flicked on their TV. Tony brought in a tray with a teapot, cups, and a plate of homemade cake.

Beth reached for a piece. "Surprised anyone had time for baking."

"Hannah made it."

"Wow, look at that!" Beth shouted, pointing at the TV after a single bite of cake. "Elected or leading in ten on the east coast. We expected four, so that's a great start, but why don't they describe the national picture?"

Tony laughed. "You're the media personality. You should know about creating suspense."

She snorted. Creating suspense should be restricted to drama. The election coverage should be about facts, not fiction. "Here come the Quebec results. Fifty!

That's twice what we predicted and a clear majority for the province. Come on, Ontario! If we get half their seats, we have it made. Only question will be minority or majority."

"Calm down. We should leave for your victory celebration, and with those trends, you're certain to attract the press."

"As soon as I see Ontario." She stared at the screen, watching it slowly reveal the results. "Yes, leading and elected in sixty-eight! We've done it. Joan Watson will be Canada's next Prime Minister, leading our first-ever Green Party government."

Tony shook his head. Her elation was understandable, but they had work to do and needed to stay focused. "Shower..."

"Yes, sir. Quick shower and then to the party before everything's decided."

Forty-five minutes later, they stood outside the West Tenth Avenue restaurant belonging to Beth's most dedicated supporter. The din was deafening, but when Beth entered, it grew by several decibels.

As Tony and Beth worked through the crowd, her campaign manager stepped up to the microphone at the far end of the room.

"Here we have it," he yelled, "at least one poll's results from all BC ridings. We're ahead in thirty." He stopped and looked around the room. "If this holds, we'll have a majority government. And here she is, Beth Manville, your Green Party candidate in Vancouver Quadra, and I'm super confident, our MP-elect."

Beth greeted a few more revellers and followed Tony, Hannah, and Michael to the platform. She grabbed the microphone. "Way too soon for speeches. We're here to join the celebration. We'll track the incoming results as we spread a little cheer and spare a few thoughts for tomorrow. Thank you, everyone, for all the hard work."

Two hours later, when the television stations decided Beth had won her seat, the restaurant crowd was bigger than ever but more subdued. The reality of having to govern the country during trying times had sunk in. Beth's speech congratulating her opponents for conducting an honest fight and thanking her campaign workers for their efforts was brief. The questions from the ever-present reporters were friendly, and the crowd soon returned to their celebrations.

*****

The day after the Canadian election, Gareth greeted Dan, Elena, and Alfredo with a sheepish grin when they arrived at his Kensington townhouse backing onto Holland Park. "My surgeon said they can take me on Thursday. I wanted this meeting before I succumb to the sawbones' ministrations."

Elena responded quickly. "Something new, a complication?"

Gareth shook his head. "Opening came sooner than expected."

"And the sooner you return to the fray," Dan added.

Gareth thumped Dan on the back as he led them into his elegant abode. He often clashed with Dan, but when it came to the crunch, they always found common ground. "I'll soon lead the company into battle." Inside his study, a middle-aged woman wearing a nurse's cap waited with a tea tray. "And join you in a proper drink. No more of this bloody herbal tea."

Elena poured drinks for Dan, Alfredo, and herself, and they got down to business.

Gareth began with the science, claiming as usual that he wanted to get the hard stuff out of the way.

"Two things worry me," Dan said after describing their ongoing success controlling temperature. "We can't succeed without input from the surveillance satellites, but why so many? In the Atlantic, we're using data from six satellites, including two Canadian ones. If we add efforts to control temperatures in the Pacific and Indian oceans, we may need data from thirty. But your colleagues at Space Technologies have launched dozens and the Americans and Chinese, many more."

Gareth looked toward Alfredo. "Is that correct?"

Alfredo nodded as he searched through his ubiquitous stack of printout. "They've launched seventy-two from the European launch facilities and received licencing fees for many more. From revenues collected, I'd estimate five hundred."

Gareth turned toward Dan, surprised by a topic they'd never discussed. "Five hundred expensive satellites. For what purpose?"

Dan shrugged. "Response to emergencies, monitoring pollution, the modern business of managing the activities of millions of citizens?"

"Does that make sense?" Gareth asked. Once again, he was frustrated by technological questions he couldn't answer. "Can they redeploy satellites designed for measuring ocean conditions?"

"Different sensors and they'd send the data to different agencies, but they're data-collecting machines."

"For spying on our citizens?" Elena asked.

"Dan?" Gareth asked again.

"We already track signals from phones and other communication devices. There's a potential for more extensive monitoring."

Gareth sighed as the light dawned. The problem was political, not technological. The Americans, the Chinese, and maybe the Russians were using the global temperature control program as a smokescreen for surveillance satellites. But what were they monitoring?

"Interesting," he said. "Something to look into once I'm released from the hospital. You mentioned a second concern."

"The global increases in carbon dioxide emissions are finally tailing off. It's a good sign, but it increases the complexity of our efforts to control temperature."

"Do we know why?"

Dan checked the notebook open in his lap. He stepped through the reasons for the decreases. They included increased carbon removal in a lower pH ocean and less coal burning in countries like China and India with air pollution problems. The improving ability to trap CO_2 discharges and either store them or convert the CO_2 to useful products completed his list. "None of these by themselves are overwhelming, but taken together, they're having an impact," he concluded.

Gareth glanced at his drinks cabinet before raising his teacup. "We're finally moving in the right direction, only twenty years too late."

"Better late than never, and we could speed up the process if the Americans cooperated."

Gareth turned to Alfredo. "The American political situation. Where does it stand?"

Alfredo, as usual, handed stacks of computer printout to everyone. "Slow, like Dan's progress with carbon emissions. We're moving in the right direction and may soon reach a point where things move more quickly."

"Summary, please," Gareth said after glancing at his pages of dense text. He understood the political and economic considerations much better than the scientific ones, but Alfredo's documentation always contained too much detail. He needed to focus on the bottom line.

"First, Venezuela oil is now part of the European supply chain. The Americans are fuming but not raising the price they'll offer for Venezuelan oil."

Gareth held up his hand. "Can't accept heavy oil imports as a positive move."

Alfredo shook his head. "Venezuela's new German advisors have applied Wolfgang Koerner's accounting principles for economic and environmental costs and priced their oil accordingly. They've built carbon recapture into the price, and they gain more revenue from sales to Europe than they did from sales to the US. When our more advanced technology comes online, the situation will improve."

Gareth turned to Dan. "Do you agree?"

Dan nodded as Alfredo continued. "The Canadian situation is similar. Their new government accepts our approach to economic and environmental management. Separating them from the US sphere will be a major coup."

Gareth fidgeted as his frustration grew. His concerns for his imminent surgery were making it difficult to focus on the discussion. "We know this, and the company is busy developing new allies in Canadian industries. What about the United States? The US political situation must be our focus."

Alfredo moved to the next page in his stack of printout. "The key to the US situation is buried in their history."

"Nonsense," Gareth said. "This is more than a reaction to their losing the global pre-eminence they've enjoyed since the Second World War."

Alfredo pointed at his printout. "Several eminent American sociologists have published assessments supporting my view. They're summarized here."

Gareth sighed. His demonstrations of impatience were not influencing Alfredo. "Give us your assessment."

Alfredo summarized the studies that attributed recent events to Fundamentalist Protestant doctrine with roots in the sects who colonized the United States. They highlighted the longstanding belief America as a country and Americans as individuals must stand on their own. Their insistence on self-reliance led to a repudiation of global organizational structures and a hunkering down on their America First agenda. He concluded by linking the sociological analysis to the Company of Gentlemen Entrepreneurs' activities.

Gareth's face turned red as he thumped the table. "The American members of the company broke ranks with the rest of us and perverted our noble cause."

"Please," Elena said, ending many minutes of silent observation. "You must remain calm. The company schism is ancient history. Focus on the future."

Gareth took several deep breaths before settling back. "We've enlisted new members, but the rogues and their Democratic and Republican party allies have a stranglehold. Their democracy has become a sham."

Alfredo resumed his exposition, describing the US economy as an unstable bubble waiting to burst. "They've had annual growth over six percent for a decade and a growing tendency to extreme measures. Their Draconian import taxes on Canadian and Venezuelan resources produced a political overthrow in Venezuela and a democratic breakthrough in Canada."

"Why did the US allow those defections?"

"Hubris. They think the Canadian and Venezuelan expressions of independence will fail. Both will return to the US fold, willing to accept even lower prices for their resources."

"The company will ensure that doesn't happen," Gareth insisted. He glanced at Dan, whose scowl showed he didn't share Gareth's newfound confidence. He wasn't concerned. The pieces, excessive surveillance, unsustainable growth, and failed efforts to manipulate neighbouring countries were coming home to roost. Their house of cards could not survive.

As usual, Alfredo had the last word. "We sit back, wait for the bubble to burst, and establish a proper working relationship with a new US government."

Chapter Thirty-Five

Sunday, October 23, 2039

Sunday evening, when Tomas Matthews returned to Lowell after a quick visit home, he rushed to Luna's dorm room without visiting his. He found her sitting at her desk, hunched over her computer.

She looked up, her sad eyes and turned down mouth signalling her disappointment. "Hoped you might make it by dinnertime."

He snorted. "Train schedules are completely screwed up."

"You learn anything?"

"Good discussion with Steve about the current situation."

Tomas began describing his stepfather's view on climate change science and the importance of coal and a cohesive American society in the ongoing commercial battle with China. Luna jumped up and dragged him out the door. She plopped onto a sofa in the third-floor conversation area.

"What's wrong?" he asked after he finished describing the weekend discussion.

"Claire has me paranoid. I'm seeing spies and surveillance devices everywhere."

"But not in this common area?"

She snorted. "Paranoia. Irrational fear they're bugging the dorm rooms."

"Hidden microphones in your room, but not here? Doesn't seem logical."

She pointed to the security camera at the head of the stairwell. "We're aware of them, but they don't record conversations."

Tomas lifted a cushion. "Maybe the sofas are bugged."

"Cut it out. You're making it worse."

"Let's go for a walk. You can start at the beginning and explain everything."

She stomped down the stairs without getting a jacket from her room and out into the clear, but frosty, night air. She said nothing until they were on the riverside path, heading east toward the large bend in the Merrimack River. "Friday, I met Claire after you went to your afternoon lab. The way she contacted me was spooky. She walked by before my lecture and dropped a note on my table without saying anything. When I met her, she demanded I return the note."

"Wow! Straight from an old spy movie."

Luna's smile was fleeting, suggesting efforts to lighten her mood would fail. She described the detailed instructions Claire gave her about a late-night meeting. They included disturbing her bedcovers with a pillow under them so a casual glance would suggest she was sleeping. "It got worse," she added. "She told me to leave my phone and ID behind and meet her in this University Avenue dive."

"They can track phones, but why your ID?"

"She says student IDs have tracking chips in them."

He shook his head. "I doubt that, but you better continue."

"She was sitting in the dingy café with three dubious-looking characters. They didn't look like students."

Luna stopped and spun around, suggesting she hoped to catch anyone following them. She sighed before continuing. "Their leader described their perspective. He said a bunch of industrialists are subverting our system. They're destroying our democracy and leaving a sham government. They plan to take over the world."

Tomas compared Claire's picture to the one his stepfather presented of America's confrontation with China. "Like what Steve told me."

"They didn't mention China or any other enemies. I might have laughed it off as a bunch of crazy conspiracy theorists, but Claire said they recruited me with no option of declining. They really frightened me."

"I'd ignore them."

She turned away and started walking back the way they came. "I can't."

Tomas hurried to catch up as Luna strode toward their university residence. "Why not?"

She described powerful people usurping governmental authority and trampling citizens' rights and freedoms. People who instituted the fucked up social structure they were living with, spying on them, turning them into mindless drones. "It makes sense, explains all the problems we've been fighting for the last two years." She paused, taking a deep breath. "And my dad's one of them."

Tomas grabbed her arm and dragged her to a halt. She was obviously upset, using swearwords she normally avoided. And he detected several inconsistencies in her description. He couldn't let her return to her room without finishing this conversation.

She shivered. "It's cold. I want to return."

He shrugged off his jacket and passed it to her before rummaging in his backpack for the sweater he'd taken to Plymouth. He pointed toward a bench. She shook her head and strode to the river's edge, where she stood, staring across the water at their university's riverfront stadium. The Big Dipper was visible near the northern horizon, and higher in the sky, the Little Dipper with Polaris at the end of its pot handle.

"Your father?" he asked.

"Yeah, they want me to be their contact with my dad."

"Why can't they send him messages like everyone else does?"

"You don't get it. Micromanaging everyone's life with constant surveillance of everything we do is central to our new overlord's ability to control us."

Tomas stared, dumbfounded. She was describing a crazy science fiction dystopia. "You suggesting they're watching everyone all the time? How can they do it? If you ignore kids, that's three hundred million Americans."

"You're the scientist, you tell me. Claire and her friends have proof we're under constant surveillance."

"Like spy satellites? They'd need thousands."

"They're doing it somehow using phones and innocuous-looking things like your university identity card."

"Your dad's in that business. He should know."

Luna nodded. "Claire's probably getting her info from him. I'll find out when I go home for Thanksgiving."

"Aren't you going home with me?"

"I was because Dad ignores me when I visit. Now I have a mission, so I'm going home."

He shook his head. Luna was his closest friend, the only person outside his immediate family who was important to him. He wanted to believe her, but her story made no sense. "We've always had business tycoons and other influential citizens meddling in government. It's never deteriorated to the situation you're describing."

"I intend to find out. And I have a plan. The perfect way to manage it."

*****

On Thursday, November 24, Luna checked her watch as her Spirit Airlines flight descended into Baltimore/Washington International. Thirty minutes late was nothing compared to her two-hour-long battle getting from Lowell to Logan.

A bus to Washington's Greenbelt Metro Station and a short ride to Riverdale and her father's apartment awaited. When Luna arrived at 7:05, she unlocked the door and entered a dark apartment. No surprise, as her reclusive father spent most of his waking hours in one room, a bedroom converted into an electronics lab. She dumped her backpack and strode into his workshop.

"Welcome home," Richard Muldoon said without taking his eyes off his computer screen. "Your dinner's in the fridge."

"I'll heat it, and we can talk when you reach a suitable breaking point." She turned at the door. "We really need to talk."

Luna was sipping tea in the darkened living room, illuminated by one tiny LED lamp beside her chair, when Richard emerged from his workshop. The glow from cars passing their building penetrated through the open-weave curtains. "You should open them and admit the daylight. Buy some plants."

"It's night, and I'd forget to water them," he replied. "Regardless, all that's become irrelevant."

"That's why I'm here. I need answers."

"I figured as much. Otherwise, you'd be celebrating Thanksgiving with your new boyfriend."

Luna scowled. She and Tomas had been together for a year, so hardly new. But she didn't want to wrangle over trivialities. "With his parents and younger sister ensuring we behaved. But you're stalling. Tell me what's going on."

Richard cracked open a curtain and stared into the gloom of a foggy evening for several minutes. "It started in 2015 when Donald Trump gained the Republican Party's presidential nomination and won the presidency."

Luna shook her head. She couldn't connect her picture of a president who accomplished very little with the current situation. "Books portray Trump as a disruptive figure who destroyed long-standing international relationships and generated political chaos."

"Disruptive, but he had a gut feeling about problems with America." Richard shrugged. "He shook up the system and set the stage for our current mess."

"No one gives him credit for solving anything, but I'm not interested in their opinions. I want your take."

Richard launched into his version of recent US history. He focused on the country's golden age from World War Two to 2100, when America led the enlightened world. A time when democracy, free markets and globalization prevailed over communism and the Soviet Union. America spearheaded the United Nations and developed international agencies like the World Bank, the International Monetary Fund, and the World Trade Organization.

He contrasted that America with a more long-standing image of a staunchly Christian country with an isolationist bent. The family, hard work, and unfettered free markets that let hard-working Americans prosper were central features of that country.

He turned and faced Luna. "Throughout our history, our democracy has been a strange beast with two political parties dominated by elites allied to the kingpins of American industry."

She joined him by the window and spread open the curtains. Despite the outside gloom, the indoor light level increased. "Okay, those are the textbook pictures of America. How do we get from there to our current mess?"

"By 2000, our experiment as an interventionist power was in trouble. China's ruthless, autocratic government with tight control of Chinese capitalism emerged as a serious threat to our predominant position in the global economy. We appeared incapable of rising to the challenge."

Luna hesitated, trying to bring together her father's picture of two different Americas and the waning of the more recent one. Globalization seemed to be the key. America may have fostered globalization but China gained most of the benefits as the US shipped more and more of its production offshore. "Our current leaders would say Americans lost their focus on family values and the American Dream and became hedonistic sycophants."

"Presidents after Mr. Trump rediscovered the characteristics that supported America through its golden age. Christian fundamentalism, unfettered free markets and government working with industrialists in a political structure that maintains the stranglehold of the political elites."

Luna frowned as she held up her hand. "It's not working."

"We're a democracy, and our leading elites couldn't openly mess with our democratic principles. They relied on the carrot of material gain. In recent years, they've increasingly resorted to more underhanded methods."

She backed away from the window and switched on a lamp. "What the hell are you trying to tell me?"

Richard paused long enough to draw a breath and glance around the room. Then he stared at his daughter for several minutes. "I suspect you understand the infringements on your liberties better than I do. I also suspect you've learned about our resistance to the status quo and expect guidance."

"Claire Fitzwilliam, a friend from freshman year, thinks they have everyone under constant surveillance." She watched carefully, hoping to pick up an indication he recognized Claire's name. His expression didn't change. "She compared it to George Orwell's Nineteen Eighty-Four but wouldn't explain. Said I should talk to you."

"The government's manipulating citizens' lives in ways liberal-minded people would reject if they understood. Its capacity for surveillance is unprecedented. They can monitor an individual's movements, but they don't have the infrastructure to watch everyone."

"So, Claire's right."

"In theory," Richard replied after Luna described the meeting that precipitated her visit home. "But only if they'd been monitoring your activities. They can't track the activities of all university students."

"But possible. And they can presumably reconstruct someone's movements."

Richard stared into the gloom for several minutes. Pauses for thought were unusual for her father. *What complicated ideas are firing his synapses but preventing him from making a quick decision?*

He broke out of his reverie. "Interesting question. I'll conduct a little experiment and give you the answer before you return to Lowell."

Chapter Thirty-Six

Sunday, November 27, 2039

Luna fidgeted on the afternoon flight from Washington to Boston. She couldn't concentrate on the *American Politics* magazine she'd purchased in University Park before catching the bus to the airport. As they descended to Logan International, she remained stuck on the first article.

After dinner in the residence cafeteria, she hammered on Tomas' dorm room door. When he didn't respond, she slumped to the floor, overwhelmed by her father's revelations on government surveillance of American citizens.

"You promised to meet me for dinner," she barked when he finally arrived.

"Sorry, Steve has an evening flight to England. I came up with him and detoured by Logan."

She took three deep breaths. Meeting for dinner had been a suggestion, not a promise. *I can't let my frustrations ruin our relationship.* "Let's get outta here. I've really important news."

He dumped his pack, and she dragged him into the cold, windy, and wet night. They crossed the Merrimack River bridge to a student hangout near the main campus. It was a simple fast-food restaurant, not a sleazy dive like the place where she met Claire's fellow revolutionaries.

Tomas purchased coffee and a submarine sandwich. Luna settled for tea. "Didn't get any dinner," he said as they cleared debris from a recently vacated table. "What's bothering you?"

"Big Brother watching everyone's activities."

Tomas pointed at a camera on the wall behind the cash. "Nothing new."

She shook her head and favoured him with a withering look. *He needs to take this more seriously.* "Much worse. You remember how Claire told me to leave my phone and student ID behind when I met her friends?"

"Yeah. I wondered about your driver's licence and other ID?"

"Don't have a driver's licence."

"I'm surprised."

"Dad doesn't own a car, so I never learned to drive. Stop getting me sidetracked."

Tomas placed his hand on hers and gave it a little squeeze before diverting into considerations of types of cards and how they could or could not be used to track someone.

"Stop it," Luna said after kicking his shin. It wasn't a serious kick, just a tap to get his attention. "You're getting us sidetracked again. I don't care how it works. What's important is they have surveillance data on everyone, and they use things like student IDs."

He leaned down and rubbed his leg. "All right, back to your story."

"You know what my dad does for a living?"

"Cybersecurity consultant. He keeps companies safe from computer hackers?"

"The federal government's his biggest client. And to do his job, he must be a super hacker."

"Makes sense. Has your father hacked into government computer systems?"

Luna paused as a scruffy-looking student started an argument with three clean-cut lads at a nearby table. The trio looked like poster children for the Campus Cooperation Council's ideal student. She waited until the fuss died down. "Where were we?"

"Your dad was hacking into government computers."

She nodded. "When I explained what Claire said about leaving my ID in my room, he said he'd investigate."

Tomas turned around after another student pushed by and joined the argument at the next table but one. He turned back to Luna. "And he found something startling?"

"More important, he pretended he knew nothing. But hell, I know when my dad's lying."

"What did he tell you?"

"The government can track my movements using my student ID. He showed me everywhere I've been since I started university."

"Do you have the records?"

Luna shook her head as she tried to dispel the image of government spies monitoring her every movement. The idea of them knowing every time she went to the bathroom was just too creepy. "Somewhere in a government building, there's a giant computer with my location every ten minutes, day and night."

"A single latitude and longitude?"

"A string of locations that spans sixty seconds, then ten minutes later, another string."

"That's it? No records of who you met, or conversations?"

Luna took a napkin and dabbed at her eyes. This is no time for weepiness, but the idea of cyberspooks following her every movement was getting to her. "If they have everyone's data, can't a computer determine where various records intersect?"

"It could, but it's an enormous dataset. Are they following the movements of three hundred million citizens?"

"Dad said they'd never accessed my records. They're collecting data on all citizens, but I don't know how many they're monitoring."

"Why would they bother with such a huge, massively expensive effort?"

"Fear. They're doing something people will oppose. This surveillance operation is part of their mechanism for controlling everyone when it's revealed."

Tomas concentrated on his neglected sandwich for several minutes. "A one-minute data burst followed by a gap sounds like satellites with narrow viewing cones. I'm guessing a lot of satellites to cover the entire country twenty-four seven. And how do they send the signal from someone's ID card to the satellite?"

"You can worry about how. I'm wondering why."

"You already explained why." He offered his take on her story; his explanation of an extensive effort to sell everyone a crock of shit. The surveillance, the garbage promoted by the Campus Coordination Council, and everyone giving up individual freedoms to contribute to their unusual prosperity featured prominently. "It's fatally flawed," he said in conclusion.

She smiled. Talking about her concerns really had helped. "And our government leaders are employing extraordinary measures to keep their house of cards from collapsing."

Tomas screwed up the plastic wrapper from his sandwich and stuffed it in his empty cup. He stood and headed toward the door. Luna followed.

"What's next?" he asked after they hurried across the bridge to their residence building. The wind was gustier than ever, but the rain had stopped.

"Claire and my father agree on my role. I should learn all I can while masquerading as a compliant student. I'll be a sleeper agent available for communication between the revolutionaries and my dad."

"That means they're including you in their ill-defined revolutionary group."

"It does," she said with an involuntary shiver. "But what about you?"

"Jessie and my dad have shown me the science problems parallel your social concerns. The country has a monumental problem we must expose, but I don't see what I can do."

"Help me understand the situation. Be ready to take part when they need us."

*****

One day earlier, Tony Atherton arrived from Vancouver on his second trip to Ottawa in five weeks, and he'd yet to see the sun. Beth's first parliamentary session was entering its fourth week. Perhaps she'd seen brighter weather than he had in the lifeless, snow-dusted wasteland that was Ottawa in early winter, but he wasn't convinced.

After a bus ride into the city and a short detour to Beth's apartment, Tony arrived at Skookum, a Byward Market watering hole. She promised to meet him there for dinner. He smiled when he saw the stylized killer whale above the door. Beth had described it as the hangout for the Green Party's BC caucus. *Did its name or logo determine their choice?*

A reporter called out as he followed the greeter to his table. "Hey, Dr. Atherton, here to advise the government on climate change?"

Tony shook his head. "Family visit *en route* to an international conference."

"High-level meeting at the Llewellyn Foundation. Something's brewing?"

Tony smiled. "Well informed, as usual, John. We must wait and see."

The reporters clustered around Beth as she entered the pub. Her arrival meant Tony was no longer the centre of attention.

He was heading to Europe to discuss two projects that provided insights into the transition from global warming to global cooling. The first, his year-long Llewellyn Foundation-funded collaboration with Achara Zhu and Olivia Grange, addressed the meeting's primary purpose, estimating the time frame for the transition. The second, a Canadian government-funded project supported his collaboration with long-time colleague Marc Lavoie. It provided insights into the transition mechanism.

Tony waited at their table until Beth wended her way through the gauntlet of reporters and exchanged a few words with patrons who were probably politicians and their staffers. She slid into her chair. "You must thank Dan and Elena for giving me a few hours' respite from the political madhouse."

"Has it been so bad?"

"Intense. It's not been a month. I'll get the hang of it." Beth glanced at the drink menu before settling on white wine. "And now a sneak peek preview of the results you'll be presenting."

Tony sighed before describing the results Achara would present on her low pH plankton blooms in the Gulf of Thailand. He went on to his calculations that help determine when those blooms will generate enough carbon removal to counteract the ever-accelerating CO_2 emissions. He passed her a few stapled-together pages. "A slow grind, but we're making progress."

She glanced toward a commotion near the door where the minister of finance was holding an impromptu scrum. "Your observations should grab their attention."

"Hope so. Impacts are years away, but the uncertainty surrounding ecological implications is mindboggling."

She laughed before folding the pages and tucking them into her purse. "No need to lecture me. I know damn well it's a threshold we must never reach." She paused when the finance minister raised his voice. "You'll provide me with a complete report when you return?"

He nodded before shifting the topic. Beth already mentioned Elena Llewellyn, a key player in both the Llewellyn Bank and the Company of Gentlemen Entrepreneurs. She would be interested in Beth's political developments. "And your first month in the lion's den? Over your disappointment at not snagging a front-line cabinet post?"

"Never a realistic possibility," she said as the waitress arrived with her wine. She described the logjam in the scramble for cabinet posts because nine of the party's fifteen re-elected members were from British Columbia. "My position as Energy Department Minister of State with responsibility for our short-term energy policy is a stepping stone to a more senior posting."

"And one with serious challenges."

"True, but it's working out beautifully. It's like we have a guardian angel looking over our efforts to get our oil and gas industry functioning responsibly."

Tony swirled the remaining ice in his drink. He was unwilling to attribute their success during the campaign and the subsequent weeks to divine intervention, but he couldn't deny they'd had extraordinarily good luck. "Recent developments?" he asked.

"Several progressive newcomers to the oil and gas industry, and we already have one major foreign buyer."

"And the environmental activists are keeping quiet."

She nodded. "Everyone's giving us a chance to develop a responsible policy."

"So short-term replacement of the single US market with diversified foreign sales and longer-term reduction in our reliance on oil and gas as an economic driver."

Beth glanced around, perhaps concerned about anyone close enough to overhear them. "It's what we campaigned on, and we're sticking to it. So far, industry has accepted our plan, including phasing out production subsidies."

"And the US reaction to your refusal to accept the American government overriding our ability to charge royalties on resource extraction?"

"They abrogated export contracts approved by the previous government and stopped our oil and gas exports. We escaped from terrible deals, and they're the ones who broke the agreements. We couldn't be happier."

Tony paused while he perused the menu. Sockeye salmon featured prominently. "As you said, you have a guardian angel looking after you."

"I wish I understood who and why."

Tony turned to the one issue that remained contentious. "What about American sabre-rattling over the Juan de Fuca Strait?"

"That issue worries the PM, but it's a nonstarter. They're shipping oil from Alaska to Washington State. Opposing our shipments from BC to Japan is hypocritical, and we have solid support from the Europeans."

"But what about the American's supposed environmental protection motive? Won't that feed into opposition from our environmentalists?"

"So far, it hasn't. As I said, everything's unfolding smoothly."

"Too smoothly, perhaps?" Tony suggested as the server approached their table.

Chapter Thirty-Seven

Friday, December 2, 2039

Dan Delacour addressed the final plenary session minutes before the scheduled noon closing of the Llewellyn Foundation carbon emissions conference at Southampton University.

"Four productive days, and we've addressed every issue we identified before bringing this august group together. Our support staff is distributing what I trust is a clean document summarizing our accomplishments. It's short, as such documents should be, and I'm convinced it represents the consensus we agreed upon earlier this morning. If you find errors, tell us ASAP, and we'll prepare a corrected version." He glanced at the clock adorning the back wall. "I won't natter on. We'll distribute all presentations and technical documents electronically. I'll close the meeting and let you get on with your pressing tasks. Thank you for your efforts this week. We've accomplished a great deal."

An hour later, Dan glanced around the empty auditorium before turning off the overhead lights. It had been a long and tiring meeting, but he had a spring in his step as he strode to his office. The conference had gone well. With fifty-two delegates from nineteen countries, including several from each of the major political powers that were constantly bickering, he expected many confrontations but encountered few. The past hour illustrated the spirit of comradery the meeting engendered. Most lingered, debating various scientific points.

Dan dropped his conference folder on his desk and joined Tony Atherton outside the Oceanography Centre lobby. They hopped into a taxi to Southampton's Central Station. Minutes later, they boarded a train to London.

Tony settled into a window seat in a standard class coach. "Good progress," he said as Dan sat beside him.

"I worried about the American delegation. Good to see Steve Matthews again and learn he's still active."

"Achara and I hoped to see Olivia Grange, but it wasn't to be."

Dan mentioned progress using CO_2 as a raw material for the production of basic hydrocarbon molecules as the train picked up speed. That report had been one of the surprise highlights of the meeting.

Tony laughed. "Plants have been synthesizing sugars from CO_2 since early in the planet's evolution. Looks like industrial man will soon manage something similar."

"Will they impact your estimates of when we reach a pH-induced tipping point?"

"Another factor in a complex web. The work of Olivia, Achara, and others shines another light on the tipping point idea. The transition appears more gradual than I imagined. Makes nailing down a date more difficult."

"Awkward," Dan replied. "Your estimate may have large uncertainty, but we needed a number." He paused, hoping Tony wouldn't ask probing questions about Elena's political activities and the forces pressing for an estimate.

When Tony stared out the window without commenting as Southampton's outlying suburbs disappeared behind them, Dan relaxed. He changed the subject. "Your research is undergoing a revival."

"Thanks to your foundation for funding unpopular research on carbon emissions, and now with these new revelations…"

"And political changes in Canada with the ascendancy of the Green Party."

"Tell me about it. You know my wife's a Green Party MP."

Dan nodded. "But few details. Elena's more attuned to the global political situation than I."

"She's a Secretary of State with responsibility for implementing energy policy. You'd call her a parliamentary undersecretary in the Energy Department."

"So, she'll be interested in the results of our meeting," Dan responded.

"Very much so. She's been an outspoken environmental advocate for decades. Now, as part of the new government, she'll see Canada contributes to defeating our carbon emission problem."

"She'll discover Britain, Europe, and other progressive countries will applaud the reversal of your rather inglorious recent past as a staunch American ally."

"It won't be easy. They're a much larger country, and our economies are highly integrated."

Dan shifted in his seat. He wanted to move the conversation away from Gareth Llewellyn and his company's meddling in the politics of foreign countries, but they kept venturing back into that quagmire. Fortunately, Clapham Junction, where they would change trains, was approaching.

At Clapham Junction, Dan accompanied Tony to his train to Feltham, the nearest community to Heathrow. Tony's connection was tight, so Dan didn't want to leave him wandering about the station.

Dan looked at his watch as Tony climbed onto the new train. "Taxi from Feltham Station. That gets you to Heathrow in ample time for your flight. Good luck with your research and Beth's political adventures."

He watched the Feltham train pull out before walking to the nearby London Overground platform and his train to Kensington.

Dan kicked errant pebbles as he dawdled from the Kensington Olympia station to Gareth Llewellyn's townhouse in Phillimore Gardens. He needed to steel himself for the transition from scientific discussions to political and economic ones.

Elena, Gareth, and Alfredo would be interested in the conference outcome. Their focus, however, would be on the Company of Gentlemen Entrepreneurs' activities. They'd want results that bolstered their fight to avoid disastrous climate change.

At the door, Elena greeted him with a welcoming embrace. "I wondered if you'd survive. Never seen you so uptight about a conference."

"Important, like the 2020s, when the company initiated the nanoparticle cure for temperature. If we don't stop increases in carbon emissions, we'll be in a similar mess."

She shook her head. "Save your eloquence for Uncle Gareth and Alfredo."

Dan cocked his head, pointing to Gareth Llewellyn's sitting-room door.

Elena nodded. "Lead on, and we'll get this discussion underway."

Dan strode into Gareth's private sitting room. "Good afternoon, Sir Gareth." He checked the old gent's appearance. He looked reasonably chipper after his recent operation. "Your sojourn at that exclusive resort you call a hospital has been good for you."

Gareth laughed, raising a glass containing an amber liquid. "Exclusive, yes, but definitely a hospital. I'm happy to report everything went well. I'm now ready to put that upstart United States president in his place."

"Hear, hear," Alfredo declared, mimicking banter from the Houses of Parliament. Sir Gareth was elevated to a life peerage years earlier but hadn't taken an active interest in the upper house until recently.

"Elena," Gareth said, "get yourself and Dan a drink, and then we must begin." He paused until Dan and Elena were seated. "Dan, important news from your conference?"

Dan described their understanding of phytoplankton growth in a low pH environment. Gareth's eyes widened when Dan added their date when oceanic plankton removal would balance increasing industrial CO_2 emissions.

He moved on to efforts to reduce carbon emissions and highlighted the developments in industrial-scale chemical photosynthesis. "Indian scientists have produced simple organic molecules from carbon dioxide. The reaction takes heat and light and uses lots of water. It's ideally suited to tropical climates."

Alfredo stared with furrowed brows. "Like algae farms?"

"Without the algae. Chemical catalysis rather than enzymes and chlorophyll. They'll produce raw materials for the production of fuels or plastics. Energy-intensive, but the methods work."

"I see a geopolitical benefit of bringing countries of Asia, Africa, and South America into the process," Alfredo added.

Gareth thumped the table, rattling his empty whiskey glass. "I distill two messages. First, we have fifteen years to get carbon dioxide emissions under control. Second, these new chemical syntheses have potential from geopolitical and environmental perspectives."

When the others nodded, Gareth turned to Alfredo. "Where do we stand with our American colleagues?"

"They remain the biggest impediment to progress."

Gareth rolled his eyes before pointing at Alfredo's documents. "You've been running the numbers for months. What's the plan?"

Alfredo passed around copies. "We've implemented the first steps. Elena and Dan won't like it, but I've crunched the numbers with colleagues in Europe and Japan. We're convinced it will work."

Gareth sighed. "Take us through it."

"Official company plan. Japan and a few European governments are onside. If we need a country's cooperation, we bring them into the picture. Otherwise, they remain in the dark."

Dan's eyebrows raised. He was constantly frustrated because the US refused to join the fight to stabilize carbon dioxide emissions into the atmosphere. But he didn't consider them a rogue state that deserved toppling. Was the Company of Gentlemen Entrepreneur's opposition a visceral reaction to their betrayal? Or a legitimate attempt to deal with the crisis?

Alfredo outlined the points of contention. He then described US government actions that eroded their cherished democratic traditions. "We'll isolate them and help their citizens re-establish their democracy."

Dan jumped up. "How can you justify such interference in a foreign country's affairs?"

Alfredo glanced at Gareth, who defended his brainchild. "First, there's no governmental interference. Second, discrediting industrialists who've subverted the system and ripped off taxpayers is our civic duty. Third, protecting the global environment is our moral duty."

"Be careful," Dan insisted. "Flaws in your temperature cure led to our current situation."

Gareth shook his head. "Perverse actions by the people we oppose, not our nanoparticle program, produced the current situation. Let Alfredo describe where we stand."

Alfredo described the American's heavy handed-approach to international diplomacy, focusing first on the Venezuelan oil situation, then on Canada.

He shuffled his papers and spread open a flow chart. He described a scheme to replace current advisors to the US government with ones counselling a return to the World Trade Organization and other international bodies. Alfredo ended with their plan to convince the American people they need to reengage with the world's progressive countries.

Dan glanced at Elena as she finally expressed her opinion. "This is where I become uncomfortable. Americans voted for a government with policies we dislike. But the American public continues to support the way their country's going."

"And despite the faults you've identified," Dan added. "America's far better than China. They're trying to replace democracies with autocracies that follow their model."

Gareth stood, leaning his hands on the table. "The situation is more subtle than you imagine. In 2016, the American government began an effort to rethink their society based on a rose-coloured recollection of America in the 1950s."

"Make America great again," Alfredo suggested.

Gareth nodded. "Our success controlling global temperatures allowed them to pervert America's democratic traditions. They produced a neo-Christian plutocracy that—"

Dan jumped in. "But Americans have free elections, and most support the society they're creating,"

Gareth ignored the intrusion. "... lulled the public into accepting their jingoistic facsimile of democracy. Unprecedented prosperity based on cheap power made this possible. Our erstwhile colleagues generated a pseudo-democracy that's no better than the one-party farce we see in Russia."

"How did it happen?" Dan asked. There was one good thing about the way the conversation was going. They were delving into topics they'd previously skirted around. He needed to keep the revelations coming.

"An industrial elite, mostly executives in major energy companies, conspired with Republican and Democrat leaders..."

Alfredo took charge as Gareth appeared to lose his train of thought. "Consider the US in the 1950s. They had a homogenous society with strong fundamentalist Christian roots and a booming economy. Citizens were following the American dream and accumulating wealth. They ignored government intrusions into their lives."

Dan sighed as he gazed heavenward. "McCarthyism and the House of Un-American Activities Committee?"

"Exactly, they accepted many intrusions provided they could pursue the good life. That ignorance of underlying problems continued until the Vietnam War woke Americans. They protested and questioned government actions. That generated some positive changes. Renewed prosperity put them back to sleep until the financial crisis in 2008. The rise of China reignited opposition."

Gareth reclaimed the initiative. "Their vaunted checks and balances hampered their efforts to challenge China. Then, in the 2020s, our American colleagues perverted our noble effort to save the world from a climate-related disaster. They seized control of their political process and generated the United States we now see. They couldn't accomplish this coup without our cure for global temperature increases."

Dan questioned Gareth's interpretation of recent US history. Could it be a rationalization designed at getting back at the renegade industrialists.? A disturbing development if his goal was saving the planet from a carbon emission crisis.

He shook his head but stifled his objections. His arguments wouldn't change Gareth's opinions, and Dan needed the company's support to make progress in the fight to lower carbon emissions.

Chapter Thirty-Eight

Tuesday, December 27, 2039

Luna Grange's feelings of isolation from her fellow human beings returned with a vengeance as she collected her luggage at Logan International Airport. During the fifteen months she'd been close friends with Tomas, her fears had been blissfully absent. Now, as she prepared to spend a week at his family home after a week in Washington with her father, they'd returned.

Was her uncertainty about social interactions and involvement in Christmas festivities responsible? Or should she blame her father's reaction the previous day when she mentioned an article in the Washington Post?

Tomas engulfed her in a bear hug when she emerged from the baggage claim area. She cringed because such a show of affection would have drawn the ire of the morality squads on their university campus. At the airport, it attracted scant attention.

He released his grip and gazed with a quizzical expression. "No armloads of Christmas gifts?"

"Tomas! I've never celebrated Christmas, never given or received a gift. You agreed, no presents if I visited."

He smiled as they headed for the subway station. "Everyone agreed, but we find it weird. Anyway, what's new?"

Tomas seemed truly happy to see her. His jokes about Christmas and gifts were just that, jokes. She, however, couldn't match his lighthearted mood. "Something really strange happened."

"Country-wide protests about our wasteful consumer society."

She shook her head. "Aren't they normal behaviour of a minority? I was referring to an investigative article in the Post about influence peddling and graft."

"Yeah. Read it online."

"Me too. It's not like my dad gets a paper copy delivered. I mean, does anyone do that anymore?"

Tomas shrugged as they stopped on the crowded subway platform. "They still print papers. Why's the article strange?"

"The reporter's secret source described meetings between this sleazy American businessman and important people in the government." She stared down the track, looking for the approaching train. It was a nervous habit she always had in subway stations. "He was living in the Cayman Islands to avoid paying US taxes."

"Okay."

"When I told my dad the description reminded me of the information the government has on our citizen's movements, he went ballistic."

"The secret information in the mysterious government computer your dad hacked into?"

She looked at him to gauge his reaction. "Exact time and date of everywhere I've been."

"I didn't think of that when I read it. Why did it bum out your dad?"

Luna sighed. *If only I knew.* "He disappeared into his office after I mentioned it. He was still there when I left for the airport twenty-four hours later."

"Odd behaviour, but I don't see its relevance. Yesterday's protests, however, could be the beginning of the unrest Claire described."

"Explain what happened."

Tomas hesitated after they boarded the Blue Line subway train to the downtown core. "If we walk from State Street to South Station, we'd go through the downtown shopping area where a protest got violent."

"Okay."

They emerged from the State Street station into a dismal late December afternoon. No precipitation, but the sky was so dark it looked like it could start raining or snowing at any moment. They headed toward Washington Avenue and its pedestrian mall with department stores and other retail outlets.

Luna stared at the debris. "What a mess. Must have been a really unruly demonstration."

"The official response was harsh."

"Were you here?"

Tomas shook his head. "Watched it on a news feed—a one-sided report. Didn't explain the protestors' perspective."

She paused, staring at one of the few unbroken shop windows. "More manipulation of how we think. What's with 'Boxing Day Sale'?"

"British tradition that involves more gift-giving and special sales. A mega shopping day like Black Friday."

"Claire's friends were protesting against rampant consumerism and our society's endless appetite for more junk."

"So says the girl who has nothing and isn't interested in giving or receiving Christmas presents."

Luna stopped abruptly and gestured with her index finger. "Not true. I have everything I need, but I don't lust after useless junk."

Tomas pulled her into his arms. "You need another hug, then onward to my parents. And I promise, no Christmas presents."

"Stop teasing. You know about my messed-up childhood and my difficulty fitting in. Spending a week at Christmas is hard for me. I'm trying, but I need your support, not teasing."

They turned onto Avenue de Lafayette and headed to the train station. "Worry you not, fair damsel. Good food and much affection, but no frivolous gifts."

She skipped ahead, wondering why her mood had suddenly lightened. "Or sensible ones, either. Race you to the station."

On Sunday, January 1, 2040, Tomas returned to Lowell to babysit a biology department experiment for two days. Luna remained in Plymouth until her dorm room came available on the third. That completed the most enjoyable week she'd experienced in her twenty-one years on Earth. She and Tomas explored the town and tourist sites celebrating early American history, knowing the family support group was always there. And a week as part of a real family was heavenly.

Her chaotic trip to Lowell on Tuesday was a huge comedown from her idyllic week in Plymouth. A power failure closed the subway platforms at South Station. That generated a forced march in Boston's sleety winter weather from the train station to the Downtown Crossing subway station.

As she crossed Chauncey Street, she slipped on a patch of ice and crumpled, crashing her left knee onto the edge of the curb. She writhed in pain, clutching her knee until another pedestrian came to her rescue.

The man, late twenties, wearing a business suit, checked the tear in her jeans. "Ruined your jeans, but no blood or any sign of a dislocation. Think you can stand?"

Luna whimpered, "hurts like hell, but I'll try."

He helped her remove her backpack before she struggled to her feet and tentatively put weight on her damaged knee. "I can manage, but it really hurts."

"Where you headed?"

"Downtown Crossing subway stop."

"I'll walk with you and carry your pack. After that test, you can decide if you need medical attention."

At the subway station, Luna, with the confidence of a twenty-one-year-old who'd always been self-reliant, decided she could cope. She thanked her Good Samaritan before she retrieved her pack and limped down the stairs.

Ninety minutes later, when she reached Lowell, the pain had hardly subsided, and her knee was immovable. She struggled from the train, more dragging than carrying her pack, and dropped it on the platform. She was thinking about a taxi to their residence building when she spied Tomas rushing along the platform.

"Whatever happened to you," he exclaimed as he skidded to a halt.

"Fell on the ice in Boston and hurt my knee."

He dropped to the ground and cupped his hands around her injured knee. "God! It's super swollen. Should we get you to the medical center?"

"I got this far, so I'll be okay. I want my room, some ice for the swelling, and rest."

"Okay. I'll take your pack, and we'll grab a taxi outside the station. You want a shoulder to lean on?"

"That more than anything else."

Luna lay propped on her bed with a blanket wrapped around her. She had her computer beside her and appeared comfortable when Tomas left to check on the experiments in his care.

"I'll bring ice, and we can decide about dinner," he said before he pulled her door closed.

Tomas returned at six with the promised ice in a portable cooler. The sun had set ninety minutes earlier, leaving the room in nearly complete darkness. She smiled, her face illuminated by her computer screen.

He placed the cooler by the bed and extracted a double-sealed Ziploc bag of ice before switching on her desk lamp.

She slid the bag under the blanket and placed it on her knee. "It doesn't hurt if I keep it still, but it's so swollen I had to slit the seam on my jeans. I don't know what I'll do tomorrow when I have classes."

"Ice this evening and in the morning should help with the swelling. And an elastic bandage—I'll buy one. We can wrap it around your knee in the morning. But what about dinner? The cafeteria's closed, and I doubt you're up for going out."

"Pizza delivery. Private party in the sitting area by the stairs."

Tomas placed the pizza order before sitting on Luna's bed, a breach of dormitory rules that didn't elicit the expected demand he stand immediately. "So, apart from the knee, how's it going?"

She sighed. "Our week in Plymouth was the happiest of my life—"

"No kidding, never seen anyone flying so high."

She smiled, imagining herself as a Japanese dragon kite flying high over Plymouth Beach. "Being together and having a family, even if it was temporary, was unbelievable. I wanted to pledge allegiance to the new social order and enjoy the happy family feeling when we enter the real world."

Tomas shook his head. "Are you joining the mindless masses who buy all the crap?"

Luna jerked upright, grimaced, and grabbed the icepack, repositioning it on her knee. "Never! During my week in Plymouth, I understood why some would. This afternoon when the subway platform was closed, and I slipped and crunched my knee, I realized it was a chimera. It must fail."

Chapter Thirty-Nine

Monday, April 2, 2040

Near the end of their junior year, Luna stood in Tomas's doorway, staring past him through his dorm room window. They were preparing for exams that would start in one week, but she couldn't concentrate. The grey weather, more like winter than spring, didn't inspire her. And the past three months, when nothing much happened, and Tomas reverted to a proper student who obeyed all the rules, had worn her down.

"Please, Tomas, can you help me resolve something important?"

He glanced up from his computer screen, knocking a pen onto the floor. He crawled under his desk to retrieve it. "One of the common rooms? That new Merrimack Street café?" he said as he stood.

Luna plopped onto his bed and laid back with her arms extended. "Here, where no one will bother us."

He closed his computer and shifted to the edge of his bed. "You're not worried about breaking more rules?"

"You joking? No one pays the slightest attention to the rules. I've walked in on my roommate in bed with two guys—"

"At the same time?"

"Different times." She shook her head, ignoring his teasing as she recalled her embarrassment when the two jerks blamed her for the intrusions. She pointed towards his door. "Leave it ajar. We'll only be stretching them a little."

He slid over and pulled her into his arms. "Is me avoiding romantic opportunities bothering you?"

She snuggled closer. "I'd really like more hugging and cuddling, but I'm not trying to push you. The problem is, I'm worried about my dad."

"Your dad? Worried when you get home in a few weeks, you'll discover a live-in girlfriend?"

She sat up, pushing him away. "Stop teasing, and anyway, he's not governed by stupid university rules. Dad said it's too dangerous for me to spend the summer at home."

"Maybe he's going away and doesn't want you living alone in big bad Washington."

"He'll be home as usual." She stood, walked to the window, and stared out for several minutes. *Why is he being so obtuse?* She spun around. "First, Claire hints he's important for their activities, and I'll be their liaison. When I tell him about Claire's concerns about surveillance, he confirms them with minimal effort. Then, his reaction when I mentioned that article in the Post, and now it's too dangerous for me to go home. What can it mean?"

"When we dug into everything, we learned something was seriously wrong. At first, I blamed a retrogressive university system, trying to force behaviour that harked back to the nineteen fifties—"

She slumped on the edge of his bed with her elbows on her knees and her chin cupped in her hands. "It's not the universities. Our entire society has turned the clock back ninety years."

Tomas nodded before pulling her back into an embrace. "America's become super religious, super conservative, and super inward-looking. And the problems with infrastructure. I attributed them to miserliness, not putting enough money into the system." He shook his head. "No longer makes sense."

She relaxed and snuggled against him, enjoying the closeness. *He's finally taking me seriously.* "Our social and economic system is out of whack. Is my dad trying to make it worse?"

"Claire and others are agitating for change. It's reasonable to assume they have undercover agents trying to push their agenda along."

"Oh, God! But my dad?" She jerked up, then settled back into his embrace. "I can't believe it."

"Then don't, because I'm probably wrong. What happens if you can't return to last year's summer job?"

She slid her hand under his T-shirt, hoping it might encourage him to do something similar. She sought a little romantic diversion, something to clear away her worries and let her focus on her studies. The discussion helped, but something less intellectual might work better. "He thinks I should spend the summer in Savannah."

"With your oceanographer mother measuring zooplankton distributions on the continental shelf. You may learn something useful."

She pushed away and perched once again on the edge of his bed. "First, you suggest my dad's a terrorist, and now you want me to spy on my mother. It's impossible. I know nothing about her science, and I won't last two weeks."

"If you spend a few days after your exams visiting your father and move on to Savannah—"

"And three weeks later, when Mom kicks me out, I'll be homeless, no job, no money. Totally screwed up summer."

Tomas sat scratching his chin for several minutes. "Here's the deal. If you spend two weeks in Washington and Savannah learning as much as possible, I'll get my parents to accommodate you for the rest of the summer."

"But you'll be in Lowell, living with the oceanography students like you did last summer."

He nodded. "But I'll have an incentive to go home as often as possible."

She left his room half an hour later, happy with the outcome. They'd gotten a little more intimate without stretching campus rules past the breaking point and addressed several of the larger problems they faced. She could now return to her room and focus on the immediate problem—acing her exams.

*****

Tomas' first opportunity for a weekend in Plymouth came on May twenty-sixth. Luna had been living with his family for two weeks after one in Washington and another in Savannah.

He packed his bag, locked the door of his summer digs, and headed for the train station. He'd learned they'd expelled sixty-seven students from their residence because they'd broken social behaviour rules during the spring term. They did it on the last day of term. Why then, and why did they identify those sixty-seven and not hundreds of other rule-breakers? The issue was certain to feed Luna's growing paranoia about their world.

Two hours later, he stepped onto the platform in Plymouth. Luna almost toppled them onto the tracks when she leapt into his arms.

"Whoa, my little lunatic, you trying to get us killed?"

"So happy to see you. Had a terrible week in Savannah, but your family's been great, and now you're home..."

Tomas's stepfather arrived, beaming. "Come on, lovebirds. Let's get going. Your mother's eager to see you."

Minutes later, Luna jangled the car keys as she grabbed the driver's side door handle. "Your dad's teaching me to drive."

Tomas shook his head while making a lunge for the keys. "Not this trip. Law says no extra passengers if you're driving with a learner's permit."

She twisted away, maintaining her grip on both keys and door handle. "Steve said I could."

"Shouldn't. You'll both get in trouble."

Steve grabbed the keys. "Back seat, both of you. I want you lovey-dovey again before we arrive home."

They were diligently patching the tiny hiccup at their reunion when Steve pulled off Main Street onto a road heading to Pilgrim's Highway. He pulled off again and parked by a pond. "Time for a beer?"

Tomas helped Luna from the car as he tried to get his mind around this surprising trip to a pub. He took her hand and followed his dad. Would it be a 'birds-and-bees' talk about their burgeoning romance?

Steve arrived at their table with three beers. "All non-alcoholic, so legal for you fledglings. We have something to discuss." He paused, staring at Tomas. "Something wrong?"

"No, sir. Didn't think Luna liked beer."

Luna smiled. "We've been practicing my driving. We tool around and come here for a beer before we drive home."

"Okay," Steve said. "If nothing's wrong, we should start. Our country's approach to climate change is causing serious problems, and I'm concerned our whole social structure is at risk."

"This is not about Luna and me behaving ourselves."

"No, Tomas, but my earlier advice to bide your time doing nothing drastic may no longer be appropriate. Everyone may soon have to choose sides."

Tomas glanced at Luna, wondering how she was responding to this bizarre conversation. His stepfather often mentioned his environmental concerns and his worries about climate change. But he'd always insisted the government had everything under control. What could have changed? "Are you talking about science questions or societal questions?"

"Let's start with the science."

After summarizing the first three decades of climate change battles, Steve paused for a swig of beer. He then resumed his lecture, ending with his opposition to America's continuing reliance on coal and heavy oil for power generation.

Tomas set down his glass and glanced around the room while he tried to gather his thoughts. Steve had never openly opposed American policies. Now he was questioning those policies and talking about choosing sides. "You've always insisted the crisis is twenty-five or thirty years away."

"That's the mantra in America. But it neglects two important realities. First, CO_2 emissions are dynamic. Recent developments have pushed the date forward. Trouble could arrive in a decade."

"And the second?" Tomas asked.

"America has thrown multinational coordination of the global temperature into disarray. We changed our protocol without consulting anyone. Last summer, our program introduced too many nanoparticles to the western North Atlantic."

Tomas' furrowed brow telegraphed his confusion. "Did the people running our temperature management program expect more upward pressure on temperature?"

Steve turned to Luna. "I suspect your mother's observations of low plankton biomass on the eastern seaboard are linked to this. But it's apparently a local aberration. It shows how temperature management can go wrong if we focus on regional rather than global observations."

"That explains why I couldn't handle Mom. She sounded like a madwoman when she chased me away, insisting the apocalypse was upon us."

"She may be closer to the truth than we realize. An imperfect engineering solution that may be running wild controls a critical environmental interaction, and our government is making things worse. You, and everyone else, must be prepared."

A few minutes later, Tomas followed Steve and Luna back to their ancient Tesla. He'd always railed against increasing carbon emissions, arguing they were putting unreasonable and unnecessary stress on natural systems and human infrastructure. Steve never disagreed with the principles, but he always argued any crisis was decades away. What had changed in the last months? And why hadn't he noticed the changes?

Chapter Forty

Three months later, Tomas arrived at his university residence at 6 p.m. after an extra weekend working at Dr. Wilson's field site. He threw his backpack and kit bag in his room, found Luna, and headed for the Chengdu Kitchen, his favourite off-campus café. He joined her at a laminate-covered table after placing his order. "God, I'm hungry. Been going flat out since eight with no lunch break. Jessie's still there. How will she manage?"

Luna pouted. "What about me? I counted on a final weekend together before we returned to this hellhole."

"I was home last weekend," Tomas replied, wondering why she was suddenly questioning his dedication to scientific research. "UMass Lowell isn't that bad. We're together and no longer in the campus thought pig's gun sights."

"But working Labour Day Weekend for free?"

Tomas sighed. She'd never understand the importance of those few days' measurements. "Couldn't leave. We'd have wasted the entire summer."

"If superwoman Jessie can now go it alone, why didn't she start Friday?"

"She can't. Dr. Wilson and another student will join her tomorrow morning. Now, what's the problem?"

Luna hesitated while a waitress delivered the food Tomas ordered. She sipped the tea he pushed toward her and reviewed the progress they made during the spring term. "Then visits to my parents made things worse, and all summer, more depressing news. Today, I learned they expelled my roommate."

Tomas stirred his bowl of chicken with mixed vegetables in hot sauce before sampling a piece of green pepper. "I suspect they forgot the hot sauce. Want some?"

Luna laughed. "You always say that. When I was stupid enough to agree, it was so spicy I damn near choked."

He smiled. His hackneyed joke worked. It brought a smile to her face. "I've been thinking about the expulsions."

"Yes."

"Massive, almost half our dorm's population has official reprimands on their student records, and sixty-seven are gone."

She shrugged her shoulders. "Everyone broke some rules. Including us, but we're still here, blemish-free."

"So, what's their goal?"

"Tell me."

He hesitated. Her refusal to offer an opinion suggested she was suffering from emotional overload, but he felt he mustn't stoop to feel-good platitudes. "Phoney charges to eliminate students who don't fit their concept of an ideal citizen."

"Makes me feel worse than ever. Underhanded psychological warfare turning us into drones who consume, consume, consume, and never question what the government's doing."

Tomas leaned over, taking her hands in his. He considered the university's brainwashing. In freshman year, they targeted misfits like him and Luna, cajoling, threatening, and sometimes forcing them to fit in. In sophomore and junior years, they watched everyone like hawks. "They're weeding out anyone they don't like."

"But my roommate? She wanted to party, study, get married, and join the unsuspecting masses. Sounds like their perfect citizen."

"Maybe she crossed some boundary that disqualified her. We don't understand their goals."

Luna pulled away, sat with her back straight, and a determined look in her eyes. "Earlier this summer, your dad said we should be joining the battle."

"He didn't," Tomas replied. "He said 'be prepared.'"

"Unfair expulsion of hundreds of students on trumped-up charges could be the trigger."

Tomas shook his head, imagining her falling into a trap, one the administration may have intentionally set. "The problem isn't the charges, they're irrefutable. The problem's their sleazy behaviour and their excessive surveillance. You lack the ammunition to tackle those. We must wait until the right issue surfaces."

She crumpled without providing any resistance. "God. I suppose you're right, but I really want to do something."

"We'll get our chance."

In October, just a week before the 2040 election, Luna tapped on Tomas's door. It was fifteen minutes before the weeknight curfew.

He called from inside. "It's open."

She pushed open the door but didn't enter. "Claire resurfaced. She appeared in the library, told me to return to my room, dump my phone and student ID, and meet her at that café."

Tomas looked up from his computer. "What did she want?"

"She said it's happening."

"What's happening?"

"The revolution. The big push to end the oppressive government intervention in everyone's lives, end our isolationist foreign policy and reengage with the world. You know, everything that's wrong."

He rose from his desk, walked across the room, and dragged her inside. "You're rambling. Breathe and take it slow."

She shook off his hand. "Sorry. We can discuss it tomorrow. I stopped because she had a message for you."

"Me?"

She ignored his question. "You're supposed to establish a presence on theRocket.com and use it to push for action on climate change."

TheRocket was a social media platform that sprouted after the government broke up the biggest social media companies. Participants post provocative questions, and readers respond. Tomas failed to see the connection. "What do they want from me?"

"She said a Bonita Sanchez would contact you."

He turned to his computer and tapped several keys. "Bonita Sanchez is the CEO of theRocket.com. This is totally getting bizarre."

Tomas's first venture onto theRocket was a question about the American government's minimal support for research into the impacts of expanding carbon dioxide emissions. It flew into the stratosphere. It wasn't the highest-flying first rocket on record, but a memorable achievement because most inaugural flights fizzled.

After reading the comments and responses his first post generated, he reviewed the guidelines he'd received from the website organizers. They stressed accuracy and documentation that supported the opinions he expressed. They claimed experts would vet all posts, comments, and replies. Inconsistencies would be publicized, and unsubstantiated claims challenged.

Fear of government retribution clearly worried the site owners, but it didn't prevent them from encouraging contributors to host material unpopular with the government. Tomas pondered as he crafted responses to comments on his first posting. Why was Ms. Sanchez confident honesty and factual integrity would protect them from a government that didn't tolerate opposition? And in this age of security breaches, could they protect their contributors' anonymity?

Tomas was staring into space, considering the surprising success of his first posting, when Luna appeared in his doorway.

She cocked her head, eyebrows raised. "Something amiss?"

"Worried about theRocket. Dad, Jessie, and Dr. Wilson say no one cares about increasing carbon dioxide emissions. I bet your mother agrees. Why did Bonita Sanchez ask me to start a discussion based on this idea, and why was it so successful?"

Luna slammed the door and sighed after plopping onto Tomas's bed. "For two years, we've bitched about the US government deceiving everyone, twisting the truth, and dragging the population into a fool's paradise. Suggesting carbon emissions aren't important is part of that deception."

"Not so! It's a worldwide phenomenon, been so since 2026 when temperature increases ended."

Luna jumped from the bed and pushed Tomas away from his desk. His chair tipped, and they tumbled to the floor. Tomas landed on his back.

She scrambled into a dominant position, sitting astride and tapping her forefinger on his chest. "Wrong, wrong, wrong! You're the scientist, and I understand this better than you do. Everywhere else, they're addressing the problem, and American citizens are finally getting the message. You're in the vanguard, leading our charge."

He reached for her arm, but grabbed the sleeve of her shirt. It was a loose-fitting affair with batwing sleeves and an oversized neck hole that often slid down over one shoulder. "Where are you getting these crazy ideas?"

She leaned back, pulling her arm into the baggy shirt. "From Claire and my mom. She's collaborating with scientists from Canada, Thailand, and Britain, and has more research money than ever." She smiled as she raised the arm inside her shirt above her head and slithered back, pulling her head through the neck hole.

Seconds later, Tomas had the shirt in his hand, and she was, once again, perched on his chest. "What the hell are you doing?"

"Me! You pulled off my shirt."

He held it out. "Here. Put it on and let me up. You trying to get us expelled?"

She grabbed the shirt and threw it onto his bed. "Oh, Tomas, you can be the most frustrating person. Our country is falling to bits, and you're worried about the university's stupid restrictions."

He pushed her off, stood, and strode to the door. He opened it a crack before grabbing her shirt. "Put it on and tell me what's bothering you."

"Just told you." She plopped onto his bed. "The country's falling apart, and you insist on living in the fantasy world our glorious leaders have created. They're toast. We no longer have to live by their medieval strictures."

"It's not dead yet. And we promised to hide within the system, ready to play our part when they need us."

His face felt hot, probably red as a beet. His roommate might arrive and find her sitting half-naked on his bed, looking like she planned to shed her remaining clothes.

She lashed out. "Stop gawking like I'm a brazen hussy. I'm twenty-two years old and forced into unnatural virginity by an emasculating regime in its death throes. We must cast off the shackles and try to lead normal lives."

He stared, puzzled why she'd suddenly chosen to abandon the cautious approach they'd maintained for years. "Be patient. We're already part of a groundswell that will bring the country to its senses. Hang in for four days. Then when we're at my parents' for Thanksgiving, anything you want. I promise."

With tears in her eyes, she pulled her shirt on before dragging him onto his bed. "I unhooked my bra so we can, you know, get a jump on next weekend without obliterating the rules."

Half an hour later, after much kissing and cuddling and more bare skin caressing than they'd previously experienced, Luna sat up. She adjusted her shirt and showed him the bra she'd completely wiggled out of. "You asked what was bothering me."

Tomas shook off images of breasts rather than shoulders emerging from the gaping open neck. "Yeah, an hour before dinner, so time for your explanation."

She leaned forward, and a nipple peeked out. "If I don't distract you."

He smiled. "I thought you wanted to discuss something."

"Yeah, really. Two days after the election, the Washington Post published a story about President Williams' re-election team planting false stories about John Miller. Then on Sunday, we had another story that showed the paper sat on it until it had no impact."

Tomas stared as Luna squirmed, obviously intent on a peep show. He resisted reaching out and giving her a hand as he pondered her musings about their current president and his Republican challenger. It must have something to do with the success of the upstart third party. "Saw them. Why would the Post publish the story after the election instead of burying it forever?"

"Until we had the election results, everyone expected either Williams or Miller would carry enough states. The Post wanted Williams re-elected, so they suppressed a story that would harm him. Ms. Taylor carried seven states, and her Progressive Party elected three senators and several dozen congressmen. That threw the election into doubt. Congress would choose the next president."

She was driving him crazy by trying to shed her clothes while conducting a serious conversation. "So, why publish the story two days after the election?"

"Because the President mentioned bringing the Progressives and Democrats together."

"I see. Anathema to the true believers running the country for decades. They, including the Washington Post, had to unify behind Miller."

"Exactly, hide any signs of an imminent collapse."

He pulled her down beside him, ending her attempts at exhibitionism. "But doesn't this breakthrough signal the end to the incestuous power-sharing between Democrats and Republicans?"

"I wish, but it doesn't. Most Democrats will side with the Republicans and make sure John Miller becomes our next president."

"So, nothing changes?"

"I'm more hopeful than that. Stories of corruption, collusion, and usurping of the democratic process are emerging. They're well researched, with irrefutable evidence that must be supported by my dad's hacking into Pentagon computers and their satellite surveillance network."

Tomas finally realized what she was getting at. "Your father's a critical player?"

"His cyberspying provides the data they need to develop their stories. If he's outed, their fight's set back years."

Chapter Forty-One

Friday, February 1, 2041

In the 2040 election, Tomas voted for Pamela Taylor, the Progressive Party's candidate for president. He'd also supported their candidates for senate and congress. He didn't give the election a great deal of thought or delve into the party positions on most issues. Tomas favoured them because their climate change policies were more compatible with his ideas. They provided a stark contrast with the continuing climate intransigence of the Democrats and Republicans.

Between the election in November and the 2041 inauguration of the new president, Tomas paid more attention to political developments. Luna, a political science student, led his re-education effort. Together, they spent many evenings digging into the shifting stances of all three parties.

A presidential election where no candidate gained a majority of the Electoral College votes was almost unprecedented. It hadn't happened since 1825. The political machinations that led to a widely criticized decision on the outcome added another lesson to Tomas's crash course in American politics.

He came away with a new perspective. The science of climate change was based on facts and logical argument. It was important, and he would continue to focus on it. The politics of climate change were even more important. It relied on an understanding of human behaviour and other social sciences. That was Luna's world, and increasingly, he suspected, his stepfather's. After the inauguration, he figured it would also become his. But for the moment, there was little he could do. He could watch the developments and try to improve his understanding. And he could launch climate change questions on theRocket.

*****

Dan Delacour hailed a taxi in the early evening gloom outside London's Waterloo train station on Friday, the first of February. He, Elena, and Carys were *en route* from Hafen Ddiogel to a dinner engagement at Gareth Llewellyn's London townhouse. Including twelve-year-old Carys was unusual. *Did it suggest a respite from Gareth's focus on his mission?*

McCribben, Gareth's octogenarian butler, greeted them at the door. As usual, he paid special attention to Carys. He promised her a diversion when the dinner conversation became too tedious before leading the little party to Gareth's library. Gareth waved from chairs clustered around a roaring fire. "The end game's afoot. We must celebrate the success of our recent efforts and develop..." He gazed into the fire, "a plan for the final action."

Dan cringed when he heard Gareth's words. He was dragging them deeper into the Company of Gentlemen Entrepreneurs' global conspiracy. Gareth fended off any potential rebuke by turning to Carys. "But first, I must hear about your adventures in Dan's laboratory."

"It's so much fun," Carys replied as she jumped onto the chair next to her great uncle's. "We have this giant map of the ocean, and sections light up if the mirrors our ships spread onto the water aren't working properly."

She paused, waiting for Gareth's reaction. He smiled and nodded his encouragement.

"The map is usually green. It should be blue because the ocean should always be blue, but it's green. If it's not quite right, it turns yellow, and if it's really bad, red."

"Then what happens?" Gareth asked.

"We send out a ship to fix the problem."

"By spreading more particles on the ocean?"

She nodded. "Particles. That's what Daddy calls them, but I call them mirrors because they work like tiny sparkly mirrors." She paused, frowning. "I can't wait to be old enough to go with them."

McCribben arrived with a Shirley Temple-like concoction for Carys before preparing drinks for the others at a side table. Half an hour later, he returned to say dinner was served.

After dinner, Carys followed McCribben to the little room off the servants' sitting room that he'd converted into a shrine devoted to his ancestral home. She would help him build the latest house in his reconstruction of his home village in the Scottish Highlands.

After Carys skipped out, Gareth returned to his preoccupation with the Company of Gentlemen Entrepreneurs climate change fight. He mentioned the previous week's inaugural address by the new American president and asked what they could do to influence his policies. He would claim they had a God-given obligation to save humanity by bringing the United States back into their fight to save the planet from environmental chaos. But could they argue the end justified the means?

Dan sat back, savouring his after-dinner glass of port as he considered Gareth's opening salvo from before dinner. "Should we be celebrating a victory? Our opponents have maintained their stranglehold on the US political system."

"Not so," Elena replied. She described Pamela Taylor's success and how it left President Williams short of the 270 votes he needed. "Choosing the next president fell to congress. Pundits expected them to give the nod to Williams. But he'd made conciliatory gestures, suggesting the Democrats and Progressives could work together. The backroom boys banded together and ensured the Republican Miller, a candidate with less than thirty percent of the electoral college votes, became president. That decision was widely criticized. It could lead to the upheaval we've been waiting for."

"The reaction of public and pundits to the Presidential Address reinforces those concerns," Gareth said after they moved from his dining room to his library. "We must plan ahead, identify our issues, and how we tackle them when that moment arrives. Dan, as usual, let us begin with the science."

Dan looked up from a private contemplation. "Nothing new. They've abandoned collaboration. Their seeding of the western North Atlantic is sporadic and follows no comprehensible pattern."

"Do you understand why?" Gareth asked.

"May be a money issue. They're not funding important infrastructure projects. More like eastern Europe after the failure of the Soviet Union than twenty-first-century America."

Elena jumped in. "If Alfredo were here, he'd produce reams of computer printout documenting the fragile state of the American economy. He'd claim they're headed for their first recession in twenty years."

Gareth laughed. "Thank you, Elena, for the economic synopsis without Alfredo's charts. Should we be exploiting their crumbling infrastructure?"

"Let them do it," Elena suggested. "The problem's obvious to the American public. It will fester without our input."

Dan bit his tongue. He wanted to jump into the conversation and encourage activities that would advance an American day of reckoning. Speeding up their transition away from their high carbon economy would be invaluable. But he was opposed to intervention in the internal affairs of foreign countries and annoyed he'd harboured such thoughts for a second.

Gareth understood his conundrum. "Dan's itching to say we should interfere, but I agree with Elena. Political interference isn't worth the risk. We can work on renewed collaboration with sympathetic American corporations."

Elena glanced at her husband, giving him a little smile of encouragement. "A task for Alfredo, I would suggest. Not one for us to consider."

"I'll stay away from rants about political interference," Dan said. "We should encourage green energy companies and electronics and technology firms."

Gareth nodded. "No problem. The high-tech industries you're referring to need financial backing. They're not getting it from US banks. European and Canadian banks are already filling this void. I can discuss expanding our involvement without breaching political interference barriers."

Dan added his begrudging agreement. "Their support will be helpful."

A few minutes later, Elena addressed the rise of the Puritanical Christians and their protestant work ethic. The discussion reminded him of an old opinion from his days as a Canadian. In those days, he thought Americans' Christian bent gave them a smug feeling of moral superiority and entitlement to the extravagant fruits of their country's prosperity.

A lull in the conversation allowed Dan to express his opinion. "Alfredo has attributed the American's acceptance of their current suppressive government to greed. The actual driver may be a sense of entitlement based on attitudes developed from their faith."

Gareth stared at the empty glass he was rotating between his fingers. Dan retrieved the port decanter and refilled their glasses.

"Interesting thought," Gareth said. "A return to religious convictions they brought to America from Britain in the seventeenth century. Another factor for us to consider."

Elena brought the conversation back to the critical issue. "We've identified the factors contributing to instability, but not how we topple their house of cards."

Gareth responded. "Scandals associated with insiders in and around the US government and the greed that drives men in power. Several major exposés over the past few years contributed to the rise of the Progressive Party. The outrageous manipulation of due process since the election must lead to further investigation of insider motives."

"The investigative reporters were surprisingly well informed," Dan added. "Rumours of insiders leaking critical information are rampant among my contacts."

Gareth summed up the situation, describing the future he imagined for the Company of Gentlemen Entrepreneurs and the world. "Exposés fueled by solid information provided by whistleblowers are our best hope for a rapid end to twenty-five years of misguided rule." He raised his glass. "Here's to those unsung heroes, and the young people who will lead the revolt."

Postlude

Autumn, 2052

As fall turned to winter, I noted changes in Pemberton's growing population. People, like my son, Michael, and his wife, Vanessa, who lived in the Pemberton Valley before 2049, remained committed to their town. Newcomers, escapees from Vancouver and elsewhere, stopped wondering when they could go home. Most accepted their new reality and joined the efforts to improve Pemberton. Some dreamed of new places where they could put down roots.

Our world was slowly expanding. We had a workable road joining Pemberton with the once-thriving resort community of Whistler, where a remnant population struggled to survive, and the more bustling town of Squamish at the head of Howe Sound.

Wildfires destroyed Squamish in 2049. Three years later, a new town was rising phoenix-like from the ashes. Its population was a mixture of indigenous people, settlers who survived the fiery onslaught, and refugees from Vancouver. They were working closely together.

Squamish represented a new dynamic, an equal sharing of effort and responsibility. It was a positive sign, pointing to a future where the indigenous peoples determined how their ancestral homeland developed.

They were building a port town on what would become a major trade route. They saw a future where they occupied a key position on the most workable route between the towns around the Salish Sea and the lands east of the Rockies.

That summer, when Zeke joined the explorers surveying the lands to the east and north, he left Hannah and me with our extensive garden to manage. I extracted a suitable quid pro quo. He promised me a careful accounting of the locations and sizes of the communities they encountered. This was important. A solid estimate of the population after the cataclysmic fires would help me assess our survival chances and better estimate our ongoing contributions to climate change. The 2049 fires produced a huge spike in carbon emissions, but our emissions since 2049 were much smaller than industrial emissions earlier in the twenty-first century. We needed to determine how much less.

In the province's southern interior, our explorers found a desolate moonscape. For decades, the region had struggled with drought and larger and more frequent forest fires. Populations were already decreasing when 2049 dealt its death blow. The area turned to desert. We would need lower temperatures and more moisture before cities like Kamloops and Kelowna, and dozens of smaller communities, could rebuild.

Farther north, settlers had re-established towns between Prince Rupert on the coast and Prince George in the northern interior. A similar rebirth occurred in the Peace River country on the eastern side of the Rocky Mountains. More communities resurrected themselves in the narrow Fraser and Columbia River valleys.

The morning after Zeke returned from their second month-long trek through the BC wilderness, he asked me if our car was available.

I looked up from helping four-year-old Alice create her breakfast. "Batteries should be charged, and everything shipshape."

"Good," Zeke replied as Hannah entered the kitchen with a scowl on her face.

"That's my man. Home for twelve hours and back on the road. May as well be a travelling salesman." She turned to Alice. "We'll make it up for you tomorrow. Promise."

"Better idea," Zeke replied. "You and Mummy should come with me. I'm seeing a man with a boat in Squamish. It won't take long. Then, we can have a picnic and drive home. You like riding in Grandpa's car, don't you?"

Alice raced off to collect her teddy, and Hannah prepared food and other necessities for their trip. Trips, even ones on the relatively safe road from Pemberton to Squamish, were still a risky adventure. No one undertook one without making preparations.

"If all's well," Zeke said before they rolled away, "I should have my report on communities and populations by tonight."

That evening, we reviewed the data Zeke collected on his two trips east and north. He presented the data collected by mariners plying the Salish Sea, and I added information Bill Robertson provided on coastal communities from farther north.

"Looks good, doesn't it?" Zeke said when we finished. "Except for Vancouver and the Lower Fraser River valley. They're important, right?"

I nodded. "Most of BC's population lived on the lower mainland. There must be a substantial remnant."

"That area was the most seriously affected by rising sea levels and the radiation spreading from Seattle."

"Not so sure. The evidence suggests radioactive contamination isn't as widespread as we initially thought."

"But flooding must be important."

"No question, and it isn't temporary flooding. The dike system was already threatened. It must now be destroyed. We'll have a permanent intrusion of seawater into most of the lower Fraser Valley."

"Give me another month. I'll get the data." He pointed at the computer screen where I'd displayed our running total. "We'll fill in this last major gap."

"Gives me hope," Hannah said when Zeke, the perennial free spirit, skipped off to entertain Alice. "Everywhere Zeke goes, he learns of more survivors, more communities rebuilding themselves. I imagine Mum struggling to survive in some shanty town or trekking across the continent looking for us."

I sighed. "You shouldn't lose hope. But it seems only a quarter of BC's population survived. It could be a few more on the prairies, but if our limited knowledge is correct, many less in the east."

"I know. A long shot. But I have this feeling. One day, when we least expect it, Mum will appear on our doorstep."

I nodded, hoping to encourage her optimistic view, but my take on Zeke's missions was more negative. I saw enemies lurking on our eastern boundary and uncertainty everywhere I looked.

Later, by the fire, I reread Dan Delacour's description of the events leading up to the environmental Armageddon we'd lived through in 2049. That background information and Zeke's compilation of remnant populations in British Columbia should provide context for my assessment of the conflict looming with a police state forming on the Prairies.

Would it lead to generations of internecine conflict? Or could we imagine a better society rising phoenix-like from the ashes produced by humanity's ultimate folly?

The End

About the author:

Alan Kemister is the pen name of a Halifax Nova Scotia based scientist experimenting with creative writing. He has a keen interest in environmental science and dabbled in yachting and golf before turning to fiction after retirement. He's written more than thirty published short stories and one poem. Several of these stories appeared in anthologies produced by Halifax's Evergreen Writers Group: *Out of the Mist: 22 Atlantic Canadian Ghost Stories* released in 2014, *Off Highway: Journeys of Nova Scotia Writers*, in 2017, and *Water's Edge*, published in the spring of 2020 at the height of the COVID-19 pandemic.

Alan has self-published *A Body in the Sacristy* and *Tilting at Windmills*, his first two Barrettsport Mysteries featuring Detective Simon Goodyear and the fictional South Shore town of Barrettsport Nova Scotia.

His current project is The Road to Environmental Armageddon, a precautionary saga about the hazards of ignoring human-induced climate change. The first volume in this series, *The Souring Seas: A climate change novel,* was published in September 2021.

Tilting at Windmills, A Body in the Sacristy, The Souring Seas, Out of the Mist, Off Highway, and *Water's Edge* are available on Amazon in paperback and e-book formats.

Links:

E-mail: alkemi47@gmail.com
Facebook: https://www.facebook.com/Phil.Yeats47
Website: https://alankemisterauthor.wordpress.com
The Souring Seas: A Climate Change novel: https://books2read.com/u/mlEv29

www.ingramcontent.com/pod-product-compliance
Lightning Source LLC
Chambersburg PA
CBHW071146170626
46809CB00002B/799